Who Owns Arizona?

✜ A Drew Steele Civil War Mystery ✜

E.E. "Doc" Murdock

H.O.T. Press

Published by
H.O.T. Press
Los Angeles, California
www.hotpresspublishing.com
Publishing Fine Books Since 1983

ISBN: 0-923178-16-3
ISBN - 13: 978-0-923178-16-1

Acknowledgments

I am indebted to the members of the Ojai Writing Workshop who provided valuable feedback as I worked through the many drafts of this book. And of course, without the help of Zoe, this book would not exist.

Dedication

On a cold winter morning in 1848, James Marshall was walking along the south fork of California's American River near John Sutter's mill when he noticed something glittering in the creek. That casual discovery led to the greatest gold rush in American history. It contributed to a nationwide fascination with the western part of the country and encouraged a steady movement of the population toward it.

Years later, after the entire map of the West had changed due to the Mexican War and the American Civil War, an old man prospected for gold in the northwestern part of the Arizona territory. He didn't have much luck finding gold, but he came back out of the desert claiming he had found something far more valuable, a single sheet of old yellowed parchment..

Each of these events, in their own way, shaped the future of the American West. This is one of the stories behind the story of manifest destiny. It is a story about the men and women who participated in the westward expansion of the union, those who found and dug up the gold, built the railroads, and developed the cities. This story is dedicated to those who suffered and died when they got in the way.

Who Owns Arizona?

Chapter 1

*H*e couldn't sleep. As he stared up into the darkness, the lonely fog horns of the ships anchored out in the San Francisco bay told him it was going to be another cold and overcast morning. According to the calendar, spring had arrived, but the rainy weather lingered on. He wondered if it might not be time for another trip, someplace warmer, someplace where the sun appeared before noon.

He got out of bed and dressed and went into his office. He lit a lamp and sat down at his desk. He picked up last week's copy of La Presse De France, and for the third time, reread the article about "the women's movement," as they called it in that newspaper. There was no mention of Stacy in the article, but he was sure she would have been involved. The story described the new women's movement as an exciting new trend, a hopeful rebirth of individuality, but an editorial in the same newspaper derided the women for their unreasonable demands and improper behavior, describing their quest for equality as defiant of God's laws. The article said five women had recently been arrested for trying to force their way into a polling place.

He put down the newspaper and smiled grimly to himself, imagining Stacy being arrested, proud and defiant, berating them even as they took her away.

His thoughts were interrupted by three loud knocks at his office door. He got up and headed for the door, but before he could get there, a loud voice called out, "Mr. Steele, are you in there? I have a case for you." Then the knocking started up again.

Someone using the name Steele instead of Smith . . . or Jones or Johnson. Time to become detective Drew Steele again. Probably it was yet another lawyer. With all the new money in San Francisco, the lawyer business, and therefore the detective business, was booming.

Steele opened the door and looked the fellow over. A middle-aged man, considerably shorter than Steele's six feet. He was wearing an inexpensive dark suit that was getting tight around the waist. Steele decided he wasn't a lawyer.

"Drew Steele?" asked the man, smiling broadly.

"That's right."

"Ah, yes, I was told you were a good-looking young fellow." He stuck out his hand.

"And you are?" asked Steele.

The man quickly pulled back his hand and took off his hat. "Oh, sorry. Name's Rudd. John Rudd. I'm a reporter for the Bulletin. Maybe you've heard of me."

Steele *had* seen Rudd's byline in that newspaper, mostly on stories about community events and the local gossip. He gestured toward the chair in front of the desk. "Have a seat."

Rudd sat down and looked around. "Nice office. I mean, a little stark, but that's all right, I guess. Nice big window with a view of the bay anyhow." He stood up to look out the window. Then he sat back down and turned to stare at Steele. "Uh, they tell me you were in the war. That where you got that scar on your cheek?"

Was this to be another case that involved the war? Steele hoped it was. Although squabbles over money were the most profitable cases, Steele was getting very tired of such nonsense. He went back to his chair behind the desk and waited for Rudd to get to his business.

Rudd fiddled with his hat in his lap, staring at Steele. "So, Drew Steele. Good name for a detective."

"That's what I thought."

"Oh, you mean it's not your real name?"

"Maybe we'd better get to the reason you came here, Mr. Rudd."

"Oh, sure. Sorry. Well, it's like this. I was told you were, uh, pretty good at finding things."

"And you need something found?"

"Yeah. Well, it's about this, uh, land document I lost. A real old one. Anyhow, now that the war's over I figured maybe it's time to go back to Arizona to see if I could get it back."

"What sort of document was it?"

"Oh, it was . . . old."

"How old?"

"Well, uh, hard to say."

Why was Rudd being so vague about the document? Steele decided to wait him out. He took out his drawing pad and began a rough sketch of Rudd. Steele outlined Rudd's round face and penciled in some shading to illustrate its fleshiness. He added a few more strokes to indicate the man's thinning hair that was brushed sideways across his head to conceal his emerging baldness.

Rudd leaned forward to look at what Steele was drawing. "You an artist?"

"Just a diversion. Helps me think." Steele pushed aside the drawing. "Mr. Rudd, if you want my help, you are going to have to tell me everything."

"Well, it's kind of a long story, but it all started when I was a school teacher there."

Steele glanced down at his drawing of Rudd. He didn't look much like a school teacher. "There? Where is there?"

"Prescott. It's the territorial capital of Arizona now, but it wasn't back then. They don't get many educated men in a place like that, and not many women either, 'cept a few Mexican women. So when I drifted into town, my one year of college back in Chicago was enough to land me the school-teacher job. They only had a handful of kids in their school anyhow. The teaching job went all right, for a while, but then I got involved in this . . . uh, situation. I ended up sort of . . . uh, losing some money. Actually, a lot of money."

"You *sort of* lost a lot of money?" Of course it would be about money. Probably another boring case about who owes who what. Still, it might mean a paid trip to Arizona. Arizona would be warm, unlike San Francisco's cold and gloomy spring weather.

Rudd hesitated. "Well, before I tell you about that . . . I mean, are you willing to take the case?"

Steele thought about it. Prescott, Arizona was undoubtedly still a small town, a rough mining town, despite it's new status as the territorial capital. Not the most exciting place to visit. "To be frank, Mr. Rudd, you haven't really told me enough to decide. And there is the matter of my fees. I require a retainer in advance, plus all expenses."

"I already know how much you charge. I checked you out. It's no problem. I have the money."

Steele stared at the man, wondering where a newspaper reporter would get that kind of money. "But there is a problem, isn't there? What is it you're not saying?"

"Uh, well, there is a little bit of a problem. The man who took the money from me sort of ended up . . . dead."

"He stole money from you and then he was murdered?"

"Yeah. Somebody got him in his sleep. Knifed him."

Steele penciled in the word murder next to the drawing of Rudd. "But that somebody wasn't you?"

"No! I swear it. Some people there probably think I did it, but I didn't. I hightailed it out of town, but it wasn't because I killed him. I didn't even find out he was dead until I read about it in a newspaper."

"Are you wanted for his murder?"

"I'm not sure, but now that the war's over and things are getting back to normal, it's probably only a matter of time before they find out where I am. So I figure I should probably go back there and clear my name. And maybe we can find out who really killed old Willig."

"The murdered man was named Willig?"

"Yeah, Dutch Willig. He was the old prospector who had the land document."

"So it wasn't your document?"

"I never said I owned it, only that I was supposed to get it. Here's the way it was. Willig let it be known that he had some kind of land document and he was willing to sell it. The big mine owner in town, a man named Longmore, wanted the document and he forced me into being the one who took the money to Willig to buy it. Old Willig liked me. He used to come by the school and shoot the breeze with me. So when he agreed to sell it, Longmore said I was the only one who knew Willig so I had to be the go-between. I didn't want to do it, but Longmore threatened to take away my teaching job unless I went along with him."

"So Willig took their money, but never turned over the document."

"That's right. That's it exactly. He showed up at my place that night and right away he got all upset because Longmore was only willing to pay a thousand dollars. A thousand dollars! Can you believe it? That's a hell of a lot of money for a piece of paper. But old Willig said it wasn't enough. I said, 'Okay, I'll take the money back to Longmore.' Well, old Willig blew up at that. Started yelling that he'd register the document at the land office himself and that bastard Longmore could go to hell. Then he said he'd show me the document to prove how valuable it was. He acted like he was about to pull it out of this dirty old pack he always carried, but instead he dumped out a couple of Cholla cactus balls right on top of my arm. Did you ever see one of those Cholla cactuses, Steele? Get stuck with one of those babies and you'll never forget it." He rubbed his arm as if it still hurt.

"So Willig used that moment to grab the money."

"Hey, that's right. You must know his type. He grabbed the money and ran out the door. He disappeared into the night before I could get my shoes on and go after him. After he was gone, I sat there picking those cactus stickers out of my arm for hours, trying to think what to do. I'd lost Longmore's money, and knowing him, he'd think I was in cahoots with Willig and stole it. Even if I didn't end up in jail, I knew my job as the town's school teacher was gone. I stuck a note on the front door of Longmore's big fancy house up on the hill saying Willig had stole the money, grabbed my few things, and got the heck out of town before dawn. I hiked on down the road 'til the morning stage picked me up and kept going until I hit this town."

Steele studied Rudd's face. He didn't look like the type who would be capable of murder, even in the heat of the moment. He must be telling the truth, or at least some of the truth. "Then Willig was killed?"

"Yep, the very next night. I guess he used some of the money to check into the local hotel. That's where they got him. Cut his throat in his sleep. It was probably the first time the old coot had ever slept in a soft bed. Mostly he lived out in the desert with his burro huntin' for gold."

Steele thought about Rudd's story. Men being killed for money in the West had become almost commonplace since the end of the war, but what kind of land document could possibly be worth a thousand dollars? "Mr. Rudd, it's hard for me to believe any kind of land in a remote place like Arizona could be worth a thousand dollars. What was it for, a gold mine?"

Rudd scooted his chair closer. "That's the thing, Steele. It wasn't a gold mine or anything like that. It was bigger than that, a lot bigger. I've been doing some checking and if the document is real, it'll be worth more than a thousand dollars, a lot more."

"What are you holding back, Mr. Rudd? You can't expect me to take this case unless you tell me what I'm looking for."

Again Rudd hesitated. "Well, I haven't told anybody else what Willig said that night, but I guess I've got to trust you. I've got to trust somebody. Okay, here it is. He said the document was a land grant, an old Spanish deed, handwritten on parchment. He said it was a really huge piece of land that had been granted by the king of Spain to a family named Rivera."

That old story. Steele sat back and shook his head. "That story's been around for a long time. The Riveras owned huge tracks of land in the southwest, but during the Mexican War they were pushed off their land. They gave up their claim and went back to Mexico."

"Mexico! That's where Willig said he got the land grant. He told me he'd got to be friends with an old guy down there. And guess what his name was? Rivera. He said old man Rivera had the document hid away and the two of them cooked up a plan to try to get the land back. Willig said old man Rivera signed the land grant over to Willig so Willig could take it back to Arizona and get it registered. But Willig didn't register it. Instead, he tried to sell it to Longmore."

Steele sat back to think about it. The Rivera family had been the dominate land owner in the southwest for centuries, but when war broke out between Mexico and the United States, they barely had time to escape back to Mexico with their lives. After the war, they tried to get compensation for their lost land, but the U.S. government had denied their claims because they couldn't prove they had ever owned the land in the first place.

"Well?" said Rudd. "Can you help me?"

"Did Willig say what land the deed covered?"

"Arizona."

"The land was in Arizona?"

"Not *in* Arizona, *all* of Arizona. Willig claimed the land grant pretty much covered the whole of Arizona territory. That's why Willig was supposed to register it in Prescott, the new territorial capital." Rudd paused for effect. "Just think of what I could do with that document if I got my hands on it."

"What could you do with it?"

Rudd sat forward, clearly excited. "I could get filthy rich, that's what. Willig said the document had been signed over to the bearer. With it, I could lay claim to the whole damn territory."

"You'd have quite a fight on your hands. The land has long been owned by others."

"Yeah, but if I got my hands on the land grant, I bet they'd pay me just to be sure they had real title to their own land. I bet they'd do it just to avoid a legal battle. Or I could sell it to Longmore, like Willig wanted to do. Come on, Steele, think about it. It'd be like a treasure hunt and you'd get paid for doing it. Let's go to Arizona and try to find it."

Steele did think about it. He turned in his chair to look out the window at the lingering fog. It didn't seem very likely that an old prospector in Arizona could have ended up with a genuine Spanish land grant that laid claim to the Arizona territory. For many years, there had been a rumor that such a document did exist. Willig could have heard about it and simply created a fake document to take advantage of the rumors. But if this man Longmore had been willing to pay a thousand dollars for it, then he must have believed it was real. And then somebody had killed Willig. Was it to get the land grant?

He turned back to Rudd. "All right, when do you want to go?"

Rudd stood up grinning. "Great. I'm ready to go right away if you are. I'll get us a couple of tickets on tomorrow's early train."

Chapter 2

*A*fter Rudd had paid the money for the retainer and left the office, Steele sat wondering why he had agreed to accept the case. Finding the land grant seemed like a long shot, but maybe it was time to go somewhere new. Arizona was one place he'd never been. It was supposed to be quite warm there in the springtime. So, why not go? There was nothing holding him in San Francisco now that Stacy had run off to Europe. It might be good to get away from San Francisco for a while.

Steele looked around his office. No need to close it down; he'd only be gone a few weeks. If anybody broke in while he was away, there was really nothing worth stealing in either his office or his adjoining bedroom.

Except for his wartime journal. He wouldn't want to lose that. He opened the bottom desk drawer and took the journal out. He would have to leave it somewhere safe, someplace Stacy could get it if he didn't make it back from Arizona. Maybe he should leave it with Chan. He could be trusted. And maybe Chan had heard from Stacy. He was the one person she might write to, besides her parents.

Steele got up and went to the file cabinet. He unlocked it and took out his little Lemat revolver. He put it into his boot holster and pulled down his pants leg over the boot. He picked up the journal and went down the stairs to the street.

Turning up his collar against the cool morning wind that was coming off the bay, Steele headed up Market Street toward Chinatown. There weren't many private carriages on the streets so early in the day, but the new two-horse cabs were already out looking for business. Steele waved them off, preferring to walk the short distance to Chinatown.

At Stockton Street, he stopped to look up toward Nob Hill. For a moment he thought about going up to Stacy's house. The legislature was in session so her father would be over in Sacramento. But maybe Stacy's maid or the butler might have some information about when she was coming home from Europe. He shook off the idea and continued up Stockton. What was the point? He knew she wasn't coming back anytime soon, and he wasn't exactly welcome in the Moran home when she wasn't there.

By the time he reached Pine Street, the fog had rolled back a bit and the sun was just clearing the tops of the buildings on Mission. He could feel its warmth reflecting off the bright red walls of the new opera house. Even at that early morning hour, carpenters and brick layers were already swarming over the foundation of another new building. Now that war between the states had come to its inevitable conclusion, the builders seemed ready to restart the fast-paced expansion of the city that had marked the gold-rush fifties.

Five blocks further on, he passed through the imaginary gates that designated the Chinese sector of the city. From that point on, the buildings were a little older, a bit more dilapidated. The walls were covered by years of overlapping Chinese posters, many with colorful, hand-drawn pictures of many different types of products for sale. The shops were already open, their bins of strange herbs and unrecognizable root vegetables giving off indescribably exotic odors, as if the Chinese had somehow managed to bring the smell of China with them.

As he turned onto Washington Street, he realized he was the only non-Chinese on the crowded sidewalk. And he was the only person not hurrying. The Chinese people always walked with purpose, head-down, moving fast, avoiding eye contact.

He arrived at Chan's shop to find it open and already doing a brisk business. Bent-over Chinese women and non-smiling old Chinese men were lined up waiting for their medicinal herb formulas to be sorted and wrapped. The renowned Chinese herbalist, Mister Lu, was at his desk in the back of the shop, and as usual, there was a line of Chinese people waiting to see him.

Steele went through the shop and pushed his way through the beaded curtain into the large room beyond. The high-ceilinged tea room was very dark and smoky, except for the center where a shaft of sunlight came down through an overhead skylight. Smoke and dust floated upward toward the light.

Some of the Chinese men looked up as Steele entered, but they quickly looked away and went back to sipping their tea and smoking their long pipes.

Steele took a seat at the end of one of the long dark-wood tables. To make sure the table was clean before he put down his journal, he ran his hand along the surface and was struck by the smoothness of the wood. Undoubtedly it had been worn smooth by many years of elbows resting on it.

The waiter, carrying a tray full of tea cups, hurried past and disappeared through a hanging beaded curtain that led to another room. Steele knew what was in that back room: men lying in wooden bunks, smoking opium. He also knew, from a single venture into that room, that Americans were not welcome back there.

The waiter soon emerged and hurried toward him. "Mr. Steele," he said, smiling and bowing. "We happy see you. You want tea?"

"Yes," said Steele nodding slightly in response to each of the man's deep bows. "Tea, yes."

The little man hurried to the big wood-fired stove that provided both heating for the room and a cooking surface. Large cans of steaming liquid covered the top of the stove, adding humidity to the warm room.

Steele wondered why the waiter always seemed so happy to see him. He doubted other Americans received this type of enthusiastic greeting. Was it because of Stacy's friendly relationship with Chan? He had never seen any other non-Chinese customers in the tea room, but Stacy liked the place. Soon after they met, Stacy had brought him there to meet Chan, the old Chinese herbalist who was treating her mother's many ailments.

"You want food?" called the waiter. "I have good cake."

"Yes," said Steele, "please."

The man poured the steaming tea into a large metal cup and hurried back to Steele. Somehow he carried the hot metal cup in his bare hand. In the other hand, he balanced an ornate blue-on-white Chinese plate piled high with pieces of yellow cake. He arranged the tea and cake on the table and was ready to move away when Steele caught his wrist. "I would like to see Chan."

The little man's smile disappeared. "Chan very busy today."

"It's important."

The man frowned. "Okay, I go see."

Steele watched the waiter hurry to the heavy wooden door that guarded Chan's quarters. He knocked, and when the door opened he went in. The door closed behind him.

Steele used one finger to hook the handle of the hot tin cup and slid it a little closer. One sip told him it was too hot to drink. While he waited for the tea to cool, he tasted the yellow cake. He always enjoyed its rich, but unusual, flavor. He had never been able to figure out what gave it that strange, decidedly foreign, taste.

After several minutes, the waiter reemerged from Chan's quarters and waved for Steele to come. Steele hurried over and was let into the dark interior. Someone unseen in the gloom closed the door behind him, and Steele moved down the narrow, dimly lit narrow hallway toward the brighter light at its end. Beautifully-carved, heavy-looking wood cabinets lined both walls.

The hallway ended in a small room where Chan sat cross-legged on cushions reading letters. He was wearing his traditional Oriental overshirt that looked as if it was made of silk. It was dark blue, with a complex pattern of gold threads subtly woven into the cloth. Chan's mustache seemed to have been recently trimmed, but it still hung down below his mouth on both sides.

Steele had never been able to determine how old Chan was: sometimes he appeared to be middle-aged, while at other times he appeared to be much older. This was the first time Steele had seen him wearing glasses. He continued to read, one of his delicate hands held up in the air suggesting Steele should wait a moment before entering. Steele wondered if one of the letters might be from Stacy. They were on the very thin onion-skin paper that was typical of foreign mailings. Several unopened envelopes were stacked on a low table next to Chan.

Chan finished reading the letter and put it down. He gestured for Steele to come closer and indicated a round, flat cushion on the floor.

As usual, Chan seemed friendly, but reserved. The deep wrinkles around his eyes suggested wisdom, and perhaps a long life of happiness—or was it self-satisfaction?

Steele approached and sat cross-legged on the cushion.

"Mr. Steele, you are welcome here. Have you been well?" Chan had what sounded like a slight British accent, and as a result, Steele had always assumed that the old man had come from Hong Kong.

"Yes, I have been very well. And you?"

"We are all well here," he said glancing away with a brief wave of his hand. Steele wondered if Chan was referring to himself, everyone in the building, or perhaps all the Chinese in Chinatown. "However, there is small-pox in the quarter."

"I have heard nothing about that," said Steele, "but if you want, I can check at the hospitals to see if there has been a general outbreak."

"My people will not be seen at this city's hospitals."

Steele wasn't sure if that meant the Chinese depended exclusively on Chan's herb shop and his staff of herbal healers, or that the hospitals would not treat Chinese. Probably both were true.

"I have contacted the authorities," continued Chan. "They claim it is not small-pox. We will wait to see." He paused and a look of concern crossed his face. "Can we get you anything? Have you eaten?"

"I have eaten. Thank you."

Chan sat back and folded his hands across his stomach. Steele knew that meant it was time for him to state his business. "I am leaving town today," he said. "It's a new case. I'd like you to keep something for me, or rather, for Stacy, if I should not return." He showed Chan the journal. "It's nothing valuable, only my writings. From the war."

Chan reached forward to accept the journal. "Your property will be safe here."

"I will be traveling to Prescott, Arizona, with a man named Rudd. A reporter on the Bulletin."

"He is known to us."

"He says he came here from Arizona."

"Would you like us to learn more about this man before you leave town with him?"

"He seems to be very much in a hurry. We are leaving in the morning."

"Is that wise?"

"He seems to be an honorable man. But there may be more to this case than he is telling me."

"Then we will make inquiries."

"I thank you for that," said Steele. "As always, I appreciate your knowledge of . . . things."

Chan made a very slight bow.

"I must go now," said Steele, beginning to unfold his long legs. But he didn't get up. He hesitated, then said, "Has Stacy written to you?"

"She has not," replied Chan quietly.

"If she contacts you, please tell her I have gone to Arizona. On a case."

"If she contacts us, we will tell her where you have gone."

They waited, as if both knew there was more to be said.

Finally Chan asked a somber question: "And what is it you yourself are looking for in Arizona?"

Steele knew this was in reference not to Arizona, but to their previous philosophical conversations. " Of that I'm still not sure. Since the war . . . Maybe I'm just looking for something different, for something to change."

"Men sometimes become lost when they change their path."

"Are you saying I'll lose my way in Arizona?"

Chan looked Steele directly in the eyes. "If a man takes a new path, he can certainly become lost. The ancient writings say as a tree grows always upward, the superior man follow the path for which he is destined."

"That may be true, but how will I know when I have found my true path?"

"Ah, the answers for which you search may not be so easy to find. You must let them find you. Then you will know."

"Thank you for that advice. I will carry it with me."

Chan remained silent so Steele decided it was time for him to leave. He got up, but decided to ask one more question. "I heard that Prescott is becoming a center of commerce in Arizona now that it's the territorial capital. Do you know anyone I might contact there?"

Chan hesitated, but then seemed to make a decision. "Ask for Cousin Wang at the Dragon House. Bring him my greetings, and refer to me as *Uncle* Chan."

Steele had heard Stacy's mother refer to Chan as Uncle Chan. Was it a sign of respect? Or something else, something to do with Chinese clans?

Chan held up a finger. "But I would ask you to be discreet in your inquiries about this man, our cousin."

Steele assumed that meant he should only speak to Chinese people. "Thank you. I will contact him privately when I get there." He bowed to Chan and said, "You have been a good friend to Stacy and her mother. I hope I can also count you as my friend."

"Stacy is a remarkable woman," said Chan quietly. He did not rise, but he leaned forward in a deep bow from where he sat.

Steele left the shop and took the bayside streets back to his office. As he walked, he thought about what Chan had said about losing his path. It seemed to be a philosophical statement, but it came in response to his question about losing his way in Arizona. Was Chan trying to warn him about going to Arizona, or was is a more general warning about trying to find something through travel when it might be better found within himself?

Chapter 3

*T*he next morning Steele woke early and pulled his old Army pack out from under his bed. He was stuffing in a few clothes when he heard Rudd's knock at the door. He took one last look around the room to see if he'd forgotten anything. Even to his eyes, his room looked stark and empty. Except for the large number of books and papers that were stacked against the walls, all of his possessions were the three drawers of the old wooden dresser the landlord had provided. He grabbed a tube of matches, his knife, and some extra shells for his revolver and went through to his office. He opened the hallway door just as Rudd was about to knock again. Rudd looked at Steele's beat-up old pack. "Is that all you're taking?"

Steele swung the pack over his shoulder. "Yes. I'm ready."

Rudd led the way down the hall, talking as he went. "It's gonna be warm down there in Arizona. This fog's got me chilled to the bone so I'm ready for some of that hot Arizona sun. I've got a cab waiting downstairs. We'd better hurry or we'll be late for the southbound train."

During the short carriage trip to the railroad station, Rudd chatted away, commenting on the fancy new open carriages, the new, more-powerful steam trains, and the changing styles of dress on the street. In fact, he commented on just about everything he saw, always tying his comments to the rapid expansion of commerce in San Francisco and the powerful men behind it all. Steele could see why Rudd had become a reporter: he was interested in everything.

With Rudd going slowly dragging his heavy suitcase, they barely made it onto the morning train to Los Angeles just as it started to move. Rudd wanted to sit on the aisle, "To keep an eye on things." Steele didn't mind sitting next to the window: he had never made this train trip south and he was looking forward to seeing the countryside.

The train was barely up to speed when Rudd pointed out the window. "Did you know this spur is owned by the Central Pacific Railroad? It's true. Eventually the big four will own everything."

Steele couldn't help but wonder if Rudd's mention of the "big four" businessmen was a way to try to get him to talk about Stacy's father. Although it was unlikely the great Nathan Moran would ever mention Steele's name in public, a newsman like Rudd might have gotten wind of the famous man's strong disapproval of Steele's relationship with his daughter. And Stacy's mother had made no secret of the fact that her daughter would never be allowed to marry a recently-arrived drifter like Steele. She constantly scolded Stacy about her low-class acquaintances, not to mention her unladylike activities regarding women's rights. But she had not hesitated when asked to pay for Stacy's trip to the women's international congress in Paris. She was probably hoping Stacy would forget about Steele while she was over there. Maybe she was right; so far, Steele hadn't received a single letter from Stacy.

Rudd rambled on about the powers-that-be, complaining that their uncontrolled building programs were ruining the city. He lit up a small cigar, blew smoke toward the ceiling, and said, "Now, where was I?"

"I believe you were about to tell me more about what happened in Arizona."

"I was? Okay, let's see. I rolled into Prescott . . . I guess it was about five years back. It was a wide-open town back then, no city government or anything like that. Not even any law. The only thing that could pass for law there was old Judge Barnes. The hangin' judge they called him. And that's what he was. If the hangin' judge said somebody was guilty, for stealing horses, or killing somebody in a bar fight or whatever, the judge called for the hangman. And the guy got hung. Or if the judge thought anybody'd broke the law, he just had a few of the local boys throw 'em in jail. There wasn't any recourse, no other courts or anything like that, old Judge Barnes decided who was guilty and that was that."

"I suppose that's all changed now that it's the territorial capital."

"Yeah, but not as much as you might think. It's still a backwater town. The old judge died last year and got replaced by a traveling circuit judge who only comes in once every few weeks. They've still only got one marshal and he has to cover that whole part of the state. There's a town council, but Longmore lords over it. He thinks he owns the town just because he owns the biggest mine."

"Tell me about Willig."

"Dutch Willig was quite the old blowhard. Short little guy. Old as the hills, with a white beard down to here." Rudd held his hand halfway down his chest to demonstrate. "He was always going on about his fabulous gold mine out in the desert. He'd tell the story to anybody who'd buy him a drink. Some folks thought he really did have a gold mine somewhere out there, but ol' Dutch never seemed to have two dimes to rub together so maybe it was all a pack of lies. Still, there was this story around town that one time he brought in some ore that assayed pretty good. He told me that's why he had to sell the land grant. To get enough money to develop his gold mine."

"What do you think? Did he really did have a gold mine?"

"You wouldn't think so. He dressed in the same old rags all the time. But who knows? He was an odd duck, and he did spend a lot of time out somewhere in the desert. He always seemed to have enough to buy a round at the bar, but nobody knew where he got the money. One thing for sure, you couldn't go by anything Willig said. He was known to stretch the truth quite a bit. That's about all I can tell you. Things might have changed in Prescott since I left there, but I bet Longmore still rules the roost." He yawned and stretched. "Hey, Steele, you know the best way to pass the time on a long train trip? Sleep. I'm gonna take a little nap." With that, he pulled his hat down over his eyes and was asleep in seconds.

As the train steamed across the grasslands of central California, Steele thought about what Rudd had told him. Had Willig really been killed for the land grant? Was Longmore the killer as Rudd seemed to suspect? If so, did he have the document? But if he had it, why hadn't he done anything with it? The more Steele thought about it, the more unlikely the whole story seemed. A genuine Spanish land grant that lays claim to most of Arizona somehow falls into the hands of an old prospector? Steele knew that in cases like this, the truth often turned out to be something completely mundane. Maybe Longmore had simply killed Willig because he had stolen his money. He confronts Willig, demands his money back, an argument ensues, and Willig ends up dead. Simple. Happens every day. But what made a rich man like Longmore think the document was real in the first place? Why was he willing to send Rudd to Willig with a very large amount of money on the hope that Willig would turn over the document to him? That was the most puzzling aspect of the case: what made Longmore think a man like Willig could possibly have a genuine Spanish land grant? Longmore must have known something that he didn't tell Rudd, something that convinced him that Willig really did have the long-missing document.

Chapter 4

*T*he train made a brief stop in the sleepy town of Los Angeles while a new engine was hooked up to take them east toward Arizona. They rolled out of town, first to the south, then to the east, following a winding path between some rugged mountains. Then there was nothing but flat, featureless desert. As they traveled on to the east, Rudd slept off and on, waking up only long enough to hike up to the food car to bring back some fruit and sandwiches. Steele drew pictures of some of the other passengers for a while and when it grew too dark to draw he leaned back and tried to get some sleep.

Steele woke up as the train lurched to a stop. It was still dark outside. He nudged Rudd and said, "We've stopped."

Rudd struggled to wake up. He leaned across Steele to look out. "Oh, it's Colorado City. End of the line. Nuthin' here but an Army fort and a couple of houses around it. Stage won't head out for Arizona until dawn. We might as well get a little more shuteye." He closed his eyes and was asleep again in seconds.

Steele looked out into the night. He opened the window a crack and enjoyed the warmth of the desert's night air. It had a strange, smell to it, an almost imperceptible sharpness, like dried weeds riding in on a gentle breeze. Whatever it was, it couldn't be more different from the air in San Francisco. He remembered the smell of the salt air on that ship bound for America and how different it had been from the dry air in Rome. It had reminded him that he was going somewhere he'd never been and that thought had excited him. From that early experience, he had grown to love that feeling of heading into the unknown. When his father had taken the job in the American embassy and moved them to from New York to London, he'd been too young to remember much about the trip, but he did remember the feeling of excitement. And then years later, after he'd made his way back to America on his own, he'd learned that to go somewhere new all you to do was make the decision and go. In America, he'd continued to seek that feeling of newness, and it kept him constantly on the move, always curious about what was over the next hill. And then came the war. He had still been a teenager then, but he wanted to know more about this new war that everyone was talking about. He wanted to know what it meant, what made men leave their homes and jobs and farms to fight each other. Would it go on for a long time? Or would it end quickly, before he could learn about it? He'd walked all the way from New York to Virginia to see it for himself. What he saw horrified him, but he still wanted to know more; he couldn't understand how men could be brought to do such terrible things to each other. Eventually, that curiosity led him to a Army field hospital in Tennessee where he'd found a way to become part of it, a way to help without having to become a soldier. Now, as he looked out of that train window, he thought about all the people he'd met during the war, and all the places he'd been to. He recognized that old feeling of being in a new place as if it was an almost-forgotten old friend. Across the river was Arizona. Another new place. Would it be a new beginning?

As soon as dawn's light began to spread across the desert floor, the people in the train started to wake up and gather their things. Steele woke Rudd up and helped him get his heavy suitcase down from the overhead rack.

As they followed the other people toward the few ramshackle buildings that surrounded the fort, Rudd began to complain about his bad back. Steele took Rudd's suitcase and carried it for him.

"Never was much good at sitting," said Rudd, holding one hand to his back. "I'd rather carry rocks all day than sit. But hey, look at this desert would you? I always kind of liked the desert. Different from just about any other place."

Rudd was right. It was different from any other place Steele had been. There were plants, scrubby bushes and low-lying cactus, but they were few and far-between. Few of the plants were taller than waist-high. The ground underfoot seemed to be made up of sandy-colored dirt and small rocks.

"So, this is it," said Rudd. "What do you think?"

"Interesting," said Steele He realized many would think such a place was pretty much barren, without much to see or think about. But, to him, that was what made it interesting. It invited thoughts about what you would do it you were alone out there. Could he survive in a place like that? Could anyone?

Most of the people from the train went to the fort. The rest were met by carriages, leaving Steele and Rudd to walk the rest of the way to the stage office alone.

"Glad to see nobody else is going to Arizona today," said Rudd. "Maybe I'll get a chance to lie down in the stage. Rest my back."

Steele waited in the street while Rudd went inside the stage office to buy tickets. After a few minutes, Rudd came out yelling at the man who was loading the freight inside the stage: "Your boss said to take that stuff out of the coach. You've got passengers today."

"Aw, damn it to hell," said the man. "I just got it loaded in there."

"Well, get it out," said Rudd. "We've got to have a place to sit, don't we?"

Begrudgingly, the man started to unload the boxes, transferring them to the top of the coach. "Going to make the whole damn thing too top-heavy," he grumbled.

"All they care about is the freight," said Rudd, loud enough for the man to hear. "They make their money on the stuff they carry from town to town. The passengers and their comfort are an afterthought."

Steele pretended to check the stage over, but he was actually looking up the street to see if anyone was watching them. Although he hadn't seen anybody on the train who acted interested in Rudd, there was always the chance that someone could have followed them from San Francisco. There were a few men sitting on the steps of the local bar, probably waiting for it to open.

After a short wait, two stage employees came out of the office. They were both dressed in leather pants and long coats. Steele noted that they were both wearing sidearms.

One of the men climbed up into the driver's seat and took up the reins. "Okay, gents, let's get this show on the road," he said to nobody in particular.

The other man took the bags and put them up top while Rudd and Steele got inside the coach.

"This may not be so bad after all," said Rudd, patting the padded seat. "Last time I was in one of these things the seat was so hard I 'bout broke my butt."

But no sooner had he spoken when they heard someone shout: "Hey, wait for me."

Steele looked out and saw a man hurrying down the street toward them. "Is that the stage to Prescott?" he yelled.

"Oh, no," groaned Rudd. "I knew it was too good to be true."

Steele looked the man over. He was probably in his early thirties, tall and thin. He had a weathered look, as if he'd been living out-of-doors.

"You got to have a ticket," yelled the driver. "Go inside and get one."

"Right, I'll do that," said the late arrival. He went inside the building, but soon he was back, waving his ticket in the air. He climbed inside the coach. "Howdy, boys. Name's Carson, but my friends call me Carse."

Rudd scowled at him.

Steele thought he heard the remnants of a southern accent buried deep under Carson's western twang. Here, sit on this side," he said, patting the seat.

Carson sat down and Rudd put a hand to his back, as if to show the new passenger why he needed to sit alone. "My name's John Rudd," he said. "No nickname. And this is Steele. No nickname there either, at least none that I know of."

The stage started to move, slowly at first, and then faster, kicking up a powdery cloud of dust behind.

"You boys headin' for Prescott?" asked Carson.

"That's right," said Rudd. "Is that where you're going?"

"You bet. I hear they got lot's of good jobs up there. Minin' and such."

Steele didn't think Carson looked like the kind of man who would want to work underground in a mine. But now that the war was almost over, a lot of men would be coming west looking for just about any type of job. He decided to probe a little. "Were you in the war, Carson?"

"Sure was, fought at the battle of Independence in 62. Nobody remembers Missouri, but we fought a bunch of mean battles back there."

"The battle for the city," said Steele. "As I remember, Independence was taken in only one day."

"That's right, by God," said Carson. "You look a mite young to have been in the big one, but you got a good scar on your jaw there. Got shot did ya?"

Steele touched his cheek. "Shrapnel. I was not a soldier. I worked in a Union field hospital."

"A hospital, eh? Guess them Federals needed patchin' up too. Me, I got some holes and they never did get fixed. Got 'em crossin' that damn wide Mississippi. Them Federals took pot shots at us while we were on the ferry. Here, look at this." He pulled up his shirt. There was a small, round scar on his left side. "That's where the ball went in." He turned and pulled up the back of his shirt. "And that's where the damn thing came out." The much larger scar on his back was oblong and ragged.

Steele understood that type of wound. He had a similar one on his back, but he said nothing.

Rudd leaned forward for a closer look. "Looks like that bullet must have hit something and came out heading downward."

"Don't know what it did in there," said Carson, pulling down his shirt. "Never got no doctor to look at it. All I know is people said I was lucky. They said if it hadn't gone clean through I'd of probably died from havin' that lead ball in me."

The stagecoach picked up speed and the clouds of fine dust began to seep in through the cracks. Rudd used his hat to try to wave it away from his face.

They had just passed the last of the houses when Steele heard someone yelling behind them. He put his head out the window and saw a buckboard coming fast. It was drawn by only one horse, but soon it caught up with the stage and matched its speed alongside. There were three people bouncing around on the wood plank that served as a seat. The driver looked like a farmer, in dusty work clothes and knee-high boots. Next to him sat an attractive young woman with medium-length blonde hair, wearing a white blouse and tan pants. On the other side of the driver was a man in a plain brown suit. "Hey, stop," the man in the suit yelled. "I got to get on that stage."

Steele leaned out the window to call up to the driver, "Wait, you've got more passengers."

"Can't stop less they got a ticket," yelled back the stage driver. Steele could see that the stage was in the deep wheel tracks of the road, forcing the buckboard off the road. It was swerving wildly, dodging cactus and bushes.

The coach driver leaned out and pointed back toward the fort. "Wait for tomorrow's stage. Tomorrow mornin'."

"I can't wait 'til tomorrow," the man in the suit yelled back. "We've got important business in Prescott."

At that moment the buckboard had to swerve violently toward the stage to avoid driving into a sand wash. The two came dangerously close together, momentarily sharing the narrow road.

The young woman was holding onto the front edge of the buckboard's bench seat with both hands, but it didn't seem to Steele that she was all that afraid.

The stage driver steadfastly maintained his speed. "Can't help that," he yelled. "I got a schedule to keep."

"I'm goin' back to the stage office to get a ticket," yelled the man. "Then you'll have to let us on."

"I ain't gonna wait," shouted the driver. "Maybe you can catch us at the ferry." He snapped the reins to hurry the horses.

The driver of the buckboard pulled back on his horse, starting a wide turn. Steele watched as they headed back toward town, then pulled his head back in.

"Do you think they'll catch us?" said Carson.

Rudd shook his head. "Not unless they get back before they get this stage loaded on the ferry. They'd have to wait for the next ferryboat and they'd never catch us out on the open road in Arizona."

The stage maintained a fast pace for several minutes and then slowed as the road began to gradually drop down toward the Colorado River. When they arrived at the river, the driver pulled the horses to a stop and yelled, "Everybody out. Nobody allowed inside while we're aloadin'."

The three of them got out, brushing the dust off their clothes. Rudd tried to beat some of the dust off of his shoulders with his hat.

Another wagon was already aboard the ferry barge and they all watched as it moved away from the bank. The tow engine chugged rhythmically, venting excess steam every few seconds. At the halfway point, the loaded boat passed the returning empty barge. The tow cable alternately sagged and snapped, but the barges moved steadily forward.

Rudd was looking back toward the west. "They're not going to make it."

"Too bad," said Carson. "That was a mighty pretty gal. I wonder if she was goin' to Prescott too."

"Yes, I suspect she is," said Steele. "The man in the suit said *we* have important business in Prescott. And there were two bags in the back of the buckboard. The driver wasn't dressed for traveling."

"That so?" said Carson. "I didn't see any of that. I was just watchin' that crazy wagon go. I thought they were going to turn the thing over."

Two men on the dock guided the returning barge into place with long poles, while another man released the clutch of the tow engine. The stage driver cautiously urged the nervous horses forward. "Take 'em slow, Charlie," he yelled down to his assistant. Charlie got between the lead horses and coaxed them onto the barge.

"Here they come," yelled Carson, pointing back toward the west. "And they're goin' like all get out."

Steele and Rudd turned to look. The buckboard was approaching fast, trailing a large cloud of dust that somehow seemed about to overtake them.

When the stage was loaded onto the ferry, the driver yelled, "Let's go, gents. Everybody aboard."

The others climbed aboard the ferry, but Steele lagged behind.

"Let's go, let's go," shouted the driver. The barge operators untied the ferry and the lapping waves began to slowly move it away from the dock.

Steele waited on the dock as the buckboard arrived and slid to a stop. Its trailing cloud of dust finally caught up and it rained down fine particles on its occupants. The man in the brown suit jumped down and grabbed both bags out of the back. He ran down the hill toward the ferry, followed closely by the young woman. She was slender and athletic-looking, running easily despite her tight-fitting pants and soft leather boots.

"Looks like you've got two more passengers," shouted Steele over the din of the barge's steam engine.

The operator pulled the engine's clutch lever and the barge stopped abruptly. The horses slid forward a little on the wooden deck. They lifted their heads nervously, their eyes open wide. Charlie stood his ground between the two lead horses, calming them with soft words.

The man and the young woman arrived on the run, out of breath.

"Just in time," said Steele.

"Thanks for waiting," said the young woman breathlessly.

"It took a while to get the stage loaded onto the barge anyway," said Steele. "I don't think the driver minded waiting a few minutes."

"Oh, good," she said. "My name's Becky. Rebecca Laird, but Becky for short. And this is my dad Lucky Laird."

Her father, a tall, gaunt-looking man with wavy dark hair, reached out and shook Steele's hand vigorously.

"Glad to meet you, glad to meet you," he gasped.

"Aw, c'mon," yelled the stage driver from the barge. "Let's get goin'. I got a schedule to keep."

"Nice to meet you both," said Steele. "My name's Drew Steele. Here, you two jump aboard and I'll hand you your bags."

"Oh, thank you," said Becky. But as she prepared to jump, she slipped slightly on the wet deck and Steele had to reach out and catch her elbow to keep her from falling. She blushed as she briefly met Steele's eyes, but quickly turned to jump nimbly across to the ferry.

Steele then steadied her father so he could also hop aboard. Steele tossed them their bags and jumped aboard himself.

During the river crossing, Laird introduced himself to Rudd and Carson. Despite their mad dash to catch the stage and the driver's unwillingness to wait for them, he was still cheerful. He described himself as a simple farmer and introduced his daughter with obvious pride. "She's the prettiest girl in the area," he said. "Look at that pretty hair." He tried to pat the top of her head, but she pushed his hand away and frowned at him. "And she was the smartest kid in her school too," he added.

"I'll tell you one thing," said Carson, "you're gonna cut quite a figure up there in Prescott. They probably ain't seen a pretty young girl like you up there since . . . well, since never."

"Have you been to Prescott recently?" asked Steele.

"Naw," said Carson with a shrug. "Never been there myself. What I meant was there probably hasn't ever been a pretty gal in those parts. Probably nowhere north of Tucson, I expect."

"Are you from Tucson then?"

"Tucson's not a bad place," said Carson taking off his hat and looking inside it. "At least it's a real city, with things to do there. They got two or three hotels and lots of bars. More than Tombstone even."

"Tucson's down in the southern part of the state," said Steele. "What brings you to this area?"

"Oh, just . . . lookin' around," said Carson. "Like I said, lookin' for a job."

"Haven't ever been to Tucson," said Laird. "We were on our way there when we saw this here big river. We decided to stop and put our roots down here, didn't we, Becky?"

She nodded and smiled at him.

"We came all the way from up north in California after Becky's mom died. When I saw this big Colorado River running through here, I said to Becky, where there's water, you can grow stuff. That's what I said, didn't I Becky?"

She again nodded and smiled.

At that moment, they reached the east bank of the river. They all got off and waited while the driver and Charlie got the horses off the barge and onto the shore. Then Charlie hurried them all back into the coach and soon they were on the road again. With the two added passengers, it was cramped quarters inside the stage. Rudd had positioned himself next to Becky, with her father seated on the other side of the coach, next to Steele and Carson.

"Glad there weren't any passengers waiting on this side of the river," said Rudd. "They'd need a shoehorn to pack us all in."

"Not many passengers on this stage ever," said Laird. "This many is unusual."

"So your moniker is Lucky," said Carson. "That your real name?"

"I spose it is," said Laird. "At least it's what my folks always called me."

Carson seemed amused by it. "Lucky Laird. Has a ring to it. Are you a real lucky feller?"

Laird just shrugged again and kept his eyes down. "Don't know about that. It's just the name I've always gone by." He paused, and then added, "My daughter here is the lucky one." He reached across to pat her on the knee. "And I'm lucky to have her."

Despite the bouncing and lurching of the stagecoach, Carson took out a bag of tobacco and started carefully rolling a cigarette. Everyone watched him as he completed it, licked the paper, and lit it up. He blew the smoke toward Laird. "Now tell me somethin', Lucky. What kind of crops could a farmer possibly grow in this here sandy desert?"

"I'll show you," said Laird. He reached into his jacket pocket and pulled out a small, greenish yellow fruit. "Take a look at that little beauty, will ya."

"What the heck is that?" said Rudd. "Looks like a little runt of an orange."

"Right you are," said Laird. "It is an orange. A mite small so far, but the trees are still little."

"Orange trees?" said Rudd, raising his eyebrows. "You're trying to grow orange trees in the desert?"

"Not *trying* to grow em. We got 'em goin' already. Almost a hundred little green trees growin' up a little bit more every day. Should have a few good oranges by next year."

Carson reached out and took the little orange. "By God. Look at that," he said. "So that's what an orange looks like."

"You never seen an orange?" said Laird. "Where you been, man? They get a lot bigger than this. And more . . . you know, orange colored. When these things get ripe they are about the best eatin' thing you ever had."

"I've eaten oranges," said Rudd. "Once. But I thought they only grew back there in Florida."

"You're right," said Laird, taking back his orange from Carson. "Florida is the only place in this here U-S-of-A where you can get an orange. That's why we decided to grow 'em out here. I hear you can't hardly find an orange out west, even in the big cities."

"They sometimes sell oranges in San Francisco," said Steele. "But they're really expensive."

Laird patted his daughter on the knee. "I'll bet we'll be able to sell them San Francisco city folks a bunch of our oranges, won't we Becky?"

She nodded in agreement, then glanced at Steele, embarrassed at being the center of attention.

"Citrus trees do well in the sandy soil of Florida," said Steele, "so they might grow here. But where will you get the water?"

"Well, I'll tell you," said Laird, "water sure was our big problem. Our place is too far from the Colorado to get it from there, and the railroads and the big boys have all the water rights tied up anyhow. But there was this valley on the upper part of our property, up in the hills. They thought it was worthless land, but Becky here explored it and she found a little tiny spring up there. Turns out, the joke's on them railroad boys. They thought they were pretty smart, selling us dumb farmers worthless desert land. But we dug out that little spring up in the hills and now it gives a pretty good flow, year round. We built water wagons and hauled water down from the spring every day to get them trees started. Haulin' it every day just about killed us, but them nice little green trees are growin' up good now."

"Won't they take even more water as they grow larger?" asked Steele.

"Yeah, but we didn't think about that at first. We bought the land with cash we had saved up, and it cost us all the rest of out money to get the little starter trees from way down in Mexico. We had to bribe just about everybody from the town mayors to the local police to get 'em back across the border. But you're right, water was our big problem. When them trees started to grow, we couldn't get anything else done but haul water. Then my Becky here came up the answer."

Becky touched his elbow. "Father, maybe these men don't want to hear about all this."

Laird looked at her and shrugged. "Well, now that we've got the water all figured out, it should be safe to tell these fellows about it. Why don't you tell 'em? It was your brains that figured it out."

"Oh father, you make such a big thing of it. The truth is, I just kind of stumbled on to it. I was up there, well, sort of . . . cooling off in the spring, when I looked up at the rocky cliff and realized it wasn't all that far between the canyon where the spring is and the next-over canyon that's right up above our farm. I got to thinking, what if we could cut some kind of hole through the rocks and divert the water over to our canyon?"

"That's right," interrupted her father. "After my smart little girl told me about her idea, I hired a couple of local fellas to try to blast a hole from that canyon through to our canyon. If we could get through, we could build a trough from there all the way down to our trees. They were willin' to try it. Dynamite is cheap in these parts."

"But it was harder than we thought," Becky said. "It took us six months."

"Yeah, but we did 'er," said her father. "You should've heard us yellin' our heads off when that first water flowed through to our canyon."

"But the water sank right into the sand," his daughter reminded him. "We had to borrow more money."

"Yeah, we ended up havin' to extend the wood trough all the way from the canyon wall where the water comes out through the rock. It's only half built now, but we'll get it done and that way we'll have irrigation water before the summer gets really hot."

"Now if that ain't a story," said Carson. "Divertin' water from one canyon to the other."

"Yep," said Laird. "we're flat broke now and our backs are busted too, but we should be able to make a go of it from here on."

"I've got a bad back too," announced Rudd loudly. Then, in an aside to Becky, he added, "But I generally don't make too much of it."

"Are your water rights registered in Prescott?" asked Steele. "Is that why you're going up there?"

"Well, we don't think we really need anything like water rights, but we got the land made legal, if that's what you're askin'. I got a handwrit deed from the railroad. We went out to talk to them railroad boys in California, but they said Arizona land is supposed to be registered in Arizona. So we got to go up there to Prescott to make sure it gets registered legal like. I sent 'em a telegram. They said I had to bring the original deed."

"Is there a problem?" asked Steele.

"Nah, I got the deed right here." Laird tapped his chest to indicate that he had it in his inside suit pocket. "It's just that the damn railroad boys forgot to register the sale in Prescott. That's what they said anyhow. Now we got to go all the way up there to straighten it out."

Steele noticed that Laird's daughter looked worried. Maybe there was more of a problem than he was letting on.

The stage slowed, made a transition to another road that curved off to the north, and sped up again.

"I'm not surprised the problem is with the railroad people," said Rudd. "They're screwing up this country good. Ever hear of a man named Moran? He's a rich and powerful man in San Francisco. He was the one who started a lot of the railroads in the north part of California."

Again, Steele wondered if Rudd knew about his connection to Stacy's father. But Rudd didn't seem to be watching him for a reaction.

Carson shook his head, but Laird said he thought he'd heard of him. "Didn't he take the railroad through the Sierras?"

"He likes to take credit for it," said Rudd, "and he made the most money out of it. But it was all done off the backs of the Chinese laborers he imported."

Laird said, "I heard there are more than thirty thousand of them Chinese here now."

"Right," agreed Rudd, "at least that many. San Francisco is full of 'em. Let me tell you a story about the great Nathan Moran. Moran had a big problem up there in the Sierras. He had his Chinese coolies blasting away rock laying track fast, but by the end of summer they came to this deep chasm. They'd have to build a bridge over it. But

Moran had used up all of his financing. He was stuck, so what do you think he did?" Rudd paused to light up one of his little cigars.

Steele could tell Rudd was enjoying himself, controlling the pacing of his story, giving his listeners time to think about what Moran was going to do.

"I'll tell you what he did. Moran ignored the experts' advice and decided to build a quick, temporary bridge. He got his coolies to start building it out of the only thing he had handy, railroad ties. When the thing was done, it was five stories tall and swayed in the wind even with no train on top of it." Rudd swayed back and forth to show them what it looked like. Becky, watching him, also swayed back and forth.

Steele took out his drawing pad and started a sketch of her.

"But somehow it held up," continued Rudd. "A few passenger trains actually made it across that shaky trestle before the government inspectors found out about it. They said no more trains would be allowed across. The trains stopped and Moran stopped making money. But did he give up?"

Like all good story tellers, Rudd was watching his audience. He noticed Becky was getting distracted by the dust that was coming in through the window. "Would you like me to close the curtain," he asked?

"No, it's so hot we'd better leave it open," she said. "Please continue with your story."

"Well, Moran wasn't about to shut down his railroad. He just had his Chinese bury the whole thing." Rudd took a puff off of his cigar and blew it up toward the ceiling while he waited for that idea to sink in. "Yep, believe it or not, he sent about a thousand of them collies up into the hills to get dirt. You know, using those poles with bags tied on each end. Bag after bag they brought dirt down until eventually they completely buried the whole five-story trestle. It's still that way today."

"Now that's what I like," said Carson, slapping his knee. "A damn good story."

"I wrote the story up in my newspaper," said Rudd. "As a result of my story, people from San Francisco sometimes take a drive up there on Sundays to see that buried bridge."

"Oh, do you work for a newspaper?" asked Becky.

"Sure do," said Rudd, smiling at her.

"Then why are you goin' to Prescott?" asked Carson.

"Well, just . . . some old business to take care of." He glanced at Steele.

"Are the buildings really as tall as people say?" asked Becky? "In San Francisco, I mean. I heard every one of the streets are paved."

"And I heard some of the people have toilets inside their houses," added her father.

While Rudd answered their questions, Steele worked on his drawing of Becky. She was a remarkably pretty girl, and she didn't seem to have any pretense or guile. She couldn't be more unlike the overdressed and overly made-up young women of San Francisco. Steele tried hard to capture her simple, youthful attractiveness. He emphasized her high cheekbones and carelessly brushed back blonde hair. Despite her youth, she seemed to have a kind of common-sense calmness about her.

"What's that you're drawing there, Mr. Steele?" asked Laird.

"Steele draws pictures of everybody he meets," said Rudd. "He drew one of me too."

"It's just a pastime," said Steele. He removed the drawing from the pad and handed it to her. "I'm really not very good at it."

"Now would you look at that," said Laird. "Never had a picture of my little girl before."

"Hey, that's pretty good," said Carson. "Really looks like her."

"That's my girl," said Laird, grinning. "Pretty as a picture."

Becky stared at the picture. "Do I really look like that? I mean, I've never seen a picture of myself." She handed the drawing back to Steele.

Steele handed it to Laird. "You can have it if you want it."

"Well, I sure would like it, if you don't mind givin' it up." He sat back to examine the drawing more closely.

By mid-morning, the stage had left the flat desert and was making its way up into the foothills. The higher they went, the rockier the ground became, and the road often skirted clusters of huge boulders. As the sun climbed higher, it turned the sky to a washed-out blue that seemed high and distant, as if it was shrinking away from the oppressive heat of the desert floor.

When they reached the higher elevations, the vegetation gradually grew more plentiful. There was a scattering of small trees that Steele thought might be a shorter variety of the tall pine trees he'd seen years before when he was traveling through Utah. He wished he would have had time to go to the library to read up on the plants and animals of Arizona before he'd left San Francisco.

The others talked or dozed while Steele drew quick sketches of the landscape they were passing through.

Becky leaned closer to see what he was drawing. "Do you also come from San Francisco, Mr. Steele?" she whispered, trying not to disturb the others who were dozing.

"Yes," whispered Steele. "Have you been there?"

"No, but I'd sure like to go there someday. I hear it's got everything there."

Just then the stage took a sharp turn, waking the others up. Dust filtered in through the cracks and rained down on them.

"Damn, this is about the dustiest I've ever seen this road," complained Rudd. He looked out the window. "Looks like we're heading up into the mountains."

"We'll be comin' to McDowell Pass pretty soon," said Laird. "People are sayin' Geronimo's the one who caused all that trouble up there."

"What trouble was that?" asked Rudd.

"Oh, maybe it's all rumor. Ever since Geronimo busted out of the San Carlos reservation, there's been lots of Indian trouble. So when some Indians robbed a stage at McDowell Pass, everybody said it had to be him."

"We published a story in my newspaper that said he was supposed to be down south somewhere," said Rudd. "In the mountains near Tucson."

"Who knows where those Redskins are," said Carson. "Those damn Indians wander all over this state like they own it."

"I believe they do think they own it," suggested Steele. "And have for a very long time."

Carson frowned at Steele. "Yeah, well they're sposed to be locked up on them reservations now. Where they belong."

"The Indians are not actually supposed to be held prisoner on the reservations," said Steele. "Technically, the reservation lands belong to the Indians."

"What?" said Carson? "How could that be?"

"The reservation lands were created by the U.S. Congress. They are *reserved* for the Indians."

"Well, how about that," said Carson, shaking his head. "Wouldn't it be just like congress to do some damn fool thing like that. Why should we have to give them anything? I thought we won the war with them Indians."

Steele didn't reply. He knew it would be a waste of time to argue with the man.

"We keep seeing bands of the young Indians on our tree farm," said Laird. "I guess they leave the reservation to hunt."

"And to steal," added Carson.

"Yes, they do some of that too," agreed Laird, "but so far they haven't taken anything of real value from us."

"Well," drawled Carson, "I haven't had much dealin's with Indians, so far, at least. But we'll see what happens when we get to this here pass you were talkin' about. I got somethin' here for that Ger-on-ee-mo." He took out his revolver.

Becky shied away from the big gun and Laird reached out to push it away. "I don't think we'll need that," he said. "There hasn't been any real trouble at the pass since last fall."

The stage made slow progress through a wide valley and up over a series of round-topped hills, but then it suddenly sped up as the road turned down toward a sandy ravine. The driver was shouting at the horses and snapping the reins to hurry them, but as they hit the sand, the stagecoach slowed and then stopped abruptly, throwing Becky and Rudd forward. Rudd ended up on Carson's lap and Becky ended up in Steele's arms as he caught her to keep her from falling. She quickly returned to her seat, blushing, but apparently not hurt.

Carson pushed Rudd back to his seat, muttering, "I knew I shoulda sat across from the gal."

Rudd leaned out the window, "What are you trying to do, kill us?"

"We're stuck," yelled back the driver. "Everybody out."

They all got out and found Charlie on his knees looking under the stage. "She's bottomed out in the sand. Stuck good."

Steele walked around the stage and saw that the front wheels were only a few inches down into the sand, but both of the rear wheels were buried up to the hubs.

"Come on, you men," shouted down the driver. "Give a push."

Steele and Laird and Carson got behind the stage, but Rudd announced he had a bad back and went to sit in the shade.

"Haw," yelled the driver. He cracked his whip.

"All at once now," shouted Steele and they all began to push. The stage rocked forward, but after a few inches of progress, the horses gave up and the wheels rolled back into the sandy hole.

The driver got down and came back to survey the situation. He took one look at how deep the wheels were buried and took off his beat-up old hat to hit the side of the stage with it. He walked around the stage swearing. He glanced toward Becky. "Sorry ma'am, but this damn thing ain't meant to carry this kind of load." Son of a bitch . . . sorry ma'am, is too heavy for this road." He hit the side of the stage with his hat again and said, "Guess we're gonna have to unload 'er, Charlie."

Charlie didn't look very happy at the prospect. "We ain't never had to do that before."

"Wait a minute, boys," said Carson. "I think we got us a bigger problem up there." He pointed toward the top of the hill.

Steele saw what Carson was looking at. Three Indians on horseback were watching them.

"Uh oh," said Rudd, getting up. "Is this that McDowell pass you were talking about?"

"Yep," said Laird. "This is it."

Rudd hurried to hide behind the stagecoach.

Laird urgently waved at his daughter. "Rebecca, get over here."

She came, but not too quickly.

Steele stayed where he was. Carson had his revolver out and the driver climbed up and got his rifle. He tossed a shotgun down to Charlie. They all watched the Indians and the Indians, high above, watched them.

"We just gonna sit here?" said Carson. "It'll be dark in a few hours."

"Well, we can't unload," said the driver. "That's what they're waiting for. The whole bunch of 'em'll come yippin' down here and grab whatever they can."

"If there are only three of them," said Steele, "I don't think they will attempt anything. And if there are more of them in hiding, then they can come down here anytime they want."

The driver didn't seem able to make a decision.

"Maybe they're not going to do anything," said Becky. "Maybe they're just curious."

"Waiting for us to make a mistake, more likely," said Carson. "So they can pick us off."

"Becky could be right," said Steele. "Maybe they're just curious about how we're going to get the stage unstuck."

"Well, we're not gonna get it unstuck just sitting here, " said Rudd, peeking around from behind the stage. "Any ideas, Steele?"

"If we had some kind of pole, we might be able to lift it up while the horses pull."

"Don't have any poles," said the driver. "But it's a good idea. The bottom draggin' under the back is what's got it hung up."

"Let's dig out the rear wheels a bit," suggested Steele. "To see what it looks like under there." He looked up at the driver. "Do you have a shovel?"

The driver untied the canvas tarp that was covering the top of the stage. He found a shovel and tossed it down to Steele.

Steele began to scoop away the sand.

Carson stayed where he was with his revolver pointed up the hill.

Laird found a stick and used it to drag sand away from the wheels on the other side of the coach. Becky got to her knees and tried to pull away some of the sand with her hands. Rudd remained in his seated position behind the stage, but he did push aside a little sand with his foot.

Once the sand had been scooped away from the wheels, Steele got down on all fours and looked under the stage. "It's no good," he said, "it's still resting on the bottom. We need to lift it up."

"We're not gonna find anything to lever it up around here," said Laird, looking around. "Nothin' but Manzanita and scrub."

"I noticed a couple of big cottonwood trees in that last dry wash we crossed," said Steele. "Maybe I can find some wood to use as a lever. I'll run back to see."

"You can't go out there alone," said Becky. "What if there are more of those Indians waiting for you out there?"

"They might be waitin' for dark," said Carson. "That's the way them sneakin' redskins do it."

"I don't see why they'd bother me," said Steele. "I'll be back soon." He turned and started to run back down the road, maintaining a steady pace. Despite the urgency of the situation, it felt good to be out of the confines of the stagecoach and running.

After about ten minutes of easy running, he came to the wash. The two Cottonwood trees he'd seen from the stage were both more than twenty feet tall. One of them appeared to be dead. There didn't seem to be anybody around. It was very quiet, except for the creaking of the dead tree in the slight breeze.

There was a fallen tree limb on the ground under the tree. He picked it up, but it didn't seem very strong. There was another limb still attached to the dead tree. He jumped up and caught hold of it. He hung there for a moment and then began bouncing up and down, trying to get the branch to break. But it didn't break; it was surprisingly solid.

He continued to hang there, resting, but then he thought he heard something. He dropped to the ground and ducked behind the tree. He heard it again. Someone was coming up the wash from the direction of the road. He reached down and took his pistol out of his boot.

But then he saw it was Laird. He was trying to hurry, but he was struggling in the deep sand of the wash.

Steele put his pistol away and stepped out from behind the tree. "Here I am. Thanks for coming to help."

Laird shrugged. "Aw, hell, Becky shamed me into it. Said we shouldn't of let you go out here alone. I tried to catch up with you, but you're too darn fast."

"Has anything changed back there?"

Laird shook his head. "One of the Indians rode away. Carson thinks he may have gone to get others."

Steele pointed to the dead branch. "Let's jump up and see if we can break that branch off. It'd make a good lever."

"I'm willin', but I don't think I can jump that high."

"It's not as high as it looks. Here we go. One, two, three, jump!"

Steele jumped up and caught the branch, but Laird barely brushed it with his fingertips.

Steele dropped down and interlaced his fingers. "Put your foot in here. I'll boost you up."

Laird put his foot in Steele's hands, bounced a few times, and then stood up. He steadied himself with his hand on top of Steele's head and then made a grab for the branch. "Got it!"

Steele jumped up next to Laird and caught hold. "Ready? Let's bounce to try to break it off."

They both began to pull up and down, getting in rhythm. But the branch didn't show any signs of breaking. "I think it's too tough," said Laird, out of breath.

"One more time," said Steele. "I think we've about got it." But then Steele heard something. He looked up and saw two Indians on horseback watching them. They were close, just on the other side of the sand wash. One of the Indians was an older man with a square jaw and dark, weathered skin. He seemed very somber, sitting quietly on his horse, watching them. He was wearing a faded blue Union Army shirt, unbuttoned to the waist, and he had a rifle tied to his back with what looked like rawhide string. The other Indian was a young boy, shirtless, and maybe still in his early teens. He had dark stripes painted on his cheeks.

Laird continued to hang on the limb. "It's not breaking, Steele. And my arms are about to give out." But then, as he gave it one more hard bounce, it broke and they both fell to the ground. Steele landed on his feet, but Laird fell over backwards, the limb landing on top of him.

The old Indian began to laugh, quietly at first, and then louder, a deep laugh from the belly. Then the boy joined in.

Laird sat up and blinked. "Oh my God, it's Indians."

"They seem to think two white men hanging from a tree is a pretty funny sight," said Steele. "Let's just take our tree limb and go."

Laird jumped up and grabbed one end of the limb while Steele got ahold of the other. They hurried up the wash toward the road.

"What if they shoot us in the back?" whispered Laird.

"If they wanted to shoot us, they could have done it while we were hanging from that limb. Let's just keep moving." Steele broke into a jog, but Laird kept stumbling. Steele shifted the load so he was carrying most of it.

"Damn, that was close," said Laird. "Wonder why they didn't shoot us?"

"Why would they? A couple of grown men bouncing on a tree limb."

Laird began to chuckle. "Guess it did look pretty funny. Specially when I fell on my ass. I bet they liked that."

With Steele carrying most of the load, they soon made it back to the stage.

Laird dropped his end of the tree limb in the sand. "Hey, everybody, we saw more Indians back there. One of them had a rifle."

Rudd jumped up and dusted off the back of his pants. "Are they coming this way?"

"Don't know," said Laird. "We got out of there fast."

"We don't know where Carson went," said Becky. "We heard a shot and the Indians that were up on the ridge went away."

"Well, let's try that pole of yours," said the driver. "We got 'er dug out as much as we can."

Steele positioned the tree limb under the stage. Then he rolled a large rock under the limb to get leverage and pushed down hard on the other end. The stage lifted a little.

"By God, that might be just enough to free 'er," said the driver. "Let's try it." He climbed back and grabbed the reins. "When I say go, you men down there push for all you're worth."

Laird and Becky got behind the stage and even Rudd came to help.

"Now!" yelled the driver.

Steele pushed down on the pole just as the driver cracked his whip and yelled, "Pull, damn you. Show 'em how it's done, Shadow."

The stage suddenly rolled forward out of the sand with surprising ease. The driver kept on urging the horses forward until the stage was completely out of the wash.

Steele rolled away the rock and threw the tree limb into the bushes before following the others as they ran to the stage.

Once they were all inside, the driver cracked his whip again and the stage started to move, but Becky cried out, "Wait! What about Carson?"

Steele opened the stagecoach door and leaned out. "Hold on, driver. We're missing one in here."

The driver acted like he hadn't heard and kept the team going fast up the hill.

Becky grabbed Steele's sleeve. "Don't fall out. Maybe Carson is waiting up ahead."

Steele started to pull back inside, but just then he saw Carson coming. He still had his revolver out and he was running for all he was worth to catch the stage. Steele yelled up to the driver, "Here he comes. Stop!"

The driver didn't stop, but he did slow down. Charlie was leaning out, looking back.

Carson finally caught up and reached for Steele's hand. Steele pulled him inside and Carson collapsed into his seat, out of breath, but laughing. "I put one hell of a scare into them Indians. Might have hit one of 'em." He waved his revolver in the air.

"Why did you do that?" said Becky. "All they were doing was watching us."

"Listen, girly, this is Arizona. There's a bounty on renegade Indians in this state. Worth a five-dollar gold piece for every scalp you bring in."

"If the bounty is paid for the scalp," asked Steele, "how would anyone know if it truly was a renegade?"

Carson stared at him, and then shrugged. "Does it matter?"

"It certainly does matter," said Becky. "They shouldn't be paying people to kill Indians in the first place."

"Oh, so you're one of that type," said Carson. "Listen, girly, if you knew what those murderin' Redskins did back in fifty-nine you'd be singing a different tune about now." He shook his finger in her face. "Down near Tucson those bloodthirsty--"

Steele caught Carson's wrist and pulled him away from Becky.

Carson jerked his arm free. "Don't be puttin' your hands on me, bub. Last man who did that to me—"

"Now, let's all just take it easy here," said Laird. "We aren't out of this yet. What if they're waiting for us up at the top of the hill?"

Carson stared at Steele for a long moment and then stuck his pistol out of the window. "Let 'em come. I'm ready for 'em."

Everyone was watching out the windows as they crested the hill, but there was no sign of the Indians. The driver kept the stage moving fast until they were over the top and starting down the other side.

When the stage slowed to its normal pace, Laird leaned back and laughed. "You should've seen us. There we were, hangin' on this dead tree limb, bouncin' away to try to break it off and up comes these two Indians. Real close. And you know what they did? They started laughin'. Pretty funny I guess, us hanging up there on that tree limb. When I fell down they laughed their asses off, especially the old one."

"Really?" said Becky. "That's all they did? Just laughed?"

"Yep, that's all they did." He turned to Steele. "You know, I've been thinking, Steele. Do you think that old guy could have been Geronimo?"

"We don't even know if he's been in this area," said Steele.

"This stage stops for the night up at Camp Verde," said Rudd. "Maybe they'll know something about him there."

"Yeah," said Laird, "and maybe the Army'll be able to tell us why all these Indians are runnin' loose around here."

By the time they reached Camp Verde, the sun was setting. A young Lieutenant met the stage and listened patiently while the driver told him about the Indians they'd seen.

Then Laird told him about the two Indians who'd watched while they hung from the tree branch. He left out the part about the Indians laughing, but described the old Indian and asked if it could have been Geronimo.

The Lieutenant shrugged and said, "It's possible. A lot of people claim to have seen him south of here, but nobody knows for sure if it really was him."

Carson let out a gruff laugh and said he was going to the bar to get a drink.

A young Mexican boy showed the rest of them to their quarters, two shacks built out of rough wood. There was one for the *Señoritas* and one for the *hombres*. The men's quarters were remarkably stark, nothing inside except for a half-dozen sagging beds pushed up against the walls. Steele assumed the women's quarters wouldn't be much better, and he had a sudden thought about how Stacy would react to such a place. Becky would be sleeping alone in the *Señorita's* shack and Steele suspected she probably wouldn't give the primitive sleeping quarters much thought one way or the other.

After they stowed their luggage, they all went back outside to find an old Mexican couple busily setting out hot tortillas and cold beans on a plank table. They politely asked for a dollar from each of the passengers.

Rudd complained that it was "a mighty high price for tortillas and cold beans," but he ended up eating a lot of it.

After eating their meal, the others headed for the shacks to get some sleep, but Steele sat on a stump in the cool night to relax for a while and think about the trip. As he looked up at the very bright stars, he realized he hadn't thought much about San Francisco, or Stacy, since they'd left the train in Colorado City.

His thoughts were interrupted when he heard someone coming up behind him. He quickly stood up. It was Becky.

"Oh, I'm sorry," she said. "I didn't men to disturb you."

"I was just looking at the stars. Will you join me?" He moved aside to give her room to sit down.

She sat down, very close, and stared up at the sky. "I love to look at the stars. And they're so much brighter up here in the mountains."

Steele couldn't see her very well in the dark, but he could smell her perfume. Or was it soap? She had probably just finished washing herself in the tin basin that was set up outside the women's sleeping quarters.

"Oh, there," she said, excited. "A falling star. Did you see it?"

"No, where was it?"

"Just above the trees. It was a long one. At home, I see them all the time. Sometimes I lay out in the desert at night just to watch for them. Last fall I saw twenty in one night."

"I read they come in groups like that every fall."

"Really? Why would that be?"

"They don't really know. But they say it happens every year."

"It must be wonderful to be educated," she said. "In the small town I grew up in, I went to a little school for all eight years, but the woman who taught us mostly wanted us to learn about the Bible. I learned to read and write, but every spring I'd get behind when I had to drop out for planting time. And it would happen again in the fall when we brought in the crops."

"You don't have to go to school to learn. In San Francisco there are several good libraries. I go there often to read."

"I want to go to San Francisco," she said quietly. "Someday."

"I'm sure you will."

"Maybe I'll marry someone who will take me there. Are you married, Mr. Steele?"

He smiled and shook his head.

"Oh darn, there I go again. I didn't mean it like that. My father says I ask too many questions."

"I don't mind."

"Oh look, there's another one." She grabbed his arm and closed her eyes.

He waited until she opened her eyes and asked, "Were you making a wish?"

"Yes. I guess it's silly, isn't it? But I've always wished on falling stars." She let go of his arm and put her hands in her lap.

They sat there without speaking for several minutes. Steele saw that the Orion constellation was almost straight up overhead. Would Stacy be looking at those same stars? But then he realized in Europe it would already be daylight.

"But I bet you have a girl, don't you? What's her name?"

"I have a . . . friend I used to spend a lot of time with. Her name is Stacy."

"Used to?"

"She's in Europe now. Has been for some time."

Becky was quiet for a while, then, "Europe. Such a long ways away."

"Yes, it is."

Becky yawned. "I guess I'd better get some sleep. My father says we've got another long day in that stagecoach tomorrow before we get to Prescott."

"Yes, I expect so," agreed Steele. "I'd better try to sleep also."

Becky hesitated and then shrugged and hurried off toward the women's shack.

Steele sat there for a while longer, watching the stars and thinking about Becky's words. How different her life was from someone like Stacy. While Stacy marched in protests for women's rights in Europe, women like Becky worked on family farms and raised children, never to see a big city, never thinking about fancy society parties and social posturing. During the war, he had met a few girls like Becky, girls who were fascinated by the war, and especially fascinated by the long lines of young soldier boys who marched right through their normally-quiet farms. To Steele, the lives of those girls had seemed so simple, but in a way their lives were more meaningful, more useful, than the complex and fast-paced lives of the people he'd met in his parent's high society back in London.

Steele pushed away those memories and got up to make his way to the men's sleeping quarters. He slipped under the rough blanket without removing his clothes and listened for a while to Laird's quiet breathing and Rudd's loud snoring. He thought about the trip so far, about the desert and its many strange plants. He also thought about the Indians who had watched them back at that dead tree. He tried to imagine what the lives of the Indians might be like. How did they survive out there in that barren desert? What did they eat? It was many hours before he felt himself growing sleepy.

Chapter 5

*I*t was already light when Steele woke up. He stared up at the sunlight streaming through the holes in the ceiling, vaguely remembering a dream about a soldier with a bullet hole in his forehead. The soldier had been following him, trying to show him where the bullet had gone in. In a way, it was somewhat similar to Carson showing them where the bullet had hit him. He'd seen many wounds like that during the war, and dreams about wounds and wounded men were almost a nightly occurrence now, along with dreams about the war, about the violence of the fighting, and about the soldiers he'd seen die in that Army field hospital. The bad dreams had started while he was still working there, and they persisted even after he'd left the war zone. They stayed with him like an unwanted companion during his travel through the West and they were still with him when he arrived in San Francisco. Then they went away for a while. They'd stayed away during the good times with Stacy, but lately they'd come back, now almost as vivid as the real horrors he'd seen during the war.

Steele shook off the sad feeling the dream had left him with and got up to wake Rudd and Laird. There was no sign of Carson.

By the time they'd collected Becky and made their way up to the stage depot, the horses were already being hitched up. "I was about to come get you folks," said Charlie. "Where's the other one?"

"We haven't seen him," said Steele.

"Well, we can't wait for him. If he's not here when we shove off, he'll have to wait for tomorrow's stage."

"Maybe he ran off to find us something to eat," said Rudd and everyone laughed. "Well, I don't think this stage line is very considerate of its passengers. They could have at least provided us with some kind of breakfast."

"Where do you think Carson went?" asked Laird. "Camp Verde isn't a very big place to disappear in."

"I'm not sorry he's gone," said Becky forcefully. But then she seemed to realize she'd spoken harshly and dropped her eyes. "I mean, I know he was a war hero and all, but he scared me. Shooting at those peaceful Indians like that. It wasn't right."

"I'm not so sure I would call him a war hero," said Steele.

"What do you mean?" said Laird. "He showed us his wounds."

"There are many ways to get wounded. Especially if you're on the wrong side of the law."

"So what are you saying?" asked Rudd. "That he wasn't in the war?"

"I'm sure he was in the war, but the battle he said he took part in was not a battle of regular army troops."

"Not regular? What do you mean?" asked Laird.

"Independence, Missouri, the place Carson mentioned, was taken during the night by a group of irregulars. I passed through there not long afterward. A large group of men shot up the town and stole as much as they could carry. They were said to be led by a man named William Quantrill. The people I talked to in Missouri said Quantrill's men pretended to be southern troops, but they were really little more than bandits."

Rudd snapped his fingers. "Yeah, that's right. I remember there was a story in an eastern newspaper about Quantrill. It accused his men of robbing a bank somewhere in Missouri."

Becky looked worried. "You don't suppose Carson is one of them do you? I mean, a hired killer?"

"Let's go, folks," said the driver.

They were hardly settled inside the stage when it started moving. Rudd said, "Looks like Carson isn't going to make it." As the dust began to filter up through the floorboards, he added, "Maybe he just couldn't stand the dust anymore."

Laird laughed and said, "Well, I can understand that."

As they headed farther north, the stage climbed steadily into the mountains. As they continued to gain altitude, the vegetation gradually changed from scrub oak to short pine trees. Within an hour, they turned west and Steele could see even higher mountains in the distance.

Steele took out his drawing pad and began a sketch of Carson from memory. He drew the man's head and shoulders, putting him in a confederate uniform and hat. As usual, he left the eyes until last. He felt he had captured Carson's sarcastic smile, but he knew he would have trouble portraying Carson's dead-calm eyes.

The coach slowed and came to a stop.

"What the hell?" said Rudd. "Why are we stopped? We're in the middle of nowhere."

Steele put down his drawing pad and leaned out the window. The road ahead was blocked by a fallen tree. Charlie jumped down to move it out of the way, but the moment he touched the tree, a shot rang out and he fell backward. When another shot kicked up the dirt next to him, Charlie tried to crawl back to the stagecoach.

"Who is shooting?" cried Becky. "What is going on?"

Steele didn't take time to answer. He threw open the door and jumped out. "Get out!" he shouted. "Get down behind the coach." He ran to Charlie and got a grip on the back of his shirt to drag him back to the stage. But two more shots hit the road and threw dirt into Steele's eyes. He fell back, but was up quickly and again began to drag Charlie toward the coach. The driver started shooting up toward where the shots had come from and that gave Steele time to get Charlie back to safely.

The others were all out of the coach and crouched down behind it. The driver was still up top, his rifle at the ready, but no more shots were coming from up on the hillside.

Becky knelt next to Charlie. "Oh my God, he's been shot."

"It's my leg," said Charlie. "Was it Indians?"

"I can't see anybody," yelled the driver. "The shooting came from up on top of the hill."

Steele tore away the cloth from Charlie's wounded leg. He'd been hit just above the knee and it was bleeding heavily. Steele hoped the bullet hadn't severed any arteries. "Who's got a clean handkerchief?" he said. "Quick."

Rudd pulled out a large red one. "You can use mine, but, uh, I don't think it's very clean."

"I haven't used this one," said Becky, producing a small white hanky.

"It'll do," said Steele. He used it to put direct pressure on Charlie's leg wound.

"We've got to get out of here," yelled Rudd. "They'll pick us off like . . . like rabbits."

"Spose you just tell me how I'm gonna get past that tree," yelled back the driver. "Somebody's got to roll it out of the way."

"Oh, right," said Rudd. "I suppose you think we should go out there and get ourselves killed."

"I'll do it," said Steele. "Here, Becky, keep this cloth pressed against the wound. Push hard."

"No, wait" she cried. "don't go out there."

Steele showed Becky where to apply pressure. He stood up and moved to the edge of the coach.

"Wait," said Laird, "you can't move that tree by yourself. I'll go with you."

"I can do it," said Steele. "Stay here." He jumped up and ran to the tree. He ducked down behind it and waited. No shots came. Maybe whoever it was had just taken a few quick shots and ran away.

He stood up and grabbed one end of the tree. He quickly dragged it to the side of the road. Then he crouched back down behind it. "Go, go," he yelled to the driver.

"Everybody in!" shouted the driver. "Get Charlie inside. Let's go!"

They helped Charlie inside the coach and as soon as they were in, the driver cracked his whip. The horses started fast.

As the coach went by, Steele jumped up and ran alongside, keeping it between him and the hillside where the shots had come from.

Laird was hanging out of the doorway. "Here, grab my hand."

Steele caught it and swung up and in.

"Man, that was close," said Rudd. "Them Indians could of swarmed down on us any minute."

Steele wasn't so sure it was Indians, but he didn't reply. He had to see to Charlie's wound. They had him lying on the floor at their feet. Becky was sitting next to him, trying her best to keep pressure on his wound.

Steele kneeled next to Charlie and used his pocket knife to cut away the rest of the cloth around the wound. He could see that the bullet was still in there, maybe lodged against the bone. Steele had seen many such wounds during the war. The bullet would have to come out, but that would take a doctor and surgical instruments.

"How bad is it?" asked Charlie between gritted teeth.

"It's not too bad," said Steele. "You'll be fine, but we need to get you to a doctor."

"There's nothing between here and Prescott," said Rudd. "Hours away."

Steele touched Charlie's shoulder. "We'll try to make you as comfortable as we can. You're going to have to hang on until Prescott." He looked up at the others. "I need some cloth to bind up his wound."

"You can have my shirt," said Becky.

"That'll work," said Rudd. "Hey, I'll buy you a couple of nice new ones when we get to Prescott."

The men turned their backs while Becky removed her shirt and put on her father's jacket. Steele cut her white shirt into strips and used them to bind Charlie's wound tightly.

Rudd folded his jacket to put under Charlie's head, but Becky thought that looked uncomfortable so she sat down against the door so Charlie could rest his head on her lap. Charlie smiled up at her and Rudd said, "Now that looks nice and comfy. Getting to put your head on a pretty girl's lap. Almost worth getting shot for."

Charlie closed his eyes and despite the stage's bouncing, he soon fell into a kind of dozing sleep.

Steele squeezed in next to Charlie and sat down on the floor, keeping the cloth pad on the wound to slow the bleeding.

Becky leaned close to Steele and whispered, "Is he going to make it?"

"If the bleeding stops, or at least slows a great deal, I think he has a good chance. But I've seen . . . ." He stopped in mid-sentence. He patted her hand. "He'll be all right."

After a while, everyone grew quiet. Steele periodically removed the cloth pad to check Charlie's wound. The bleeding seemed to have slowed somewhat. He sat back and thought about the many leg wounds he had seen during the war. It still troubled him to remember the men that were only slightly wounded, but died anyhow. The doctors called it "shock." For Steele, the hardest part of working in the field hospital was seeing the ones that seemed like they were going to make it, but didn't. After a year of following the battles with a young man's fascination, the hospital had seemed to be a backwater of calm in the midst of the war's madness, but he saw more death there than he had seen on all the battlefields combined. The officers who ran the hospital had willingly accepted his offer to work as a volunteer in exchange for food and shelter, but the two years that followed were a very sad time for Steele, a time of hard work, but also a time of watching and thinking, of trying to understand what could be worth so much misery and death. He had learned a lot about medicine and the treatment of wounded men and hadn't expected to have to use that knowledge after the fighting ended. But sitting on the floor of a swaying and bouncing stagecoach, trying to hold back the bleeding of yet another man wounded by gunfire, it almost felt like he was back in another war. He couldn't help but wonder what else might be waiting for him in this remote territory.

Chapter 6

After what seemed like a very, very long ride, they finally rolled into Prescott just as the sun dipped behind the hills to the west of the town. It had been a fine day and quite a few people were still out sitting in the town square. The driver slowed the stage and yelled to them. "We got a wounded man in here. Somebody go get the doc. We're takin' him to the hotel."

At the hotel, Steele opened the stagecoach door and called to a man that was sitting on the hotel's front steps: "We've got a wounded man in here. We need a blanket to carry him."

The man jumped up and ran inside the building and he was soon back with the blanket. With Laird's help, Steele was able to get Charlie out of the stage and onto the blanket. Steele got on one side of the blanket and with the stage driver and Laird on the other side, they carried Charlie into the hotel and put him down on the floor.

"This man's been shot," yelled the driver to the young clerk behind the counter. "We need a room."

The young man grabbed a room key and came out from behind the counter. He looked down at Charlie's ashen face. "Is gonna die? Who was it, Indians?"

"Yeah, Indians," said the driver. "They're all over the place out there. Which room?"

The clerk led the way up to a room on the second floor and they managed to get Charlie into the bed without banging him around too much. Through it all, Charlie kept his eyes closed and his teeth clenched. The young man ran out, but soon came back with extra blankets. Becky took the blankets and waved him away.

The stagecoach driver looked down at Charlie for a long moment, then shrugged and said, "Well, I got to get the stage back to the depot. I'll be back." He left quickly, not looking back.

Steele sat in the chair next to the bed and tried to stop the bleeding that had started up again during the move.

"What should we do?" said Rudd.

"There's nothing we can do," said Steele. "I'll try to slow the blood loss until the doctor gets here."

"Okay, well, how about if I go down and get us rooms then?"

Laird said he'd go with him and Becky shooed the curious onlookers out into the hallway.

She came back to the bed and looked down at Charlie. "He's brave," she whispered. "It must have been really painful to lie on the hard floor of the stagecoach with it bouncing all over like that."

Steele nodded in agreement. "It's surprising what the human body can take. We're stronger than we realize."

Several men and boys stood outside the door, peering inside. The boys whispered and giggled to each other. Becky put her finger to her lips and they quieted down.

Steele was worried about Charlie's color. He seemed too pale. His lips were almost blue. Was he bleeding internally? "Are you cold?" he asked.

At first, Charlie didn't seem to hear. Then his eyes fluttered and Steele repeated the question. Charlie shook his head no, but Steele wasn't convinced. The man was taking shallow breaths through an only slightly-open mouth. He seemed to be having trouble keeping his eyes open.

The doctor finally arrived and rushed into the room. He was a fairly young man, probably in his thirties. He was very short, under five feet and as a result, his head appeared too large for his body. Without a word to anyone, he sat down on the edge of the bed and began to unwind the bloody bindings around Charlie's wounded leg. He threw them to the floor and leaned close to look at the wound.

"The bullet may be lodged in the bone," said Steele.

The doctor glanced up at him. "So you're an expert on bullet wounds, are you?"

"I had some experience with wounds," said Steele. "During the war."

"Is that right? Where was that?"

"Field hospital. Tennessee."

The doctor opened his bag and got out a ivory-handled probe tool that must date from before the war. He wiped the blade on his sleeve and began to probe at the wound. "So, what were you? A medic?"

"I was only a volunteer. My name is Drew Steele."

"Okay, Steele. So you were patchin' up the Federals in Tennessee while I was down in Georgia patchin' up the ones your boys shot. Lot of good either one of us did. Fast as we'd fix 'em up they'd just bring in more, right?"

Steele nodded.

The doctor probed deeper and Charlie suddenly woke up and yowled. The doctor ignored him. "My name's Fletcher, Jacob C. Fletcher from a nowhere place called Baxley, Georgia. Folks around here just call me Doc. So, you were a volunteer, eh? Not a soldier, I guess?"

Steele shook his head.

"Okay, volunteer. Why don't you volunteer to go tell somebody to get us some hot water? That bullet's got to come out."

"I'll do it," said Becky. She ran out of the room.

"So you think you know about leg wounds, do you, Steele? Well, tell me this, what're we gonna do if that bone in there is shattered?"

"Not much we can do, doctor. Immobilize it and hope for the best."

"That's right. And hope he don't get gangrene. In the war, we'd cut their damn legs off right away, just to make sure."

"I hope you don't have to do that this time."

"Well, I cut off a hell of a lot of them, that's for sure. I still think about all those boys sometimes. Hoppin' around on one leg. How're they gonna plow their fields or hunt rabbits, or whatever they do?" He jabbed at the wound again and Charlie again cried out. "Pipe down," said the doctor. "You think that hurt, just wait 'til I go in after that bullet."

Becky came back leading a young boy who was struggling to carry a bucket full of steaming water.

The doctor picked up the bloody cloth from the floor and used some of the water to wash the blood away from the wound. Charlie's leg was greatly swollen. The swelling was shrinking the bullet hole and slowing the bleeding, but Steele knew there could still be bleeding within the leg.

"Well, let's get it out," said the doctor. "If I know anything, it's how to take out a damn bullet. I sure dug out a lot of 'em in my time." He stood up and took off his coat. He turned to the group crowding around the door to the room. "What are you all looking at?" he said. "You all act like you never seen anybody shot before. Somebody close that door."

Becky ran to close it.

The doctor took out a scalpel and began to widen the wound.

Charlie cried, "Jesus, doc, what're ya doin' down there?" He tried to sit up, but the doctor pushed him back down.

"Everybody around here seems to like to shoot each other," said the doctor. "This is the third bullet I've dug out since . . . let's see, since Christmas. One gut shot, other two back shot. They all died, but this fellow looks like he might make it if his leg doesn't get infected."

He began to rummage through his bag. It sounded like he was pawing through a drawer full of silverware. Finally he pulled out a battered pair of forceps. "But I guess their shootings keep me in business, that and accidents up at the mine. Other than that, it's mostly farmers calling me to save their animals. You want to know something about the doctoring business, volunteer? Sometimes it seems like they care more about their animals than they do for their wives. They call me when it's time for a calf to be born, but when it's their wives' time, they call for the midwife. You know why?"

"The midwife is cheaper."

"That's it exactly. They don't mind paying if it's a calf. A calf is worth something." He picked up another one of the bloody rags from the floor and dipped it into the bucket of hot water. He tried to swab out the wound, but the blood was flowing so fast it didn't do much good. "There are so few women up here you'd think they'd realize a woman has some value too." He used the scalpel to dig around in the wound.

Charlie screamed and tried to sit up again.

"Can't you give him something for the pain?" said Becky.

The doctor nodded toward his bag. "There's some stuff in there that might help. Get him a bottle."

Steele looked in the doctor's bag. There were several bottles of dark liquid. He took one of them out. "This?"

"Yeah. It's got a little bit of Laudanum in it, and a lot of cocaine. Give him that."

Steele handed the bottle to Becky.

"How much should I give him?"

"As much as he wants."

"Out of the bottle?" she asked.

"Sure," said the doctor with an impatient wave of his hand.

Becky held the bottle up to Charlie's mouth and he eagerly drank it all.

Steele knew from personal experience how painful it was to have a bullet dug out so he wasn't sure how much the doctor's potion of Laudanum and cocaine would help. But it was better than nothing. During the war, it had been almost impossible to get Laudanum in the field, leaving the patient to suffer through the most horrific surgeries, even amputations, without anything to dull the pain. Despite standing orders against drinking on the battlefield, soldiers often arrived at the field hospital drunk because their buddies gave them whiskey as they were carried away on the stretcher. The whiskey helped the pain, but Steele had learned that it raised their blood pressure and slowed their recovery. They would have been better off to just endure the pain.

Without waiting for the painkiller to take effect, the doctor went back to work. With each probe of his instrument Charlie jumped and groaned.

"Bullet's still in there," said the doctor. "I can feel it, but I can't quite get ahold of it. Guess I'll hafta make the hole bigger."

When he began to cut, Becky had trouble holding Charlie down so Steele changed positions with her and held Charlie's wrists. It brought back old memories of the many times he'd done the same thing during the war.

Finally, the doctor pried the bullet loose and pulled it out. He held it up for them to see. Outside the door, someone began to clap and soon a few more joined in. Steele realized they must be peering through the keyhole.

"Could I keep that bullet?" asked Steele.

"Sure," said the doctor, handing it to him. "Why do you want it?"

"Maybe we can tell what kind of gun it came from." He looked at the mostly intact bullet. "Forty-four, I think. Could have come from a pistol."

"They told me it was Indians," said the doctor.

"We didn't see any Indians. The shots came from up on a hill."

"Well, who knows. Like I said, they shoot each other out here left and right. See if you can find me a needle and thread in my case while I hold the wound closed."

Steele found an already-threaded needle in the bottom of the bag and the doctor used it to quickly sew up the wound.

Becky winced with each new stitch, but Charlie had stopped fighting and seemed to have passed out. The doctor's potion was finally taking effect.

The doctor dipped the bloody strips of cloth from Becky's shirt in the hot water and used them to rewrap Charlie's leg. Then he wiped his hands on the bedsheet and stood up. "That should do it. Now, who pays me?"

"This man is a stage line employee," suggested Steele. "And he was wounded in the performance of his job."

"Well, then I guess I'd better go see the stage company." The doctor took two more bottles of the dark liquid out of his bag and handed them to Becky. "Have him drink some of this whenever he comes to. I'll be back tomorrow."

Steele walked to the door with his hand on the doctor's shoulder. "Thank you for coming so quickly, doctor."

"No problem. All we can do now is wait and see. Keep an eye on that wound to see if it festers. I spose you know about that."

"I do."

"Yeah, well, let's hope it doesn't happen."

The doctor opened the door and the group outside parted to let him through. He took out one of his bottles of liquid and held it up for the group to see. "That man in there is much better now. Owes it all to this magic elixir. Only twenty cents the bottle. Fixes whatever ails a body. Now, who wants some?"

A few of the men were reaching into their pockets as Steele closed the door.

Becky was sitting by the bed, stroking Charlie's forehead. "He looks kind of pale. Do you think he'll be all right?"

"Only time will tell," said Steele. "You look tired. You'd better go find your father and get checked into your room."

"I'm all right," she said, rubbing her eyes with the back of her hands.

"There is one more thing you could do. Could you ask that hotel clerk to bring me a clean sheet. I don't like the fact that the doctor used the bloody cloth to rewrap Charlie's wound."

She left but was soon back with Rudd and her father. She handed Steele a clean sheet.

"I got us some rooms," said Rudd. "Just down the hall. Is he gonna be all right?"

"The doctor took the bullet out. If there's no infection, he should pull through.." He sat down on the edge of the bed and carefully removed the bloody bandages while the others watched. Charlie groaned and turned his head to the side, but he didn't wake up. The area around the wound was very red and swollen, but that didn't necessarily mean it was infected. Steele knew there was no way to tell which wounds would get infected and which wouldn't. He remembered a black woman who worked in the field hospital's kitchen who tried to sell the wounded soldiers good-luck charms to keep the infection away. Most of them bought one, just to be on the safe side.

Steele tore the sheet into strips and carefully rewrapped Charlie's leg.

Rudd put his hands to his stomach and said, "Well, now that that's done, what do you say we all go get something to eat? Do you have any idea how long it's been since we ate?"

Just then, there was a knock at the door and it opened before anybody could get to it. It was the stage driver. "Is Charlie all right? He isn't dead, is he?"

"He's just sleeping," said Steele. "Doctor Fletcher gave him some medicine."

"Oh, yeah, the doc's magic elixir. That stuff'll knock out a horse. Well, I'll stay with him now. You all can take off."

"We were just about to go down to get something to eat, "said Rudd.

"Then go. I don't have to head back down south 'til tomorrow. I hired a Mexican woman to come in and watch over him. She's a hell of a cook too. We'll take care of him."

"See there," said Rudd. "Everything's taken care of. Now let's go eat before I fall over." He herded everybody out of the room and down to the hotel's restaurant.

There were only four small tables in the restaurant, but two of them were still empty. Rudd and Laird pushed the two tables together and they all sat down.

"Well, we made it," said Becky. "It's hard to believe everything that happened since yesterday."

Everyone nodded in agreement. They were all silent until Rudd made a cheery suggestion that they should order some wine. "To celebrate our escape from those Indians."

"I'm not sure it was Indians," said Steele. "We didn't see who did the shooting."

"Well, whoever it was, we're lucky to be alive," said Rudd. "Let's drink to that."

As it turned out, the restaurant didn't have any wine. But they did have beer, so Rudd ordered a couple of pitchers of beer along with their meal. Steele wasn't sure if it was the beer, or the long frightening trip, but as soon as the others had finished eating, they suddenly seemed very sleepy.

"We'd better get some sleep," said Laird, yawning. He put some money on the table and stood up. "I got a long day tomorrow."

After Laird and Becky had left the restaurant, Rudd leaned toward Steele to whisper: "I can hardly believe I'm back here. I went out for a short walk after I got us rooms and nobody even seemed to recognize me. Maybe they aren't looking for me after all."

"Still, we'd better go talk to the authorities. Before they come looking for you."

"Time enough for that tomorrow," said Rudd. "I'm sleepy. By the way, did you notice that row of bars on our way in? Right across from the town square. They call it Whiskey Row. That's where you get news in this town. We'll go there tomorrow and see what's what."

"I expect those bars will be open tonight. We could go down there and talk to people now."

"Don't you ever get tired?" protested Rudd. "We've been on the go since we left San Francisco."

"I am tired, but I expect people saw you come into town. You said you might be wanted for murder in this town. Don't you want to go find out?"

"If they want me, they know where to find me. If you want to go look around, go ahead. Me, I'm going to bed." He took out some money and put it on the table. Then he stood up and stretched. "I had them take our bags up. You're in room eight. I'm in nine." He tossed a room key to Steele and started to leave. But then he hesitated and turned back. He leaned close to Steele and spoke in a whisper. "By the way, if you're going out to look around, take my advice and be careful. This place only looks peaceful. Under the surface, there's still a lot going on here. I can feel it."

Chapter 7

After Rudd left, Steele sat at the table for a few minutes deciding whether to go upstairs and try to get some sleep or go for a walk. Despite the long trip, he didn't feel at all sleepy. He decided to go out and look around a bit, get a feel for the town. Maybe he could find that place Chan had mentioned, the Dragon House.

He left the hotel and headed up the main street toward the group of bars Rudd had referred to as Whiskey Row. The row of bars was fronted by a fairly new-looking board sidewalk with an overhanging shingled roof. He stood on the board sidewalk and listened to the piano music coming from inside the bars. He thought about going in to one of them, but decided against it. He felt the stiffness from sitting up in the stagecoach and from carrying the heavy tree branch the day before. He felt hot and sticky. He wondered if they had baths at the Dragon House.

Just then a big man stumbled out of one of the bars. He yawned and leaned up against the building to unsteadily roll a cigarette. He got a small, crooked one finished and struck a match on the back of his trousers, but the wind caught the flame and the match went out before he could get the cigarette lit.

"Excuse me," said Steele, "can you tell me how to get to a place called the Dragon House? I believe it's a lodging house."

The man looked up, but seemed to be having trouble focusing on Steele. He rocked back on his heels, but then he noticed the tobacco was falling out of his cigarette. He licked the paper again, but he got it too wet and fell apart, leaving the cigarette paper stuck to his fingers. He shook his hand until the paper detached and floated away in the slight breeze. He stared at Steele and then laughed. "Lodging, you say. At the Dragon House? Haw, that's a good one." He tried to give Steele a hard slap on the back but Steele turned slightly to ward off the blow and the drunken man nearly fell off the raised sidewalk. Steele had to catch his arm to keep him upright. The man grinned and turned unsteadily. He pointed to the north. "Go down there where the sign says . . . " He hiccuped. "Blacksmith. Then ya turn left and go down toward . . . the crick. You'll see the . . . place . . . down there." He gave a little wave of his hand and staggered away down the street saying, "Say hi to them Chink ladies for me."

Steele followed the drunk's directions until the dirt street turned into a narrow path. It led through a small grove of trees to an isolated two-story frame building that seemed to have been built in stages without any concern for consistency.

There was no lantern on the porch of the building, but there was dim light coming from one of the windows. Steele saw the shadows of several people moving in there. He pushed the door open and stepped in. The only light in the hallway was from a wall lamp that gave out very little light because the glass was black from years of accumulated soot.

The narrow hallway led to a much larger room that was dimly lit by a single hanging chandelier. The place was overly warm from a roaring fireplace and the air was hazy with cigar smoke. A few tables and chairs were arranged around a dance floor, but there was no music nor any sign of a place for musicians. Several men dressed in dirty gray uniforms and stained gray caps were seated at the tables. Steele assumed they were miners. A pretty Chinese girl dressed in a long formal gown that might have been made of pure white silk was sitting alone at a small table in the corner. She looked very young.

A long bar dominated the far wall and a thin Chinese man in western dress was behind it, watching Steele. Steele started in that direction, but he was intercepted by a very old, very tiny Chinese woman who had jumped up from a chair that was in the shadows next to the wall.

She grabbed his arm. "You come," she said, pulling at him. She was bent over from the waist which forced her to turn her head to one side to look up at him. "You new here, yes? Not see before, yes?"

Despite her tiny size, her hands were strong. He let her tug him toward the table where the young woman was waiting. "You take Mi-mee. You like." The young woman stood up as they approached. Steele realized the Dragon House was not a place of lodging.

"Uh, no thank you," said Steele, stopping. "I'm looking for a man named Wang."

The old woman continued to tug at his sleeve. "Mi-mee take care of you. Very cheap."

"No, I want to see Cousin Wang."

The old woman suddenly released his arm. Her feeble attempt at a smile disappeared. "No Wang here. You go." She began to try to pull him back toward the front door. "You go now. Bye bye." She wasn't having much luck at budging Steele, but she kept trying. Out of the corner of his eye, Steele saw the Chinese man come out from behind the bar and head toward them.

"What you want here?" demanded the man before he even reached them.

He was a small man, but he didn't seem afraid of Steele, despite their great difference in height. Steele looked for any kind of bulge beneath the man's clothes, but saw nothing that might indicate a hidden weapon.

"I'm looking for a man named Wang. Cousin Wang. I come from San Francisco."

The man's stern expression suddenly turned into a smile. "Ah, yes. You must be Steele. Uncle Chan say you come." He waved the old woman away and she hobbled back to her seat, frowning and mumbling to herself.

"Uncle Chan said I should contact Cousin Wang when I got here."

"Yes, yes, we know." He led Steele to the bar. "My name Teng. Cousin Wang not here. You want drink?"

Steele shook his head and sat down on one of the bar stools.

Teng went behind the bar and poured him a drink anyhow. It looked like whiskey.

"Honorable Cousin Wang, he not here. He up at mine."

"Is he a miner?"

"He was miner. Before. Many Chinese work at mines before. Now mines not allow Chinese. Other miners say no work if Chinese come in."

"So what is he doing up at the mine?"

"Not know. You meet Cousin Wang here tomorrow?"

"All right, I'll come back tomorrow."

"You want something now?" asked Teng. "Food? Girl?"

"You don't happen to have baths here, do you?"

"Yes, yes, we have nice bath here." He signaled to the old woman who came hobbling over.

Teng said something to her in Chinese and the old woman disappeared through a door. She soon returned with a Chinese girl in tow. She was a little older than the other girl, but even more attractive. She was wearing the same type of long white silk gown.

The old woman pushed the girl forward. "Su-zee for you. You like."

"Uh, thank you," said Steele, backing up a step, "but I was just trying to get a bath."

Teng smiled. "It all right. Su-zee show you way. Baths in back." He pulled the girl aside and spoke to her in Chinese.

The young woman bowed to Steele and led him through a door and down a narrow hallway. She stopped at the last door in the hall and opened it. The tiny room contained only a large metal bathtub and a narrow table.

Steele followed her inside, ducking under the low doorway. Suzie leaned back out into the hallway and called out something in Chinese. A young Chinese boy came scurrying with several towels in his arms. Without looking at either of them, the boy put the towels down on the table and hurried out again. But he soon returned with a bucket full of steaming water which he poured into the bathtub before hurrying back out.

The girl pointed to the tub. "You take off clothes now."

When Steele hesitated, she giggled and turned her back. He was completely undressed by the time the boy came with another bucket of hot water.

Steele eased down into the water. It was very hot, but it felt wonderful.

Suzie moved behind him and began to rub his neck.

"Ah, that's very nice," he said. "Thank you."

"You not from here?"

"No, I just arrived today. My name is Steele, Drew Steele."

"Hello mister Drew Steele." She held out her hand.

Steele took his hand out of the water and shook hers.

She went back to rubbing his neck. "Wang say you important man. Know Uncle Chan."

That was interesting. Could Chan's influence extend all the way to this remote Arizona town? "Have you met Uncle Chan?" he asked.

"Yes. Uncle Chan help me. When I come this country. All alone."

"How long have you been here, Suzie? In Prescott I mean."

"Here?" She stopped rubbing his shoulders and thought about his question. "I here . . . four year. I think."

It was hard to tell how old she was, but she couldn't be more than twenty. "You must have been very young when you came here."

"Yes," she agreed. "I young girl. Not know how old."

A girl that young, thought Steele. Alone in a foreign land. Who had brought her here, and for what reason? Was it because of her pretty face and attractive figure? Had she been brought to this country just to please men in a place like this?

They both remained silent as she continued to rub his shoulders. The boy continued to bring buckets of water until the tub was full. Then she waved him away.

"Why you come this town, mister Drew Steele?"

"I came with another man, a man named Rudd."

"Rudd? School teacher Rudd?" She seemed very excited. "Rudd come back?" Then she frowned. "Some people mad at him. Maybe he better not come back."

"Did you know him when he was the school teacher here?"

"Everybody know school teacher Rudd. He friend of poor Dutch Willig."

"Oh. Did you know Dutch Willig?"

"Oh, yes. mister Dutch come in here all time. But he die."

"I heard he was killed. Do you know how it happened?"

"In hotel. It night. I hear men in here talk. Some say it very sad, but some say he get what he deserve. They say he cheat people. He killed in bed. With knife."

"Did anybody say who might have killed him?"

"No, but when it happen, everybody go down to hotel to look. I go too. Everybody stand on street in front of hotel. Look up at window where it happen."

"I see. You say he was killed in bed with a knife. Did the doctor say what kind of wounds he had?"

"No doctor. No doctor in town then. Horse doctor come here later."

"Horse doctor?"

"Yes, little horse doctor."

"Oh, you mean Doctor Fletcher, the doctor that is here now."

"Yes, he doctor for horses and cows. And for people too. Chinese people not like him."

"What else can you tell me about Dutch Willig? Did he have any other friends, except for Rudd, that is?"

"No friend. Poor mister Dutch. No friend except Crazy Billy."

"Crazy Billy? Is he a local man?"

"He crazy. Sit all day in park and look up at birds. Mister Dutch sit with him all time." She stopped rubbing his back and reached for a bar of soap. "Now I soap you."

"Actually, I can do that for myself," said Steele, holding out his hand for the soap.

Suzie frowned and pulled the soap away from his outstretched hand. "No, I soap. Teng say we honor you. You like me do soap. Very nice."

Steele gave in and sat back to accept her attentions. She was right. It was very nice.

After his bath, she dried him with a thick towel. As she rubbed his back vigorously, she said, "You stay with Su-zee tonight? Teng say no charge."

He declined politely and got dressed while she watched. He gave her two silver half dimes and thanked her several times for the bath, bowing in response to each of her deep bows.

She showed him to a sagging door at the back of the building and he stepped out into the night. The cold mountain air was a sharp contrast to the steamy bath room. He waited in the darkness until his eyes adjusted and then made his way around the building and up the path to the street. As he walked back to the hotel, he thought about what Suzie had said. At least one of the men who frequented the Dragon House had suggested that someone had been hired to kill Willig. The killer must have been after the land grant. But would Willig have kept the land grant with him? And if he didn't have it with him, why would the killer kill him without finding out where it was? Maybe they were just to keep him quiet. Did it mean they thought the document was genuine?

The streets were empty as he passed Whiskey Row, but he heard loud voices coming from inside every one of the bars. He stopped to look in the window of the first one, a place named "Ham's Saloon." Inside the smoky room, there were about a dozen men, most of them lined up on stools along a long bar. There was a piano player in the back beating out a fast-paced tune, but no one seemed to be listening to him. Four men were playing cards in a dark corner of the room, lighted only by a single lamp hanging above the card table.

Steele continued on down the street toward the hotel. The temperature was dropping rapidly; what had been a pleasant evening was turning into a rather cool one.

There were several horses tied up in front of the bars, but nothing was moving on the street. It looked like a peaceful little mountain town, but he remembered Rudd's warning about what lay beneath the surface. As if in response to that thought, there was a sudden flare of a match on the other side of the square. Someone was lighting up a cigarette over there in the doorway of a closed store. There was no light on the street so Steele couldn't see anything but the glow of the man's cigarette. Was he being watched? Steele shook off the thought. It was probably nothing more than man out for a smoke before going to bed.

When he got back to the hotel, he stopped in the middle of the street to look up at the windows on the second floor. Suzie had said the people stood in the street looking up at the room Willig had been murdered in. There were four windows up there that faced the street.

Which one of those rooms had Willig been in? There were no balconies or adjoining rooftops, so it didn't seem likely that anyone could have come in through the window to kill him. But if Willig knew somebody was after him, he would have made sure his door was locked. Did he know the killer and open the door to him?

Steele went up to his room and sat on the edge of the bed to take off his boots. He put his pistol on the table next to the bed and turned up the lamp. He took out his drawing pad and began a quick sketch of Susie. Then he did one of Teng. When he had completed the two rough sketches, he turned down the lamp and lay back on the bed, thinking. Suzie said Willig was known to have cheated people. Was that what he was doing with the land grant, trying to cheat people? But maybe his death had nothing to do with the land grant. He might well have been killed for some other reason. The place to begin would be to find out as much about Willig as he could, find out if it was possible for a grizzled old prospector and probable con man to have actually come into possession of what could turn out to be one of the most valuable documents in U.S. history.

Chapter 8

*T*he next morning Steele woke up trying to remember a dream about being trapped in a dark place. It was the cave dream again, and as always, there was a sense of danger in that cave. He'd never been in a cave, or even a mine, but he often dreamed about being trapped in one. Maybe the dream was about being trapped in general, trapped in one place, unable to make a decision. Or it could mean the opposite, becoming trapped when his own restlessness put him into a dangerous situation from which there would be no escape.

He pushed away those troublesome thoughts, dressed, and went down to the restaurant. There was no need to wake Rudd or any of the others. He'd get an early start on his investigation.

He was surprised to find Lucky Laird already seated at one of the tables. He was looking through some papers.

Laird waved him over. "Cook's not here yet. They say he must have got drunk last night. But they've got some really bad coffee. Have some." He pushed the dented metal pot toward Steele.

"You're up early," said Steele, pouring himself a cup of the thick brew.

"Yep, got to go to the territorial land office in the court house. Get this thing about my property straightened out."

"Exactly what is the problem? If you don't mind me asking."

"No real problem. I bought my land from the railroad and that's that. I tried to get it officially surveyed to make sure the water was really on my property, but they said I had to get it registered at the land office first. That's why I'm here. To get it straightened out."

Steele took a sip of the coffee. Laird was right, it was terrible. "Sounds like it could be a big problem if you can't prove you own the land."

"Nah, there's no problem. I got a legit bill of sale, handwrit. There's no arguing with that. Those railroad boys own so much desert land in Arizona Territory they probably just forgot to register the sale. Hell, they got so much land from the government during that land-for-rails scandal, what do they care about my little patch?"

"The newspapers back east are questioning the entire land swap deal."

Laird stared down at the table and rubbed his temples. Then he looked up at Steele. "Well, don't tell Becky anything like that. We've put so much into that land it's all we got now."

"You say you have an original signed bill of sale from the railroad? Did you bring it with you?"

Laird looked around, then leaned forward. "I got it right here under my shirt," he whispered. "It's all I got to prove my claim so I'm not about to let it out of my sight."

"Maybe you should put it in the bank."

He sat back and shook his head. "After what happened in that last bank crash? No siree. I don't trust banks." He took another drink of his coffee and leaned forward to speak quietly: "Becky's worried about it though. She worries about things, just like her ma did. On her deathbed, she was in a lot of pain, but all she thought about was how we'd get along without her." He took a drink of his coffee. "A lot of water under the bridge since then. I raised up Becky best I could. A woman's hand would have been better, I spose. Becky growed up more like a boy than a girl, until recent anyhow. Now she's changin'." He looked up at Steele. "You know what I mean."

"She's an attractive young woman."

"Yeah, I guess she is. I been wantin' to talk to her about . . . uh, getting grown up and all, but I—"

Just then Rudd came into the restaurant and called out, "There you are, Steele. I been knocking on your door." He came to the table, but he didn't sit down. He looked toward the kitchen. "What's to eat? I'm famished."

"They say the cook is hung over," said Laird. "Didn't show up this mornin'. That's why we're sittin' here drinkin' this bad coffee."

"Hung over? What, they only got one cook in this town? Hell, I'll go back there and cook us some eggs myself." He headed straight for the kitchen door.

Steele glanced at Laird smiled. "When Rudd gets ready to eat, he's ready to eat."

But Rudd was soon back, laughing. "The cook finally showed up. He's back there with a wet rag on his head, but he says he'll cook us some bacon and eggs. And they've got some bread baking."

"Sounds good to me," said Laird.

Rudd sat down and gestured toward the window that faced the street. "Well, what do you think of my town, Steele? Not much compared with San Francisco is it?"

"It's an interesting little town. Very small for a territorial capital."

"Yeah, that's what Tucson said when they moved it here. Nobody could figure out why they did it. No way to even get here but by stagecoach. Bout broke my back, that stage ride. I could hardly get out of bed."

"What this town needs is a railroad," said Laird. "That'd put it on the map."

"Yeah, they got all that land from Congress," said Rudd. "Why don't they put some of it to use?"

"We were just talking about that," said Laird. "About how they got so much land for free."

"The railroads!" snorted Rudd. "Don't get me started on that. Free land from the government on a promise to build a railroad. Someday. Ha! But the eastern newspapers are on to them now. It's only a matter of time before they get to the bottom of it."

"Laird is worried because he bought his land from the railroad," said Steele.

"Hey, that's right," said Rudd. "You bought some of that railroad land, didn't you?"

Laird was about to say something, but Becky had entered the restaurant and was coming toward them. He leaned toward Rudd. "Don't say anything to Becky about railroads or land. It'll just get her to worryin'."

Steele rose to pull out a chair for Becky.

"Good morning everybody," she said, sitting down gracefully. She carefully straightened the skirt of her brightly-patterned yellow dress. It was the first time Steele had seen her in anything other than a shirt and pants. The dress was cut low enough to reveal the upper part of her small breasts and as a result, she was getting plenty of attention from the other men in the restaurant.

He father frowned at her. "Why are you wearing your Sunday dress, hon? We're not goin' anywhere special today."

"Oh, father. It's such a beautiful day I thought I'd wear something nice for a change."

"I didn't see nuthin' wrong with what you usually wear."

"Well, I for one think she looks really nice," said Rudd. "Did you sleep well, Becky? Was your bed all right?"

"Yes, thank you. But I woke up in the night worrying about poor Charlie. Has anybody looked in on him yet?"

"I thought I'd check on him before I went out this morning," said Steele.

"Oh, good idea," she said. "I'll go with you."

The food arrived and Rudd launched into one of his stories about how fast Prescott had grown up after somebody struck gold in the hills. He described the first buildings, all made out of logs, and how they'd used long teams of mules to haul the mine machinery up all the way from Tucson.

Steele noticed Laird was hardly paying attention to Rudd's story. He quickly gulped down the last of his eggs and stood up. "Got to go."

"Oh," said Becky, "should I go with you?"

"No," said her father, "you go on up and check on Charlie with Steele here. I probably won't be too long." He hurried toward the door.

They finished eating and Rudd pronounced the meal the best he'd had since he left San Francisco. Then he announced he was going to order the same thing and start all over again. "Before they run out," he said, winking at Becky.

As Steele and Becky got up to leave the table, Rudd called out to Steele. "As soon as I'm done eating, I'm going up the hill to see my old pal Ed O'Brien."

"Shouldn't you go see the town authorities first?" asked Steele.

"They must know I'm back in town and nobody has come looking for me yet. Let me go talk to O'Brien first. He'll know everything that's going on in town. I'll meet you back here for lunch."

"All right," said Steele, "but it may be lunchtime before you finish breakfast."

Becky covered a smile with her hand.

"Very funny," said Rudd. "I'm only hungry because I didn't hardly get anything to eat all the way here." In an aside to Becky, he added, "Steele never eats, you know. No wonder he's so skinny."

Becky squeezed Steele's upper arm. "Oh, he's not all that skinny."

Becky kept ahold of Steele's arm as they left the restaurant and headed up the stairs. "Why did you say Rudd should go see the town authorities?"

"Some legal matters he needs to clear up."

"Is that why the two of you came to Prescott?"

"That's right."

They went upstairs and Steele knocked on the door to Charlie's room. From inside, a woman's voice said "Entre."

Steele opened the door and was heartened to see Charlie sitting up in bed. A smiling Mexican woman was sitting in the chair next to the bed, knitting.

"Well, you're looking much better," said Becky.

"I got a real sore leg," replied Charlie. "That's for sure. But Mrs. Sanchez here brought me some good eats and I'm feelin' some better."

Steele asked if he could look at the wound and Charlie gladly obliged. Steele loosened the bandages and leaned close. There was no new blood; that was good, but the wound was quite swollen, with a bit of white puffiness around the edges. "The next time Doctor Fletcher comes, why don't you ask if he has some ointment to put on your wound?"

"The doc came in early this morning," said Charlie. "Said there wasn't nothin' else he could do for me."

"Well, be sure to drink a lot of water," said Becky. "You lost a lot of blood."

Charlie looked at Steele. "Is that right, doc? I should drink a lot of water?"

"It's good advice, but I'm not a doctor."

"Yeah, well, that Doctor Fletcher said you worked in an Army hospital. He said you knew your stuff about wounds."

"Did he say anything about damage to the bone in your leg?" asked Steele.

"Nope, just took a quick look and said he had to go help some farmer deliver a calf."

Steele rewrapped the wound, and said, "Maybe you'd better not put too much weight on that leg until we see how it's healing. Be patient and stay in bed, even if you're starting to feel better."

"Whatever you say, doc. You don't see me complaining, do ya?"

After they left the room and started down the stairs, Becky grabbed Steel's arm. "Oh, I'm so happy he's feeling better."

Steele didn't reply.

"What's the matter," she said. "He does look better, doesn't he?"

"Overall, he does look better than he did yesterday. But during the war I saw many men improve dramatically after they'd been wounded, only to succumb to infections later."

Becky stopped abruptly at the bottom of the stairs. "Oh no. Did his wound look bad?"

"It didn't look too bad, but there was some discoloration though."

Becky looked worried. "Maybe you should go talk to the doctor."

"I'm not sure he'd want to hear what I have to say. I've been reading about some research in Europe. Most doctors in this country still believe infections come from air-borne gasses so they don't think sanitation is all that important. They say to keep the patient indoors, and out of drafts. But in Europe they're suggesting infections could be caused by an infestation."

"Infestation? You mean like with bugs?"

"Something like that, but very small. They are seeing it under very strong magnifying devices. Whatever it is, they think it gets into wounds and causes problems."

"Maybe doctor Fletcher should bleed him. When my father was sick two years ago, they bled him and he got better."

Steele didn't reply. He was remembering the time the doctors had repeatedly bled Stacy's mother, first using steel clamps and then leeches. When Steele had suggested that improving her diet would do more than leeches, it had led to an argument with Stacy.

Becky interrupted his thoughts. "Let's go see him every day. We'll make sure he's recovering well."

"Good idea."

She pulled him toward the hotel's front door. "Now, how about that tour of the town?"

"I have some things to do, Becky."

"Just for a few minutes. It's such a nice day."

As they walked toward the town square, two men on the other side of the street noticed Becky. One of them whistled and they both pulled off their hats and waved. Becky ignored them, but she smiled, just a little.

The two men didn't seem aggressive. Steele assumed they were just happy to see such an attractive young woman in their little town.

When they reached the park-like town square, an old Chinese man took off his hat and bowed as they passed. It was the first Chinese Steele had seen outside of the Dragon House and he thought about stopping the man to ask if he was Cousin Wang. But the old man lowered his head and hurried on.

Becky clung to Steele's arm, still smiling.

"Looks as if they don't get many pretty young women in this town," said Steele. "At least not as pretty as you."

"Oh, quit kidding." After a moment's reflection, she added, "I'll bet that's a side you don't show many people. Kidding, and things like that."

Steele didn't say anything, but he had to agree she was right. When they came to a bench, Becky suggested they sit for a while. Steele knew he should be trying to find out more about the town, but he decided it wouldn't hurt to sit with Becky for a while. It was quiet in the park, except for some crows that were chattering noisily in the highest branches of the huge elm trees.

Becky leaned away from Steele, staring at him. "No," she said, "I don't think Drew Steele is much of a kidder. I think mister Drew Steele takes things very seriously."

"I suppose that's true. Maybe I forgot how. During the war."

"Yes, I've heard other men who were in the war say that. It must be hard to . . . " She didn't finish the sentence and they were both quiet for a while.

Steele didn't want to think about the war. He wanted to think only about what a nice day it was, a nice day to be sitting in the park with a refreshingly direct and honest young woman. She was very different from the aggressive and calculating women of San Francisco. She seemed unconcerned about cleverness and coy pretenses, which made her as different from the young heiresses of San Francisco as the little town of Prescott was different from San Francisco with its imposing stone buildings.

"Gee, that question sure took you away," said Becky. She leaned her head against his shoulder. "What were you thinking about?"

"Oh, nothing. Just . . . remembering."

Becky closed her eyes and leaned back to enjoy the sun. Steele could smell some kind of scent on her, probably some kind of fancy scented soap. Now where would a farm girl like Becky get something like that? She'd probably found it at the hotel. And she was wearing a pretty yellow dress, tight fitting enough to show off her youthful figure. No wonder the local men were whistling.

He thought about her comment that he wasn't much of a kidder. After the things he'd seen in the war, it had been hard to find humor in anything. Stacy had helped him rediscover some lightness, but then she got involved with a group of women who protested at how women were treated in America and her lightness went away. He supported what she was doing, but it had saddened him when it began to lead her away from him. After she left for Europe, he'd stayed away from the social scene on Nob Hill and he soon found himself mostly alone again, once more the quiet man he had been during the war, the observer of things rather than a participant in them. He accepted very few cases and kept himself busy reading and doing library research. Often he just sat at his second-story window, drawing pictures of the people who passed by on the street below.

He turned to Becky. "Can I draw a picture of you in your nice dress?"

She opened her eyes. "Oh, yes, I'd like that. But you don't have your drawing pad."

"I have a smaller one." He reached into his coat pocket and extracted a small pad of drawing paper and a short pencil. He held them up. "You never know when you'll encounter a beautiful scene."

"There, you did it again. Maybe you are a kidder after all."

He posed her sitting very upright at the end of the bench, looking slightly toward him. The pose eliminated the shadows from her face and neck, and it emphasized the sharp outline of her breasts. For a fleeting moment, he thought about what it would be like to draw her in the nude, as he had drawn the hired nude models at the school in Paris in his youth. He shook off the thought and began to sketch her in full figure. But she looked too staged. It wasn't like her. He told her to relax, to watch the people going by and forget she was being drawn.

In his drawing, he tried to capture her essence. He didn't know very much about her, but he knew she liked to go for long rides in the hills by herself. She had mentioned taking secret dips in the cool creek, probably naked. She was what she was and nothing more, a simple country girl who probably liked to go to harvest dances and hoe-downs. Did she have a beau? The local boys would certainly be chasing after a beauty like her. She was attractive enough to turn heads even in a place like sophisticated San Francisco, let alone in Arizona. She was not an educated girl, but she was calm and thoughtful. He tried to capture some of that calmness in his drawing.

"Can I talk," she said, being careful not to move.

"Of course."

"Why do you draw pictures? I've never met an artist before."

"I'm not really an artist. I draw to see things more clearly. It helps me in my job."

"Your job? On the stage, Rudd talked a lot about his job, working for that newspaper. But you never did say what your job was."

"I'll tell you, but I'd rather you didn't say anything to anyone else."

"Oh, a secret. Okay, I promise."

"I'm an investigator. I investigate things."

She frowned. "Is that a job?"

"It is. People in places like San Francisco often need someone to investigate things."

"So, is that why you're here in Arizona? Are you investigating something here?"

"I'm here to help Rudd with a legal matter."

"Which you're probably not supposed to talk about."

"It would be better if I didn't."

"Okay, but how did you get started drawing things? Did you go to school to learn how to do it?"

"When I was young, my parents sent me to a school in Paris. Of all the classes I took there, I liked art the best. But my mother saw some of the nude drawings we were doing and sent me to a new school in Rome. There we mostly drew classical architecture."

"Wow, all those places. So how did you get here? To this country, I mean?"

"I got tired of school and sneaked onto a ship bound for America."

"Really? By yourself?"

"Yes. At school we were hearing about a big new war starting in America. I had to see it."

Becky was silent for a few minutes. Then she turned to look at him. "You've been all those places. I've never even been to San Francisco."

"Look straight ahead," he said gently, "just for a few more minutes." He drew her neck and shoulders. She was strong, undoubtedly from the years of hard farming work and he tried to show it in his drawing. He put a few finishing touches on it and handed the pad to her.

She studied it for several minutes. "Is that what I look like? To you, I mean?" She turned the drawing for him to see.

"It's not very good. I'll do a better one for you later."

"Oh, no, that's not what I meant. I think it's very good. I just meant, when you look at me, do you . . . " She stopped in mid-sentence when she saw her father coming out of the courthouse across the street. She stood up and called to him.

He waved, but he didn't smile.

"Something's wrong," Becky whispered. "I know that look."

But as he arrived, Laird managed a tight smile. He reached out both hands to greet Becky. "And how's my little girl."

"What's the matter father, you look worried."

He waved away her question. "Oh, it's nothing, really. It's just those railroad boys. The land office says the railroad never registered the sale of our land. So I have to meet with the district judge when he comes to town to show him our deed. He has to legalize everything. They made me leave our deed at the land office 'til he gets here."

"But what if the judge won't recognize it?" said Becky.

"Now don't get all worried," said her father. "He'll recognize it. They sold it to us legal, and we got the deed."

"Did you give them your only copy?" asked Steele.

"Well, there is only one copy, the one the railroad wrote out to me when I paid 'em the cash down in Yuma. But the land office wrote me out a receipt for it. I got it right here. He pulled the piece of paper out of his pocket and unfolded it. It was a professionally printed land office form, with the date and a brief description of the land written in.

"Keep that in a safe place," warned Steele.

"I'll do that," said Laird, carefully refolding the paper and putting it back into his pocket. "Well now, how is my little girl this fine morning?"

Becky frowned at him. "You know I haven't been a little girl for a long time, father."

"I know, I know, but to me you'll always be my little girl."

They walked a ways down the street until Becky stopped. "Father, what will happen to us if they don't honor our deed?"

"Don't honor it!" her father roared. "How could they not honor it? It's a perfectly good deed. And we've already built on the land, and planted our orange trees. They have to honor it." He started to walk again.

Becky reached grabbed his arm and stopped him. "But what if the railroad says they didn't really sell it to us?"

Her father didn't want to hear it. He refused to answer and waved for them to come along. Becky looked at Steele and he wondered if she had ever before seen her father not know what to do. She frowned and hurried ahead to catch up with him. Steele stayed behind to let them talk. He could tell Laird was very worried. Maybe there was something going on beyond what he had told them.

Chapter 9

*B*ack at the hotel, Laird cheered up and suggested they go to the restaurant for some coffee. The restaurant was crowded, but there was one free table next to the window. They were hardly seated before Rudd came through the door and hurried over to join them.

"Just in time," said Becky. "We just got here."

"Of course I'm just in time," said Rudd. "I have an unerring instinct to be wherever and whenever food is available." He winked at Becky. "I'll have two of whatever you're having."

Everyone laughed except Laird. He seemed preoccupied.

Rudd put his hand on Steele's shoulder. "Can I talk to you for a minute?"

Steele followed Rudd out into the lobby.

Rudd leaned close to whisper. "I found my old pal O'Brien and he says I don't have a problem. When I left town, everybody thought I was the one who did in Willig, but the next time the stage came though town, the driver said he'd picked me up out on the road early in the morning. Willig wasn't killed until that night."

"So they know you didn't do it. What about Longmore? Does he still think you stole his money?"

"O'Brien says he never mentions it. More important, he never swore out an official complaint against me."

"That's interesting," said Steele. "Maybe he doesn't want the issue to come out in open court."

Rudd shrugged. "Could be. O'Brien says he still owns the only operating mine left in town, but the word is his vein is running out so he spends most of his time down in the middle of the state. A place they call Phoenix. O'Brien thinks he's starting some kind of new business down there. Anyhow, it gives us some time to try to find the land grant before he gets back."

"And if we do find it? What then?"

Rudd looked around to make sure no one was close enough to overhear. "I've got a thousand dollars hid in my money belt, under my waistband. If we find the land grant, I'll pay Longmore back the money and then it's as much mine as anybody's."

"Has O'Brien heard anything about the land grant?"

"I don't think so. At least he didn't say so. He's invited me to go out horseback riding with him later today. I'll talk to him more about it then."

"Did he have any thoughts about who might have killed Willig?"

"He says pretty much everybody in town suspects Longmore had something to do with it, but he hasn't been charged or anything. O'Brien says it's because this town depends so much on Longmore's mine."

Steele nodded. "All right. You go on that horseback ride with O'Brien. Find out what you can from him. Enlist his help to ask other people. Somebody must know something, either about the document or about Willig's murder."

"All right. What are you going to do?"

"I'm going to try to find out more about Willig, and about why he was killed."

"What do you mean? Don't you think he was killed for the land grant?"

"I suspect his murder did have something to do with *his claim* to have the document, but if the killer got it from him that night, why hasn't anybody heard about it? Why hasn't the person who killed him used it?"

"Yeah. Well, that's good news for us. I bet it's still around here somewhere. If I know old Dutch Willig, he wouldn't have kept it on him. He was too smart for that."

"Maybe."

"I bet old Willig hid it away somewhere and . . . well, that's why I hired you. If anybody can find it, you can. Now how about that lunch?"

They rejoined Becky and her father in the restaurant.

"What have you been up to, Rudd?" asked Becky cheerfully.

"I found my friend O'Brien up at his big house on the hill, but the old house isn't in such good shape now. He's fallen on hard times. He used to be the second biggest mine owner in town, but a while back his mine started taking in water and he had to shut it down. That mine was all he cared about after his wife died."

"Oh, that's terrible," said Becky. "His wife died and now he's got problems with his mine?"

Rudd nodded grimly. "Yeah, a bad streak of luck. He's been trying to pump the water out of his main shaft, but it keeps coming back in. He's just about gone broke because of it."

"You hear about that all the time in Arizona," said Laird. "Somebody hits a big strike, makes a lot of money, and then the ore runs out. I'll stick to farming any day. As long as you got water, things will grow."

Rudd nodded. "Yeah, but don't mention water to O'Brien. He claims there's still plenty of gold down deep in his mine, but they can't get to it because of all that water."

"Too much water," said Laird, shaking his head. "Ain't that somethin'. We break our backs trying to get water to our little orange trees and up here they got so much water they don't know how to get rid of it. Too bad it's too cold up here to grow orange trees. We could make a deal to take that water off of his hands."

"O'Brien has a plan to get rid of the water by putting in a shaft on the other side of the hill to drain it off," said Rudd. "But it would be expensive. He's been trying to find investors, but no takers so far. This afternoon we're going out on his horses to take a look. Even though he's about broke now, he still has his fancy horses. Couldn't bear to sell 'em off. We're goin' over to the other side of the hill so he can show me where he plans to dig his drainage tunnel."

"It sounds like a good idea," said Becky.

"Yeah, it sounds good," agreed Rudd, "on paper. But it would take a lot of money. Who's gonna invest that much money in a scheme that might not work when it's all said and done?"

"Some might consider it a scheme born out of desperation," suggested Steele

"He is desperate," said Rudd. "He hates what he's become. He liked being a rich mine owner. He liked spending all that money, and he liked being one of the leaders of this backwater town."

"Is he a nice man?" asked Becky.

"Sure is. Wait 'til you meet him. He was a good guy, even when he was rich."

Laird finished his coffee and stood up. "I gotta go send another telegraph message to those railroad boys. I keep sending them messages, but they never answer."

Becky stood up and said, "I'll go with you."

"No need. I can take care of it."

"No, I want to help."

"All right, Have it your way."

After they left, Rudd said, "What's that all about?"

"Some trouble with their land claim," said Steele.

Rudd looked toward the door. "Boy, it would be too bad if they lost their land after all the work they've put into it."

Steele nodded. It would be too bad, but it wouldn't be unusual. In San Francisco, a boom in land fraud had accompanied the boom in land prices that had followed the gold rush. Many of Steele's cases had to do with land swindles. A lot of well-meaning people had lost a lot of money to clever swindlers.

Rudd had managed to get the attention of the waiter and was pointing to one of the pies behind the counter.

"Where is the land office in this town?" asked Steele.

Rudd turned back to him. "It's in the courthouse. Right across from the town square. "Why, are you going to try to help them?"

"I was planning to visit the land office anyhow. You said Willig had threatened to register the land grant in his own name. If he did, they should have a record of it in that office."

"Good idea," said Rudd as his pie arrived. "I'll see you later tonight."

Chapter 10

*O*n his way out, Steele stopped at the hotel desk to ask for directions to the local newspaper. But instead of going directly to the newspaper office, he detoured down past the creek to look at O'Brien's mine. With the mine shut down, grass was already starting to grow up through wood platform that surrounded the crusher. The steam-powered lift was protected by a wooden roof, but the cables that led down into the mine shaft were already starting to rust.

As he walked away from the mine, he noticed a narrow path that led back toward town. He followed it and found that it curved through the trees, staying close to the creek. It eventually led to the back doors of the Whiskey Row bars. The name "Ham's Saloon" had been hand-painted above the closest door. Steele went through the door and into the dark barroom. At that time of day, there were only two customers seated at the bar. They turned on their stools to watch him with unmasked curiosity as he passed through on his way to the front door.

Out on the street again, the bright sunlight made Steele squint. A block later, he found the newspaper office, even thought there was no sign out hanging front. The office was identified only by a small sign in the window that advertised low-cost printing. Steele entered and found only one man inside, a short fellow with a bushy mustache and ink-stained hands. "Are you the publisher?" asked Steele.

"Yep, publisher, writer, typesetter, and floor sweeper."

"I just arrived in town yesterday," said Steele. "I was hoping you had some of your old newspapers so I could read about the town's history."

"The town's history? This town doesn't have a history. It wasn't hardly even a town until they hit gold a few years back. Then the government up and named us the territorial capital, and now everybody thinks we're a town. But I do have a couple stacks of the old papers out back. I'll get 'em."

He disappeared through the door, but soon returned with a stack of tattered copies of old newspapers. He pushed them across the counter to Steele and nodded toward a narrow table in the corner.

Steele sat down at the table and leafed through the stacks. "It looks as if they only go back six years. Don't you have anything older than that?"

"That's when the paper started. Before that they only had a monthly two-pager that the church put out. But nuthin' much happens in this town anyhow. Those'll pretty much tell you what's been goin' on around here. Take your time. I'll be in the back room."

After the man left, Steele began to examine each newspaper, starting with the oldest. It reported mostly news about the mines, plus church news and social events, but after an hour's reading, he ran across a story headlined, "Prescott's Violent History." It listed past murders and shootouts, and had interviews with residents about them. There was a short paragraph about Willig's murder, followed by a mention of another very similar murder in the hotel soon thereafter. In both cases, a man had been murdered in his sleep. The story described Willig as a prospector and said the other victim had also been a prospector, an Easterner, newly arrived in town, who had falsely claimed to have discovered silver at Jerome, a small town to the north. An editorial in the same issue complained about increasing violence in town, suggesting it was due to the proliferation of bars along Whiskey Row and what it called "the drunken carousers" that had come to town with the opening of the mines.

Steele took the rest of the afternoon carefully going through each of the newspapers, trying to get a feel for the town. In one of the more recent issues, he found an editorial complaining about "outsiders" who came to buy up the land without contributing anything to the community.

Steele got up and took the paper into the back room to find the publisher. The man was setting type on an old typesetting machine, a complex pedal-powered iron instrument of clanging wheels and levers.

Steele showed him the paper. "Did you write this editorial?"

The man stopped the machine. "I suppose if it's in there, I wrote it." He glanced at the paper. "Oh, that one. What about it?"

"Your editorial said outsiders were coming in to buy land here. Can you tell me who they were?"

The newspaper man scowled at him. "So, you come in here wantin' to look at old papers. Then you only ask about that one piece. Maybe you'd better tell me why you're wantin' to know."

"I too am interested in buying some property in this town." He handed the newspaperman a printed business card that provided only the name "Drew Steele" and the address of his San Francisco office. "I'd like to get in touch with the investors you referred to in this editorial."

The man looked at the card. "Another San Francisco investor, eh?" He handed the card back to Steele. "Well you can't get in touch with him. And it wasn't investors, it was only one guy. A fancy lawyer in a fancy suit. He showed up in town and bought up what we all thought was worthless property. Then he went right back to San Francisco."

"Worthless property?"

"Yeah, desert land southeast of town. Nuthin' much out there but cactus and sand. But a few months later they named us the territorial capital so maybe he wasn't as dumb as he looked."

He thanked the newspaperman for the information and left the office. Why would someone send a San Francisco lawyer to Arizona to buy up local property? Even if they had inside information that the town was about to be named the territorial capital, why would they think that would make the land more valuable?

Chapter 11

Steele left the newspaper office and as he passed the town square, he noticed a young man sitting by himself on a bench under one of the largest trees. He was looking upward. Steele suspected it might be the man Suzie had referred to as Crazy Billy, Dutch Willig's friend.

Steele crossed the street, and as he drew nearer, he saw that the young man had a vacant look in his eyes and appeared to be mumbling to himself. He was wearing a dark shirt that had been patched many times and dirty brown pants that were too short for him. His face was so smooth and unwrinkled he could have been a teenager, but Steele suspected he was quite a bit older than that. He had seen a boy in Tennessee who looked remarkably like this young man. That boy had wandered the streets aimlessly and was called "Dummy" by the people of the town.

Steele sat down next to him. "Are you Billy?"

The boy stopped mumbling, but he continued to stare up into the branches.

Steele followed the boy's eyes. What was he looking at up there? The birds?

"It's a beautiful day, isn't it?"

Billy didn't respond.

For several minutes they both sat quietly watching the birds flit around in the highest part of the tree. When a blue jay flew in, Billy got very excited and pointed. He made a guttural sound that might have been his attempt to say the word "mean."

"It's a blue jay," said Steele.

"Mean," repeated Billy, and he began to rock rhythmically, forward and back.

"Is he a mean bird?"

"Mean."

"Does he pick on the other birds?"

Billy nodded, and for the first time he looked at Steele.

Steele could see that Billy understood what he was saying. "Someone told me your name was Billy. Can I call you Billy?"

Billy began to rock even faster, staring at his own hands.

"Look," said Steele, pointing. "The blue jay, the mean bird, flew away. I wonder where he's going?"

"Eat," mumbled Billy.

"Do you think he's going home to eat? Is it time for his lunch?"

Billy didn't respond. He continued to rock and a little bit of drool slipped out of the corner of his mouth. Steele took out his handkerchief and wiped it away. Billy didn't resist. Maybe the thought of food had made Billy hungry and that's why he'd started to drool.

Steele continued to sit with Billy, occasionally offering a word or two of comment. But the young man seemed barely aware of him.

Suddenly, Billy stood up. "Go time." He hurried toward to street. He stopped to let the wagons and horseback riders pass, then he hurried across.

Steele followed him across the street and up the steps of the courthouse. Inside, Billy raced across the wide lobby and out another door. Steele caught that door before it closed and saw that Billy was headed for the outhouse. The young man may have been odd, but he knew how to get to the outhouse on his own.

After a few minutes, Billy came back. He passed right by Steele without looking at him. Steele followed him back to the bench and sat down next to him. "Well, any new birds up there since we left?"

Billy shook his head. "Go time."

"Go time? Do you mean they've gone to their own outhouses?"

Billy didn't respond. He went back to his rhythmic rocking, staring at his fingers.

"Billy, I want you to try to remember something. Do you remember your friend Dutch Willig? He used to sit here with you. Do you remember him?"

Billy wasn't paying any attention. His focus was on the birds above.

Steele decided it was too complicated a concept for Billy. Or maybe he didn't remember things that had happened in the past.

Steele took out his watch to check the time. It was getting late. He'd better get going to meet Cousin Wang at the Dragon House.

Billy suddenly reached out to touch the watch, but he quickly pulled his hand back.

"It's pretty, isn't it? said Steele. He held the watch up so the ornate carving in the gold case would catch the sunlight.

Billy's eyes never left the watch.

"Do you want to hold it?" Steele put the watch in Billy's hand.

Billy brought the watch up very close to his face and stroked it.

Steele reached over and opened the case so Billy could see the jewel-encrusted watchface. He pointed to the slowly moving second hand under the glass. "See, it moves. It tells us the time of day."

Billy stared at it, transfixed. When the minute hand reached the hour, the repeater started to chime. Billy cried out with excitement. He began rubbing the watch against his cheek, cooing like a pigeon.

It made Steele smile to see him so happy.

But when the chiming stopped, Billy looked very disappointed. He held the watch out toward Steele making urgent sounds.

Steele pointed at the watch face. "When the big hand is up, the watch makes the sound. It chimes. But when both hands are up, it plays a little song. Do you want to hear it"

Billy looked confused.

"Here, let me show you," said Steele, reaching toward the watch.

Billy pulled it away.

"All right, you can hold it. Just let me reset the hands." Steele pulled the watch's stem out and reset the hands to one minute before twelve. "Now we wait."

Billy looked at him questioningly.

"Just wait. You'll see."

Billy stared at the watch. When the two hands came together, the watch began chiming out a little ditty. Billy squealed with delight and held it up to his ear.

Steele hadn't been able to find out the name of the tune, but Stacy was sure it was part of a nursery song that was commonly sung to children in Germany.

When the melody ended, Billy stared at it in dismay. He shook the watch and held it up to his ear. Finally, he held it out to Steele. "Sing."

Steele again reset the hands to one minute before twelve and handed the watch back to Billy.

Billy stared at it for a few seconds and then tried to give it back to Steele. "Sing."

"We have to wait."

When the watch began chiming again, Billy laughed loudly and bounced up and down. He held it up to his ear until the music stopped. Then he immediately handed it to Steele again. "Sing."

Steele took the watch and reset it to the correct time. "It will sing twice a day, Billy. But now I'm afraid I have to go. I'll come back later so you can play with the watch again."

But as he stood up, Billy began to wail. He reached out toward Steele, his fingers clawing at the air. A few passersby looked in their direction.

"Tell you what," said Steele. "I'll let you keep it for a while. I have to go to an appointment, but when I come back, I'll make it sing some more." He handed the watch to Billy.

Billy was very happy to have the watch back in his hands again and seemed content just to stroke it.

"You wait. The chimes will come every hour."

Steele patted Billy on the shoulder and headed for the Dragon House. He hoped Billy wouldn't lose the watch while he met with Cousin Wang. It was a gift from Stacy and he was sure it had been very expensive.

At the Dragon House, he found Teng waiting for him. "Cousin Wang be here soon. You want drink?"

Steele shook his head and sat on one of the stools to look around. There were only a few men in the place.

Soon, an old Chinese man came out of the back room. It was the man who had tipped his cap at he and Becky in the park.

"Cousin Wang?" asked Steele.

The man sat on the barstool next to Steele. "Please forgive me for not identifying myself in the park today. But you were occupied with the young woman."

Steele recognized the man's crisp accent as being very much like that of Chan's. "Are you originally from Hong Kong, Wang?

"Very long time ago."

Steele wondered if Cousin Wang was actually a cousin of Chan's. Maybe they had come to America together. "Uncle Chan said I should come to see you. I need some information about this town."

Wang glanced toward the men at the tables. "Perhaps better if we talk in back," he whispered. He led Steele to the same back rooms where Suzie had given him the bath the night before, but he went farther down the hallway and opened a door. He bowed. "Please be welcome to my humble room."

The room was very small and the only furniture was a narrow bed, a small bedside table, and a single straight-backed wooden chair. Steele had thought Wang was the owner of the Dragon House, but the tiny room seemed to indicate otherwise.

Wang closed the door and sat on the low bed. He gestured for Steele to sit on the chair.

Steele pulled the chair closer to the bed and sat down. "I bring greetings from Uncle Chan. He sends you his regards."

"And how is Uncle Chan? I have not seen him in some time."

"He is well. He said you might be able to help me. I came here with a man named John Rudd. Do you know him?"

"He was the school teacher here."

"Can you tell me what people in this town think of Mr. Rudd?"

"I know little of such things."

"Uncle Chan said you would be able to help me."

Wang made a slight bow but his stoic expression didn't change. "If I can."

Steele leaned back in his chair and reached for his drawing pad. "Would you mind if I drew your picture while we talked? It's a habit of mine."

"If you wish."

"I'm seeking information about a man named Willig," said Steele as he began the drawing. "He was killed in this town. Do you know anything about that?"

"I do not."

Steele roughly sketched in the man's features: a narrow face, high cheekbones, thinning black hair. "I have heard someone may have hired the killer."

Wang did not reply.

"It may have been because he cheated some important people out of money."

Wang still did not reply so Steele left the drawing unfinished and stood up. "Apparently you are not the person I need to talk to. I will tell Uncle Chan you were not able to help me."

Wang raised one hand. "I have heard . . . men speak of it."

Steele sat back down.

"Men . . . in here . . . said Dutch Willig should have known better."

"Better than what?"

"Than to cheat important man."

"Important man? Did they say who they were referring to?"

"They did not."

Steele penciled in the man's strong jaw. It hardly seemed to fit his narrow face. "Do you think they might have been referring to Longmore?"

After a long pause, Wang said, "This is a small town. The important men are well known."

"One last question. Do you know anything about a man who came here from San Francisco to buy property?"

Wang shook his head. "I know nothing about that."

Steele closed his drawing pad and stood up again. "I thank you for your time, Cousin Wang. If you think of anything else related to these subjects, will you tell me?"

"I will," said Wang, standing up and bowing.

On the way back to the town square, Steele thought about Wang's apparent reticence to provide information. Both Suzie and Teng had been willing to talk openly to him, probably because he'd told them it was Uncle Chan who had referred him. Why was Wang so guarded?

Chapter 12

*S*teele headed straight back to the town square, but the bench where Billy had been sitting was empty. Had he run off with the watch? It was already getting dark, so maybe he'd just gone home. At any rate, there was nothing he could do about it tonight. Steele headed for the hotel.

As he passed the row of bars, he noticed that most of them were relatively quiet. But Ham's Saloon was noisy with the voices of many men and an out-of-key piano. Steele pushed open the door and peered into the dark club. A little bell attached to the top of the door jingled softly, but no one seemed to notice. The place smelled like most bars, a mixture of old beer, sweat, and cigars. Through the haze of tobacco smoke, Steele saw that most of the men were gathered around someone at the bar. It was Rudd. Not surprisingly, he was telling one of his stories and he had the full attention of the other drinkers. When Steele got closer, he realized Rudd was telling the story of how they had all almost been killed by wild Indians during the stagecoach ride into town.

Rudd finished his story with, "So the guy says, 'All the same, I'd rather get shot in the butt.'"

The group broke into appreciative laughter.

But Steele noticed that two of the men didn't laugh. One was heavy set, with a thick beard. The other was unusually short with angry, dark eyes. Both were wearing sidearms, identical Remington 46s in identical tooled-leather holsters. Expensive weapons for Arizona cowhands.

Something about the way the two men were watching Rudd made Steele decide it was time to get him out of there.

Just then Rudd noticed him. "Steele!" he yelled. "There you are." He waved his half-full beer mug. "I was just telling these boys about how we almost got killed yesterday."

An old man with a white beard waved him over. "Come on and join us, mister. Have a drink." He unsteadily held his mug out toward Steele.

Rudd pointed his cigar toward the back of the bar. "Hey Steele, you'll never guess who ducked out the back door as I came in. Carson! I only saw his back, but I'm sure it was him. He ran out as soon as he saw me come in."

Before Steele could reply, the short man pushed his way through the crowd and grabbed Rudd's arm, roughly spinning him around. It made Rudd spill some of his beer down the front of his shirt. He looked down at the little man, surprised, but smiling. "Be careful, friend. You made me spill my beer."

The little man jabbed his finger into Rudd's chest. "I'm tired of your stories you old blowhard. Why don't you just shut up and let us drink in peace."

Rudd stared down at him, still smiling. "No harm done, friend. I was just tellin' about our stage trip yesterday. We got chased by Indians."

"Indians," scoffed the short man. "What a bunch of bull. I say you're making it all up."

"Well, I'll admit I'm feeling pretty good what with the fine beer this establishment serves," said Rudd with a wink to the others, "but I think know what I saw."

The little man jabbed him in the chest again. "I can't stand a man who can't hold his liquor. Makes me sick."

Rudd was no longer smiling. "I'm not drunk, mister. Not yet, anyhow."

Steele quickly moved between them. "We were just leaving anyhow, weren't we Rudd? About time we headed back to the hotel for some supper. Right?"

"Who asked you to butt in?" said the short man, glaring up at Steele. "I was talkin' to your fat friend here."

"Now let's not get personal, shorty," said Rudd leaning around Steele.

The little man pushed Steele out of the way. "What'd you call me, asshole? Only my friends can call me that."

Rudd looked a little confused, but then he shrugged and stuck out his hand. "Nothing meant by it. It's just that I don't know your name. My name's John Rudd."

Before Steele could react, Shorty delivered a lightning fast blow to Rudd's throat. Rudd gasped and slid to the floor, his hands to his throat, trying to catch his breath.

The rest of the men moved back.

Shorty looked like he was about to hit Rudd again, but Steele moved fast and caught his wrist. The man turned and threw a wild right, but Steele leaned back and used the man's own arm as leverage to make the blow miss.

Shorty jerked his arm loose and stepped back, glaring at Steele.

Steele was about to go to Rudd's aid, when he felt something cold and hard against the back of his head. He heard the unmistakable click of a pistol's hammer being cocked back. He realized it must be Shorty's companion. The man threw his big arm around Steele's neck, choking him and pulling him away. "Stay out of it," he hissed in Steele's ear.

Steele tried to pry the arm away from his throat, but with each movement the man pulled him backwards, pressing the barrel of the gun harder against his head. Steele watched helplessly as Shorty stood over Rudd. "What's the matter, fat man? Can't back up your big talk?"

When Rudd tried to get up off the floor, Shorty was ready. He kicked Rudd in the side of the head, hard. Rudd slumped down against the brass foot rail, apparently unconscious. Blood trickled down the side of his face.

Rudd was on his back, his eyes closed, completely vulnerable. Shorty stood over him, ready to strike again.

Steele tried to break free again, but the big man pulled back harder. Steele let his legs go limp, forcing the man to hold him up. When he felt the pressure change from his throat to his chin, Steele stood up fast and twisted sideways. Before the man could react, Steele was able to thrust his left hand up inside the man's arm. He could finally breathe. "Rudd is done for," he gasped. "Stop him."

The old man with the white beard stepped forward. "Yeah, that's enough. Old Rudd has had it."

"That's right," said the bartender. "Enough's enough."

The others muttered agreement, but Shorty said, "He don't get away that easy." Before anybody could stop him, Shorty stepped forward and stomped down hard on Rudd's throat.

Steele suddenly realized this was more than a bar fight: Shorty knew exactly what he was doing. He was trying to kill Rudd by collapsing his trachea. One more blow to Rudd's throat would probably do it.

"Come on now, young feller, Rudd's had enough," said the old man. He grabbed Shorty's arm.

Shorty jerked his arm free. "Don't tell me what to do. This fat pig deserves what he's gonna get." He pushed the old man aside and moved toward Rudd.

"You're all witnesses," shouted Steele, holding tight to the bar so the big man couldn't wrestle him away. "These two are trying to kill him. Look over here. Look at me. Why is this man holding a gun to my head? All I want to do is pick up my friend and get him out of here."

The bartender leaned across the bar. "Let that guy go, mister. I won't have no shootin' in here."

The big man hesitated just long enough for Steele to get a grip on his wrist. He found the space between the two tendons and squeezed as hard as he could. The man yelped and jerked his arm away.

Steele resisted the strong urge to knock the big man down and instead hurried to Rudd's side. He pulled him up to a sitting position, keeping himself between Rudd and Shorty.

Shorty laughed and strutted over to join his partner. "I guess that'll teach the fat pig a lesson."

Steele pinched Rudd's cheeks and his ears, squeezing hard. It was a trick he had seen doctors at the army hospital do when they were trying to bring wounded soldiers back to consciousness. Rudd roused a little and shook his head. He opened his eyes and looked at Steele, blinking. He seemed as confused as a little boy who'd been hurt and didn't know why. He put his hand to his throat, trying to get a full breath, but he didn't seem to be getting much air. Steele hoped Rudd's throat was not becoming completely sealed off by the swelling.

The old man came over and kneeled down next to them. "Is he gonna be all right?"

"We've got to get him out of here," whispered Steele. "Can you help me?"

"Sure," said the old man. "Let's get him up."

"Come on Rudd, you've got to stand up," said Steele. With the help of the old man, he was able to get him up and walking. With Steele supporting most of Rudd's weight against his hip, they got him out the door.

The cool night air seemed to revive Rudd slightly. But when he tried to speak, nothing came out but a thin whistle.

They made slow progress up the street and Rudd soon lapsed back into unconsciousness. It made him almost impossible to carry. They sat him down on the edge of the board sidewalk while they rested.

"Thanks for what you did back there," said Steele, breathing hard. "I think you saved his life."

"Those boys sure had it in for Rudd," gasped the old man. "And I don't reckon it was just for sport either."

Steele glanced at him. "You called him by name. Do you know him?"

"I reckon I knew of him. He was the schoolteacher back when I was mostly out prospectin'. My name's Gibby. Rudd called you Steele. You a friend of his?"

"That's right, but we'd better keep moving, Gibby. They might decide to follow us."

The old man started to say something else, but ended up coughing. "Just a second there . . . young feller . . . think I swallowed some . . . teebaccy juice." He spit into the street and cleared his throat. "Okay, let's do 'er."

They got Rudd up and moving again. The old man was red-faced and puffing hard, but together they managed to get Rudd back to the hotel. They sat him down in the middle of the hotel lobby and Steele bounded up the stairs. He knocked on all the doors shouting, "Are there any strong men in here? We need help."

One-by-one, the doors began to open. People peered out. Laird opened his door, rubbing his eyes. "What's the matter, Steele?"

"It's Rudd. He's been hurt. Can you help me get him up to his bed?"

"Sure, just let me throw some pants on."

Becky leaned out of her door looking sleepy eyed. "What happened?"

Steele was heading back down the stairs. "It's Rudd. He's hurt."

By the time he got back down to the lobby, Gibby was looking worried. "He don't look so good, Steele. Kind of blue like. I don't think he can breathe."

Rudd's face was pale and contorted. Although he was still unconscious, his mouth was moving, as if he was trying to say something.

"He's still getting a little air, but we have to get him upstairs fast," said Steele.

Laird and two other men came hurrying down the stairs and Steele waved them over. "Hurry, he's hurt bad."

With the help of Gibby and the other men, they got Rudd up the narrow stairwell to his room.

"Becky, go through his pockets," said Steele. "Find his key."

While the men held Rudd up, Becky started to pull things out of his pockets. They were full of junk: a tin of tobacco, a half-smoked cigar, an assortment of papers and notes, some loose matches. Finally she found the key and fumbled at the lock. Her hands were shaking.

They carried Rudd in and put him on the bed.

"Somebody light the lamp," said Steele. "And go get Doctor Fletcher."

Steele unbuttoned Rudd's shirt and felt along his throat. It felt intact, but very swollen.

"Is he going to die?" whispered Becky.

"Now don't get all fret up," said her father. "You know how you get." He turned to Steele. "What the hell happened to him?"

"He was attacked in a bar. A man known as Shorty was trying to kill him."

"Weren't you there?" said Becky, wringing her hands. "Why didn't you help him?"

"A big guy held him back," said Gibby. "Held a gun to his head."

"Oh, I'm sorry," said Becky. "I knew you'd help him if you could." Tears welled up in her eyes and she was rubbing the sides of her head with both hands.

"Somebody oughta get the marshal," said Laird.

A small crowd was gathering outside the door. "He's out of town," someone shouted. "As usual."

"The doctor is the important one," said Steele. "Get the doctor."

"Why is he so pale looking?" asked Becky. "It's like he can't breathe."

"He's getting a little air," said Steele, "but not much. Where is that doctor?"

As if to answer Steele's question, a man rushed into the room, out of breath. "He's gone out to Blue Springs. Won't be back 'til mornin'."

'Then everybody get out of here," said Steele. "Except you, Becky, and you, Laird. Stay and help me."

"You don't have to shout at everybody," said Becky. She burst into tears and turned to her father. "Oh why did we have to come to this terrible place? It's . . . " She stopped and looked down at Rudd. Then she fell to her knees beside the bed. "Oh my God, he stopped breathing." She looked up at Steele. "You have to do something!"

Steele put his ear close to Rudd's mouth. She was right. He wasn't getting any air at all. The swelling around his trachea must have reached the point where it had closed off his airway completely.

"Oh no, look!" cried Becky. "Look at his fingers. He's turning all blue."

Her father moved forward and tried to pull her away. There's nothin' we can do for him now," he said gently. "He's gone."

"No!" shouted Steele. "Not yet." He took out his pocket knife and opened it.

Becky's eyes widened. "What are you going to do?"

"I've got to open his air passage."

"Jesus," said Laird. "Do you know what you're doing?"

"I learned how to do this procedure during the war," said Steele. He didn't tell them that he had only been allowed to do it when the doctors had abandoned all hope and moved on to the next wounded soldier. He felt along Rudd's trachea, searching for the spot the doctors had taught him to penetrate. Without hesitation, he pushed the point of the blade in, making sure it didn't penetrate too deeply. A thin stream of blood spurted out and Steele reached behind Rudd's neck to lift him up to make sure the blood didn't flow back into his airway. He enlarged the incision slightly and then turned the blade sideways to keep the hole open.

But Rudd still didn't start breathing. "Get over here, Lucky. Push on his chest."

Becky turned away.

"Becky, you can't faint now," said Steele. "You have to come over here and help me."

"I'm all right," she said, wiping away the tears with the back of her hand. She hurried over to the bed.

"She won't faint," said her father. "She helped me deliver a calf, more than once."

When they were both in position, Steele held the knife steady to keep the air hole open and said, "Now push and then release, Lucky. Becky, when he releases, you lift up Rudd's arms."

They both did as they were told and Steele felt a little coolness on his fingers as a tiny amount of air come out of the hole in Rudd's throat.

"Do it in rhythm," said Steele. "Count one, Lucky pushes. Two, you lift his arms, Becky." He guided them until they got into the same rhythm he had been taught in the hospital where he had often been in the role of the pusher or the puller. A few times it had worked and soldiers who had died on the operating table were somehow brought back.

But this time Rudd was not responding. He wasn't taking up the breathing on his own. Steele could see that Becky was getting tired. "You have to be strong, Becky. Keep up the rhythm." He wanted to touch her hand to reassure her, wanted to push back that lock of hair that kept falling in front of her eyes, but he had to keep his hands steady. He had to keep the little hole in Rudd's airway open. The technique still might work. He had seen it fail many times, but once in a while the man would suddenly start breathing again. "Just a little longer," said Steele. "See, his color is already improving." He could still feel a little bit of coolness on his fingers as the air came out. "Keep going."

"Suddenly, a wheezy breath whistled in through the hole. Rudd coughed, then he took another wheezing breath. Half conscious, he seemed to realize someone had ahold of his arms and he began to struggle.

"Don't stop. It's working."

After a few more minutes of it, Rudd was breathing on his own and Steele told them they could stop. "I need something to keep the hole open. Some kind of tube."

"How long does it need to be?" asked Laird.

"Only an inch or so," said Steele. "How about your revolver? Does it use paper cartridges?"

"No, I had my old Colt converted to use store-bought metal shells. But I think I've still got a few of the old paper ones. Should I get one of them?"

"Yes. Hurry."

"I'll be right back." Laird rushed out of the room.

Several people were still in the hallway. One young man leaned in through the door. "Is he dead?"

Steele ignored the question, concentrating on keeping the knife in position to maximize the amount of air Rudd was getting.

"Stand clear," said Laird pushing his way back into the room. He closed the door and hurried over to Steele. "Will this do?" he said, holding out the paper cartridge.

"Yes. Now cut the end piece off of it and dump out the black powder."

Laird took out a pocket knife and did as he was told. He handed the tube to Steele.

Steele carefully slid the paper cartridge into the incision in Rudd's throat and removed the knife blade. He dabbed at the seepage of blood around the edges of the tube. He leaned forward to listen at the end of the tube. Rudd was getting air.

"Is he breathing?" said Becky.

"So far it seems to be working."

"Oh, I hate this town," she said. "First it was Charlie and now poor Rudd."

"Now don't trouble yourself, honey," said her father. "Rudd will be all right. Won't he, Steele?"

"We'll have to wait and see. It depends on if there's any permanent damage to his trachea. I'll be able to tell more when he wakes up. Why don't you two go get some sleep."

"Oh no," protested Becky, "I'm going to stay and help take care of him. There must be something I can do."

"You could clean him up a little. Get rid of some of the blood on his head."

"Yes, I'll do that. He'd like that. I've got some water and a washcloth in my room."

"Do you happen to have a needle and thread in there too?"

"I think so. Why?"

"He's going to need some stitches."

She grimaced. "I'll be right back." She hurried out the door.

"She worries too much," said Laird. "Always has. Her mother was like that too." He watched Rudd for a few moments, and then said, "Listen, Steele, would you do me a favor and hang onto this receipt for me?" He pulled out the receipt the land office had given him when he'd registered his property.

"Why? Have you been threatened?"

"No, nothing like that, but after what happened to Rudd . . . well, it's got me thinking. This is the only thing that proves I really did have a deed for our property. If something happened to me, well, the farm is all Becky would have. I hated to give up my deed to the land office, but that's what they said I had to do. At least I was able to write out a copy of the deed before I gave it to them. It's nice and safe in my room, but I'd just feel better if you held onto this here receipt."

Before Steele could respond, Becky rushed back into the room and Laird stuffed the receipt into Steele's pocket.

"I went down to the kitchen and got some nice warm water," she said. "And I found a needle and thread." She handed them to Steele and sat down on the edge of the bed and began to gently wash the blood off of Rudd's face and neck.

"Well, don't stay up too late, Becky," said Laird. He headed for the door, but hesitated before opening it. "And don't worry so much. Steele knows what he's doin'."

Steele called out to him. "Make sure you lock your door tonight. And your window."

"That's right," said Becky. "There are bad things happening in this town."

"I'll be fine," said her father. "Last night I discovered somebody'd cut a groove in the floor. The chair leg fits perfect in there so you can wedge it against the door. Nobody could get in even if they could get the door unlocked."

After her father left, Becky continued to gently wash the blood off of Rudd's face. "The bleeding seems to have stopped. Do you think his head is hurt bad?"

"Head wounds often look a lot worse than they are. I think his throat is his biggest problem."

"But why would somebody do something like this to poor Mr. Rudd? He seems like such a . . . gentle man." She stared at him. "And he's so funny, with his stories and all. Why would anybody want to hurt him?"

"Do you remember I said I'd come here with Rudd to help him with a legal matter?"

"Yes."

"I'm not sure if that's why Rudd was attacked tonight, but it could be."

"Why did you tell my father to lock his door. Could something happen to him too?"

"It doesn't hurt to be careful."

"He's worried about our property. He doesn't say anything, but I can tell."

Steele continued to focus on keeping Rudd's airway open.

Becky put the wet washcloth on Rudd's head. "We put everything we have into that land, and those orange trees. We'll have nothing if we lost our land."

"Your father acted in good faith. The sale should be legal."

Becky got up and began to rub Steele's shoulders. "You must be exhausted," she said. "You've been through so much in the past few days."

"I'm all right," he said, reaching back to pat her hand. "But it's time for you to get some sleep now."

"I'd rather stay with you." She left her hands on his shoulders.

"There's nothing more we can do for Rudd now. I'll stay with him tonight, but I may need your help to watch over him tomorrow."

"I could stay here tonight. I mean . . . we could watch over him . . . together." She still had one hand on his shoulder.

He hesitated, and then said, "It would be better if you stayed in your own room. You know how people—"

"People talk? I don't care about that. But if you don't want me . . . "

He wanted to stand up and hold her in his arms, make her understand that he was not rejecting her. He wanted to tell her he was feeling very close to her, that he . . . But it was late and they were both probably reacting to the trauma of what had happened to Rudd. "Becky, it's not that. It's just that—"

She quickly removed her hands "It's all right. I understand. I'll come back in the morning. Just take good care of Rudd."

"Lock your door and don't let anybody in."

"All right. If you need help, you will wake me, won't you?"

"I will."

She left the room, closing the door gently.

Steele leaned back in his chair and watched Rudd for several minutes. "Well, Rudd, you got yourself into quite a fix this time."

He got up and locked the door. Then he went to the window. The dark night reminded him the room would look very bright from out there. He turned down the wick on the lamp until it barely flickered and then he went back to the window. It looked down on a deserted street: a few small houses, no lights in any of the windows. The whole town must be asleep.

He was about to turn away from the window when he saw the flare of a match down below, followed by the glow of a cigarette. He remembered the glow of a cigarette he'd seen his first night in town. Someone had been on the other side of the street, smoking in the dark. Was it the same person? Was someone watching him? Shorty and his partner could be out there. If they really had been trying to kill Rudd, they'd probably know by now that they hadn't finished the job. And what about Carson? Rudd said he saw him in the bar. If he was coming to Prescott anyway, why did he get off the stagecoach in Camp Verde?

Chapter 13

Steele watched over Rudd for the rest of the night. The side of Rudd's head was gradually turning a dark purple-blue. He wasn't showing any sign of waking up and that worried Steele. It could be a sign of brain swelling. He put his hand on Rudd's forehead, but it wasn't too hot. He pulled back Rudd's eyelids. The pupils were dilated, but at least they were both of the same size. He brought the lamp closer. Rudd's pupil's constricted, as they should.

He squeezed Rudd's hand hard, but there was no response. "How about it, Rudd?" he said very loudly. "Ready to wake up?" Nothing. He tried pinching Rudd's ears again. Still no response. At least he seemed to be breathing normally. The swelling in his throat looked like it had gone down a little. Hopefully, it meant there was no permanent damage to the trachea. Was it time to take the tube out? Steele put his finger over the end of the tube. Rudd continued to breathe normally through is mouth.

Steele went to the wash basin and thoroughly washed his hands. He returned with the needle and thread and sat down on the edge of the bed. "I might as well do this while you're sound asleep, old fellow." He removed the breathing tube and stared at the ugly hole in Rudd's throat. "I hope you don't mind that I've never done this on a living person before." One of his primary jobs at the field hospital had been to sew up the corpses. When an emergency tracheotomy failed to save a soldier, the doctors didn't have time for such niceties as sewing up the hole. It was more important for them to quickly move on to the next wounded man so it was left to Steele to take care of the bodies. In time, he had become very adept at neatly stitching up the incisions so the bodies would look a little better before they were sent home to loved ones.

Rudd barely moved during the stitching, and that was another worrisome sign. If there was damage to Rudd's brain, he might stay in a coma for a long time. Eventually, he would develop pneumonia, and that would be the end of him.

Steele stayed in his chair for the rest of the night, watching over Rudd. He kept his knife at the ready in case he had to hurriedly cut out the stitches. But Rudd slept on quietly, breathing normally, blissfully unaware of the troubles of the world.

It was still dark outside when Steele smelled acrid coal gas seeping up through the floor. It must mean they were stoking up the furnace downstairs. Soon the odor of food cooking also drifted up through the floorboards. Steele looked down at Rudd, wishing he would wake up wanting breakfast.

Soon Steele heard men going past the room and down the stairs. Probably miners, heading up to the mine for the morning shift. He wondered why neither Laird nor Becky were up yet. Laird was a farmer, undoubtedly used to being up at dawn's first light.

He was about to go check on him when there was a knock at the door.

"Who is it?"

"It's me. Becky."

Steele got up and opened the door for her. She was wearing the same yellow dress from the day before. She smiled at Steele, but then she glanced toward the bed and frowned. "Oh, his face looks so sad all bruised like that. Did he wake up?"

Steele shook his head.

She looked back at Steele. "Why doesn't he wake up? Once my father got kicked in the head by a horse, but he woke up after only a few minutes."

"Every head injury is different, Becky. We'll just have to wait and see."

She glanced toward the door. "I thought my father would be in here with you. I knocked on his door, but he didn't answer. I looked down in the restaurant and he wasn't there either. Where could he be?"

"Let's go see. Maybe he just overslept."

She shook her head. "You don't know him. He's never overslept in his life."

They went out in the hallway and Steele knocked at Laird's door. There was no answer. Steele leaned down to look through the keyhole, but it was blocked. He turned back to Becky. "It looks like the key is still in the lock. He must still be in there."

Becky looked worried. "How could that be? If he's still in there, then why . . . " She frantically began to knock on the door. "Father, it's me. Open the door now."

"Wait here," said Steele. He hurried to his room and dug into his pack to find his lock-picking tool kit. He grabbed a newspaper from the top of the bureau and hurried back to Laird's room.

"What are you going to do?" asked Becky.

"I'll see if I can turn the key and push it out. He got down on his knees and slid the newspaper under the door. He opened the leather case and took out a small tool. He carefully inserted the tool into the lock and after a few tries was successful in knocking the key out. When he heard it hit the floor on the other side of the door, he carefully pulled out the newspaper with the key on it. He grabbed it and unlocked the door. But it wouldn't budge. "He's wedged a chair or something against the door."

"That means he's still in there," said Becky. "So why doesn't he answer?" She was wringing her hands. "Something's wrong. I can feel it."

"I'll have to go around outside. Maybe I can get in through the window. Why don't you go into Rudd's room and wait."

"No, I want to go with you."

"Listen, Becky. Maybe your father just isn't feeling well. I'll try to get in there and check on him. But someone needs to stay with Rudd. He could wake up at any time."

She frowned. "All right. I'll go stand in his doorway and watch him. But open this door as soon as you get in there."

Steele bounded down the stairs, three at a time. As he ran out the front door, the young man behind the hotel desk yelled, "What's the matter?"

Steele ignored him. He stopped in the street and looked up at the windows on the second floor. The window of Laird's room was wide open. Why would he leave the window open?

At the corner of the building, Steele found a drainpipe that went all the way up to the roof. Could someone climb up that pipe to get to the second floor ledge? Then he noticed a series of large rusty nailheads near the pipe. He got ahold of the pipe and pulled at it. It seemed to be securely bolted to the side of the frame building. He put one foot on the first nail and pulled himself up. He soon discovered that the nails were in exactly the right place to serve as footholds and within seconds he was on the second floor ledge.

"What the hell are you doing up there?"

Steele looked down. It was the desk clerk.

"My friend won't answer his door," Steele yelled down. "It's blocked from the inside."

"Yeah, well maybe he wants his privacy. Didja ever think of that?"

Steele ignored the man and moved carefully along the ledge. When he got to Laird's window, he thought about taking his gun out of his boot, but surely if someone had gone in through Laird's window, they would be long gone by now.

He looked into the dark room and saw what looked like the shape of a person in the bed. As he climbed in through the window he detected a familiar odor; it was the stink of bodily fluids that are released when muscle and sphincter can no longer hold them inside. He had smelled that odor often during the war. It was the smell of death.

He hurried to the bed and found what he expected: Laird was lying on his back, his eyes fixed open with the distant stare of a man who no longer saw this world. His throat had been cut. The pillow, once plain hotel white, was now stained dark red with Laird's blood.

He looked toward the door. It *had* been blocked by a chair. Becky would be waiting out there. How would she deal with her father's death? He looked back down at Laird's body. Had he been murdered because of his land? It was strangely similar to the murder of old Dutch Willig. He too had been murdered in this hotel, probably because of a land deed.

He felt Laird's forehead. There was the clamminess of death, but there was still some warmth under the skin. He hadn't been dead long. His body was covered by a blanket, but his bare arms were outside the blankets. Steele lifted one arm and saw that there were deep gouges in his forearms. At least he'd put up a good fight.

But why did he leave his window open? Steele went to the window to look closely at the sill. There were no pry marks. And the glass was unbroken. Why wedge the door shut and leave the window open? It didn't make sense.

He went to the door and kneeled down to look at the deep groove that had been cut into the floorboards. The leg of the hotel chair fit perfectly in the groove so it could be used to wedge the door shut. It had taken a big knife to cut that groove, and a lot of time. He squatted down and ran his finger the length of it. There was old yellowed floor wax in it. That groove had been there a long time. It made Steele wonder how many frightened men had used the chair to wedge the door shut. Was it there when Willig had been killed? Suzie had said that after Willig was killed, everyone went down to the hotel to stand in the street looking up at a window on the second floor. Could it have been the same room?

"Father, are you in there? Please open the door now."

It was Becky. What was he going to say to her?

He pulled the chair loose from under the doorknob and opened the door.

Becky seemed surprised to see him. "Oh, you got in. How is my . . . " She stopped in mid-sentence, seeing the look on his face. "What is it?"

He put his arm around her shoulders and tried to lead her away.

She shook off his arm and turned back. "What's the matter? He's not . . . " She pushed past him before he could stop her and stood in the doorway staring at the bed.

She seemed to be trying to catch her breath, trying to talk, but nothing was coming out. He put his arm around her and led her out of the room. He pulled the door closed and gently led her across the hall to Rudd's room and sat her down in the chair. She slumped forward, her head in her hands and whispered, "Why, why?"

Steele knelt down in front of her. "I think they may have been looking for his land deed. Listen, Becky, I've got to go back in there."

She took his hands. "Our land deed? They . . . did that for our land deed?"

"I think so."

She pulled Steele's hands up to her face and sobbed into them. "His throat . . . He . . ."

He took her in his arms, trying to think what he could say to console her. "I know, I know." He stroked her hair and let her cry against his chest.

When her crying began to subside, he said, "I have to go back in there. Will you be all right for a few minutes?"

She nodded.

He went back into Laird's room and locked the door. He walked around the room, looking for anything out of the ordinary. Laird's things were on the bureau: his hat, some loose change, a handkerchief. His clothes were draped over the chair. The pants pockets were turned inside out. Laird must have had some money. If so, it was gone.

He went to the bureau and opened each of the drawers. They were all empty. Laird had said he had a converted Colt, but there was no sign of it. No holster, and no bullets either.

Laird had said he'd made a copy of his deed, but there were no papers of any kind in the dresser. Had the killer taken it? Steele searched every potential hiding place in the room, but found nothing.

He took the land receipt that Laird had given him out of his pocket and looked at it. It was a numbered land-office form with a brief description of the location of Laird's land. Was this what the killer was looking for?

Steele put away the receipt and continued to look around the room He was again drawn to the window. Why had Laird left it open? He tested the window's lock. It worked smoothly. He turned to look at Laird's body. The gash in his throat looked like a terrible second mouth, downturned and unhappy. "Why did you open the window, Lucky?" whispered Steele.

Steele sat on the sill, looking at the room. Why would a person open a window? Could it have been too hot in the room? No, there was no heat source at night in the hotel. It had been quite cool all night and it was still fairly cool in the room. The smell of goal gas was strong. Steele had smelled it from Rudd's room early that morning. It must have come from a furnace downstairs somewhere. But the odor seemed stronger in this room. Steele looked at Laird again. "Was that why you opened the window? Was the smell of coal gas especially strong in here?"

Steele got down on his hands and knees and began to search the floor for cracks or holes. But he found nothing. What was below this room? The furnace? He went out and locked the door. He went down to the hotel desk.

"Well, if it isn't the wall climber," said the desk clerk. "What happened, did your friend have one too many? Couldn't get him awake, eh?"

Steele stared at the young man. "He's dead."

The desk clerk's eyes grew wide. "Dead? How could he be dead?"

"He was murdered. Tell me, why was he put in that room?"

"What kind of question is that? You think it had something to do with that room?"

"Someone climbed into his window, as if they knew which room he would be in. I want to know if someone specifically placed him in that room."

"Gosh, mister, it wasn't my fault. He must have wired ahead for a reservation because his name was down for that room. He must have asked for it." The young man turned the registration book so Steele could read it. "See there, his name was already in the book and down for that room when I came in to work. I asked my uncle if he'd taken the reservation and he said he thought I'd done it."

Steele looked at the name: "L. Laird." The handwriting was noticeably different from the other writing in the book. "Is the book always here on the counter?"

"Sure. In case anybody needs to look up which room folks are in."

Steele pushed the book aside. "Does this town have an undertaker?"

"Sort of. The carpenter takes care of it."

"Well, somebody better go get him. Where's your furnace?"

"The furnace? Whatta you want with that?"

Steele waited.

"I guess you can look at it if you want. It's right down the hall. Second door."

"Show me."

The clerk led Steele down the hallway. He opened the door, but stepped back to waving his hand in front of his face. "Kind of smoky in there today. Damn thing must be acting up again."

"Who takes care of the furnace?"

"Old man Swill. But I don't 'spose that's his real name. He hits the bottle pretty heavy."

"Where does the coal come from? There's not much here."

"Swill brings it every mornin'. In his wagon. Nobody can keep this old furnace goin' 'cept Swill. It hardly ever works right. But it keeps the place warm and my uncle is too cheap to buy a new one."

Steele looked up toward the ceiling. The room would be directly beneath Laird's room. "So this man named Swill brought coal this morning and stoked up the furnace. What time did he get here?"

"Seems like he came in a little early this mornin'. About an hour before dawn, I guess. Why?"

"You didn't see anyone else around here at that time?"

"Naw, old Swill came in and fired up the furnace. Nobody else. Then he went back to see the cook. They probably shared a bottle back there."

"Do you know how long he stayed?"

"I guess they were back there in the kitchen for a couple of hours. He doesn't usually stay that long. That's why I figured they were tyin' one on."

"And did this man Swill come back into this furnace room before he left?"

"Yeah, he did. I guess he wanted to throw a little more coal in."

"I think I'll look around in here for a few minutes. You should get back to your duties."

"Uh, I'd better stay here with you. What are you looking for anyhow?"

"Close the door on your way out."

The desk clerk hesitated. "Oh, right. I guess it's about time for my morning break anyway."

After the young man left, Steele climbed up on top of the coal barrel to get a closer look at the ceiling. He soon found something unusual in the corner: one spot was the same color as the ceiling, but it was soft to the touch, like putty. He picked at it and the putty came away in his hand to reveal a hole about one-inch in diameter. It must go all the way up into the room above, Laird's room. Who had drilled the hole? The man named Swill? And how long had that hole been there?

He pushed the putty back into the hole and hopped down from the barrel. He went back upstairs to Laird's room and went to corner of the room where he thought the hole from downstairs would come through. But there was nothing there. He wondered if it could be hidden behind the molding. He took out his knife and carefully pried the molding away from the wall. And there it was. The hole had been carefully drilled right next to the wall, specifically so it could be hidden by the molding. By unplugging the hole from down below, the coal gas could be directed up into this room. It explained why Laird had opened his window. If the gas was strong enough, it might even have made him groggy, an easier-to-handle victim. It meant the murder had been carefully planned.

Steele closely inspected the hole. It was not new. The edges of the wood inside the hole were dark from age. That hole had been there a long time.

Steele replaced the molding and stood up. He looked at Laird's body and thought about old Dutch Willig. Had he been killed in this same room? Steele imagined Willig sleeping in that same bed, getting up to open the window just as Laird had, and then going back to bed, groggy from coal gas. Two men murdered in the same room, both with throats cut. Most likely, the same person had murdered them both.

Chapter 14

Steele went back to Rudd's room. Becky was sitting next to the bed holding Rudd's hand. When Steele entered the room, she stood up. Her eyes were red from crying. "He won't wake up. I've been talking to him and telling him it's time to wake up, but he won't."

Steele put his hands on her shoulders. "It's all right, Becky."

"No, no," she cried, "it's not all right. We've got to help him. We've got to do something."

"There's nothing we can do but wait."

"Wait? But somebody tried to kill him . . . I mean, what if they come back and . . ."

"Becky, you've got to calm down. He's safe here."

"How can I calm down? My father is in there. . . He wasn't safe. It's this town. I know it. First Charlie gets shot, then Rudd gets attacked. Then it's . . . my father. He never hurt anybody. He . . ." She dropped her head and began to weep uncontrollably.

He took her in his arms, but he couldn't think of anything to say to comfort her. He held her and let her cry.

"He never hurt anybody," she whispered. "He didn't even go to the war."

"I know," whispered Steele. "He was a good man, a gentle man."

She looked up into his eyes. "Please, tell me what to do. I don't know what to do."

"There's nothing we can do for your father now, Becky. We have to be strong."

She turned away. "I don't know how. I don't know what I'm supposed to do."

Steele felt like he should be able to say something to help her. During the war, so many had died senselessly that after a while, nobody talked about it anymore. Everybody at the field hospital just did their jobs, focusing on the living. Maybe that would help her. "Becky, you have to be strong because Rudd is going to need your help. Our help."

"Where am I?"

They both turned toward the bed. Rudd had spoken and his eyes were open, blinking. He tried to speak again but couldn't get anything to come out. He put his hand up to his throat, confused.

Becky hurried to his side. "Don't try to talk. Your throat has been hurt." She turned back to Steele. "He shouldn't try to talk, should he?"

Steele sat down on the edge of the bed. "Don't talk. Just nod your head. Can you breathe all right?"

Rudd swallowed hard and nodded. "What . . . happened?" he croaked.

"Don't try to talk," repeated Steele. "Just whisper. Do you remember anything?"

Rudd shook his head. "Bar"

"That's right. You were attacked in the bar."

"Shorty."

"Yes, the man you called Shorty attacked you. He kicked your head, and your throat."

Becky took Rudd's hand. "Steele tried to help you, but a man held him back. With a gun."

Rudd nodded, but he looked confused. He looked at Becky and then back at Steele. "Crying? For me?"

Becky nodded and kissed his hand. "A lot of things have happened while . . . while you were asleep. But we can talk about that later. Now we need to get you strong again." She turned to Steele. "Can he eat?"

"Only liquids. In the Army hospital we gave soldiers with throat wounds a mixture of milk, and eggs, and touch of whiskey."

"Whiskey," whispered Rudd. "Forget . . . milk."

"At least you haven't lost your sense of humor," said Steele. He touched Becky's arm. "If you can stay with him for a while, I have a few things to take care of."

"Do you have to leave now?"

"There's something I have to do."

She walked with him to the door. "But why? Where are you going?"

"There's a man named Swill who might know something about this. I want to talk to him."

Becky looked worried. "Do you think he had something to do with . . . "

"He might have."

She touched his arm. "Be careful. Promise me you'll be careful. I couldn't stand it if—"

"I'll be careful." He squeezed her hand. "Lock this door behind me. I'll stop at the kitchen and have them make up the liquid diet for Rudd. I'll have them send up something for you too."

She shook her head. "I'm not hungry." She turned back to Rudd and said, "I'll take care of him. Just come back as soon as you can."

Steele went out and hurried down to the hotel desk. Several people were gathered around the desk clerk. He saw Steele come in and pointed toward him. "There's the man who found him. Ask him?"

The people turned to Steele "How was he killed?" one of them said. "Was he shot?"

Steele ignored the man and took the desk clerk aside to describe the food he wanted made up for Rudd. The young man said he would take care of it. "Did you get word to the undertaker?" asked Steele.

"Yeah. He'll be here soon."

"I want to talk to this Swill fellow? Where can I find him?"

The clerk looked worried. "What are you going to do?"

"I said, where can I find him?"

The young man shrugged. "He lives out past the edge of town, raises a few pigs out there. Go past the sawmill. You'll see a trail off to the left. You'll smell his place before you see it. You goin' out there to kill him?"

"I just want to talk to him. Give me a can of that tobacco."

The clerk retrieved the can. "I'll put it on your bill. But I don't think you should kill old Swill. Doesn't seem to me he'd have the grit to kill your friend."

Steele turned to go.

"And he don't much like visitors," the clerk called after him. "Specially those he don't know."

Steele found the sawmill and the path the clerk had described. It led up over the ridge and down into a narrow valley. From the top of the hill, he could see a dilapidated log cabin in the middle of a swampy clearing. A few pigs wandered around the yard, rooting through the mud. A worn-out looking wagon with mismatched wheels was parked next to the building. A scrawny horse wandered nearby, nibbling the new spring grass.

Steele took out his pistol and went closer. He moved along the side of the cabin until he got to the window. There was no glass in it, only a dirty curtain inside. He moved the curtain aside and looked in. The floor inside was dirt, with trash and soiled clothes piled against the far wall. All of the other corners of the room were piled high with coal. In the middle of the floor, a man was sleeping on his back on a filthy mattress, snoring. Despite the cool weather, he was not covered.

Steele went to the door and kicked it open. Something ran across the floor. Steele pointed his gun at it, but it was only a rat.

"Who's 'at?" said a slurred voice from the darkness.

Steele went closer. The man was trying to sit up.

"My name is Steele. I have a few questions for you."

The man finally managed to sit up. "Questions? Get the hell out of here before I—"

"I have a pistol, Swill. I want to ask you about what happened this morning at the hotel."

"I don't know nuthin'. Go away."

Steele saw a lamp hanging from a nail in the wall. He took it down and lit it.

The man put his hand up to ward off the light. "Jesus! Why can't you let a man sleep?"

Steele held the lamp up high and looked the man over. He was unbelievably filthy, probably from the constant handling of coal. He was wearing stained long underwear that once might have been white.

"You delivered some coal to the hotel this morning. And you lit the stove there."

"So what? I didn't do nothin' wrong."

"I think you did do something that was wrong. I think you unplugged a hole in the ceiling and made smoke go up into the room above."

"Get outta here," yelled Swill. He reached for something under the mattress. Was it a gun?

Steele stepped behind the thick post that was holding up the sagging roof and pointed his pistol at Swill.

But the man wasn't holding a gun; it was a large knife.

"No need for that," said Steele. "I don't want to hurt you. I just want to know who paid you to do it."

"Son of a bitch," growled Swill, trying to get to his feet. "I'll cut yer damn guts out and feed 'em to my pigs."

Looking for something to ward the man off with, Steele saw a worn shovel sticking out of one of the piles of coal. He put his gun away and picked up the shovel. As Swill staggered toward him waving the knife in the air, he brought the shovel down hard on the man's wrist.

The knife went flying and Swill dropped to his knees. "Ow! God Damn! You broke it. You broke my damn wrist. What'd you have to do that for?"

Steele pushed the shovel blade against the man's chest. "I asked you a question, Swill. Who paid you?"

"It wasn't my fault. I just did what they told me. I didn't know what they was gonna do."

"Who are they? What did they tell you to do?"

"He'd have hurt me if I didn't do what he said. The hole was already there in the ceiling. I didn't put it there."

"Who would have hurt you?"

"I didn't know the guy. He was a stranger. And he had a gun. He came out here and said he'd pay me twenty bucks if I opened up the hole and made the furnace smoky. I didn't want to, but he said I had to do it or else."

"What did he look like?"

"Just a regular guy. Kind of tall, like you. Skinny."

What color hair? Eyes?"

"Hell, I don't notice things like that. He had a gun, I noticed that. What was I supposed to do?"

"You knew what he was going to do. You knew when you sent the smoke up through that hole in the ceiling. You knew what happened the last time."

"Last time? I don't know what you're talkin' about, mister. What last time?"

"Didn't you send smoke into that same room once before?"

"You're crazy. I never done it before. Never even noticed that hole in the ceiling 'til that guy told me about it yesterday. I only been here since last fall. Came here all the way from Colorado to take over my cousin's coal-deliverin' job after he got killed in a fight."

Steele threw the shovel into the corner. "Don't try to leave town, Swill. The marshal will deal with you when he gets back in town."

"What about my arm? I think you broke my damn arm. How'm I gonna deliver the coal?"

"I'll send Doctor Fletcher out when he gets back."

Steele hurried back toward town, thinking about what Swill had said. It was clear he was telling the truth. A stranger had paid him to send smoke up into Laird's room. But how could the killing be so identical to Dutch Willig's murder if Swill hadn't even been in town at the time. The hole in the ceiling of the furnace room must have been drilled back when Willig was staying at the hotel, or even before. But who was the stranger who had paid Swill? How would someone from out of town know about that hole in the ceiling of the furnace room? From Swill's vague description, the stranger could have been anyone, but it sounded a lot like Carson. Was this why Carson had come to Prescott? Rudd said he'd seen Carson duck out the back door of the bar. Was he trying to stay out of sight until he'd done the job he'd been brought to Prescott to do?

While Steele was still outside of the town limits, he ducked into the woods. The weeds underfoot were wet from the night's dew fall and the warmth of the spring sun had triggered a new hatch of some kind of tiny insect. Steele waved them away from his face and continued on until he got to a thick grove of aspen trees. He sat down on a large stump and took out the receipt Laird had given him. He tore a sheet out of his drawing pad and carefully copied down all of the information on the receipt. He folded the paper and put it into his inside coat pocket. Then he took out the can of tobacco and dumped out the contents. He stuffed Laird's original receipt into the can and used his knife to dig a hole next to the stump. He buried the can and smoothed the ground over.

That done, he hurried back to town and went up to Rudd's room. He knocked on the door and identified himself. Becky opened the door. "Did you find him?" she whispered.

"Yes."

"Did he . . . do it?"

"I don't think so. But he had a part in it. He said a stranger had paid him. From his description, it could have been Carson."

"Carson? From the stage?"

"It could have been. I'm not sure yet."

"But why? Why would he want to hurt my father?"

"I don't know, Becky. Maybe someone hired him."

She looked confused. But then, with a sigh, she turned to look at Rudd. "He's feeling much better."

Rudd opened his eyes and waved weakly.

Steele went to him. "How are you feeling old man?"

"Headache. Hell of a headache."

"That's to be expected. You got hit pretty hard. Several times."

Rudd pointed toward Becky. "Won't let me eat . . . anything. Drink." He pointed to the half empty glass on the table next to the bed. "Awful . . .stuff."

"That's my fault, I'm afraid," said Steele. "It's a concoction we used in the Army hospital. It's supposed to make you heal faster."

"Need . . . real food."

"You may want solid food, but your throat isn't ready for it. Give it a few days."

"Few days? I'll . . . starve."

Steele patted Rudd on the shoulder and glanced at Becky. She was sitting quietly staring at her hands in her lap.

Rudd gestured for Steele to lean closer. "She's . . . sad. Been crying."

"Yes, I know. We'll talk about it later."

Steele went to Becky. "How are you holding up?"

She shrugged and wiped away the tears with the back of her hand.

"I've got to go . . . make arrangements."

"Hey," said Rudd, "what's all the whispering?"

Steele turned back to him. "I've got to go out for a while. I'll be back soon. Will you be all right?"

"In good hands," he said, pointing at Becky."

Steele checked across the hall and saw that Laird's body was gone. The mattress had been turned down and the bedclothes removed.

He went down to the hotel desk and rang the bell for the desk clerk who came out of the restaurant chewing on something. "So you're back. Well, did you find Swill? Did you kill him?"

Steele ignored the question. "I see the undertaker came for Laird's body. Where can I find him?"

"Down the street. Across from the general store. Sign out front says carpenter's shop."

Steele walked to the carpenter's shop. There was no one in the shop, but he heard sawing in the back room so he went through and found a man sawing the end off of a board. Laird's naked body was lying face up on a table in the middle of the room.

"I'm here to see about him," said Steele, pointing toward the body.

"Oh, yeah. I'm makin' his box now. You come to pay? Twenty bucks."

"Yes, and to make the arrangements."

"That's good, 'cause it's no credit on buryin's. It's pay in advance."

Steele counted out twenty dollars. "Make him a good coffin, and line it with something inside."

"Line it? With what?"

"Put some cloth in there so he isn't just lying on the wood.

"Okay, guess I can get my old lady to do somethin' like that. We usually bury 'em right away before they start to stink. I think I can scare up a couple of diggers by noon tomorrow. How's that?"

"Noon tomorrow is fine. You can get his suit from his room at the hotel. Put him in it."

"Guess I can do that. Graveyard is out north of town. Follow the main road."

"And if anybody asks you about him, tell them to come see me. My name is Steele."

"Whataya mean, asks?"

"I think the killer was looking for something in his room. But they didn't get it. I already had what they were looking for."

"Oh, yeah? What was it?"

"A land document. I carry it with me for safe keeping." Steele pulled the paper part way out of his inside pocket to show him.

"You say this guy was killed for those papers and you're carrying them around?"

"That's what I said."

"Doesn't seem like a very good idea to me, but it's your funeral, and that means more business for me." The man went back to sawing.

Chapter 15

As he passed the town square, Steele noticed that Billy was back on his usual bench, staring up at the birds. Steele crossed the street and sat down next to him. "Well, how are the birds today, Billy?"

Billy glanced at him and went back to looking up.

"Have you finished playing with my watch, Billy? I'd like to have it back."

Billy became very fidgety, staring at his hands and shaking them.

"Billy, do you have my watch?"

Billy looked away and scooted to the end of the bench.

Steele assumed Billy had lost the watch. Too bad. Stacy would be upset at the loss of her expensive gift.

Steele started to get up, but saw a heavy-set woman in a faded black dress heading toward them. She was red-faced and scowling. She walked with long, deliberate strides. She walked straight up to Steele and pulled the watch out of her pocket. "This yours?"

"Yes, it is."

Billy saw it and reached for it, wiggling his fingers.

"No, Billy!" she scolded, shaking her finger at him. "I tol' you a hundred times, you aren't supposed to take things from people."

Billy put his head down and stared at the ground.

She turned back to Steele. "Did you give it to him?"

"He wanted to play with it."

"You can't give him things. He'll just lose 'em."

"He liked it so much I didn't want to take it away from him."

"Here." She held out the watch and Steele took it.

"Keep it in your pocket and he'll forget about it. He wouldn't steal anything. He's a good boy. He just doesn't understand."

Steele noticed that she called Billy a boy, despite his age. "He is a good boy," he agreed. "We've been sitting here looking at the birds."

"Yeah, he likes the birds. I bring him here every morning. I take in wash since his father run off and the boy gets in the way. So I bring him here. He don't cause no trouble. Everybody knows him." She pulled out a wadded up handkerchief and used it to wipe the thin line of drool that trickled down the side of Billy's mouth.

"Yes, I noticed he was here often. My name is Drew Steele. I sat down to ask him about a man he used to know, a man named Dutch Willig."

"Did you know old Dutch? He was real nice to Billy." She leaned closer to Steele and whispered, "He don't know where old Dutch went. Misses him real bad."

Billy squirmed in his seat, wringing his hands and making little moaning sounds.

"Do you know what they did together?" asked Steele

"Oh, just sat here mostly. But old Dutch learned him how to go over to the toilet, over there behind the courthouse. Didn't he, Billy?" She beamed at the young man, as proud as any mother of any child.

Steele wondered why Willig had taught Billy to go through the courthouse to use their outhouse instead of using the one in the park.

"Well, I got to get back to my work," she said. "You be good, Billy."

"I think I'll sit here with Billy for a while. He doesn't seem to mind."

"Yeah, he don't seem to mind you bein' here. Some people, he don't like at all. But he likes you." She leaned close to Steele to whisper, "Sometimes he ain't so dumb as he looks. He seems to know which ones are the good people and enough to stay away from the bad ones."

"Then I'm glad he likes me," said Steele. "Is there anything I can get for him? Something he particularly likes?"

"Oh, that's easy to say. He likes that hard candy they got over there at the general store."

"Is it all right if I buy him some?"

"Oh sure. He'd like that. Well, I got to go." She turned to Billy. "You be good now and maybe this nice man will buy you a candy."

As soon as she was gone, Billy stood up.

"Do you want to go to the store with me, Billy? Your mother said I could buy you some candy."

Billy led the way to the store, constantly glancing back to be sure Steele was still following him.

At the store, Billy went in and headed straight for the row of glass candy jars on the counter. He stood there waiting.

The proprietor looked up from his job of stacking canned goods. "Why, Billy, haven't seen you in here for quite a while."

"His mother says he likes hard candy," said Steele. "Do you know which ones?"

"Oh, you don't have to worry about that. Billy knows which ones he wants. Don't you, Billy?" He turned back to Steele. "He only likes the red ones. How many you want? Two for a penny."

"How many does his mother usually buy for him?"

"She don't. Last person I remember buying him any candy was old Dutch Willig. But he's dead now."

"Why don't you give him one and put a dozen in a bag for me."

The man reached into a jar and pulled out a handful of the red candies. Billy held out both hands and the man gave him one. Then he counted out a dozen into a small paper bag and handed it to Steele.

As Steele paid the storekeeper, he watched Billy suck on the candy for a few moments before spitting it into his hand. He rolled it around in his fingers, and then put it back into his mouth.

"Let's go, Billy." Steele led Billy outside, but instead of going back to the park, he took Billy by the hand and led him to the courthouse. "Let's go in here, Billy."

Billy was so busy with his piece of candy he didn't seem to care where he was being led.

"Billy, do you remember coming here with your friend Dutch Willig? The old man with the beard." Steele stroked his chin.

Billy looked at him, puzzled. Then he mimicked Steele's stroking of an imaginary beard.

"That's right. Dutch Willig. You remember his white beard, don't you? What did you do in this building with him? Can you show me?"

Billy squeezed one eye shut like he was thinking. Then he turned and immediately started up the stairs.

Steele followed him, but half the way up Billy stopped to look back at him. "What's the matter, Billy? Am I supposed to stay down here?"

Billy turned and again started up the stairs.

Steele waited until Billy disappeared and then bounded up the stairs, reaching the top landing in time to see Billy go into one of the rooms at the far end of the hall. The sign above the door said "Land Office."

Steele hurried down the hall and looked through the open door. A man and a young boy were waiting in front of a polished-wood counter while a clerk wearing a green visor looked up something in a thick ledger.

The clerk looked up at Billy. "Why, if it isn't Billy. Haven't seen you up here in a long time."

Billy turned away and headed back toward the door without a word.

Steele hurried back down the stairs to wait for Billy in the lower lobby.

Billy came down the stairs and hurried to Steele's side. "Man. Boy."

"That's good, Billy. I like it when you talk to me. So you saw a man and a boy up there?"

Billy nodded and put out his hand.

Steele understood. He gave Billy another red candy.

Billy popped it into his mouth and headed for the door.

As they walked back across the street to the park, Steele thought about Billy's actions. He had obviously been trained to go up to the land office and report back who was in there. Dutch Willig must have trained him to do that, using the same red candies as a reward. But why? If Willig wanted to know who was in the land office, why didn't he just go up there to see for himself?

He sat next to Billy for a while, watching the people pass by as Billy happily played with his sticky red candy. Why would Willig teach Billy the complicated game of who is in the land office? Billy didn't report about the employees in the office, only the visitors. Willig must have been scheming to do something in that office. If

Willig's story was to be believed, a member of the Rivera family had signed over the land grant to him so he could register it in that office. But if that was what he was planning to do, why not just do it? Why take all the time to train Billy to report who was in the office?

Steele stood up. "I've got to go, Billy. I'll come see you later." He handed the sack full of candies to Billy and headed back to the hotel. As he walked, he watched both sides of the street to see if anyone was following him. Everyone on the street seemed to be going about their business. He stopped a few times in front of shop windows, checking the reflections in the glass to see if anyone was watching him. No one seemed to be.

Back at the hotel, Steele knocked on Rudd's door and an unfamiliar man's voice said, "Who's there?"

Steele thought about taking out his pistol, but decided against it. The killer wouldn't come in the daylight; his style was to strike in the night. "It's Drew Steele. Let me in."

"Okay, okay, I'm coming," said the gruff voice.

Soon the key turned in the lock and the door opened. A short man, a little unsteady on his feet, stared at Steele. He squinted and said, "I bet you're Steele. Rudd's been telling me about you. I'm O'Brien." He stuck out his hand and Steele shook it.

O'Brien seemed older than Steele had expected. He had a ruddy face and the wide, pock-marked nose of a long time whiskey drinker. He was wearing a pin-striped suit that looked expensive, but it was beginning to show the wear of years.

O'Brien took Steele's arm and led him to Rudd's bed. "I've been telling Rudd here some stories about the old days. He can't talk so good so I'm doin' the talkin' while I can. Isn't that right, Rudd?"

Rudd smiled weakly. "He . . . always did . . . most talking."

"I came right over soon as I heard about what happened to Rudd. He says you had to cut open his throat to get him breathin' again. Good thing you knew how to do that. Damn shame what's been happening to this town. Good folks movin' out, no-accounts and drifters hangin' around in those bars, attacking innocent people. Like I been tellin' Rudd here, the law should have done something about it a long time ago."

"As if there was . . . any law," croaked Rudd.

"Easy on that throat," said Steele. He picked up the glass from the table next to Rudd's bed. This doesn't look like milk."

"We were just havin' a few little drinks," said O'Brien. "For old times sake."

"Yeah," said Rudd. "Old times . . . sake."

"Where's Becky?" asked Steele.

"Oh, she went to her room to rest,'" said O'Brien. "She looked real tired. What's wrong with her?"

Steele went to sit on the edge of Rudd's bed. "Didn't she tell you about her father?"

Rudd looked surprised. "Her . . . father?"

"She didn't say anything to us," said O'Brien. "She left as soon as I came in. What about her father?"

"Her father is dead," said Steele. "Murdered."

"Jesus Christ!" said O'Brien. "Was that her father? I heard somebody got killed, but everybody said it was just some stranger in town."

Rudd stared at Steele, his mouth open. "Lucky is . . . dead?"

"I'm afraid so. Somebody came in through his window in the night. Cut his throat."

Rudd grabbed Steele's sleeve. "Throat? Like what happened to Willig?"

Steele nodded. "Exactly like Willig."

"Hey, that's right," said O'Brien. "Old Dutch Willig was knifed in this hotel too." He looked toward the door. "Poor girl. We didn't know. She just said she wanted to go lie down."

"I'll go see her," said Steele. He stood up, but looked back at Rudd. "Go easy on the whisky. You're throat needs time to heal."

"I'll take care of him," said O'Brien, moving to the chair next to the bed. "He's a tough old bird." He gently patted Rudd's chest. "You know what this old bird told me once? He said he'd outlive me. Said he'd dance at my funeral. Ever since that day, we had a bet. A case of Ireland's best to the one who lives the longest, or drinks the most, whichever comes first." He laughed and lightly punched Rudd's shoulder. "I almost won this time, didn't I?"

"Too tough . . . for 'em," said Rudd. He coughed and put his hand to his throat.

"I'd suggest you let O'Brien do the talking," said Steele. "I'll be back soon."

Steele went down the hall to Becky's door, but hesitated. Maybe he should just let her sleep. He tapped lightly to see if she would respond.

"Who is it?"

"It's me."

After a few moments, she opened the door. She hadn't changed out of her yellow dress and it was very wrinkled. Steele hoped it meant she'd been sleeping.

"I'm sorry I left Rudd," she said, "but his friend O'Brien came. I thought it would be all right to leave them together."

"Yes, I just met O'Brien. Rudd seems to be recovering more quickly than I thought he would. How are you doing?"

She shrugged. "I don't know what to do with myself. I was thinking maybe I should go see how Charlie is."

"Maybe you should just rest."

"But I feel . . . on edge, like I should do something to keep from thinking about . . . "

"All right, let's go see Charlie."

They went down the hall to Charlie's room and knocked. A woman's voice said, "*Un momento.*"

Soon, a very short Mexican woman opened the door. "*Sí?*"

"*Perdon, Señora.* My name is Steele and this is *Señorita* Becky. We were with Charlie on the stagecoach. *El diligencia.* How is he doing?"

The woman stood back and pointed toward Charlie. "He is not good, *Señor* Steele. Will you look?"

Steele hurried to the bedside and gently squeezed Charlie's arm.

Charlie opened his eyes and blinked. "Mornin'. It is mornin', isn't it?" He was sweating excessively.

"How are you feeling, Charlie?"

"All right, I guess. Feelin' kind of . . . tired. Sleepy."

"Would you mind if I looked at your wound?"

"My what? Oh, yeah, sure, go ahead. But the bullet's not in there anymore. They said the doctor came and took it out."

Steele unwrapped the bandages. The wound was red and swollen, which was to be expected. But the area around it was cool to the touch, despite the fact that Charlie was sweating. Not a good sign. Steele had seen the same thing many times during the war; it could mean infection was setting in. He re-wrapped the wound and checked Charlie's pulse. It was fast, but not irregular.

"Well, whatta ya think, doc?" asked Charlie.

"I think Doctor Fletcher should take another look at it. I'll go see if he's back in town yet."

"Whatever you think, doc."

Steele didn't correct Charlie's reference to him as a doctor. The fact that Charlie didn't seem to recognize him and didn't remember anything about them taking out the bullet was worrisome.

He instructed the Mexican woman to make sure Charlie drank plenty of water and then he led Becky out of the room.

In the hallway, she grabbed onto his arm. "What's the matter? Is his wound getting infected?"

"Yes, but it doesn't look too bad so far. The doctor should evaluate it. If he's back in town, I'll get him to come and he can check on Rudd too."

"I'll go with you."

"I'd rather you stayed with Rudd, if you're feeling up to it. I'm a little worried his friend O'Brien might be tiring him out." He tried Rudd's door and was surprised to see it was unlocked. He opened the door to find O'Brien in a fit of laughter and Rudd holding his throat, desperately trying not to laugh.

O'Brien turned and waved a half-full bottle of whiskey at Steele. "Hey, if it isn't your old buddy, Steele, back again. Come on in here, Steele, and have a drink with us."

Becky hurried to the bedside and pushed away O'Brien's attempt to put the bottle into her hands. "You shouldn't be giving him alcohol, O'Brien. He's barely started to recover."

"A little touch of Ireland's best never hurt a man, missy. Make him forget his troubles."

"Becky is right," said Steele. "That whiskey won't help him recover. On the contrary—"

"Relivin' old times," whispered Rudd. "No . . . harm done."

"Suit yourself, Rudd. But try to drink more of that milk and eggs mixture. I've got to go see the doctor. I want him to come look at you and Charlie."

"Charlie bad?" whispered Rudd.

"I don't like the looks of his wound, but we'll see what the doctor thinks. I'll be back soon."

"I got to get back up to my place anyhow," said O'Brien. "I'll walk a ways with you."

Becky said she'd stay with Rudd so Steele went out with O'Brien.

"I sure did miss old Rudd," said O'Brien as they walked the two short blocks to the downtown area. "This town's got nuthin' but blowhards and roughnecks. Nobody to sit down with to have an intelligent conversation."

"And have a drink with?"

"Now, don't give me trouble about that, Steele. I was just tryin' to make him feel better. Can't believe anyone would want to hurt old Rudd. Why do you think they did that to him?"

"I'm not sure. What do you think?"

"Oh, I got an idea who was behind it. You bet I do. I expect Rudd told you about a man named Longmore here."

"The mine owner. So you think Longmore hired those men to attack Rudd."

O'Brien stopped at the corner. "Who else? Everybody in this town liked Rudd. But Longmore claims Rudd cheated him out of some money. He won't say what it was all about. Did Rudd tell you?"

"I expect Rudd will tell you all about it when he's feeling better. But let me ask you about something else. I heard someone was in town a while back trying to buy property. Has anyone approached you about selling your mine?"

"Yeah, some out-of-town lawyer. But I sent him packing before he got out ten words. No way I'm gonna sell my mine to a bunch of San Francisco investors, no matter what they'd have offered me. I know there's plenty of gold still down there under all that water. Soon as I get it drained, it'll be the most productive mine in Arizona."

"Did you find out who the lawyer was representing?"

"Naw. Some investment group, that's all I knew. Didn't matter to me. I'm not sellin'. Well, I got to go feed my horses. The doc works out of his house. Follow this street and you'll see his sign."

The doctor's office turned out to be in a small, somewhat-run down house. He knocked at the door, but got no answer. He leaned in and called, "Anybody home? Doctor Fletcher?"

The place was a mess, with left-over food on the table and papers stacked against the wall. The floor had recently been swept, but the resulting pile of debris had never been picked up. An open bottle of the doctor's patent medicine was on the table next to an empty glass. Doctor Fletcher was nowhere to be seen, but there was a partly-open door leading to another room.

Steele went to the door. "Is anyone here?"

There was the sound of a bottle hitting the floor. "Who's there?"

"It's me, Drew Steele."

The doctor came out wiping his hands on a soiled rag. "Oh, it's you, the volunteer medic. What is it this time? Somebody else get shot?"

"You haven't heard?"

"Heard what? I just got home."

"My associate, John Rudd, was attacked in a bar last night. He nearly died. And this morning a man was killed in the hotel, a man who came in on the stage with us."

"Two in one night? Didn't I tell you? All the men around here do is get drunk in those bars and shoot each other."

"He was in bed. His throat was cut."

The doctor took his glasses out of his pocket and put them on. "Throat cut? That's different, but I've seen it before. Guy gets into a fight in one of those bars and later the other guy comes after him for revenge."

Steele shook his head. "No, I believe it was a hired killing. It was carefully planned."

The doctor went to the table and filled the glass with dark liquid from the patent medicine bottle. He took a sip. "Well, I just got back and nobody told me. Last night, they dragged me all the way out to Blue Springs just because some prize cow wandered into the clover and got herself all blowed up like a balloon. I had to stab the poor old girl with a butcher knife to get the gas out and then I hadda wait 'til mornin' to sew her back up."

"I had to do an emergency tracheotomy on Rudd to save him."

The doctor looked surprised. He took another drink. "So I'm out in the desert messin' with some old cow while you're in here doing a tracheotomy on a human being. Well, guess it was damn lucky you were here. Sounds like you learned your lessons well in the Army hospital, volunteer. But I'm surprised they'd let a volunteer do tracheotomies."

"They'd already given up on them."

"Oh, I get it. They were pretty much already dead."

Steele nodded.

"Did it ever work?"

"No."

"Thought so. Well, sounds like it worked this time. I'd better go take a look. Who knows what damage you did to his trachea."

The doctor grabbed his bag and they headed for the hotel. On the way, the doctor rambled on about the war and how many soldiers he'd tried to save doing things like tracheotomies. "Sometimes the wounded were coming in so fast they told us we had to pick the ones we thought we could save. And you know what that really means."

"Which ones to let die."

"Right. I still think about those boys, the ones I had to leave lying there on those stretchers. What about their families back home? What was I supposed to tell them? And for what? What did it all mean anyhow?"

The doctor looked at Steele as if he expected an answer, but Steele didn't know what to say. He'd had the same thought many times.

"When my time was done, I packed up and came out here. Just couldn't face any of the people back home."

They walked for a while without talking, but then the doctor touched his own cheek and said, "Where'd you get that scar? Looks like shrapnel."

"A shell came though the roof of the hospital. It killed the doctor standing next to me, and the soldier he was working on."

"Sounds like you were pretty lucky."

Steele nodded. He knew the doctor was right. When he woke up, he was patient in his own hospital. They did what they did for any other patient in wartime, dug as much of the metal out of his cheek as they could and put him in a bed. But two days later they needed that bed so he got up and went back to work.

"I thought coming out here might help me forget all that," said the doctor. "It hasn't. It's like they're still having their own little war out here. Half the men on the street carry a gun and some of 'em know how to use it. I might as well have stayed back home."

When they reached the hotel, Steele suggested they go see Charlie first.

"Why? asked the doctor. "I just saw him yesterday."

"I don't like the looks of his wound, and he seems feverish."

"Uh oh. Well, if it's getting infected there's not much I can do about it."

"Maybe you could drain it."

"That what you did in your field hospital?"

"When they had time."

The doctor shrugged. "I've seen it done. Doesn't seem to do much good. If gangrene sets in, we'll have to take his leg."

"I know."

Upstairs in Charlie's room, Steele waited while the doctor examined Charlie. Then, as they walked back down the hall to Rudd's room, the doctor said, "You were right. Looks like infection might be setting in. If it gets worse I'll reopen the wound, like you said."

Steele knew infections were often worse than the wounds themselves. But there was usually nothing the doctors could do. Sometimes the body would rally and fight off the infection; sometimes it wouldn't. The last resort was amputation, trying to stay ahead of the infection. Steele had seen soldiers suffer through two, or three, or even more progressively more drastic amputations, and even then, sometimes it didn't save them.

When Steele knocked on Rudd's door, he heard Becky cry out," Drew, run!"

The door was thrown open to reveal a husky man holding a short-barrel Colt 45.

Steele jumped to the side and pulled his own pistol out of his boot. Was it the killer? Was he holding Rudd and Becky hostage?

"Don't shoot, Steele!" yelled the doctor, waving his hands. "It's the marshal."

Steele moved a few feet further down the hallway in case the man tried to shoot through the wall. If it really was the local marshal, why was he in Rudd's room with his gun out? Steele looked at the doctor. "Tell him to put his gun away."

The marshal peered around the doorway, but when he saw Steele's gun, he quickly ducked back into the room. "Christ! He's got a gun."

"Well, of course he's got a gun," said the doctor. "You pointed a gun at him first."

"Stay out of this, Doc. I have to take that man into custody."

"Into custody? That's a pretty fancy word for you, Johnson. Quit waving that gun around and let's talk about this."

"The time for talkin's over with. That man killed Swill."

The doctor looked at Steele. "That right? Did you shoot poor old Swill?"

"No, I didn't. I went out to his place to talk to him about Laird's murder. He admitted he was involved and I left him there. I told him he should not leave town before the marshal got back."

The doctor turned back to Johnson. "See there, Steele didn't kill him. He only talked to him."

"Then he's got nuthin' to be 'fraid about. Tell him to throw down his gun."

"Why don't you both just put away your guns and talk to each other? I feel like a telegraph machine passing messages between the two of you."

"What's goin' on up there?" It was the desk clerk at the bottom of the stairs. Several other people were behind him, all peering up at Steele.

"Who's that out there?" came the marshal's voice.

"Just a bunch of people wondering why you're being so stupid," said the doctor. "They're waiting for you to stop this nonsense." He turned to Steele. "Why don't you just give the marshal your gun? If you didn't do anything to Swill, we can work this out."

"I did not kill Swill, but I intend to find out who did. I won't sit in jail while Laird's killer is still on the loose."

The doctor turned back to the marshal. "Sounds like he's not going to put down his gun, Johnson. Guess you'll have to come out here and take it away from him."

"Me?" said the marshal. His voice sounded shaky. "You know I never asked for this job. You all said I only had to do it until they brought in a new marshal from Tucson."

"Well, you got the badge so if you want to arrest this man, you'd better cock your gun and come out shooting."

"Shootin'? Hey, how do I know he's not some kind of hired killer that Rudd brought in here from San Francisco? I didn't sign on to shoot it out with no hired gunslinger."

"Well, then I think you'd better put your gun away. We'll come in and talk." He looked at Steele and Steele nodded.

The doctor led the way into Rudd's room with Steele following. The marshal had holstered his pistol, but he stood warily near the wall.

Steele put his little revolver into his pocket, but kept his hand on it.

"He came in here and said you killed a man," said Becky. She started toward Steele, but he held up one hand to stop her.

"I told him you . . . came here with me," whispered Rudd. "Told him you wouldn't kill anybody. Would you?"

Steele turned his attention to Marshal Johnson. "Swill admitted that he forced smoke up into Laird's room from the furnace to make him open the window. The killer was waiting outside."

"I get it," said the marshal, pointing at Steele. "You wanted revenge. They told me you went out there to get him and you did. By the time I got out to Swill's place, he was already dead. Shot right through the head."

"I didn't shoot him. If he's dead, it must mean the same person who killed Laird came back to make sure Swill couldn't reveal his identity."

"See there," said the doctor. "I knew Steele couldn't have done it."

"All I have is his word about that," said the marshal. "Why should I believe him?"

"Well, I believe him," said the doctor," but if you want to try to take him to jail, go ahead."

The marshal hesitated. "Well, he'd better not try to leave town." He seemed confused for a moment, then he frowned and headed for the door, not looking back.

As soon as the marshal was gone, Becky hurried to Steele's side. "I was afraid he was going to shoot you. What if he comes back with help?"

"He doesn't have any help," said the doctor. "It's our own fault. We talked Johnson into taking the marshal's job and it's been an easy monthly salary for him. Mostly all he does is lock up drunks. Lately he hasn't even been doing that. Been spending most of his time down in a new place called Phoenix. Word is he has a girlfriend down there."

"Thank goodness you were here, Doctor Fletcher," said Becky.

"Yeah, thanks, doc," whispered Rudd.

The doctor shrugged. "Didn't want to see any more men get shot. Now, let's take a look at that throat." The doctor moved to Rudd's bedside. "How's it feel?"

"Hurts."

"I'll bet it hurts." He felt along the sides of Rudd's throat. "You're damn lucky someone was here that knew how to open it up." He glanced at Steele. "Even if it was a volunteer medic. Expect you'd be dead now if he hadn't done it."

"Steele is a . . . handy fellow," whispered Rudd.

The doctor nodded. "Looks like he did it right. Comes with practice I guess, even practice on stiffs."

Rudd looked at Steele. "Stiffs?"

"Never mind," said the doctor. "How's your breathing? Not your throat, I mean, your lungs. Do they feel tight?"

Rudd shook his head.

"That's good. Maybe you didn't get too much blood in your lungs." The doctor opened his bag and took out two bottles of his homemade patent medicine. "Drink some of this every once in a while. You'll be fine." He stood up and headed for the door.

Steele got there before him and opened the door to check the hallway. It was empty. He went out into the hall with the doctor and closed the door. "Before you go to see Charlie, doctor, can I talk to you for a few minutes? We could talk in my room."

"Sure, what's up?"

Steele led the way to his room. He invited the doctor to sit in the only chair while he sat on the bed. "I'd like to confide in you, doctor. I came here with Rudd to help him clear up some things. I know Rudd left this town about a year ago, before you came here, but have you heard anything about it?"

"I do remember somebody saying something about a schoolteacher stealing some of Longmore's money and skipping town. I guess that was Rudd."

"If that was true, why hasn't Longmore filed charges against him?"

"Good question. So you're saying Rudd didn't steal Longmore's money?"

"Rudd *was* involved in some money dealings with Longmore, but he told me a man named Dutch Willig took the money. And then Willig was killed."

"I've heard about Willig getting killed, but it was before I got to this town. Wasn't he supposed to have been killed right here in this hotel?"

Steele nodded. "I believe he was killed in an identical manner as Laird. It can only mean the same person killed them both, or the same person set up the killing. I think it had something to do with land. You're one of the important people in this town. I was wondering if you'd heard anything about anybody trying to acquire land."

"Hah! Me important?" The doctor waved off the idea with both hands. "In this town you got to have money to be important. Hell, I left home before I could grow whiskers and had to work my way through medical school. By the time the Army was done with me, I didn't have a penny to my name. You got any idea what it costs to set up a medical practice in a place like this? I'm in debt up to my ears."

"The town must have been grateful to get a doctor."

"You'd think so wouldn't you? You want to know how grateful this town was? I tried to borrow money from the bank and they just laughed at me. I didn't have anything to get started with except the doctoring tools I brought with me, stuff the Army let me keep. The only reason I've got a house to work out of now is because one of my old patients died and left it to me. Then the owner of a local business loaned me money against the house to set up my surgery, meager as it is."

"A local business?"

"Yeah, the local whore house. Place called the Dragon House. That's pretty funny isn't it? The only reason this town has a place for me to do surgery is because the miners spend so much money on them Chinese whores."

"Who owns the Dragon House?"

"Beats me. Some San Francisco outfit."

"You don't know the owner's name?"

"I guess it's called the CTL Consortium. That's what it said on the paper I signed anyhow."

"You didn't deal with the owner?"

"No, they did the whole deal long distance. Never actually met anybody from the consortium. Hell, you don't look a gift horse in the mouth. They offered me cash money when I needed it. To tell you the truth, when they said the owner didn't want to be identified, I said fine with me. I was scared they were going to back out of the deal."

"But someone from the company must have brought you the papers, and the money."

"Nope, they just used a runner. Some Chinese guy named Teng. He said he didn't know who the consortium was either. Said he was just an employee of the Dragon House doing what he was told to do."

Steele thought about what the doctor had revealed. It was an extraordinary idea, a mysterious consortium from San Francisco loaning money to people in this remote to Arizona town and managing to keep their identity secret.

"You could help me, doctor, if you'd ask around and find out if anybody else has had any land dealings with this consortium."

"Why? Does it have something to do with why you and Rudd are here?"

"I'm not sure. But doesn't it strike you as odd that an anonymous group from San Francisco would be loaning money in this remote town?"

"I figured it was because we're now the territorial capital. Maybe they just think this town is going places."

"It's possible, but why be so secretive about it?"

"Yeah, I see your point. I'll ask around."

After the doctor left to go look in on Charlie, Steele remained in his room, sitting on the edge of the bed. There was something going on in Prescott, something that had to do with land. Was the mysterious San Francisco consortium operating in this town back when Willig was killed? The consortium didn't seem to have anything to do with Rudd's quest for the old Spanish land grant, but both issues did seem related to the ownership of land. And Laird's death seemed likely to have been about land also. On the stagecoach, Laird had said he owned his land free and clear, so it didn't seem like his death would benefit anyone. The land was now Becky's, and there was a handwritten deed to prove it. The deed was safe in the Arizona territorial land office. Or was it?

Without stopping at Rudd's room, Steele hurried out of the hotel and down the street toward the city hall. He saw Billy sitting on his usual bench, staring up at the trees, and once again it made Steele wonder why Willig would have trained Billy to report on who was in the land office. If Willig really did have the long-lost Spanish land grant, would he have registered it in the land office? Maybe he did that in preparation for a legal battle over ownership of the land.

Steele went into the courthouse and up the stairs to the land office. As he entered, he saw that the clerk who had talked to Billy was still sitting at the front counter, bent over a ledger. He stopped writing and looked up at Steele. "Can I help you?"

"I'm here to see about a land claim."

"That's what we're here for. Mining claim?"

"No, a friend of mine named Laird brought in his original bill of sale yesterday. It was for his farm down in the southwest part of the state."

"Property number?"

"The number on the receipt is 3317. I have it here in my pocket."

The clerk held out his hand. "Let me see it."

"I'm keeping it safe for the owner."

"All right, whatever you say." The clerk took a small piece of paper out of a little wooden box on the counter and wrote the number on it. He got up and went to a large, multi-drawered cabinet. He dragged his finger down across the labels on the front of the drawers until he found the one he was looking for. He opened that drawer and thumbed his way through the files. Then he closed the drawer and came back to the counter. "Yep, property form says it's a small farm down by Yuma. Came in yesterday. Man by the name of L. Laird."

"Can I see the deed?"

"Not here. They're taken downstairs to records every night. They've got a fireproof vault down there."

"Can you get it?"

"Nope. The owner has to fill out a request. Then somebody'll bring it up the next day."

"I'm afraid that won't be possible. The owner is dead."

The clerk lifted his eyebrows. "Dead? But you said he just registered it yesterday."

"He was murdered last night in the hotel. Surely you heard about it."

"That was the guy who got killed?"

"Can his daughter come in and fill out the request to see the original deed?"

"Sure, but she'll have to get the district judge to transfer legal ownership first. He'll be here next week."

"All right, I'll tell her. One more thing. Do you remember an old man named Dutch Willig?"

"Sure. Who could forget him? Quite a colorful character."

"Did he ever register a deed in here?"

"Sure he did. Lot's of them. Mining claims, from all over this area. He'd register them here and then try to sell the claims to people. Most of his claims were invalidated because they were on government land, but he kept on trying, even after old Judge Barnes had him thrown in jail for thirty days for perpetrating land hoaxes."

"Did he ever register any land claims?"

"Oh, you must be talking about that land he tried to register just before he died. He came in here saying he had something important to register, lots of land, way too important for a plain little clerk like me. Said he had to have at least two independent sworn witnesses to make sure there wasn't any funny business."

"What was he trying to register?"

The clerk shrugged. "Never did find out. Just then the judge showed up sayin', "I been lookin' for you, Willig." The judge said this time he was gonna lock old Dutch up and throw away the key. Dutch was cryin' and moanin,' sayin', 'What for? I didn't do nuthin.' The judge said, 'You know what for. You're up to your old land fraud tricks again, aren't you?' He dragged old Dutch out of here, but he must have let him loose later that day because Willig ended up in the hotel that night and that's where he got killed."

"Would Willig's claims still be down in the vault?"

"I guess so. The judge had them brought up when he was gonna file charges against old Dutch, but I guess they all ended up back in the vault when the judge was done with them."

"Are they safe down there? What about break-ins?"

"So you heard about that, did you? Somebody did get in and they tossed things around a bit. But nothing seemed to be missing. I think they were looking for money so when they saw it was only old records they got out of there as fast as they could. The judge had the combination on the vault changed and there haven't been any more break-ins since then."

"When was that break-in?"

"Let's see, late last fall, I guess it was. About the time the snows came, I think."

"One more thing," said Steele. "Can you think of any reason why anyone would want to kill Laird for his land. Do you think it has any special value?"

"Let's see, you said it was down by Yuma. Don't know why it would be anything special. Unless maybe it's in the path of the new railroad."

"The new railroad?"

"Yeah, just announced down in Phoenix. They're gonna put in a new line from there to link up with the railroad at Colorado City. Does the land have water?"

"It does."

"Well then, there you have it. There's not a spec of water between the Colorado River and Phoenix. Them steam trains need a lot of water. If that property is in the path of the new line, this man's daughter is probably going to be a rich woman."

Steele thanked the man and left the office. So that was it. Becky's discovery of how to get water from the mountains down to their desert land had suddenly made their little farm very valuable, but only to someone who knew where the new railroad was going to go. O'Brien had said Longmore was spending all his time down in the new community of Phoenix. Did he know about the new railroad line?

As he walked back to the hotel, he thought about what he should tell Becky. The deed to her property was apparently still locked away in the record department's vault so her claim to the land should be safe. She should go before the district judge to prove her claim to the land as soon as possible. But now she might be in as much danger as her father had been. Whoever had killed her father would still be trying to get her land.

His thoughts turned to what the land clerk had said about Willig, that he had come in to register 'something important' shortly before he died. It must have been the land grant. That was why he had trained Billy to check to see who was in the land office. He was ready to register it, but didn't want to take it in until he knew who was in that office. But was it just another one of his land fraud schemes? Apparently the judge thought so, and was ready to arrest him as soon as he brought it in.

But somebody must have taken it seriously enough to break into the records vault to look for it. That had to be what they were looking for. The clerk said the break-in had occurred late last fall. That would've made it after Willig's murder. Did they find the land grant? If so, why hadn't it surfaced? Maybe they did find it, but soon realized it was just another of Willig's hoaxes, the grandest one of them all.

Chapter 16

*B*ack at the hotel, Steele found O'Brien sitting beside Rudd's bed reading from the local newspaper. When Steele came in, he lowered the newspaper. "Hey, Steele, glad you're back. Your patient here is trying to talk me into taking him down to the restaurant to get something to eat."

"Starving," whispered Rudd.

"Maybe the restaurant could make you some soup. I'll go down and check."

"Soup?" said Rudd, "Hell with soup. Need . . . meat."

Steele shook his head. "No meat. Not yet. Maybe tomorrow. I'll go down and get you some soup."

"Bread?" begged Rudd.

"Maybe a little bread. I'll be right back. Is Becky in her room?"

"She said she was gonna lie down for a while," said O'Brien. "Poor little thing."

Before going down to the kitchen, Steele stopped at Becky's room and tapped softly on her door. After a few moments, she opened the door a crack.

He could tell she'd been crying. "I'm going down to the restaurant to get Rudd some soup. Would you like me to bring you something?"

She shook her head. "I'm not hungry."

"You have to eat."

"Maybe later."

"I went down to the undertakers. He said he would arrange for your father's funeral tomorrow at noon. Is that all right with you?"

"I . . . guess so."

"Shall I come get you tomorrow when it's time?"

"I guess so."

"Get some rest."

She nodded, but then as he started to turn away, she said, "Drew?"

"Yes?"

"Could you stay and talk to me. Just for a . . . little while."

"It's really not appropriate for a man to visit a woman's hotel room, Becky. This is a small town and people . . . "

"I don't care what they think."

Steele hesitated. "I understand. What you're going through is very hard."

Becky stared at the floor. "It's just that . . . I don't know what I'm . . . supposed to do. My father took care of things. Now . . . I mean, do I just go back home? Or do I stay here to find out who . . . "

"I expect you have others at home, people there who will help you. Relatives, or friends?"

She shook her head. "No, there's nobody. The nearest neighbors are twenty miles away and we haven't been there long enough to get to know people very well. After my mother died, he wanted to leave California. Try someplace new."

"I understand, but there are your orange trees to consider. Is somebody tending them?"

She turned to look toward the door. "I guess so. We weren't supposed to be away very long."

"I think you are going to have to stay in this town until the district judge comes next week. You have to transfer ownership of your land into your name. I can help you send a telegraph message to Yuma in the morning. Someone could ride out to tell your employees the situation."

Becky looked confused. "I guess so. I hope they won't just run off. Sometimes Mexican workers can be . . . unreliable. But maybe they'll stay. My father never told me how to . . . do anything. He took care of everything. Never wanted me to worry. I guess I should have learned more from him."

"There's time enough to think about that tomorrow. Right now, you should get some rest. We can talk more in the morning."

"All right. You'll come for me? In the morning, I mean."

"I will."

Steele closed her door and went downstairs to the restaurant thinking about the copy of the land receipt he carried in his pocket. The original land receipt he'd buried in the forest might be the only thing of real value Becky had now. Laird had said he'd spent all his money getting the orange trees started. What kind of arrangement had he made with the workers? If she didn't have enough money to keep the orange farm going, the workers would soon leave. Then she'd have to sell the land. Was someone counting on that? If she didn't know the railroad was coming through her property, she'd be glad to sell the property to them for anything she could get. But who could that someone be? What about that San Francisco lawyer who'd come to town to buy any available land? And O'Brien had said Longmore was involved in some kind of new business down in the middle of the state. Maybe it also had something to do with land or water.

At the restaurant, he asked the cook for some soup and bread for Rudd. He also asked them to take some up to Becky.

Back in Rudd's room, O'Brien jumped up as soon as Steele entered. "Listen, Steele, I just came up with a great idea. How about if tomorrow morning we move all of you up to my place? I got plenty of room. Rudd would be more comfortable up there anyhow. And why waste the money on this place?"

Steele glanced at Rudd who was already nodding.

Steele turned back to O'Brien. "Is there an appropriate place for Becky there? After what happened to her father, I think she needs to be protected."

"Of course. She's welcome and I'll be glad to keep a close eye on her. She could stay in my wife's old room. Nobody's been in there since she passed away. Real nice room. Somebody ought to use it."

"I think Becky needs to rest tonight. And her father's funeral is tomorrow at noon. How about if we move everyone up to your house after that?"

"Good plan," said O'Brien. "I'll come to the funeral to pick you all up."

After O'Brien left, the kitchen boy arrived with the soup and bread and Rudd eagerly devoured it while Steele stood at the window looking out at the gathering darkness. Maybe a few days of rest up at

O'Brien's house would be good for both Rudd and Becky. And with O'Brien there to watch over them, it would give him a chance to spend some time looking for whoever had killed Laird. Steele remembered the glow of a cigarette he had seen outside Rudd's window last night. The killer must still be out there somewhere, watching and waiting.

Chapter 17

The next morning, Rudd insisted on getting up to go to the funeral. After they picked up Becky at her room, Steele helped Rudd down the stairs and stopped at the front desk to ask the clerk to have their things sent up to O'Brien's house. Rudd paid the bill, insisting on paying for Becky and Laird's room also. Then they made their way to the telegraph office where Steele took Becky aside to explain to her what the clerk had said about her land.

She stared at him and tears filled her eyes. "You mean that's why they killed him? Because our land might be more valuable if the railroad comes through there? People would kill a man for something like that?"

"I'm afraid so, Becky. Many have been killed before because of such things."

She wiped away the tears. "Well, they won't get it. Even it isn't worth anything, it was his dream. I'll register the land in my name when the judge gets here and I'll keep it going. For him."

Steele helped Becky compose and send a brief telegram to tell the farm employees about her father's death. In the telegram, she said she would be back as soon as matters were finished up in Prescott.

They found O'Brien waiting at the cemetery next to a beat-up one-horse carriage. The casket, still smelling of new wood, was resting at an odd angle next to two Mexicans who were still digging the hole.

Nobody said anything while they waited for the men to finish their work.

Finally, just as the men were finishing the grave, the carpenter-turned-undertaker came hurrying up the hill. He took off his hat and mopped his brow with a dirty handkerchief. "Didn't know if you folks were going to show up. Ready to put him in?"

Steele turned to Becky. "Would you like to see him one last time?"

"If it's not too much trouble."

"No trouble," said one of the workers.

The undertaker scratched at the back of his neck. "Ya sure you wanna do that?"

But it was too late. The worker had already pried off the top of the box to reveal Laird, lying on his back, stark naked. The terrible gash in his neck had turned black.

Becky gasped and turned away and O'Brien took her arm and pulled her back.

Rudd stepped forward to look, but he too quickly turned away, obviously shaken.

Steele felt his anger rising up against the undertaker, but he tried to keep his voice calm. "I told you to get his suit from the hotel."

"How was I to know you were gonna open up the box? Besides, we always take off their clothes before the burryin'. Helps cover the costs."

"You have already been paid. You were to—"

"It's all right," said Becky. "Just close it. Let him rest." She was twisting her handkerchief into a tight knot. "

"Well, I told ya not to open it, didn't I?" complained the undertaker. "We didn't even know if anybody was gonna show up. You're all strangers here. I thought maybe you'd already gone out on the mornin' stage."

"You will return his possessions to Miss Laird," said Steele.

The undertaker shrugged. "Whatever you say." He turned back to the two workers. Put him in, boys."

The two men fitted the cover back onto the box and wrestled it into the hole. But before it was fully in, one of the men lost his grip and the box caught, half way down. One of the men kicked at it until it fell the rest of the way into the hole with a thud.

"Well, that's done," said the undertaker. "Should we fill it in?"

Steele turned to Becky and found her staring straight forward with glassy eyes. He touched her arm. "Should we say some words over him?"

She nodded.

"I'll do it," said O'Brien, stepping forward. "I mean, if you want me to."

Becky nodded again.

"Uh, dear Lord," O'Brien began, "take this good man and . . . uh, he was a good man, like I said. As I understand it, he was a farmer and didn't ever hurt anybody. And, well, this kind of thing shouldn't have happened to him. He, uh . . . ."

"May he rest in peace," said Steele.

"That's right," said O'Brien. "May he rest in peace. Amen."

"He was a good man," whispered Rudd. He went to Becky to pat her hand.

"Thank you," said Becky. "All of you."

They all stood there for several minutes staring down at the coffin. Then O'Brien said, "Well, now I think we should all go up to my place and get you settled in. I bet Cook's fixed up somethin' good for us."

"You've got a cook?" asked Rudd.

"You bet. I trade him room and board for cookin'. And he's damn good at it."

O'Brien helped Rudd to the carriage and Steele took Becky's arm to follow them.

The four of them barely fit into the small carriage, but it was only a short ride up the hill. They stopped in front of an ornate, many-windowed two-story house; it was the largest house on the street. Steele could see it had once been a showplace, but now it was beginning to show signs of neglect. The paint was peeling and several windows were cracked and unrepaired.

As they got out of the carriage, a big brown, friendly-looking dog came loping out to greet them. It went immediately to O'Brien's side, shying away from the others.

"Oh, what a nice old dog," said Becky, her eyes still glistening with tears. She bent over and stroked his head. "What's your name, doggie?"

"My wife called him Roy, but he'll answer to just about anything," replied O'Brien. "He's old, but maybe not as old as he looks. He's just kind of sad. Has been ever since my wife passed on."

"Oh, poor old Roy," said Becky, squatting down to scratch the dog's ears and nuzzle him against her cheek.

The dog seemed happy to have her attention and stayed with her as O'Brien led them up the steps onto the broad porch. "This is it," he said with a flourish. "Such as it is." He led them into the large front room and sat Rudd on the big overstuffed sofa.

"Comfy," said Rudd, testing it. "Maybe I'll just stay right here."

"You can stay anywhere you want," said O'Brien. "My house is your house. Now why don't you all just sit a spell. I'll go see what Cook has rustled up for us. Then I'll show you your rooms."

After O'Brien had left the room, Becky helped Rudd lie back and busied herself arranging the pillows behind him. Steele could see that she seemed to be comforting others as a way of comforting herself. It wasn't a bad approach.

Although the elegant furniture was showing some wear, Steele could see that it had originally been the best that could be brought in from San Francisco. He stood in front of the wide bay window that overlooked the town below, wondering how much of O'Brien's wealth had been spent building and furnishing the huge house.

O'Brien returned holding a large cake on a fancy cut-glass platter. "Look what I've got here. Cook says it's even got apples in it."

"Apples?" said Becky. "At this time of year?"

"Says he used dried apples. Says his mother taught him to bake this kind of cake."

"Well, let's have some," said Rudd.

Steele smiled. "Sounds like your voice is coming back."

"Just need solid food," said Rudd. "Like cake."

O'Brien went to the huge ornate sideboard and took out a stack of dishes. "Would you help me. Becky? I'm not so good at this sort of thing."

She got up and went to help him cut and serve the cake.

When everyone had a piece, O'Brien stood in the center of the room to get their attention. "We should have a wake. Back in Chicago, people looked forward to wakes. Life was hard for my people back there, for the Irish, I mean. A lot of people saw us as foreigners, unwanted newcomers. So when someone died, it was a chance for everybody to get together and, well, support each other. You know what I mean?" He was looking at Becky.

"It sounds like a nice tradition," she said softly.

"Right," said O'Brien, beaming at her. "A tradition. And you can't have a traditional wake without Irish whiskey. He went back to the cabinet and pulled out a dusty bottle. He wiped the top of the bottle with his sleeve. "I been savin' this one. For an occasion." He opened it and filled the three glasses. He took one to Rudd and he held out another to Steele. When Steele shook his head, O'Brien thrust it into his hand anyway. "C'mon, it's an Irish wake. We all have to drink a toast to the departed." He held up his glass toward Becky. "Ladies excepted, of course."

"I might try a little of it too," said Becky quietly. "My father used to let me have a little drink now and then, when he and the others were drinking."

O'Brien hesitated, but then said, "Well, by God, in this house, ladies can have a little drink too." He got out another glass and poured a tiny amount of whiskey into it. He handed it to her and held his glass high. "Here's to the departed. At least his cares have gone away."

Everyone lifted their glasses and drank.

"Good old Irish whiskey," said O'Brien. "Makes the cares of the world go away. That's what my father always said before he drank. And it took away his cares every day of his life." O'Brien chuckled. "Probably put him in his grave a little early though, stone dead before he hit forty-five."

"Oh, that's too bad," said Becky. "I'm sorry."

"Nothin' to be sorry about," said O'Brien, going to sit next to her. "He lived his life the way he wanted to. Came over on a steerage boat and headed right out west. In those days, out West was Chicago. He started a bar on the bad side of town, at first just servin' shots out a window to the people on the street. Eventually he got a real bar goin' and it made him good money."

"So what brought you out here?" asked Becky.

"Me? I wasn't interested in the bar business. I wanted to find gold, like most everybody else back then. I took off for the real West before I was hardly old enough to shave. And I done alright too. Got here before the real gold rush started and staked my claim." He stared down into his glass lost in thought for a moment, but then he recovered. "But hey, that's not why we're here. We're here to drink to the passing of a good man, Lucky Laird." He lifted his glass and downed it all in one gulp.

The others remained silent. Becky was staring at the floor.

"C'mon everyone," said O'Brien "This is supposed to be a good old Irish wake. The idea is to be happy."

No one responded. Both Rudd and Steele glanced at Becky who stared into her drink.

O'Brien tried again. "Hey, we're all supposed to think of fond memories. That's how these wakes are supposed to go."

At first there was only continued silence, but then Becky softly said, "I remember one time when we were still back in California." She paused to take a sip of her drink. "One of the ranchers lost his oldest son. We all came together to help him get his crop in."

"That's the spirit," said O'Brien. "I'll drink to that. To helping each other."

Chapter 18

*F*or the next few days, the center of activity at O'Brien's house was around Rudd's place on the sofa. He was recovering quickly, happy to have so much attention and happy to have a cook in the house who seemed eager to fix him anything he wanted to eat.

Becky spent most of her time sitting with Rudd, listening to his infinite supply of stories. When Rudd slept, she often talked to O'Brien. Sometimes she went out to help him feed and groom his horses.

Steele used the time to interview some of the townspeople about their memories of Willig, asking if they'd seen anything the night he'd been murdered in the hotel. No one seemed to have much to say about either Willig or his death. Apparently, everyone knew him, but few had ever talked to him.

Steele also asked people about the man who had come from San Francisco to buy property. Several had sold the man large sections of their unused land, what they described as worthless desert. They all said the same thing: the buyer was a lawyer from San Francisco who foolishly paid cash for their land deeds.

Steele also spent one afternoon back at the hotel, speaking to every one of the employees about the night Laird was killed. Steele described Carson to them, but nobody seemed to remember seeing anyone fitting that description. If Carson was still in town, he was staying well hidden. But they were all sure Swill hadn't been a willing participant. "He wasn't brave enough to get mixed up in anything like that willingly," said the young hotel clerk. "The killer probably got him drunk and promised him a lot of money."

Next, Steele headed for Ham's Saloon, the bar where Rudd had been attacked. Before he went in, he shaded his eyes and looked through the dirty window. There were two men sitting at the bar. He recognized one of them as Gibby, the old prospector that had helped him get Rudd back to the hotel. Ham, the bartender, was not behind the bar; he was sitting on a stool at the far end, slowly turning up playing cards one after the other.

As Steele entered, both of the men at the bar turned to see who it was. The bartender stopped his card game for a moment to look Steele over, but then went back to focusing on the cards.

Gibby slid off his barstool, staggered a little, but recovered and held out his hand to Steele. "Halloo there, young fella!. I been wonderin' how old Rudd was gettin' along. I was afeared he was a gone coon."

"He's doing much better," said Steele, shaking Gibby's hand. "A gone coon, eh?   I haven't heard that one since the war. Back in Kentucky."

"Well, I allow I spent some time back there in ol Kentuck. But that was a mighty long spell ago. Not since I was a b-hoy back there." He paused and took a gulp of beer, looking at Steele over the top of his glass. "Ya know what a b-hoy is?"

Steele shook his head.

"That's what some of the big toads in the puddle called us little bugs back then. Til we set 'em straight one dark night." He gestured toward the bars' front door with his beer mug. "The next day I lit out for the West." He chuckled and plopped back down on his bar stool.

The other man sitting next to Gibby looked Steele over, rubbing his chin with the edge of his beer glass. He looked sleepy and seemed about to tip backward off of his stool.

"Join us," said Gibby. "Never too early for a good ol anti-fogmatic."

"I'll buy you one," said Steele. "I' just came in to ask if you'd seen any more of that man who attacked Rudd.

"Did you hear that? said Gibby, lifting his mug toward the bartender. "The man said he'd buy a round."

The bartender got up without expression and went behind the bar to refill Gibby's beer mug. He also refilled the other man's mug, but the man didn't seem to notice; his head was down on the bar and he was snoring.

"Can't say I have seen that Shorty character since that night," said Gibby. "You seen him in here, Ham?"

The bartender shrugged and busied himself wiping out glasses.

"That means no," said Gibby. "Old Ham, he runs this bucket shop, but he don't talk much. Probably claim to see even less, if you were to ask him straight out."

"I see," said Steele. "Had either one of you ever seen Shorty or his companion before?"

"Not me," said Gibby. "How about you, Ham?"

The bartender shook his head.

"Ya know what?" said Gibby. "Maybe that Shorty guy came in here just to get old Rudd? Whatta ya think about that?"

"It's possible," said Steele. "Let me ask you something else. Do you remember the man who came out of his room at the hotel that night to help get Rudd upstairs? His name was Laird."

"Uh, don't rightly remember him. I had my share of whiskey that night, I guess."

"He was killed last night in the hotel. You probably heard about it."

"That was the guy? Sure, we all heard about that." He turned to the other man who was still snoring, head down on the bar. "We were just talkin' about it, weren't we?" Gibby jabbed the man with his elbow.

The man lifted his head to stare at Gibby with glazed-over eyes. "What?"

Gibby turned back to Steele. "So are ya thinkin' there was a connection between that and what happened to Rudd?"

"It's hard to say. Laird was here in town to see about his land claim. I think whoever killed him was after the receipt for his registered land claim."

"No kiddin'. Did they get it?"

"No, I have it right here," said Steele, pulling out the folded piece of paper. "He gave it to me for safe keeping." He held it up to be sure the bartender saw it.

Gibby looked at the paper and then at Steele. He leaned closer. "Uh, feller, if they was after that there piece of paper, I'd be gettin' rid of it if I was you."

"No, I think I'll keep it right here in my pocket. If anybody wants it, they'll have to get it from me."

"Suit yourself," said Gibby, "but it seems a mite foolhardy for a man who don't even pack a pistol."

Steele felt the weight of the little revolver in his boot, but he was careful not to glance down. "It could be that the killer has done his job and has already left town, but if you see any strangers in town, men who don't look quite like miners or prospectors, will you let me know?"

"Sure nuff," said Gibby. "I'll keep my eyes open."

After he left the bar, Steele headed for the Dragon House. He found Teng behind the building, cutting firewood. Even after he saw Steele, Teng continued to chop the wood, driving the axe hard into each piece. Finally, he lowered the axe and turned to face Steele. "You want Su-zee?"

"No, I'm looking for Cousin Wang."

"Cousin Wang have business in Jerome. He come back soon."

"What sort of business?" Steele remembered reading the story in the town newspaper about the man who had been killed in the hotel after claiming to have discovered silver at Jerome, a small town north of Prescott.

Teng went back to chopping wood. "I not know. He back soon."

"Could you tell him I want to talk to him? I'm staying up on the hill at a man named O'Brien's house."

Teng stopped chopping and again turned to face him. "Ah yes, I hear. Young woman very pretty. No worry. Suz-ee our secret." Teng was smiling, cradling the axe in his arms. It was the first time Steele had ever seen the man smile.

Steele decided against replying and turned to go without the usual formal bow. He followed a well-worn path that seemed to lead from behind the Dragon House back toward town. Why had Teng made that comment? It seemed to imply that he thought something was going on between him and Becky, and that Becky wouldn't approve of his visits to Susie. It was a surprisingly aggressive statement, coming from a Chinese. It also meant that someone had already told Teng about their move up to O'Brien's house. He had seen only one other Chinese since he came to town, one of the kitchen staff at the hotel. Was that who was reporting back to Teng?

After only a short distance, he realized the path was not leading back toward town. It led into the woods. Soon he came to an old stone building with no windows that seemed to be gradually sinking into the ground. Was it a storage building used by the Dragon House? If so, why was it so far back in the woods, a good quarter mile from the main building? The cabin seemed very old, but it was still solid. The walls were much thicker at the base, tapering up to the top. Despite the apparent age of the building, there was one part that was new: the door. It looked heavy. It was made out of planed wood with a thick coat of new-looking paint and a new, well-oiled lock. What was so valuable in the old cabin that you'd have to have a lock like that?

He headed back down the path toward the Dragon House, this time watching for footprints. There were several, but most noticeable were the deep heel marks of a man's large boot. The footprints were too large for a Chinese. Whoever the man was, he had traveled this path several times since the last rain. Steele moved on a little farther and then stooped down to examine a very different set of footprints. The impressions were faint, hardly noticeable. They were the tiny footprints of a very small person, probably a woman wearing shoes without heels, maybe something like a slipper.

He got off the path and cut through the woods back to town thinking about those large boot footprints. Why would a large man, obviously not a Chinese, be going back and forth between that windowless locked building and the Dragon House?

Chapter 19

*B*ack at O'Brien's house, he found Rudd sitting on the front porch. The dog was at his feet. "Hey, Steele, come and sit with me. Becky and O'Brien are helping cook whip up some supper. They left me out here all alone."

Steele sat down and stretched out his legs. It was warm, but the sun had gone behind the edge of the house and there was already a little of the evening coolness in the air. "I'm glad to see how quickly you're recovering."

"You bet. Feelin' great. So, what did you find out today? Anything on who might have killed Laird?"

"Nobody seems to have seen anything. It's as if the killer did his work and disappeared."

"Do you think he left town?"

"It's possible, but if he was after Laird's land receipt, he didn't get it."

"So maybe he hasn't left town. You think he'll try again."

"It seems likely. I've been letting it be known that I have the receipt to the Laird's land deed."

"Hmm. I see. You're letting people know you have it so they'll come after you."

"That's what I'm hoping. And I also want everybody to know Becky doesn't have it."

Rudd shook his head. "I get it. Well, no one could ever say you don't earn your fee. But I'd hate to see you end up in that shabby graveyard where they put Becky's father."

"They won't find me as easy to handle as Laird was."

Rudd was silent for a few minutes. Then he said, "I've got something to tell you, Steele. I probably should have told you about this before, but . . . well, I'd just met you and . . . Anyway, seeing how close they came to putting me in that graveyard, I guess I better tell you now. The truth is, that night Willig came to my place to sell me the land grant, he left something with me."

"Something?"

"Yeah. Remember I told you he got all upset when they were only willing to pay him a thousand dollars for the old Spanish deed. He claimed he wasn't being selfish, only that he needed the money to develop his claim out in Gold Valley."

Gold Valley?"

"Yeah, it's this wide valley out in the desert, maybe forty miles from here. Pretty dry out there, all cactus and sand, but the valley's got water from a couple of little trickles that come down from the snow melt in the mountains. A lot of the old prospectors used to pan for gold in those streams. There were some big strikes in that valley back in the old days, but now everybody says it's all played out. There's still a few small-timers out there, old prospectors like Willig, but they don't ever bring much gold into town."

"So what did he give you, a treasure map?"

"Hey, that's right. How did you guess?"

"From what I've heard about Willig, he probably had a pocket full of such maps. All of them fakes."

"Maybe, but I don't think this one is a fake. That night, he got so excited about his big gold discovery, he just had to lay out his secret map for me to see. He kept on jabbing at it with his finger. 'Right here," he kept on saying, 'right here. More gold than any of 'em has ever seen.' Willig said he had to sell the land grant to get the money to make his discovery legal before they took it away from him."

"They?"

"He wouldn't say who they were. Only that they were all after him, after his gold. And he was right, wasn't he? The very next day he got killed."

"So you think that means he really did have a fabulous gold mine out there?"

"Well, it's possible, isn't it? At least he might have hit a gold vein and had high hopes for it. But let me tell you what I think. I think he might have hid the land grant out there in his mine."

"In his mine? Why would he do that?"

Rudd frowned. "Don't say it like it's such a crazy idea. He was like that, always thinking somebody was going to take away whatever he had. Let's say maybe he really did have the old Spanish deed. If he knew somebody was after him, wouldn't he hide it?"

"Maybe. But I had a talk with the clerk at the land office. He told me something else you apparently forgot to tell me. Willig had been tried and convicted of trying to sell fake land deeds."

"Oh yeah, that. But it doesn't mean everything he did was crooked. I knew old Judge Barnes had him locked him up for a month in the jailhouse, but the judge was probably only doing what Longmore told him to do. Longmore had the power to get a lot of people arrested. He thought he ran this town."

"Longmore brought charges against Willig? Why didn't you tell me that?"

"Didn't I mention that?"

"No."

"Well, I must have forgot. But the important thing is Willig left the map on my table when he ran off with the money. I take it out and look at it sometimes and wonder what I might find out there."

"And you brought it with you."

"Sure." He patted his beltline. "I've got it right here in my money belt."

"Let's see it."

There was nobody in sight, but Rudd looked around as if he was really worried. "You mean right here? Somebody could come along."

"Let's see it."

"Well, all right." He took an old, yellowed piece of paper out of his money belt, unfolded it and spread it out on his lap. "See here, there's a big arrow. That has to be where his mine is"

"Or where he left his favorite frying pan."

"Frying pan? Don't make fun of me, Steele. I've looked at this map so many times I've about wore it out. Willig drew in that big arrow just past where these two lines meet up. I think those are supposed to be where two rivers come together. And see these straight-up lines? Looks to me like he was trying to draw a cliff, but it's got a lying-down V-shape in the middle of it? What do you think that's supposed to be?"

"He might have been trying to draw some kind of cut in the cliff."

"Yeah, like part of the cliff fell away or something. Maybe that's how he found the gold vein. And see these wavy lines up at the top of the map? I think they could be a line of mountains northwest of a place they call Gold Valley. O'Brien and I went out there once to hunt doves. I think I could find it."

Steele thought about it. The map looked a little too obvious to be real, but so far he hadn't turned up anything else that might lead him to Rudd's lost land grant, or to Laird's killer. Maybe he should go out there and take a look. The murders of both Willig and Laird seemed to be related to land claims. Maybe he should follow up on anything related to Willig and land. It was better than sitting around waiting for something to happen. "All right, if O'Brien can supply me with a horse, I'll ride out there tomorrow and take a look."

Rudd shook his head vigorously. "You're not going out there without me. I know that area, you don't."

"You're in no shape to ride, Rudd. Besides, you said you'd only been out there once. I can find the spot as easily as you."

"Nope, I'm going too. It's not my butt that got hurt. I might as well be sitting on a horse rather than sitting around here."

"I'm afraid it would be too tiring. You need time to—"

"Well, then we'll stop and rest sometimes. Listen, Steele, this is why I came here. Maybe I should have told you about this map, but can't you see that it's the only clue Willig left? Maybe he didn't leave it accidentally. Maybe he wanted me to have it, in case anything happened to him."

"All right, if O'Brien can provide you with a gentle horse, let's ride out a ways tomorrow. But if you get too tired, we'll turn right back."

Rudd refolded the map and put it back into his money belt. "I won't get tired. You'll see, I'm tougher than you think."

Chapter 20

*A*t supper that night, when Rudd told Becky they were going to go for a ride out into the desert the next day, she wouldn't hear of it. "You are definitely not ready for anything like that, John Rudd. You've been hurt badly. You shouldn't even be up and around yet."

"Now, now," said Rudd reaching across the table to pat her hand. "I appreciate your concern, Becky, but I'm feeling fine. You worry too much."

The tears welled up in here eyes. "Worry? What do you expect me to do? With what's been happening in this terrible town, I . . . "

She didn't continue, but everyone knew what she meant and it cast a pall over the rest of the meal. Before anyone else was through eating, Becky excused herself and went up to her room.

When O'Brien and Rudd went out to the front porch to smoke, Steele went up to make sure Becky was all right. He tapped lightly on her door

"Come in."

He opened the door and saw that she was lying on the bed, her arm over her eyes. He stayed by the door and said, "Are you all right?"

She rolled over to face him. "Will you come in and talk to me . . . for a while?"

Steele glanced back toward the empty hallway.

"Just for a minute," she said. "I need to talk to . . . somebody. I don't know what's the matter with me. I feel afraid all the time. And . . . angry."

Steele went in and quietly closed the door. He sat on the edge of her bed. "You've had a great loss, Becky. It will take time to recover."

"I know, but I feel like something's terribly wrong here. In this town, I mean. I keep on thinking I'll die here too."

Steele touched her hand. "You're going to be fine. You have a long life ahead of you. Opportunities, happiness, even though it doesn't feel like it now."

"I guess so. But I keep on worrying about . . . you. I mean about all of us. Maybe bad things will just keep on happening." She twisted the sheet in her hands. I know it's just a feeling, but I hate this town. I want to leave, to go back home, but I don't think I can. It just doesn't seem right to . . . leave him here . . . in that terrible cemetery. And now you and Rudd are going out to the desert. I keep thinking something bad will happen."

"There's nothing to worry about. We'll be back by tomorrow night."

He started to get up, but she grabbed his hand. "I'm really worried about you, Drew." She flushed red and released his hand. "And poor Rudd, of course."

He took her hand in his. "Why don't you rest for a while. You'll feel better in the morning."

"Would you stay with me? Lie down with me?"

"I don't think that would be appropriate, Becky."

"Just for a little while. Maybe you could draw me again. That would make me feel better. Do you have your drawing pad?"

"I have a small one in my pocket, but let's wait until we can go out into the sunlight."

She released his hand and picked at the bedspread. "You said you drew women in the nude in Paris. What was that like?"

Steele smiled. "Now don't go getting ideas."

"No, really, what was it like to draw those nude models. Were they beautiful?"

"Some were, but most weren't. And we didn't just draw women. We drew men too, sometimes old men. We were studying the human body, muscles, bone . . . the inherent shapes of the body and the spirit. The teachers were trying to teach us to see beyond the surface, to the essence of the human form."

"The essence. What do you think my . . . essence is?"

"I'm not sure I know what you mean, Becky."

"I mean do you think I'm . . . you know."

"Beautiful?"

She nodded, but then got embarrassed. "Never mind. I'm just being silly. But I really would like you to draw me again. Just like I am now, before I change. I can feel myself changing, Drew. I'm afraid. Afraid of what I'll become with all this sorrow inside me."

"Anyone would certainly describe you as beautiful. Yow saw how those men in the park reacted to you. I'd be glad to do a drawing of you, but it would be better if I went to get my larger drawing pad."

She held his hands tightly. "No, don't go. Maybe I just want you to look at me. To tell me . . . I don't know, tell me who I am. Talk to me."

"I can tell you that you are a very attractive young woman who has her whole life ahead of her. You will recover from this and undoubtedly go on to find a husband and raise your own family."

"Will I?"

"I'm sure you will."

"And will it be on a small farm in Arizona? Not in a big city, or someplace like Paris?"

"You can go anywhere you want to. Do anything you want to."

"If I was in Paris, would you want to draw me? I mean . . . like you drew those other women? Without their clothes?"

Steele laughed. "Tell you what, if someday you go to Paris to be an artist's model, I'll do my best to get over there to draw you."

"But not now?"

"Not now."

"And what about your friend, Stacy? Wouldn't she mind if you ran off to Paris to draw me?"

"Becky. Where are you going with this?"

"I was just . . . wondering."

"If I'm going to draw you, maybe I'd better get started. Just lie back and find a comfortable position."

"Can I pose any way I want to?"

"Of course."

All right, turn your back while I decide."

"Why should I turn my back. What are you up to?"

"I just want you to see me the way I am."

"All right, but keep your clothes on."

"I will."

He turned his back and after a few seconds she said, "You can turn around now."

She was mostly under the blanket, but her shoulders were bare.

"You said you would keep your clothes on."

"I'm under the blanket. You can't see anything. I want to pretend like I was asleep and you drew me without me knowing it. I never wear clothes when I'm sleeping."

"All right. Close your eyes then."

She did as she was told and he started the drawing. She was lying on her side, as if asleep, her blonde hair spread across the pillow. She really was a beautiful young woman, but as he started to develop the drawing he worried about why she had taken her clothes off. Was she offering herself to him? She was undoubtedly still a virgin, and yet she seemed very willing. As he shaded in the contours of her lovely face, he decided she must be grasping for something to replace the terrible loss of her father. She probably wasn't sure what she really wanted, but she wanted something powerful enough to make the hurt and the loneliness go way. He wondered what would happen to her when she finally faced up to the fact that she had to go back down to her ranch. She might marry the first man who asked her. But maybe she wouldn't. Maybe now that she was alone in the world she would feel free to try a completely different kind of life. Maybe she really would go to Paris someday.

She opened her eyes. "I'm not sleepy."

"You're only supposed to be pretending to be sleepy."

"I don't want you to draw me sleeping, I want you to draw me looking at you, like this." She threw off the covers. She was completely naked, lying on her side, facing him. "Tell me how to pose. How did the women in Paris pose?"

Steele hesitated. He knew it was completely inappropriate, but he had to admit he really would like to draw her that way. "I would like very much to do that kind of drawing of you, Becky. You have a beautiful body, but such drawings are not often done in this country, not even in art schools. It would be a problem for you if anyone saw it."

She quickly pulled the covers back up, suddenly embarrassed about her nudity. "You don't have to. I just wanted you to see me . . . that way."

She looked away and was silent for a few seconds. Then she turned back. "Do you really think I'm beautiful? I mean do you think my body is . . . beautiful? Nobody ever told me that before."

He smiled. "Have others seen you that way."

She smiled in return and shrugged. "Not really."

Steele put his drawing pad back into his pocket and stood up. "I think you would be the most popular nude model in Paris. But I'd better go now. I think you should get some rest."

"Just come sit beside me. For a minute."

He stayed where he was. "Becky, we have . . . time to get to know each other. When I get back from the desert tomorrow, why don't we do some walking, and talking, like we did that first day?"

She turned down her eyes. "I know, I'm too forward. My father always said I was. Besides, you should be faithful to Stacy."

Steele moved back to the bed and kissed her on top of the head. "It's not that, Becky. It's just that it's too soon for us to be together like this. You need to . . . get your feet back under you."

Suddenly, she sat up and threw her arms around him and clung to him as she began to cry. He felt the heat of her naked body against him, but tried to push the feeling of attraction away. He just held her, not saying anything, letting her cry for as long as she wanted to. When it subsided, he gently lowered her back down and covered her with the sheet. "Get some rest. We'll talk when I get back from the desert."

"All right. I'm sorry. I shouldn't have tried to . . . "

He stood up. "Nothing to be sorry about. We'll do that drawing later, all right?"

She nodded and he went out and closed the door quietly. He was grateful not to run into anybody in the hallway. He went to his room and sat on the bed to look at the unfinished drawing of her peeking out from under the blanket. Looking at it, he felt very close to her, closer than he had felt to anyone before, except Stacy. The odd thought crossed his mind that Stacy would like Becky. She would probably take Becky under her wing and . . . what? Teach her how to deal with men? He shook off the thought and took out his pencil to work on the drawing. He spent several minutes trying to capture that look he had seen in Becky's eyes. What was it? Pain at the loss of her father, uncertainty, but also . . . longing. Yes, that was it. Longing, hoping, wanting something more. He stared at the drawing. It was so different from the drawing he had done of her in the park. In that drawing, she had simply been who she was, a young woman enjoying the sunshine, enjoying being the center of his attention. Now she looked older, sadder, and clearly worried. He could only hope time and better days ahead would take that worry out of her eyes.

Chapter 21

The next morning, Steele went downstairs and found Rudd already up and busily preparing for the trip out to Gold Valley. He turned to greet Steele with a broad smile. "O'Brien is out getting the horses ready. He thinks we'll have to get going pretty quick if we're going to be back before nightfall."

"I'm ready."

They went out to the corral and were packing the supplies into the saddlebags when Becky came running out of the house. She hurried to Steele's side. "You weren't going to leave without saying goodbye, were you?"

"The sun is barely up," said Steele. "I thought you needed your rest."

"I still wish you wouldn't go," she said. She leaned close to Steele and whispered, "I had a dream. A terrible dream. You were—"

"Don't worry about us," said Rudd cheerfully. "We'll be back tonight. You probably won't even miss him. Uh, I mean us."

Steele frowned at Rudd, but he just turned away to wink at O'Brien.

"But I do worry about you," she said. "Especially you, John Rudd. You take it slow and easy out there. Stop to rest if you get tired. It's going to be another hot day."

"Everybody's worried about me getting tired," complained Rudd. "Me and O'Brien used to ride out there all the time." He turned to O'Brien for support. "Didn't we?"

"We sure did. More than once. Nothing to worry about, Becky. They've got everything they need, food, water, matches, even scarfs to keep the biting flies off their necks. I got 'em both a good hat and that pistol Rudd's packin' is my good old Army Colt."

"What does he need that for?"

O'Brien laughed. "Nothing to worry about. It's just in case they stumble across a . . . a rattlesnake or something."

"He needs a pistol for rattlesnakes?"

O'Brien shrugged. "Aw, they'll be back in time for supper, but not if you don't let them get on the trail."

She stepped back. "Then go, you two. But be careful. Do you have enough food and water?"

"I packed enough in those saddlebags for two trips," said O'Brien. They don't have a worry in the world."

But as they rode out of the corral and onto the trail that led up the side of the hill, Steele wasn't so sure there was nothing to worry about. The sun was just clearing the top of the mountains to the east and the air already had a bit of warmth to it and he was worried about how Rudd would handle the heat in his condition. And then there was the desert itself. Steele had never been in the desert, but from what he had seen during the stage ride from Yuma, it seemed to be an alien and forbidding place. Part of him was looking forward to the exploration of someplace new, but there was also a feeling of concern, especially for Rudd. He watched Rudd riding up ahead, already squirming to get his large bulk comfortable in the saddle, and wondered if maybe he should have insisted on going alone.

At the top of the hill, they stopped to look back down. Becky and O'Brien were still at the corral, leaning against the fence. When she saw them stop, Becky waved and Rudd took off his hat and waved back enthusiastically. Steele waved once and turned his horse back onto the trail.

Minutes later, they were over the top and starting down the other side, heading west. Soon the cedar trees and dry grassland changed to sandy desert. Ahead of them was seemingly empty terrain. There were no houses, no trails, no indication that civilization had ever encroached into the lonely desert landscape.

Rudd stopped to wait for Steele. "You seem to be doing all right. Where'd you learn to ride a horse?"

"Stacy's father has horses."

"Who?"

"You know who. Nathan Moran."

"So you *were* involved with his daughter. I heard rumors, but I didn't know if it was true. Sorry about those cracks I made about him back there when we were on the stagecoach. But then I heard you and him don't get along all that well anyhow. Is that true?"

Steele spurred his horse forward. "We'd better keep moving."

Rudd caught up "Okay, I get it. Sorry. Just my nosy reporter's nose." He pointed toward the lowest part of the valley. "Hey, that's where we're going. That's Gold Valley, way down there."

Steele estimated it was at least thirty miles. It was going to be a long hot ride. With Rudd's weakened condition, Steele was already wondering if they really could make it all the way down there and back in one day.

Rudd urged his horse on ahead and Steele dropped far enough back to keep out of his dust. It was hot, but Steele found himself enjoying his first ride out into the desert. From a distance, the many bushes and cactus gave the desert a dusty green look, almost lush, but up close, those green plants were usually cactus or spindly, thorny bushes, thinly scattered across an almost colorless background of sand and rock. It seemed a miracle that any plants could survive out there at all, but survive they did; a few of the cactus plants were even in bloom. One type of cactus had long thin arms that extended upward and outward from a central base and each of the thorn-covered arms was tipped with a brilliant red flower.

Steele reached back and took his drawing pad out of the saddlebag. As they moved slowly down toward the valley, he tied the reins off on the saddle horn and drew quick sketches of some of the stranger-looking cactuses.

After a few hours, he turned to look back. They had come maybe ten miles, slower going than he would have expected. There was a thin line of dust some distance back and he wondered if it was another of the small dust storms he had been seeing, swirling little gusts that sprang up out of nowhere only to disappear just as quickly. On the other hand, the wisps of tan against the blue sky could be other riders heading in the same direction they were going. He decided to look back often, just in case they were being followed.

After several more hours, they began to come across deep ravines and they were forced to detour around them. The heat was intense. Up ahead, Rudd seemed to be struggling. He was leaning forward in the saddle, almost as if he was falling asleep. Steele urged his horse forward to catch up. "Problem?"

"What?" Rudd jerked up straight and turned to look at him, blinking. "Oh, no, just feeling . . . a little sleepy."

"Let's stop for a while."

"No, I'm all right. We'd better keep going or we'll never get there."

"That valley still seems a long way off. Are you sure we're going the right way?"

"Yeah. Pretty sure. The route seems a little different than I remember, but I guess if we just keep on going we'll get down to the river sooner or later."

"It's very peaceful out here," said Steele. "Beautiful, in its own way."

"It's peaceful all right," agreed Rudd. "But I don't know about beautiful. This place'll kill you if you don't know what you're doing."

"You mean the heat."

"That's one way it'll get you. It can get way over a hundred in the shade out here, if there was any shade. And you won't find a drop of water out here either, not 'til you get clear down to the river."

"How did prospectors like Willig do it?"

"Beats me how he did it. You'd think that sun would kill just about anybody after a while."

As they went on, Steele kept a close eye on Rudd. It grew steadily hotter and Rudd was riding slower and slower. Finally, he came to a stop.

Steele rode up next to him. "How are you doing?"

Rudd slowly turned to face him, trying to focus his eyes. "Oh, it's you, Steele. Uh, what'd you say?"

"It looked like you were sleeping."

"Sleeping? No . . . not really. Just a little . . . tired."

"Maybe we should stop. How is your throat feeling? Are you drinking enough water?"

Rudd shook his head to clear it. "No, I'm all right. Actually, it's not my throat that's bothering me, it's my back. It's killing me. Guess I forgot how long it's been since I was on a horse." He took a long drink from his canteen. "But I can make it. I'll get to feeling better as soon as we get to that river." He spurred his horse forward.

Steele wondered if he should try to force Rudd to stop and rest. He had recovered well from the beating, but the sun was unrelenting and the constant detours around sand washes and rocky ridges slowed their progress. The day was passing and it looked like they still had a long way to go. Steele took out his watch. Not many hours left before sunset. They certainly weren't going to make it back before dark.

When they topped a small hill, Steele turned his horse and stood up in his stirrups to look back. That wispy dust cloud was still back there, but it wasn't getting any closer. Was it riders? Were they being followed? It could be just an illusion, heat waves rising off the desert floor. There was nothing to do about it but keep going. He turned his horse and hurried to catch up with Rudd.

After another hour's traveling, they came to a deep sand wash and Rudd pulled up his horse. He seemed a little more alert. "I think we're almost there. Let's try following this wash. They usually lead down to the river."

"Let's hope so. These horses need a drink."

"Me too," said Rudd, shaking his canteen. "I've been out of water for an hour."

They followed the wash for some time until it eventually widened out and disappeared. Rudd was disappointed, but he still refused to get down off horse and rest. Steele gave him the rest of his water and that seemed to liven him up a bit. They continued in the same direction until, late in the day, they finally saw the sun reflecting off water in the distance.

"There it is," shouted Rudd. He urged his horse forward and the horse must have smelled the water because it began to run.

"Uh, oh," yelled Rudd, "I don't think I can hold him."

Steele's horse also began to gallop and Steele let him go. When they reached the river, both horses ran right into the water and stopped to dip their snouts into the slow-moving stream. The river wasn't very deep or very wide, but the water looked clean.

As the horses drank, Rudd got out Willig's map to study it. "I think we have to go further upstream." He showed Steele the map. "I think we're still downstream from where the two rivers come together."

Steele dismounted. "Let's rest here for a minute and fill up our canteens."

"Good idea." Rudd slowly got down from his horse. He leaned forward against his horse and put a hand to his back.

"You all right?"

"Yeah, damn back tightens up on me. I'll be okay in a minute."

Steele filled the canteens while Rudd went to sit on a rock.

Steele remounted his horse, and Rudd got up and struggled to do the same. But the horse suddenly moved away and Rudd fell forward onto his knees.

Steele jumped down to help him, but Rudd waved him off. "Just give me a second." He took several deep breaths and finally made it up onto his feet. He dusted off his pants and sighed. "I'm all right. Too hot, that's all. Let's see if we can find where the map shows that other little river coming in."

Steele took out his pocket watch and showed the time to Rudd. "It's clear we're not going to make it back to town tonight."

"Hey, that's some watch. Where'd you get it?"

"The point is, we're running out of light. Maybe we should stop and camp here. We could look for Willig's mine in the morning."

"But we're almost there now," protested Rudd.

"I think you need to rest."

"I'm okay. Like I said, it's too damn hot. And maybe I've gotten a little too fat."

Steele helped Rudd get aboard and then mounted his own horse. He looked back in the direction they had come from, but the long shadows on the hillside made it hard to see much detail back there.

"See something?" asked Rudd.

"No, but earlier I saw some dust, quite a ways back behind us. I can't figure out if it was other riders or just heat waves."

"Maybe it was somebody headed for the miner's shanty town. It's a ways south of here."

"Maybe."

They headed north, staying close to the river. The going was much easier in the dried mud flats next to the water and soon they saw the narrow canyon where the other river came in. "That's it," shouted Rudd, "just like on Willig's map. Willig's mine should be just a little ways from here, right next to that little creek."

As they moved slowly along, looking for signs of Willig's camp, the shadows grew longer.

"We'd better find a place to camp," said Steele."

Rudd hurried his horse forward. "Just a little farther. It's got to be right along here somewhere."

They went on and Rudd didn't want to stop even after the sun had gone behind the mountains. Rudd kept on looking at Willig's map, puzzled. "I was sure these straight lines were supposed to be some kind of cliff, but there's nothing like that out here."

They kept going and finally they saw it in the distance, a steep cliff, just as the map had indicated. The middle of the cliff had fallen away into a pile of rubble.

"There it is!" yelled Rudd. "And that's what the V shape on the map was. There's a place where the cliff broke off."

Rudd kicked at his horse to force it into a gallop. By the time Steele caught up, Rudd was already off of his horse and looking at the ground. "Look here, Steele, it's his camp. We found it."

There was a ring of charred rocks with a dusty pile of firewood next to it. Nearby was a small barrel that was falling apart and there were some rusty tin cans piled up next to the cliff face.

Rudd ran to the base of the cliff. "And look here. It's his diggings."

Steele tied up both horses and joined him. He leaned down to look inside the hole. "Somebody has been digging here, but it doesn't go very far back into the cliff. Looks like he barely got started."

Rudd frowned. "You know, you're right. Doesn't look much like a real mine does it? But maybe this is just one of his test holes. His mine must be further back in this crack in the cliff. Let's go look."

They crawled over the fallen boulders and worked their way into the cut. It led to a dead end. There were no more diggings. The walls of the cliff went straight up on both sides.

"There's nothing here," said Rudd, obviously disappointed. "So where the hell is his mine?"

"Maybe this isn't the right place," suggested Steele.

"It has to be. It's just like on the map."

"Well, we can look around more in the morning. Right now, we need to find a place to camp."

They walked back to the fire pit and Steele squatted down for a closer look. "It does look like the type of camp a prospector might establish, but it doesn't look like anyone stayed here very long. There's not much trash around except for those few cans."

"Maybe this was just his first camp. Maybe the real mine is somewhere nearby."

Steele shook his head. "This is clearly the place the map was referring to. He was using the map to lead you here. Why would he do that if this is not the right place? Was he using the map to lead you astray?"

"Lead me astray? I don't get it. Why would he want to lead me to a damn pile of tin cans?"

"We can look around more in the morning. I think we should go up on top of the ridge and find a place to camp."

"Why not here? The sand is nice and soft here. It's all rocky up there."

"What if someone was following us? Remember, I saw that dust in the distance. From down here we can't see anyone coming."

Rudd looked up at the cliff and then back at Steele. "Naw, that could have been anybody. Besides, if somebody was following us, they were so far behind us they'd never find us here. I'm tired and my back hurts. I'm staying right here. We should stay here next to this cliff. It'll keep us out of the wind." He went to his horse and started to unpack his saddlebags.

Steele silently unpacked his own saddlebags and bedroll. It would probably be all right to stay where they were as long as he kept watch throughout the night.

He turned to find Rudd starting a fire. "Wait a minute, Rudd. I don't think we should start a fire. A fire can be seen from a long ways off at night."

"Hey, it's getting dark," said Rudd, throwing more wood onto the fire. "You don't know how cold it gets out here. It's still warm now, but just wait 'til later. You'll see. It gets damn cold in the desert at night."

"Well, let's keep it low then. O'Brien didn't pack anything to cook anyhow."

"Yeah. I wish he'd of packed us a coffee pot. I could use a strong cup of coffee right now."

"What you need is some sleep."

"Maybe so. I was sleepy all afternoon, tryin' to stay on that damn horse. But now, for some reason, I'm wide awake."

Steele sat down and dug into the saddle bags to see what O'Brien had packed for them to eat. There were some chicken sandwiches, several dried apples, and a few baked potatoes. He imagined O'Brien's cook happily preparing the picnic.

He handed the package to Rudd who went right for the dried apples. He ate several and licked his fingers. "Hey, this is pretty good. Reminds me of that cake O'Brien's cook made for us the day we buried Laird."

"You should eat a sandwich too."

"Right, right, I will. It won't go to waste. You know me. But, if all we had to eat in this world was that apple cake, I think I could live just fine. Wish he'd sent something like that along." He ate several more dried apples, washing them down with large gulps from a pocket flask.

"You know, that stuff doesn't help your thirst."

Rudd shrugged. "Yeah, I guess, but it damned sure helps my sore butt." He picked up a sandwich and took a bite. "You know, I used to be able to ride all day. Me and O'Brien used to ride all over the place and I never had a backache like this." He ate a little more of his sandwich. "You know Steele, I was talking to O'Brien this morning. He thinks it was Longmore that sent that Shorty guy after me to try and get his money back."

"Shorty was trying to kill you. He wasn't after money."

"Kill me? How would that help Longmore get his money back?"

"It wouldn't."

Rudd thought about that. "Well, maybe he thought I had the land grant. Maybe he thought I got it from Willig."

"And how would killing you help him get it?"

Rudd stopped eating to think about that. "I guess it wouldn't."

"On the contrary," said Steele, "if he thought you had the land grant, he would want you alive. He would probably have you arrested and say it was his money that paid for the land grant so it was rightfully his."

Rudd frowned. "But who else could have sent that Shorty guy after me? I don't have any other enemies in Prescott."

"Not that you know of. Lucky Laird didn't think he had any enemies either."

Rudd got quiet after that and ate his sandwich in silence.

Steele began to cut up one of the baked potatoes with his pocket knife, thinking about what Rudd had said about having enemies. Laird didn't know he had enemies. But he was worried about his land claim, so he turned over his land deed to the territorial land office. Then he was killed, that very night. Was it possible Willig had done the same thing? Did he take the land grant document to that same land office, just before he was killed? Longmore had been trying to get his hands on the land grant. Could he also be involved in Laird's death?

"What are you thinking about?" asked Rudd.

"I'm wondering if Longmore could have had anything to do with Laird's death."

Rudd looked puzzled. "I don't see how. Besides, he was out of town."

"There's something going on in Arizona, something related to land. If somebody is trying to acquire land in this area and they will go to any lengths to get it, wouldn't Longmore know about it?"

"Yeah, but I can't see him killing somebody to get a little patch of land down by Yuma. I never liked the man, but it just doesn't seem like something he would do."

"Maybe not," said Steele. "Let me show you something. He picked up a stick and drew a square in the dirt. "Let's say this is Laird's land." He drew a line leading away from the square. "He travels to Prescott to register his deed at the land office." He drew another square to represent the land office. "Then he goes to the hotel where he's killed." He looked up at Rudd. "What if Willig did the same thing?"

Rudd stared at the drawing. "What are you saying? Willig took the land grant document to that land office?"

"That's right. He might have been killed after he deposited it there, just as Laird was killed after he registered his land deed in that same office."

Rudd leaned forward, excited. "So you're saying the old Spanish document might have been in that land office all this time? How do we get our hands on it?"

"The courthouse vault was broken into soon after Willig was killed."

Rudd sat back, disappointed. "So it's gone. They've already got it."

"Maybe so."

"But wait a minute," said Rudd, picking up a stick to tap on Steele's drawing in the dirt. "If they got it, why haven't they done anything with it?"

"Maybe they took one look at it and discovered it was a fake."

"Aw, don't say that, Steele." Rudd threw down the stick in disgust. "I came all this way to get it back. I can't believe it was a hoax all along." He dug into the pack, mumbling to himself as he searched for something else to eat.

Steele sat back to think. Could there be another explanation? What was he overlooking? It seemed likely that the courthouse break in was to try to find the land grant document. It took place soon after Willig was killed. But there was a problem with that theory. If they knew Willig had deposited the document at the land office, why bother to kill him? To keep him quiet? But would they worry all that much about what he said? He was a convicted land swindler. Would anybody believe him?

"You got quiet again," said Rudd. "What about Laird's killing? Are they going to break into the vault again to get his deed?"

"They changed the combination on that vault and I suspect it is better protected now. In Laird's case, they may try to cast ownership of his property in doubt. Or maybe they thought with him dead and having no sons, they could buy it cheaply from his daughter."

"But why would anybody want a little orange farm down there enough to kill for it?"

"It lies directly in the path of a proposed rail route. And it has the water that the steam engines will need."

Rudd let out a low whistle. "The railroads. The damn railroads. I should have known. They'll do whatever it takes to get what they want."

"There's no reason to believe any of the railroad companies are behind it. They do try to buy up land along their proposed routes, but would they commit murder to get it?"

"I wouldn't put it past 'em," said Rudd, biting into another sandwich. "But I guess it means Laird's death didn't have anything to do with the Spanish land grant, did it?"

"Only that both murders may have had something to do with land."

Rudd shrugged and went back to eating his sandwich. But then he stopped eating. "Hey, maybe it was Carson that killed Laird. You said he might have been a killer during the war and I saw him in the bar that same night."

"If it was Carson, he either left town immediately or he's in hiding. I've described him to people all over town. No one remembers seeing him."

Rudd yawned and lay back on his bedroll. "Well, all I know is I'm frustrated. I thought Willig's map would lead us to something important out here. But if his mine doesn't really exist, them maybe we might as well give up and go back to San Francisco."

"You can go if you want to, but I'm not going until I find out who killed Laird."

"For Becky's sake?"

"For her sake, and to try to keep anybody else from being killed."

"You think they'll kill again?"

"There's no reason to think they won't."

Rudd was silent for a few moments. "So, tell me the truth, Steele, do you think they got the land grant?"

"There is no way to know for sure."

"So it's possible they didn't get it."

"It's possible."

"In my gut, I'm just about sure they didn't . I still think Willig could have hid it out here somewhere. Tomorrow we should examine the map more closely. Maybe we aren't looking at it right."

Neither of them spoke for a while and the only sound was the soft murmur of the nearby river. Then Steele thought he heard a slight change in the sound of the flowing water. He turned to stare into the darkness.

"That Willig," said Rudd. "He was a strange old—"

"Shush," whispered Steele.

"What? Did you hear something?"

Steele got up silently and moved toward the river. He reached down and took his pistol out of his boot. He couldn't see anything moving, but he got the feeling that whatever it was had heard him and stopped in their tracks. He moved a little further upstream to get away from the firelight. Then he saw something move out in the middle of the river. There were at least three shadows out there, but they were not moving. They seemed too large to be humans. Was it horses? He looked back toward the fire and saw that Rudd was building it up. As the fire grew brighter, Steele could see that it did look like horses, but there were no riders. Could horses survive out here? But then they started moving downstream and as they came into the firelight, he saw that it wasn't horses, it was burros. A whole herd of them. He stood up and as soon as they saw him they bolted, splashing noisily through the water and up the hill on the other side of the river. There were some young ones mixed in with the herd and the older burros seemed to be trying to keep them in the middle of the pack.

"Burros!" yelled Rudd, pointing. "A whole bunch of them."

Steele moved back to the campsite. "I wonder what they're doing out here. We didn't see any ranches nearby."

Rudd laughed. "Nah, they don't belong to anybody. They're wild." He sat back down next to the fire. "O'Brien and me used to see stray burros out here all the time. When the prospectors are done with 'em, they just let 'em go."

"Looks like they've been breeding. There were some young ones."

"Yeah," agreed Rudd, "they seem to do pretty well out here. Wonder what they eat. Cactus?"

"Whatever they eat, they need water. If we get lost, we can follow them to their water sources."

"Right, and if we get hungry enough we can shoot one of 'em for breakfast."

"They'd probably be a little tough."

Rudd yawned. "Yeah, I guess. Well, I'm ready to turn in. How about you?"

"In a few minutes. I think I'll take a hike up the hill."

"Right, you do that." Rudd pulled off his boots and pulled the blanket up over his legs.

Chapter 22

Steele stood up and moved away from the fire to look up at the stars. The big dipper was bright in the north sky. He thought about Willig sitting next to that same firepit looking up at the stars. Did he really have a mine out here somewhere? Why had he drawn the map? Was it all just another one of his hoaxes?

He started back toward the fire, but just as he moved, he saw the muzzle flash of a shot in the darkness and heard the bullet glance off the hillside behind him. He dove to the ground. "Rudd!" he yelled, "get away from the fire."

Rudd struggled to get out from under his blanket. Two more shots rang out and Rudd fell forward, his feet tangled in his bed roll. Another shot barely missed him as he jumped up and ran to the cut in the cliff. He made it, but before he could take cover, another shot came, knocking him down.

Steele jumped up and ran to join Rudd as more shots kicked up the dirt around his feet. Behind the boulders, he found Rudd lying on his stomach, groaning.

Steele kneeled next to him. "Are you hit?"

"I think so. My shoulder. In the back."

Steele felt Rudd's shirt. It was wet, but not soaked. "Turn over onto your back. Try to put direct pressure on the spot where the bullet hit."

"All right, if you say so." He rolled over. "Ouch, that hurt's like hell."

Steele reached down to touch Rudd's arm. "Hang on, old man. Don't move. The bleeding will stop."

Steele took out his revolver and moved to a position where he could see between the boulders.

"Who the hell is shooting at us?" asked Rudd. "Can you see him?"

"It sounded like two different guns."

"Two of 'em. Damn, I bet it's that Shorty again, and that big guy who was with him at the bar. What do you think they want?"

"They want us dead."

Another shot came. The bullet ricocheted off of the boulder they were hiding behind and whined away into the darkness. Steele immediately fired back toward where he'd seen the muzzle flash, just to let them know he was armed. But he couldn't waste any more shots. His extra shells were back at the campsite in the saddlebag.

"What're they doing now?"

"I can't see them. Do you have your revolver?" whispered Steele.

"No, it's back by the fire. Jesus, Steele, I think they got me good. What a place to die, out here in this god-forsaken—"

"Shh. Something's moving." Steele readied his pistol. He aimed toward where he'd seen the movement. There was no sound except for the faint crackling of the fire as it died down.

"Hey, mister. We got no quarrel with you. We just want to talk to your fat friend there."

Steele realized they didn't even know who he was. They were after Rudd.

"It's him," whispered Rudd. "It's Shorty. I knew it."

"Why don't you just come out of there, fatso?" came the voice again. "Come on out and we'll talk."

"What do you want to talk about?" yelled Rudd.

"Just wanted to see if you were still alive and kickin'. I bet I got ya didn't I?"

"Who's out there?" yelled Rudd. "Is it that little runt, Shorty?"

"That's right, fatso. Did ya miss me, sweetie?"

"You're mama wouldn't even miss a runt like you," yelled Rudd. "Why didn't she drown you when you were born like she should have?"

Two quick shots rang out. Both glanced off of the top of the boulder.

"You might as well come out and take it like a man," yelled the voice, angry now. "You and your dumb friend are trapped in there. We can wait."

"He's saying we," said Steele. "It means he's not alone."

"What should we do?" whispered Rudd.

"As soon as the fire goes out, I'll try to crawl back over and get your pistol and some more cartridges for my gun."

"No, don't do it. They'll pick you off for sure."

"I've only got four bullets left and we're trapped in here. I've got to do something."

Rudd groaned. "My shoulder is really starting to hurt now."

"Yes, but you're still talking. At least we know the bullet didn't hit your lungs. Can you still move your arm?"

"Yeah, but it hurts like hell. What are they doing now?"

"They're not coming any closer, but they're making quite a bit of noise."

"Noise? What kind of—"

"Wait, it looks like they're starting a fire."

"A fire? What the hell?"

"They're building it up, throwing more and more wood on it."

"Why?"

"I guess they want to be able to see us, to make sure we don't try to get back to our campsite, or to the horses."

"Damn, we're trapped like a couple of mice behind these rocks. What're we going to do?"

"We wait."

"So this is it then."

"They haven't got us yet. Let's sit tight and see what they do."

Rudd was quiet for several minutes, then he said, "I'm glad I got to know you, Steele. I mean, even if we didn't find the land grant, we had an adventure, didn't we?"

Steele didn't reply. He was watching the two men build up their fire. Once in a while, he could see an arm come out as they threw more sticks onto the fire. He might be able to wing one of them, but at that distance it wasn't worth wasting a bullet.

"Maybe I should never have got you into this. I guess I've been thinking about coming back to Arizona ever since I heard about Willig's death. Should have known it was a wild goose chase."

"Are you feeling dizzy? Can you still see all right?"

"I'm not dizzy or anything. You know, it hurts like hell to get shot, but not as bad as I'd have thought. Maybe the bleeding has slowed some."

"It's important that you don't move. If you've got the bleeding stopped, you don't want it to start up again."

"Right, right, but it probably doesn't matter now anyhow. All they have to do is wait us out. We don't even have any water."

"We're not dead yet."

"Listen, Steele, I'm going to take my money belt off. Don't let them get the map or the money. Bury it somewhere before those bastards come and finish us off."

"Don't move. Don't get the bleeding started again."

"I got it off. Here, bury it." He threw the money belt toward Steele. "There's a lot of money in there, all my savings. I want you to bury it under this big rock and if either one of us makes it out of here, we can come back and get it."

Steele scooped out the sand under the rock and buried the money belt as deeply as he could. Then he went back to watching Shorty and the other man build up their fire. The cut in the cliff was a good place to hide, but there was no way they could get out of there without being seen. All they could do was wait. But what good would waiting do? When it got light, it was likely they'd get up on top of the cliff to fire down at them and that would be the end of it. He turned to look at the cliff. In the flickering firelight, its sheer face loomed high above them. Could it be climbed?

He kneeled down next to Rudd. "I'm going to move back further into this cut. There might be a way to climb out."

"Not a chance. It's straight up."

"I've got to try. If you hear shots from up on top, it means I was successful."

"Or that they got you too."

"One or the other," agreed Steele.

He moved along the face of the cliff, hidden from the men, feeling for handholds. The cliff seemed to be made up mostly of solid rock, but there were places where it came apart in his hands. That was going to be a problem. Even if he didn't fall, the sound of falling rock might tip them off. But it was their only chance. He had to try.

He put his pistol back into his boot and found his first handhold. He pulled himself up and felt for a foothold. As he got up a little higher, be began to find fractures in the rock. He jammed his hands into them and found he could make some progress by following the cracks upward. But when he was only half way up, the cracks ended. He found a crevice, but it would take him out toward the front of the cliff. Out there, they might be able to see him. Still, he had no other way to go so he inched along the crevice until it petered out. He paused there to catch his breath. From there, he could clearly see their fire and the cluster of rocks the two men were hiding behind. They were too far away to risk taking a shot at, and besides, even it he hit one of them, the other might be able to pick him off before he could fire again.

He moved back in the direction he'd come from, feeling for any kind of handhold up above. His fingers were cut and bleeding from jamming them into the cracks, and his calves were aching and threatening to cramp up. He felt a slight ledge, but when he put some weight on it, it gave way, sending a shower of small rock fragments bouncing down the cliff face. He held still, hoping they hadn't heard the rocks falling.

He turned his face to look in their direction and saw one of the men standing up. It was Shorty, shading his eyes from the firelight with his hand.

"Hey, he's up there! On the cliff."

The shots started coming fast and furious. Steele flattened himself against the cliff. With each shot, he was showered by rock fragments.

"Get up above him," yelled Shorty. "Get a torch."

The big man grabbed a stick out of the fire and ran up the hill, holding his torch high.

"There he is," yelled Shorty. "I see him. Get him."

Steele knew he had to act fast. There were no handholds nearby, but the light from the man's torch had showed him there was a ledge a short distance below. If he could jump down to that ledge, he would be at least partially hidden. But if he missed, or if the ledge wasn't solid, it was a long fall back down. When the next shot came, he felt something hit the upper part of his left arm. He had to act. He jumped.

When his foot hit the ledge, the loose rocks gave way and he started sliding down the cliff. He grabbed for anything he could find and caught hold of some kind of plant. Thorns penetrated deep into his hands, but he was able to hang on just long enough to get his feet under him again. He flattened himself against the cliff, trying to catch his breath.

"Where'd he go?" yelled Shorty. "Did he fall off?"

Steele stayed still, his legs shaking from the exertion. More shots came, but they were hitting above him. They didn't realize he'd jumped down. He tried to find a way to move farther back on the ledge, but suddenly he saw a light above him. Shorty's partner had gotten up above him. It was the big man from the bar, the one who'd held a gun to his head. He was leaning out over the edge, holding the torch. Steele pulled out his gun and flattened himself against the cliff wall, hoping the man hadn't seen him.

But then he heard a shot from below. The torch bounced down the face of the cliff, narrowly missing him.

"I think I got him, Steele," yelled Rudd.

Somehow, Rudd had made it back to the camp to get his revolver.

"Get down!" yelled Steele. But it was too late. A shot rang out and Rudd fell to his knees. Steele looked up and saw the man standing on top of the cliff. He was taking careful aim at Rudd, ready to fire again.

Steele aimed quickly and fired twice to drive the man back. He looked down at Rudd. He was still on his knees, staring down at his stomach as if he couldn't believe he'd really been shot there.

"Get behind the boulder," yelled Steele, but it was too late. Shorty was running toward Rudd. He fired twice as he ran and Rudd fell forward onto his face. Shorty looked up at Steele and laughed. He was out in the open, defying him to shoot. Steele took careful aim, but before he could pull the trigger, another shot came from above. It hit the ground just above his head, spraying dirt into his eyes. He pulled the trigger anyhow, hoping to hit Shorty, but by the time his eyes cleared, Shorty had dived for cover. Steele wasn't sure it he'd hit him or not.

He looked down at Rudd, hoping to see any sign of life. But Rudd's body lay still. No matter how many times he had seen it during the war, Steele had never been able to quite come to terms with how quickly life drained out of human bodies when they died. He realized he hadn't known Rudd long, but his death felt like an old friend passing. His first thought was what he was going to tell Becky and O'Brien; that is, if he somehow made it back alive, which right now didn't seem very likely.

His first problem was the man on the top of the cliff. He'd lost his torch, but it wouldn't take him long to make another one. There would be plenty of tinder-dry brush up there. Steele rested his gun against the rock, aiming for the last placed he'd seen the man. He wondered if he'd hit Shorty. If not, it would only take him a few minutes to get up there also.

He put his gun back into his boot holster and ignoring the pain in his arm, he moved slowly along the face of the cliff, feeling for anything he could get behind if they started shooting again. His fingers found a narrow ledge just above his head. He quickly climbed up to it. It was solid, the first solid footing he'd found on the side of the cliff. If only he could get a little farther away before they came.

But then he saw a flickering light moving up above. Steele flattened himself against the cliff. Then he saw another torch coming and then they were both on top of the cliff, both leaning out holding their torches high.

"Do you see him?" It was Shorty's voice.

"Maybe he fell off," said the other voice.

"Naw, we'd of heard him fall," said Shorty. "You work your way down there. I'll keep you covered."

Steele heard rocks and dirt tumbling down the cliff face. The man was coming down. Steele moved along the ledge, feeling for any possible place to hide, but there was nothing. Then his hands felt some kind of hole. The entrance was filled with brush and dirt. Was it an animal's burrow? The light of the torch was coming closer. The hole was his only chance. He tore furiously at the brush and crawled inside. The hole went in deeper than he expected. He crawled farther in. If the hole had been made by an animal, it must have been a large one. He just hoped he wouldn't have the bad luck to come face-to-face with it, whatever it was.

There was another shower of loose rocks from above. "Hey mister. You down there?"

The voice was close. Steele didn't move.

"You got no place to go, ya know." It was Shorty's voice again, from higher up. "Your fat friend, Rudd, got it. Now it's your turn."

Steele stayed perfectly still. The sound of his own breathing seemed loud inside the hole.

A shot glanced off the rocks outside the hole. Then another and another. What were they doing? It sounded like they were shooting randomly. Were they trying to flush him out? Maybe he *should* go out. Maybe it was better than getting trapped inside the hole if they found it. The light from the big man's torch was coming closer. He had to decide fast. Maybe if he came out shooting, he could get one of them. But counting back, he realized he had only one shot left.

"Come out, come out, wherever you are." It was Shorty's voice again.

They wanted him to come out. It meant they would be ready for him. Better to crawl back deeper into the hole. The hole was so small they would have to crawl in after him one at a time.

He moved further in, but soon came to something solid. Was it the end of the hole? But if it was an animal's burrow wouldn't there be debris, some kind of nest? He clawed at the dirt and discovered the hole had been blocked by a thick piece of wood. This was not an animal's burrow. Someone had dug the hole and then blocked it with a board that had been cut to fit. It must be a miner's tunnel. Was it Willig's?

He pulled the board loose and immediately felt a cool breeze come out. Was it Willig's mine? If so, why was the entrance half way down the cliff? Every time Willig wanted to go in, he'd have to climb down the cliff and crawl through the small entrance hole. Willig must have been an extraordinarily secretive person to have done such a thing.

Steele crawled a little farther on, but then it seemed like the tunnel made a slight turn. This would be a good place to make a stand. If they fired into the hole, their bullets would go on past and into the dirt. He stopped and took out his pistol. He waited.

The aching pain in his arm soon reminded him that he'd been wounded. He put down his gun and felt along his upper arm. He winced at the pain. He tore away the shirtsleeve. The bullet seemed to have gone clear through, but there was so much pain he suspected it might have glanced off the bone. There was too much swelling to tell how badly the bone had been damaged. The wound was still bleeding, but not excessively. He used the torn cloth to wrap the wound, using his teeth to pull it tight. He hoped the pressure would stop the bleeding. If not, he'd have to make a tourniquet.

Voices from the tunnel's entrance told Steele they'd found the hole. He picked up his gun and got ready.

A torch was thrust into the hole, but Steele knew they wouldn't be able to see past the curve in the tunnel. He cocked his revolver and waited.

"Do you really think he went in there?"

"Let's find out."

The shots were so loud inside the small space, Steele had to force himself not to scramble back further. He had to take a stand. He flattened himself against the tunnel wall and waited. He pointed his gun toward the light. It was coming closer. Only one shot left. He would have to make it count. When he saw movement behind the flickering torch, he aimed and squeezed the trigger. He heard a scream and the torch fell to the ground. Then there was only silence. The torch gradually burned out, leaving the tunnel in darkness.

Steele was sure he'd hit the man, but with no bullets left, he couldn't go forward to find out. He turned and scrambled farther back into the hole. Soon the tunnel widened out and he felt a definite change in the air; it was not only cooler, but damper, like . . . a cave. He took out one of the matches O'Brien had given him and struck it with his thumbnail. It flared and he held it up high. He *was* in a cave. Whoever had dug the hole in the cliff had broken into a natural cave. In one direction, the passage went upward, getting narrower as it went. In the other direction, the tunnel got larger as it led downhill.

The match burned out and he was again in darkness. Should he go on, or wait there? It must have been Shorty's partner that he'd shot.

That man was now either dead or badly wounded. It meant Shorty would be the one coming in after him. Steele was out of bullets, but he still had his folding pocket knife. He took it out and opened the blade. He would wait for Shorty next to the entrance hole.

Time passed but Shorty didn't come. Maybe he was planning to wait him out. Without food or water, he couldn't last long in there.

Steele took out his pocket watch, but decided against striking another match to look at it. Holding the watch in his hand reminded him of how much Billy had wanted to hold it. Rudd had also admired it. Poor Rudd. He had ended his days where Willig had spent most of his, out in the desert, looking for something precious. Too bad Rudd never got to see that Willig's map was real. The cut in the cliff was the real location of the mine, but the opening was halfway up the cliff. Rudd would have been excited, eager to explore the cave. Steele stared back into the darkness. How far did the cave extend? Had Willig really found gold somewhere in the cave? And was the lost land grant in there as Rudd had hoped?

His thoughts were interrupted by scraping sounds from within the entrance hole. Shorty must be getting ready to come in. Steele held his knife at the ready.

But then he smelled the smoke.

"How do ya like that, you son of a bitch? See if you can breathe this."

It was Shorty's voice again. He must have built up a big fire and then blocked the entrance so the smoke had nowhere to go but into the tunnel. The smoke poured into the cave and soon Steele began to cough. He had no choice but to go further down.

He put away his knife and began to feel his way deeper into the cave. But no matter how far he went, the smoke followed. It was rapidly filling up the entire cavern. He continued to move farther and father down the passageway, but unexpectedly he felt his foot hit water. He pulled his foot back. Why would there be water in the cave? Was he below the level of the river?

He struck another match and saw that it was an underground lake. He looked back up the tunnel and saw the smoke coming. He was trapped. When the match went out, he lit another. The smoke was getting thicker. His eyes were tearing so much he could barely see. He dropped the match and got down on his stomach next to the water. It wasn't much better down there; he could barely breathe. He had no choice but to crawl into the water. The water was surprisingly cold and it made his wounded arm ache. He'd almost forgotten about that. He hoped the cold water might help stop the bleeding.

He waded further in, getting as far away from the smoke as possible. At first his feet could still touch the bottom, but as he moved further out into the water, the ground underfoot slanted away and he had to start swimming. He only swam a short distance before he ran into a rock wall. It was as far as he could go. The smoke was getting so thick, every breath was a painful rasp. His eyes burned. He ducked under the water and at least it made his eyes feel a little better. Being under the water made him realize he was thirsty. He had the absurd thought that he might drown, but at least he wouldn't die of thirst. He waited, holding his breath. But what was the use? He knew that within a few seconds he would have to come up for air, and there wouldn't be any air, only smoke. But something felt a little different at the top of his head. It didn't feel quite as cold. He put his face up against the overhead rock and felt a thin a pocket of air. He took a breath and didn't cough. There didn't seem to be any smoke there.

He felt along the ceiling to see how far back it went and discovered that the farther he went, the more space there was between the water and the rock above. He paddled on, breathing with his face up against the rock, and suddenly he couldn't feel the rock ceiling any longer. He coughed and heard an echo. He must be inside some kind of large chamber. It was completely dark, so dark he might as well have his eyes closed.

But he was away from the smoke. The next problem was finding a way to get out of the water. His clothes, and especially his boots, were weighing him down, threatening to pull him under. He felt along the wall for some kind of handhold, but the rock was smooth and wet. He realized he might have been saved from the smoke only to drown in a water-filled cavern with no way out.

Chapter 23

Steele swam the perimeter of the chamber, feeling for any place he could pull himself out of the cold water. Finally, his hands felt a small ledge. If he could only pull himself up onto that ledge, he might be able to stay there long enough to warm up. He knew if he stayed in the cold water much longer his body would start to shut down.

He tried to pull himself out, but his injured arm wasn't much help. Using mostly his other arm, he managed to thrust himself up far enough to get his elbows onto the ledge. But it was slippery and his damaged arm gave out. He slid back into the water. Once again, he swam around the chamber, feeling for any way out of the water. There was nothing. The water had worn the rock smooth. He felt his way all around the chamber wall until he again came back to the small ledge. He had to try to get up there again; it was his only chance. This time, he readied himself and used all his strength to explosively pull himself out of the water. The moment he was clear of the water, he threw himself onto his side, hoping the friction of his clothes would keep him on the shelf long enough to find another handhold. It worked and his fingers found a small nick in the rock just as he was about to slip back. He held on despite the pain in his arm. He didn't dare move lest he slide right back in. He was shivering and he was afraid that might make him start sliding again. He might end up back in the water and he wasn't sure he had enough strength left to get out a second time. He carefully felt for anything other than smooth, slick rock. His hands found another ledge just above the one he was lying on. It felt like a step. He slowly sat up, making sure he didn't start sliding. He pulled himself onto the next shelf. That one was not so slick and he no longer felt like he might slide back into the water. He felt above that ledge and found another one. It was almost like stairs. Could somebody have carved steps into the rock? The next ledge was much wider. He was able to stand up. He moved cautiously away from the water, reaching out into the blackness like a blind man.

After only a few steps, he bumped into something. It felt like . . . wood. He touched it, felt it, but his mind had trouble accepting what it was; could it really be a wooden chair? How could a chair have gotten to the bottom of a water-filled cave? He moved around the chair and felt the top of a table. It didn't make sense. He took out his remaining three matches and laid them out on the table. He picked up one and blew on it to try to dry it. After a few minutes of blowing on the match, it felt fairly dry. He carefully struck it on the tabletop. It flared for a moment and went out. Only two matches left. This time he would wait until they were completely dry before he tried again.

In the brief flare of the match, he had seen enough to realize he was in a small cavern with no outlet. There was the chair, a rough wooden table, and a bed with a filthy mattress on it. How did those things get there? The only way into the cavern was through that water, by swimming under the rock wall. How could anybody have brought the furniture in through that water? And how would they have discovered the room in the first place?

As he stared into the blackness, he thought about the smoke out in the main tunnel. Shorty would wait for the smoke to clear and then he would come in, expecting to find Steele's body. What would he do when he didn't find it? Would he suspect Steele had gone into the water? If so, would he assume that Steele must have drowned? Or would he wait to see for sure. Steele's best option was to wait. Without any bullets left, he couldn't confront Shorty in the cavern. It was very unlikely that Shorty would dare venture into the water. He doubted there was anything to eat in the room, but at least he had plenty of water to drink. He would wait until he was sure Shorty had gone. Then he would go back out.

He felt for the bed and sat down on it. The mattress felt damp. He shivered. Too bad there weren't any blankets. He had to get warm, had to stop the shivering. How long would it take his clothes to dry in the damp chamber? Should he take them off? No, they would dry faster from his body heat.

And what about his arm? It was hurting even more, maybe because of the cold. He felt it. It didn't seem to be bleeding very much. Nothing he could do about it anyhow. The important thing was to get warm.

He stood up and ran in place for several minutes. That helped, but how long could he keep it up? His arm was hurting, and he was beginning to feel drowsy. What time was it? He took out his watch and held it up to his ear. Still ticking. He opened it so it would chime at the next hour.

He sat down on the bed again. Maybe he should lie down for a while. He stretched out on the soggy mattress. In the damp air of the cavern, lying down felt even colder than standing up. He couldn't stop shaking. If only he had a blanket. The mattress was lumpy and smelled terrible, but at least it was fairly soft. But then he had the thought that it might be warmer under the mattress than on top of it. He took off his boots and crawled underneath it. Still cold, but better. The rough wood under him wasn't very comfortable, but at least it blocked some of the cold air coming up from the damp rock floor. Soon he stopped shivering and started to feel sleepy. Maybe he was going to survive this after all.

Chapter 24

Steele awoke feeling as if he was being suffocated. It took him several seconds to remember he was under the heavy mattress. Its dank smell was suddenly so overpowering he had to push it away. But then he immediately felt the cold and had to pull it back over him. He turned on his side, trying to get comfortable on the hard wood and felt something under his shoulder. He touched it. Paper. He had the sudden memory of Rudd saying Willig could have hidden the lost Spanish land grant in his mine. But no, this felt like ordinary paper, not parchment. In the darkness, Steele smiled grimly at the thought of Willig hiding a piece of paper under the mattress. It was an absurd idea. If was very unlikely anyone would ever find the entrance to the mine, let alone discover how to swim into the secret room. Willig must have been a very, very cautious person. But maybe whatever was on the paper was that important to him.

Steele stared into the darkness, wondering if the matches were dry yet. Would they ever dry in the damp, cold cavern? He resisted the impulse to get up and find out. Better to wait a while longer. He pushed the paper back down under the mattress and turned over to get a little more sleep.

He woke up to the chiming of his watch, left with the remnants of a dream about the soldiers who had frozen to death while marching toward Chattanooga. In the dream, they seemed to be already dead, but they were still walking, all together, all in rhythm. No matter how fast he walked, they followed, close behind. He knew he'd have to keep walking to keep from freezing and becoming like them.

He stared up into the darkness and felt the sharpness of the cold air. He began to shiver again. Why was he so cold? His clothes were still slightly damp, but the heavy mattress on top of him should be keeping him warm. Something was wrong. Was his wound festering? He touched his arm near the wound. It felt hot and sweaty. That wasn't right.

He pushed away the mattress and swung his feet out onto the rock floor. Suddenly, he was dizzy. Something was definitely wrong. He felt for the chair and steadied himself with it. He stood up. In the absolute darkness, it was hard to tell if he was standing steady. He felt like he was rocking forward and back, about to fall down. Why was he so dizzy? He sat down on the chair. That helped, a little. He felt along the tabletop for the two matches. What if they didn't light? He picked up one of them and carefully struck it against the table. It sputtered and went out. He picked up the last match, but hesitated. Maybe he should wait a while to let it dry longer. How long had he been in the cave? If only he could see the face of his watch. He had heard it chiming in the darkness, hadn't he? How many times had it chimed? He couldn't remember. Maybe the match would never get completely dry in the damp cave.

He decided to take the chance. He struck the match. It sputtered, but he cupped his hand around it and it stayed lit.

He held up the match and saw the stub of a candle on the table. With shaking hands, he carefully lit the candle. At first it sputtered and threatened to go out, but soon the wax caught and it burned steadily. Guarding the flame with his hand, he held it close to his watch. Just past five o'clock. Five in the morning? Was that the real time? The watch must still be working because he'd heard it chiming in the darkness. It meant he'd been in the cave all night. Would Shorty still be waiting out there?

He turned to look at the water and was shocked to see that it was right at his feet; it had risen at least two feet while he slept. It meant the chamber was filling up with water. Would it eventually fill the entire room? Maybe that was why the mattress stank so badly; maybe it had been underwater. If so, it would be filled with mold. Was that why he'd felt so dizzy? Or was it the cold? Maybe his body was going into shock. And why was his wound hurting so much? Had the mold gotten into it? It was hurting even more than it had right after he'd been shot. That didn't make sense. Wounds were very painful at first, because of the swelling, but the pain usually subsided as the swelling lessened.

He leaned his arm close to the candle and saw that it was badly swollen, bulging out from under the tightly wrapped cloth. Why hadn't he remembered to loosen the bandage after the bleeding stopped? He wasn't thinking clearly.

He put the candle down and used his teeth to untie the cloth and take it off. In the weak candlelight, he looked closely at the wound. As he had suspected, the bullet had gone clear through, but if it had hit the bone on its way through, there would undoubtedly be lead fragments left in there. When he got back to Prescott, he would have to ask Doctor Fletcher to reopen the wound and clean it out. If he ever got back to Prescott.

He squatted down next to the water and used the bloody cloth to wash the wound as best he could. Then he re-wrapped the wound, not so tight this time. He sat back down at the table, staring at the flickering candle. When it burned out, he'd be in darkness for as long as he was in the cave.

He looked at his watch again. Before long, it would be getting light outside. The smoke should have cleared from the cavern by now. Would Shorty be in there looking for him? He glanced toward the water. Now that it was so much deeper, there would be no chance of Shorty finding his way in. In fact, it wasn't going to be very easy to get out.

When the candle flickered, he looked at the bed. He was starting to feel very cold again. Maybe he should just get back under that terrible mattress and wait, mold or no mold.

Then he saw the piece of paper sticking out from under the mattress. He grabbed it and held it close to the candle. Handwriting, in Spanish. An uneducated scrawl that wandered across the paper. The paper was so faded, Steele could only read a few of the words. Translated from the Spanish, it read, "These lands . . . in perpetuity. By order . . . king of Spain . . . be it known . . . and all its territories." At the bottom was a date, 1756, or maybe 1786.

Was it a handwritten copy of the land grant? More likely, it was only Willig's rough attempt to write out a forgery of what he thought a Spanish land grant might look like. But why would Willig bother to hide it under his mattress? No one would believe this rough, handwritten scrap of paper was worth anything. Steele folded the paper and put it in his pants pocket.

The candle started sputtering. It wouldn't last much longer. He took a quick look around. There was a wooden box under the table. He pulled it out and lifted the lid. Dynamite, maybe a dozen sticks or more, with primers and cord. He closed the box and pushed it back under the table.

The candle almost died, flared up, and went out. But just before it went out, Steele had seen something sparkle in the wall behind the table. Could it be gold? Had Willig actually stumbled onto a valuable vein of gold? Maybe that was why he was trying to raise money, to pay for mining equipment to follow a vein of gold that had been exposed by the water running though this cave. He wished he had another match so he could take a closer look at whatever was in that wall.

For now, the important thing was to get warm. He crawled back under the mattress, trying not to think about the overpowering odor of mold and decay. How long would he have to stay in the cave? How long would Shorty wait out there? All day?

Steele tried to sleep, but the smell of the mattress almost seemed to be getting stronger. He stared up into the darkness and waited. Hours passed, marked by the chiming of his watch. When the watch struck seven times, he suddenly wondered if the water was still rising. He put his hand down to touch the floor, but all he felt was water. The water was rising fast. It must be all around the bed. He suddenly remembered his boots were still on the floor. He felt for them. They were soaked. He felt for the table and put them on top. The thought of all that water made him feel even colder. He shivered and pulled the mattress up over himself again. As much as he hated the idea of putting that moldy mattress over his face, he had no choice. If his body didn't get warm, it would shut down completely. He remembered the soldiers they brought in half-frozen. The doctors didn't have time to deal with them so all Steele could do was wrap them in blankets and hope they would recover. Often they didn't.

Steele woke up hearing chimes. His first thought was to wonder how there could be chimes in a dream about drowning. There are no chimes underwater. But what if it was a dream about a watch? Billy had loved the sound of those chimes.

He woke up again. Another dream, this time about running. He couldn't get away. His legs wouldn't work right. Then those damn chimes started up again. He'd better get up and find out what they were. He sat up but instead of a floor, his feet found water. Why was there water on his feet? It was too cold to have water on your feet.

He tried to stand up, but he was too dizzy and had to sit back down again. His feet were so cold, he decided he didn't want them in the water anymore. He pulled them up and sat there with his legs crossed, shivering. What should he do next? The chimes had stopped, but why was he just sitting there? It was so cold. He had to get warm.

His feet felt like they were about frozen. Where were his boots? Why didn't he have his boots on? For some reason, he thought they might be on the table. It didn't seem very likely, but just in case, he reached over and felt along the top of the table. There they were. He pulled them on and put his feet down. There was a splash. Oh, no, now his feet were in water again. That wasn't good. And his arm hurt too. He touched it and the sharp pain reminded him: he'd been wounded. He'd been shot. He was hiding in a cave because somebody'd shot him. Shorty. Of course, Shorty was out there waiting for him. What was the matter with his thinking? He shook his head to clear it. He had to concentrate on the danger. Would Shorty still be out there? Maybe not. Maybe it was daylight out there and Shorty would be gone. The sun would be shining. The nice warm sun would stop the cold, stop the shivering. He stood up and held onto the edge of the table to steady himself.

And then the chiming started again. Then he remembered what is was: the chiming was coming from his watch. Billy liked to listen to his watch. Steele felt for it, found it, and put it in his pocket. Time to go out into the sun. Time to go out and get warm.

But which way was out? Pick a direction. He took three steps but with the third step his foot found no more floor. He fell forward with a splash. He was in deep water. He was swimming. The water was unbelievably cold, but it helped him remember. The way out was to swim. But after swimming only a few strokes, he ran into a solid rock wall. That's right, he had to swim under the rock wall? He ducked under, expecting to find some kind of underwater tunnel. But his hands found nothing but more rock. He came back up to the surface. What had happened to the way out? The water must be deeper than he remembered. He took a big breath and dived down deeper. He swam under the rock wall and eventually found he could go forward. He kept on swimming, but it was taking too long. He was running out of breath. Had he gone the wrong way? Should he turn around and go back? But which way was back? And back to what? To the cold? To that terrible mattress? He had to keep going.

Finally, he broke through and felt the air. He gasped for breath. He sank back down and swallowed some water. He fought back up to the surface again, choking and coughing. But then he was swimming again, going forward further into the darkness. How far did the water go on? Would he have to swim forever? But soon his fingers brushed the bottom. He pulled himself forward and soon found himself crawling on a smooth rock surface. He stood up and steadied himself against a rock wall. Finally, he was out of the water.

He took a few steps up the sloping rock floor, feeling his way along the wall. But then he smelled smoke and he remembered. This was where the smoke was. Shorty had made smoke to drive him out. He took a cautious breath. Most of the smoke was gone.

He felt his way along the wall until the tunnel turned and he saw a tiny spot of light ahead. It had been so long since he'd seen light, he'd almost forgotten what it meant. It meant the sun. That spot of light was the sun, shining in through the entrance hole. It had been dark when he came in, but now it was light out there. The sun, warmth. But would Shorty still be waiting out there to kill him?

Steele reached down and took out his pistol. But the feel of it in his hand made him remember the last time he'd used it; he'd shot a man and there were no bullets left. He put the pistol back in its boot holster and kept going. The hole got smaller and he had to get down on his hands and knees to crawl. The circle of light was not far ahead. Maybe he should wait for dark. No, then it would get cold again. His clothes were still wet. He had to get out into that warm sun. He kept on crawling toward the light. He was almost there when he saw something ahead. He stopped to let his eyes adjust to the light. It was a man, lying on his face, with both of his arms pinned beneath him. He wasn't moving. Steele crawled closer. It was the man he'd shot. He was dead.

Steele crawled over the man and out into the sunlight. It felt warm and good. He stood up, but when he looked down he realized he was on the side of a cliff. It made him feel unsteady, as if he could topple off. It was a long way down. He leaned back against the cliff and looked up at the sun. It felt very warm, but he knew he couldn't stay there. He had to get off that cliff. Shorty was out there somewhere.

Using his good arm, he began to carefully work his way up to the top. When he finally made it off the cliff, he looked back down. He could see the boulders near the campsite where he and Rudd had been hiding. It was where Rudd had been killed. But Rudd's body was gone. Shorty must have taken it away. But why? Shorty hadn't bothered to drag his companion out of the tunnel, so why bother with Rudd? Did he have to take Rudd's body back to Prescott to prove he'd killed him?

Steele slowly worked his way back down to the campsite, watching for any movement. But the desert was silent. No wild burros, no birds, nothing. Maybe the heat of the day had driven them into shade somewhere.

When he got back down to the campsite, he saw that everything was gone. Shorty had taken the supplies, his hat, the horses; even the bedrolls were gone.

He went to the spot behind the boulder where he'd buried Rudd's money belt. Would it still be there? He dug into the sand with his hands and soon found it. He opened it. It was there. The map was inside, along with a lot of money. Poor Rudd. He'd come all that way to clear his name and to try to find the lost land grant, only to die out in the desert.

Steele stood up and put the money belt on, hiding it beneath the beltline of his pants. He knew he shouldn't stay there long; Shorty could come back at any time. He looked at the distant mountains to the east. Prescott was up there. It would be a long walk. Could he make it? Why not? Hadn't he walked all the way from New York to Virginia to see the war? And then he'd walked all the way to Tennessee. He was younger then, but he was still strong. He picked out a distant mountain peak that he thought might be near Prescott and started walking toward it. All he had to do was keep on going until he came to that mountain.

He walked as fast as his strength would allow, trying to get as far away from the river as possible. But wait, shouldn't he have gone down to get a drink from the river? No, that's where Shorty would wait. He was all right. He'd drank some water in the cave, hadn't he? Better not go back. Better to just keep walking.

Time passed and he didn't feel like he was making much progress toward those mountains. He checked his watch. Past noon. How long had he been walking? Just keep going.

As he walked, he sometimes checked his watch. The time was passing quickly, but the distant mountains didn't seem to be getting closer. And it was hot. Even when the sun moved into the western sky, it didn't seem any cooler. Not having a hat made it seem even hotter.

He searched his pockets, looking for something to put on his head. The only thing he found was the piece of paper he'd found in Willig's cave. He looked at it again. In the bright sun, the writing was a little easier to read. There was a description of lands, with rivers and mountain ranges as landmarks. He folded the paper down the middle, tucked in the ends, and put it on his head. If it really was a copy of the famous land grant, it seemed like a funny idea to use it as a hat. But it would do. Steele focused his eyes on the distant mountain and started walking again.

Sometime later, the sun was much farther down in the western sky and his feet were really starting to hurt. He could feel that they were blistering. He'd treated a lot of foot blisters during the war. The doctors wouldn't bother with it. They told Steele to drain the blisters and send the soldiers back to the line. Maybe that's what he should do: stop and drain the blisters.

He sat in the shade of a tall cactus and took off his boots. His socks were all bunched up and there were blisters on both feet. Some of them looked like they were already infected. How could that be? He hadn't walked that far, had he? Maybe they were already like that from being constantly wet in the dank cave.

He took out his knife and carefully punctured the edges of the blisters. He squeezed out the fluid and put his socks back on. It hurt his feet terribly to pull his boots back on, but he knew he had to do it.

He started to put away his knife, but thought about his wounded arm. Maybe he should look at it also. He untied the cloth and was shocked to see how bad it looked. It was not only swollen, but an angry color of red surrounded the wound. In places, the skin was patchy white, in other places it was very dark. Steele knew what that mean: it was festering, and gangrene might be taking hold. How could it have happened so quickly? Was it the damp cold in the cave? The mold in that mattress? The swelling should have gone down somewhat by now, but it looked even more swollen than it had in the cave. He knew he would have to drain the puss out of it. He got a good grip on his knife and gritted his teeth. It would hurt, but it had to be done. He had watched the doctors do it many times during the war. Sometimes the soldiers had screamed so loud the nurses had to put their fingers in their ears. The doctors always told the patient to think about something else. Steele tried to think about a cool breeze, one of the blustery spring days when he and Stacy used to sit by the ocean and talk about the future. But that was before she ran off to Europe. He shook off that memory. Better to just do it and get it over with. He plunged the blade deeper into the wound. Puss and blood leaked out and he immediately smelled a terrible, familiar odor. In the Army hospital that smell often came before death. Sometimes when the wounded soldier had that smell coming out of their wounds, the doctors just said to move him out into the yard. The yard meant heat and flies and screaming. The yard meant no hope.

Was he dying? If the wound continued to fester, he wouldn't have much of a chance out there in the desert. He watched the blood run down his arm. Letting it drain was all he could do until he got back to town. Then what? Would the doctor have to cut off his arm? It was a terrible solution, but it often saved the soldier's lives. There was nothing more he could do about it now. He decided to stop thinking about it. He rewrapped his arm and stood up. Time to get back to walking.

When the night finally came, the cooler air made Steele feel a little better. A sliver of a moon came up and when he looked back he saw Venus near the western horizon. Its familiar presence up there gave him a little reassurance. He kept walking, constantly taking note of the position of the moon and the rising stars of the Orion constellation to be sure he was still walking toward the east. The moon wasn't providing much light, but he wanted to keep going to cover as many miles as possible in the cool night. Sometimes, stumbling forward in the darkness, he ran into cactus. He picked out the stickers and kept walking. At least he was out of the terrible cold of that cave. The cold of the night was nothing compared to that. All he had to do was keep on walking. That would keep him warm. Soon the sun would come up and then he would see Prescott in the distance.

But by the time the sun did start to brighten the eastern sky, he was disappointed to see that the mountains looked about as far away as they had when he'd started. He felt very thirsty. His mouth was so dry it felt rough, like sandpaper, and there was some kind of crust on his lips. He realized he hadn't peed all night. That wasn't good. It meant his body was starting to conserve moisture. He remembered conversations with wounded soldiers who'd told him they often forgot drink during the heat of battle. Sometimes the battles would go on all day and wounded soldiers were brought in so dehydrated they weren't thirsty anymore. They didn't want to drink even when he offered them water. Those were the ones who usually died.

As the sun rose higher in the sky and the air began to heat up again, Steele knew he wasn't going to make it if he kept going. He would have to find some shade and wait for night.

He found one of the tall, thick cactuses and sat down in its shadow. He sat facing the east, hoping to see some dust on the horizon. It might mean O'Brien was out looking for him. But it could also be Shorty. If it was Shorty, he would be leading the extra horses with Rudd's body on one of them. That many horses would raise quite a bit of dust.

Steele turned to look back down toward the river valley. Was he leaving a trail that could be followed? Could you follow a man's trail across the sand of the desert? There was nothing he could do about it now. He'd just rest for a bit and think about it later.

He woke with a start and found himself lying on the ground. How long had he slept? The sun had moved a little toward the western sky, but not much. It seemed even hotter. He decided maybe he'd feel better if he got moving again.

Standing up was a bit of a challenge, but once he got going he made good progress. He was feeling dizzy again and he wasn't sure why. Maybe it would pass.

He checked his watch often and the time seemed to be moving very slowly. He got into the habit of checking his watch every time he came to a new landmark, such as a small hill or a ravine. But the minute hand seemed to hardly move. He held the watch up to his ear. It was ticking. How could he have walked so far without the time changing? Maybe he hadn't walked as far as he thought. In fact, the tall cactus he'd come to looked a lot like the one he'd been sitting next to that morning. Had he gone back to that cactus to get out of the sun? But that didn't make sense. Why would he go backward?

He shook his head to clear it. He told himself not to forget the mountains. He had to always go toward the mountains.

He stumbled on, sometimes feeling like he was getting closer to the mountains, but at other times he was overwhelmed with despair when they didn't seem any closer. The bright glare of the sun was bothering his eyes so much he took to walking with them closed, but that didn't work very well because he kept walking into cactuses. Several times he had to stop to remove the painful Cholla cactus balls from his pants. And once he nearly stepped on a snake that rattled its tail at him. It took him a moment to realize that it was a rattlesnake. He stared at it for quite a while, then made a wide detour around it and continued on.

The sun got hotter and hotter, but it didn't matter—he had to keep going. As he walked, he thought about the war, about then leaving the war to go to California. He thought about meeting Stacy in San Francisco. How he wished she was there with him. Sometimes he was almost sure he could hear her voice talking softly in his ear. Or was it Becky's voice, whispering to him, enticing him? He remembered that last night when Becky had wanted him to draw her in the nude. Her body was so beautiful, so young and—

"Hey *amigo*, you lost?"

Steele stopped and turned toward the voice. He tried to make his eyes focus. Was it an Indian? It looked like an Indian. He was young, sitting on a small horse, with a large knife hanging from his waist. Was he smiling?

"Where you go, *amigo*?"

Maybe he wasn't a real Indian. Maybe it was a dream Indian. Steele turned to walk away.

"Hey, *amigo*, come back. *Espera*."

Steele stopped and looked back. Maybe it wasn't a dream Indian. And now there were two other Indians coming. They were on horses too, but they weren't smiling like the first Indian.

Steele was sure he had seen one of them before. Where was it? Then it came back to him. It was the old Indian he'd seen back when the stagecoach got stuck, the one that looked like Geronimo. And the Indian boy had been there too. They had laughed when he and Laird bounced on the tree limb trying to break it off.

"Sit, *amigo*. You want water? *Agua*?"

Water? Was it really water? He thought about what he'd told Rudd, that Burros would always lead the way to water. "Burros," he said, but his throat was so dry it came out like a cough. He tried again: "No burros."

"Burros? No, *es agua*. Here, you drink." The boy held out an old U.S. Army canteen.

Steele stared at it. Maybe Indians were like burros. Maybe they always knew how to find water too. A great chief like Geronimo would know where to find water. "Geronimo. Great chief," he said out loud, surprised at how raspy his own voice was.

"You know Geronimo? *Goyahkla*? Here, drink." He thrust the canteen into Steele's hands.

Steele fumbled with the top until finally the boy finally got down from his horse and opened it for him. Then Steele drank and the water tasted so good it made his head ache. The water was cool. How could the water be cool when everything else was so hot? He drank again and handed the canteen back to the boy. "Thank you. *Gracias*."

"You lost? *Perdido*?"

Steele stared at him. Was he lost? Maybe he was. He looked up at the old Indian chief. He seemed very tall on his small spotted pony. Steele pointed toward the old Indian. "He was at the tree."

The boy smiled. *"Es verdad.* We see you at big tree. *Goyahkla* call you hombre-who-hang-from-tree. You funny man. Make chief laugh."

The chief spoke again and the boy turned back to Steele. "He say you have funny hat."

"My hat?" Steele pulled the piece of paper off of his head and looked at the writing on it He tried to think how to explain it to the chief. He held it up. "No hat. Used paper."

The chief just stared at him.

The young man pointed at Steele's arm. "You hurt?"

"Si," said Steele. "Shot. Some men. Bad men. *Hombres muy mal.* Killed my friend, Rudd."

The young Indian turned to say something to the other Indian, an old man with very long gray hair. His skin looked like old leather and he was cradling a rifle in his arms.

The chief nodded and the old man got down from his horse. He handed the rifle to the boy and said something to him.

"He say take off *paño.*"

"My bandage?"

"He fix."

"All right." Steele put the paper back on his head and untied the bandage.

The old Indian roughly grabbed Steele's arm and leaned close to look at his wound. Then he untied a bag that was around his neck. He took out something that looked like dried leaves. Then he grabbed Steele's arm. Startled, Steele tried to pull his arm away, but the old man's grip was too strong. He pressed the dried leaves into the wound. Then he grabbed Steele's other hand to place it over the wound. He said something to the young Indian and got back on his horse. The two old Indians rode away.

"He say wrap wound. *Tela. Comprende?*"

"I should put the cloth wrapping back on? Are those leaves some kind of medicine?"

"Si. Keep wound wet," said the young Indian.

Steele sat down on the ground and being careful not to disturb the damp plant mixture that covered the wound, he rewrapped the cloth around his arm and tied it. He wondered what kind of leaves they were. Did they really have healing powers? He wished he could get more of them. He could take them back to show Chan. Maybe they were something like Chan's Chinese healing herbs.

The boy pointed back down toward the valley. "*Agua*. That way."

"No, I can't go that way," said Steele, standing up. "A man is down there. *Hombre*. He wants to kill me."

"*Uno hombre. Tres* horses?"

"That's him."

"He not by river. He come." He pointed.

"He's coming this way? Is he close?"

"*Si*. Close. Maybe I go get *hombre's* horses."

Steele shook his head. "No, he is dangerous. *Peligroso*? You understand? You don't have a gun. He will shoot you."

The young man stared in that direction. Then he turned back. "You have knife? *Cuchillo*?"

"*Si*," said Steele, reaching into his pocket. "A small one." He held it out. You want it? In exchange for the water?"

The Indian shook his head. "Come." He walked away.

Steele followed the boy until they came to a fat round cactus that grew close to the ground. It was covered in curved spines. The young man took out his big knife and stooped down to cut a large chunk out of it. He handed it to Steele. "*Agua*."

Steele took the chunk of cactus and looked closely at it. Was this the way the Indians got water? From a cactus? It did seem quite wet.

"In mouth. *Boca*. Get *agua*. Spit out." He pretended to chew and then turned his head to spit. Steele bit off a piece and chewed it. It tasted terrible, but there was some moisture in it.

"Spit out. No good. Make *estómago* bad. *Agua*, okay."

"Thank you," said Steele, chewing the cactus, trying to get as much moisture out of it as possible. "*Gracias*."

The young man nodded and turned to go. Steele watched him trot back to his horse and ride away. Steele hoped he wouldn't go anywhere near Shorty.

Steele turned back to look at the distant mountains. He had to get moving. Now that he knew Shorty was after him, he would have to move fast, and he should try not to leave any tracks. He would keep going until he got to the mountains, not stopping for anything. Now that he knew how to get moisture out of cactus, he was sure he could do it. All he had to do was keep walking.

Chapter 25

A voice, faint, as if from a great distance, but urgent.

"Drew. Can you hear me?"

Something touched his arm, or was it a dream?

"It's all right, Drew. You're safe now."

Somebody was holding his hand. He tried to open his eyes. Too bright.

"You're all right now. We're with you."

He opened his eyes just a little. A face. Was it the Indians again?

"Doctor Fletcher was here again this morning. Can you hear me? He said he'd check back this afternoon."

He knew that voice. Was it Stacy?

"He said you were lucky to be alive."

Becky? Her face was still hazy. He closed his eyes again. He was no longer in the desert. He was lying on something soft.

"The doctor said you might not remember much. He said he'd seen it before. Heat stroke. That's what he called it."

So if he wasn't in the desert, how did he get here?

"Where's Rudd?"

A different voice. Asking about Rudd. Was it O'Brien?

"We found you, but we couldn't find Rudd. We looked all over for him. We found you wandering on the mountainside. Actually, it was old Roy who found you. We were on our way back here when he started barking and ran off into the trees. You didn't even recognize us. You kept on trying to walk, even while we were putting you up on a horse. Just tell us where Rudd is and we'll go back out and get him."

"Dead," whispered Steele.

He felt Becky's hand tighten around his wrist. "Oh, no. Don't say that, Drew. Maybe he's just lost."

He opened his eyes again. It *was* Becky, sitting next to the bed in her pretty yellow dress. O'Brien was standing next to her, his hand on her shoulder.

"Shorty," whispered Steele. "Shot him. Gold Valley."

"Shorty?" said O'Brien. "Damn it to hell, it's Longmore's doing. Didn't I tell you, Becky? I got worried as soon as I heard he was back in town."

Their voices faded and time drifted by. It was dark. Was he in the cave again?

"Can you see me?"

Another voice. Insistent. Something touched his eyelid. A face. All blurry. Was it the doctor?

"Glad to see you awake, Steele. They said you woke up for a while. Can you see me?"

"Blurry."

"I expect so. The sun has damaged your eyes, but if you can see at all maybe they'll get better. But your arm . . . not so good. I dug out some of the bullet fragments."

"Gangrene?"

"Fraid so. I've been draining it, but it's going to have to come off sooner or later. I've just been waiting 'til you're a little stronger."

Steele didn't reply. Part of him knew it would probably have to be amputated, but he couldn't let himself think about that while he was out there in the desert. The desert. How long had he walked? There was so much he couldn't remember. The mountains seemed so far away. And there had been Indians. A young Indian boy had helped him. And two old men. Could it really have been the great chief, Geronimo? Maybe that was only a dream. Maybe this was a dream. Maybe he was still in the cave. He felt himself slipping back into the darkness.

"Can you feel that?"

Steele was sure he'd slept, but the doctor was back again, squeezing his fingers. "Yes. My fingers."

"How about this?"

"My thumb."

"Good, good, at least you've still got feeling in the hand. I've been trying to keep your wound drained, but it's not any better. Like I told you yesterday, it doesn't look good."

"When?"

"When will I take it off? How about tomorrow morning. I can do it here."

"Tomorrow morning?"

"The sooner the better. The gangrene is spreading. Your wound had a dirty cloth wrapped around it. Some kind of leaves in there."

"Indians."

"Indians? You ran into Indians?"

"Gave me water. And medicine. On my arm."

"Well, you're lucky they didn't take your scalp. You just rest easy now and drink plenty of that tonic I left for you. We'll get that arm taken care of in the morning."

After the doctor left, Steele stared up at the ceiling, thinking about what life would be like without a left arm. Because of the war, there were many men now living without arms or legs. Many of them were living productive lives. But he'd read an article in an eastern newspaper complaining that there were so many crippled men begging on street corners they were becoming a nuisance. Was that how people would see him. As a nuisance?

There was a light tap on the door and Becky peeked in. "Oh, you're awake. The doctor said you might be sleeping."

"Come in."

She was carrying a tray. "I thought you might like some soup. Cook said he made it special for you."

"I'll eat it later."

She put the tray on the dresser and came to the bed to sit lightly on the edge. "Oh, Drew, the doctor told me about your arm. I'm so sorry."

"It has to be done."

"That's what he said. Just like poor Charlie."

"Charlie? So he had to cut off Charlie's leg?"

"Yes, he did it yesterday. But he said Charlie will get better now. And he said you'd get better afterwards too. At least you'll be alive. We were so worried when you didn't come back."

"I'm sorry I couldn't bring Rudd back too."

"Oh, Drew, are you really sure he's dead. Did you see it?"

"Yes. Shot twice."

"Oh, poor Rudd. He was such a nice man. Always telling jokes and . . . well, you know."

"Yes, I know."

"But you don't have to talk about it now. The doctor said you should rest."

"I don't mind talking."

"All the time you were lost out there, I kept on telling Edward how nice you are, so smart, and a great artist."

"I'm not a great artist. But I wish I could draw your picture right now. When I was out there in the desert, I thought about that last night before I left. When you wanted me to . . . draw you."

Becky flushed and looked down at the floor. "I'm sorry about . . . being so forward like that. I know you wanted to be true to Stacy. I shouldn't have—"

"It wasn't that. It was . . . Anyhow, as things turned out, I'm glad I didn't draw you that way. Someone might have found the picture while I was gone."

"I don't care. I just wanted you to . . . Oh, never mind. I should let you rest." She stood up.

"You don't have to go."

"I should. Edward is going to show me where he wants to put in his new mine shaft, on the other side of the hill."

"Going on horseback?"

"Yes, he loves horses as much as I do."

"That's good."

She hesitated at the door. "I could stay with you, but the doctor said you needed to sleep."

"Before you go, Becky, did I have a money belt when you found me?"

"Oh, yes. Edward noticed it when we were undressing you. I mean when he . . . I mean I only helped . . . a little. Anyhow, he put it in the dresser. Along with that piece of paper you'd made a hat out of. Do you want them?"

"No, as long as they are safe. The money belt belonged to Rudd. You go on for your ride with O'Brien now. I'll be fine."

"Well, if you really think so. Oh, by the way, a Chinese man named Wang came by this morning. He wanted to see you, but Edward chased him away."

"If he comes back, I'd like to talk to him."

"Oh. All right. But not until you're stronger. By the way, that Chinese man said he would notify Uncle Chan of your condition. Does that make any sense to you?"

"Yes. Chan is a man I know in San Francisco."

"Oh, all right. Well, bye then. I'll come and see you as soon as we get back."

After Becky left, Steele was left wondering why Wang had wanted to talk to him. And why had he mentioned Chan's name? He had been unwilling to say much before. Had he been in touch with Chan?

Chapter 26

"*D*rew, Drew, wake up."

It was Becky, excited, squeezing his hand.

"Is it time?"

"Time? Time for what?"

"My arm."

"Oh, yes, it's morning. But no, the doctor came, but I wouldn't let him do it. We got a telegram from Stacy. She's coming."

"Stacy?"

"Yes, she says she's arranged for a special stage in Yuma. She's bringing a man named Mister Lu. The telegram said 'Stop, do not amputate arm.' It said somebody named Uncle Chan was sending his best doctor, this Mister Lu person. Oh, Drew, isn't it wonderful? She's coming, all the way from San Francisco."

It was hard to believe. Stacy was back from Europe? And she was coming to Prescott? "Did the telegram say when?"

"I guess it came in last night. The boy just got around to delivering it this morning. Doctor Fletcher was already here, sitting on the porch with Edward, waiting for you to wake up when it came."

"And he went along with the idea? Of waiting, I mean?"

"Not really. He said we should go ahead and amputate. That delays could be dangerous. But the telegram said she was leaving right away so I said it couldn't hurt to wait another day or so. Edward said if she hires somebody in Yuma who knows the area, they could come up by the river route and be here maybe by tomorrow."

"If anybody can do it, Stacy can."

"Oh, I so much want to meet her. What's she like?"

"You'll like her. She's . . . strong willed, competent."

"Oh, such a big word to describe the woman you love. I mean, you do love her, don't you?"

"We have a lot in common."

"Then she must be very wonderful. I'll have to get busy to get ready for her. She can have my room. That is, unless she wants to stay in here with you."

"She might."

"Oh, right. Well, okay. Anyhow, I hope this doctor she's bringing is very good. I hope he really can save your arm"

Steele had met Mister Lu at Stacy's house. He was supposed to be the best Chinese herbalist this side of China, but he'd been treating Stacy's mother for years with little sign of improvement. It was hard to imagine the little man coming all the way from San Francisco to treat what might be a lost cause. But it was very much like Stacy to arrange it. Once she got an idea in her head, there was no stopping her. And she wasn't above using the power and authority her father commanded when it suited her purposes.

"That took you away," said Becky. "What are you thinking about?"

"I was thinking about how Stacy makes things happen. She's far away in San Francisco and she's already making things happen here."

Becky stood up. "I can't wait to meet her. But right now, we've got to get you healthy and strong. The first thing you have to do is start eating. You never touched that soup Cook made especially for you. I'm going to go down to get you some more and this time I'm going to sit here and feed it to you."

"Yes, dear."

"So you're back to making your little jokes again. That's a good sign."

"I am a little hungry. I can get up."

"No you can't. The doctor says your feet are badly blistered, and badly infected. You wait right here. From now on, if you need anything , I'll get it for you."

She did come back with hot soup and she did insist he eat it. While he ate, she told him that O'Brien was having the house cleaned from top to bottom, telling everyone who'd listen about the upcoming visit from the famous Nathan Moran's daughter.

The doctor came back that afternoon and he made no secret of his disapproval of the delayed amputation. "You know as well as I do, Steele, if that gangrene spreads, it could hit your heart and kill you."

"I know that."

"And you're still willing to wait for this Chinese witch doctor?"

"He's not a witch doctor, he's an herbalist."

"Yeah, yeah, I've heard all about it. Ancient Chinese medical secrets. Not a bit of it has ever been proven scientifically."

"Maybe this will be a good test of it."

"A test with your life at stake. Did you ever see any of your Federal soldier boys recover once the gangrene set in?"

"The doctors never gave it a chance. They amputated immediately."

"And they were right to do it. Mark my words, this Chinese herbalist won't be able to do any more than I can. In the end, you're going to lose that arm. Delay too long and you're a dead man."

"Can you drain the wound and keep it open until he gets here?"

"If that's what you want. I'd advise you to drink a whole bottle of my tonic every few hours. Maybe it'll keep you alive until I can do what you know I'm going to have to do with that arm." Without another word, the doctor removed the bandages and lanced the wound. It hurt, but not as much as Steele would have expected. It meant he was already losing feeling in the arm.

The doctor rewrapped the wound, closed up his bag, and left.

Becky took his place at Steele's bedside. She was cheerful and chatty, feeding him soup and homemade bread. She insisted he follow the doctor's orders and keep on drinking plenty of the tonic. Steele tried to listen to her constant talking, but his mind kept wandering off, thinking about Stacy out there in that same desert that had almost claimed his life.

He must have fallen asleep while Becky was still there because he didn't remember her leaving. It was dark and cold in the room and his arm was throbbing. The smell of his wound was strong in the room. He stared up into the darkness, remembering the penetrating cold of the cave. So cold, so alone. The memory of lying under that stinking mattress suddenly made him want to get up and move. How long had he been lying in that bed? Too long.

He swung his legs out of bed and was immediately hit by a wave of dizziness and nausea. He realized it must be the gangrene in his system. He waited until the dizziness subsided and stood up. But his feet hurt so bad he had to sit right back down again. He had a vague memory of cutting open the blisters on his feet. When was that? In the cave? Or when he was out in the desert?

He tried standing again and this time he was able to stay upright by putting both hands against the wall. It felt good to be up. He kept one hand against the wall and moved slowly to the window. It was very dark out there. Everyone in the town must be asleep. He looked down at the roofs of the dark houses and wondered if Longmore lived in one of them. O'Brien had said Longmore was back in town. Was he really the one responsible for Rudd's murder?

He was about to head back to the bed when he saw the glow of a cigarette down there, near the back fence. This time he knew it was somebody watching him. That lone cigarette smoker at the town square might have been just a man out for a walk in the dark, but that same glow in the dark below Rudd's window at the hotel and now below his window at O'Brien's house confirmed it: he was definitely being watched. But there was nothing he could do about it now. As soon as he got better, arm or no arm, he would find that smoker, find out why he was always out there in the dark watching.

Chapter 27

*I*t was easy to hear the moment Stacy arrived. Becky was sitting next to the bed, reading out loud to him and they both heard the commotion downstairs. Becky jumped up to open the door.

Steele heard her familiar voice. "Where is he?"

Stacy was never one to waste time with formalities. Steele heard her coming up the stairs, two at a time.

Becky met her at the door and held out her hand. "You must be Stacy. I'm—"

"Where is he? In here?"

She burst into the room and came straight to the bedside. She was dressed like some kind of cowgirl, in a plaid shirt and dusty chaps. It made Steele smile to see her like that.

"So, you're not dead after all. I go out of the country for a few months and this is what you do to yourself."

Steele shrugged. "Sorry."

"None of your jokes, Drew. They tell me you got yourself all shot up. Didn't you get enough of that in the war?"

"I wanted to give them another chance at me."

"Always the joker."

"Only when you're around."

"All right, fine, make a joke out of it. Uncle Chan said his man in this town sent him a telegram. It said they were about to hack off your arm. Looks like they didn't get it done."

"Not quite." It was good to see her. Steele had almost forgotten how beautiful she was, and how strong her personality was.

"Well, thank goodness for that. I brought Mister Lu with me. He'll get you fixed up." She turned back toward the door. "Mister Lu, where are you?" she yelled. "Get up here." She sat on the edge of the bed and kissed Steele's cheek. "Seriously, Drew, how bad is it? Were they really going to take off your arm?"

"They may still have to."

"Not if I can help it." She turned back toward the door again. "Mister Lu. I said get up here. Now!" She sized Becky up. "And who's this? Your nursemaid?"

Becky stepped forward. "I'm Becky Laird, Miss Moran. I'm glad to meet you."

"Nice to meet you too, Becky." She turned back to look at Steele. "I expect she's been taking good care of you."

"She sure has."

Stacy smiled and waved Becky over. "Come here, dear. Let me take a closer look at you." She took some time to look Becky over. Then she smiled. "Well you certainly are an attractive young lady, aren't you? But I'll bet Drew has already informed you of that."

"No, actually . . . " stammered Becky.

"Well, plenty of time to talk about that later," said Stacy. "You and I probably have a lot to talk about" She jumped up. "Now, where is that man?" She headed for the door, but stopped close to Becky. "Poor Mister Lu is probably in the outhouse. That horse about shook his guts out. He'd never been on a horse before in his life. We had to pull horses along behind the wagon so we could ride the last part. There's no good way to get to this God-forsaken town. You from here, dear?"

Becky started to explain that she was also new to town, but just then Mister Lu appeared and Stacy guided him to Steele's bedside with both hands on the little man's shoulders. "Look at his arm. Can you fix it?"

Mister Lu immediately sat down in the chair and removed the bandages to examine Steele's wound. After only a few seconds, he turned to Becky and said, "Water? Hot?" Then he began unpacking various vials and pouches of herbs from his leather bag.

"Why don't we leave Mister Lu to his business?" said Stacy. She took ahold of Becky's arm and guided her to the door. "I'm starving. Maybe we can get something to eat and have a little talk."

"Oh, I'd like that," said Becky.

For the rest of the afternoon Mister Lu didn't leave Steele's side. Never saying a word, he frequently bathed Steele's wound with something that looked like very dark tea, but smelled more like dank earth. He applied hot compresses that were made up of some kind of leaves that he had cooked down in a tiny pot that was heated with a wax burner. He insisted Steele drink a terrible-tasting tea that was made from herbs that were so strong the whole cupful had to be downed quickly in one gulp.

Steele doubted that Mister Lu knew all that many English words, other than "Hot water," which he called for often.

Later in the afternoon, Doctor Fletcher stopped by, but stayed by the door watching. After a while he shook his head and left without a word.

Stacy and Becky didn't come back for hours, and then they only stayed for a few minutes to watch Mister Lu work. They often leaned close to each other to whisper.

That night, Stacy came in with a tray of food. She chased Mister Lu out and pulled a table close to the bed. "What do you say we have a picnic, like we used to. Remember?"

"Of course I remember. Once you even tried cooking something yourself."

She laughed and sat on the edge of the bed. "You don't have to worry this time. Cook fixed all of this for you. Everybody here wants to take care of you, especially Becky."

"She's a fine young woman," said Steele.

"A fine young woman. Is that all you can say about her? Are you trying to pretend you weren't interested in her?" Before he could answer, she said, "Here eat this" and forced a large piece of bread into his hands. "And eat lots of this soup. Cook says you'll like it."

"She lost her father. He was murdered soon after we arrived here."

Stacy nodded grimly. "Yes, O'Brien told me. And he told me about the attack on the man you came here with. The man named Rudd, and he told me how you saved him by cutting into his throat so he could breathe. It was a good thing you were there." She stared at him. "How do you always get yourself into these situations?"

"It's my job."

"Your job. If you really wanted a job, my father would have given you a job that paid ten times as much as you can make detecting."

"In some place like Colorado. Anywhere, as long as it was far away from you."

"That was my mother's doing. You know that."

"We've been through this before, Stacy."

"Yes, we have, but I still think your opening that detective office was nothing more than a way to get back to the kind of danger you experienced in the war. You love it. You're addicted to it."

"So you've told me."

"Well, this time you almost went too far. This time you could have come back with more than bullet holes in you, you could have come back to me without an arm."

"Will you still love me if the doctor has to take my arm?"

"Is that supposed to be another one of your little jokes. It could happen. Mister Lu hasn't saved your arm yet."

"You didn't answer my question."

"I do love you, despite your wanting to get yourself shot all the time. But I want you in one piece. As soon as you're recovered enough to travel, I'm going to pack you up and take you back home with me."

"You're mother will love that."

"I had a long talk with her before I left San Francisco. I told her I was going to bring you back with me and she might as well get used to it."

Steele took her hand. "Listen, Stacy, I have to stay here for a while."

"But why? You could have died out there in the desert. They said you were half dead when they found you. Why would you want to stay here any longer?"

"There are still—"

"I know, I know, you want to find whoever killed her father. Becky told me. These people act like you're the savior come to deliver them from all their problems. Especially Becky. She thinks you walk on water."

"Her father was murdered. I was right across the hall. And Rudd was shot down like a sick dog. I have to do something about that, don't I?"

"No, you don't. Why does it have to be you? Don't they have any law in this God-forsaken town?" Tears welled up in her eyes, but she angrily wiped them away. "Oh, why aren't you eating? Eat."

They ate in silence and when they were finished, she kissed him on the forehead and picked up the tray. "Mister Lu should be finished eating by now. I want him to come back and work on your arm some more. I don't want him to stop until it's all healed."

"Is he supposed to stay with me all night?"

"I know what you mean by that, but you're not well enough for . . . that. I'll come sit with you tonight, but you have to behave. We've got to get you all healed up first."

"Then send him back up. The sooner he fixes me, the better."

She frowned at him. "Very funny. You haven't changed at all."

Chapter 28

*S*tacy did come back to sit with him that night. Steele told her about everything that had happened since he'd arrived in Prescott, about meeting Lucky Laird on the stagecoach, about the night Rudd had been attacked in the bar, about finding Laird dead in his room, and about the tragic trip out to Gold Valley. After that, they talked for a long time about her trip to Europe. She told him all the things she had seen there, and about the exciting women's movement that was rapidly spreading across the continent.

Steele awoke in the middle of the night and saw that she was still in the chair, but leaning against the bed, sound asleep. Using his good arm, he managed to coax her into bed without fully awaking her. She turned toward him and seemed as if she was about to wake up. But he stroked her hair softly and whispered for her to go back to sleep. She snuggled up against him and was asleep again in seconds.

For much of the night, he lay as still as possible, listening to her breathing, happy to just have her there. For the first time since he'd come back from the desert, he felt optimistic. His arm would get better. He would convince Stacy that it was necessary to stay in Prescott for a while until he could learn why Laird and Rudd had been killed. Maybe she would stay with him, maybe she wouldn't, but he knew he could not leave this town until he uncovered the truth behind the murders.

The next morning, Stacy hurried in, suddenly cheerful and full of busy plans. "Becky is going to show me the town, what little there is of it. And Uncle Chan asked me to pay his respects to his Cousin when

I got to town. A man named Wang who runs a hotel or something here. A place called the Dragon House."

"It's the local whore house run by the Chinese. They've brought in young Chinese women."

"Is that right? Well, visiting a place like that should be an experience. Maybe I'll have a talk with those Chinese women about their rights." She hurried off to find Mister Lu.

Becky soon came in with a tray full of food, bubbling with excitement about showing Stacy around. "She's so smart, Drew. And so experienced. She's been telling me all about London and Berlin and Paris. Did you know they have a museum in Paris with paintings and sculptures that go all the way back to the ancient Romans?"

"Yes," said Steele, munching on the toast and jam she'd fixed for him, "I was aware of that."

Becky picked up a piece of toast, but she didn't eat it. She just held it while she looked off toward the window. "She has a small apartment in London, or at least her father does. She said I could come there to visit her some time."

"I'm sure you'd like that, Becky. London is a wonderful old city. A very large city."

"Really? Bigger than San Francisco? Have you been there?"

"Much bigger. I lived there, when I was younger."

"Really? What was it like?"

"Have Stacy tell you. Or better yet, take her up on her offer to visit her there."

Becky nodded thoughtfully. "Maybe I will. Someday."

For the rest of the day, Mister Lu worked on Steele's arm. He was not only constantly applying hot compresses and massaging the damaged arm, but he had started sticking tiny pins into various locations on Steele's body, even in places that were some distance from his arm. The pins didn't hurt much, but being forced to sit in bed all day was making Steele very restless. Whenever Mister Lu left the room, Steele got up to walk to the window, trying to get a little of his strength back. Once he was still at the window when Mister Lu came back and that got the little man very upset. As he guided Steele back to bed, he noticed how painfully Steele was walking and after he got Steele back into the bed, he insisted on looking at his feet. He took one look and let out a shriek. He immediately moved his chair to the foot of the bed and went to work on Steele's feet with his compresses and massages, muttering to himself in Chinese. For the rest of the day, he was in and out of the room constantly, working first on Steele's arm and then on his feet.

For the next few days, Stacy and Becky took turns sitting with Steele. They both asked him frequently if he was in pain and each time he lied, claiming that it hardly hurt at all. Once, when they left him alone for a little while, he began thinking about the last time he had been confined to a bed. It was when he was still in the Army hospital in Tennessee, after he had been wounded by the exploding shell that came in through the roof of the surgery. The doctors removed the shrapnel and sent him to bed. At first, the nurses had fussed over him, brought him special treats, and stayed to talk to him. But soon new battles at the front brought in more wounded and no one had time for a patient who was in the process of healing. That experience had taught him how to be alone with his pain. He learned to find that secret place of refuge where pain was only a curious, if powerful, sensation—something new to learn about.

From time to time, O'Brien stopped by for a visit. He always seemed a bit uncomfortable and Steele wondered why. Maybe it was because Steele's debilitated state reminded him of his wife's long illness and eventual death. He usually walked to the window, cheerfully describing the weather outside. He sometimes talked about Becky, once describing her as "a wonderful young woman, the kind of woman who would someday make a man very happy."

At night, Stacy slept close to him, but she insisted he not tire himself by any sort of lovemaking. "There will be time enough for that when you're better," she said firmly.

Mister Lu spent his nights at the Dragon House, but every morning, he arrived early to patiently to tend to Steele with his potions and his pins. All through the day, he came often to check on Steele.

In time, Steele realized that whatever Mister Lu was doing, it was working. The swelling in his arm was very gradually going down, and the skin, although badly damaged, was slowly healing.

One day, he could no longer tolerate being in bed. The next time Stacy came in he said, "Find my clothes. I'm getting up."'

"Now don't get restless," she said. "Even if your arm is healing, your feet need time to recover. Mister Lu said your feet were in just about as bad shape as your arm, if not worse."

Steele slid out of bed and stood up. "Either find my clothes or I'll have to go downstairs naked. My arm is healing and so are my feet. They will heal just as well sitting on the front porch."

Stacy tried to talk him out of it, but she finally admitted that his clothes were in the top drawer of dresser. He got up and went to it. His clothes had been cleaned and pressed and the money belt was on top of them. He fastened the money belt around his waist and was still dressing when Becky rushed in.

She saw he was half undressed and quickly turned away. Without looking back at him, she said, "What's this I hear about you getting up? Mister Lu is going to be very upset."

"Mister Lu can administer his magic just as well with me sitting in a chair like a normal person."

When he was fully dressed, Stacy told Becky she could turn around now. Then, with Stacy on one side and Becky on the other, they helped him down the stairs and out onto the front porch. While Stacy leaned against the porch railing, watching, Becky brought pillow after pillow to make sure Steele was completely comfortable. "Can I get you anything else?" she asked. "Are you hungry?"

"No, I'm fine."

"You may be fine, but you have to eat if you are going to get your strength back. I'll go get you something." She hurried away.

"She hovers over you like a mother hen," said Stacy, smiling.

"She'll make somebody a fine wife."

"When did you figure that out? On those cold nights when I was so far away in Europe."

"Well, she *was* here, and you weren't."

Stacy chuckled. "Just as I suspected. I suppose you used the old trick of telling her you were an artist, telling her you could draw her much better if she'd just remove her clothes."

Steele glanced at Mister Lu.

Stacy also looked at the little man. "He doesn't have any idea what we're talking about. Well, what do you have to say for yourself? Taking advantage of a young girl like that."

He smiled and shrugged. "What could I do? As you said, the nights were cold."

Stacy laughed again and came to sit beside him. She leaned close to whisper in his ear. "Becky told me all about it, how she wanted to pose in the nude for you. But you were such a gentleman you wouldn't hear of it."

"She told you about that, did she? I'm surprised."

She patted his hand. "My dear, if you only knew what women talk about when you men aren't around."

Just then Becky came back with a tray full of sandwiches and Stacy sat back in her chair to watch as Becky tried to get Steele to eat something.

When Steele finally agreed to eat half a sandwich, Becky sat back, looking satisfied. "I remember the last time Cook made chicken sandwiches for you. It was before you went out into the desert." She paused for a moment, then said, "Edward says he's sure Longmore was behind Rudd's death, but nobody is going to do anything about it."

"Is that right?" asked Stacy. "He's sure?"

Becky nodded.

Stacy turned to Steele. "What do you think?"

"I'm not sure. As soon as my feet heal a little more, I plan to go talk to him."

"Right back into the breach, eh?" said Stacy. She shook her head and looked away.

After several moments of silence, Becky got up and went to the door. She opened it and looked back. "Edward says Longmore is a very evil man. Do you think he had anything to do with . . . I mean, my father didn't even know him. So why . . . "

"I don't know, Becky," said Steele. "But I won't leave this town until I find out."

Becky looked like she was about to say something else, but changed her mind and went inside, closing the screen door carefully behind her.

Stacy looked at Steele for a long moment, but then shrugged and turned away.

Steele knew there was nothing else to say. As soon as he was able to walk, he would go see this man Longmore. It was time for some answers.

Chapter 29

*T*hat night, when O'Brien returned, they all ate together in the dining room.

"What a pleasure to have so many around this old table again," said O'Brien. "It's almost like the old days when . . ." He left the sentence unfinished and lifted his glass of whiskey. "Well, anyhow, here's to good company and better times ahead." He drained his glass and refilled it. "And speaking of good company, I'd like to drink another toast to Miss Becky Laird here, as good a company as a man could ever hope for."

"Now Edward, you promised to cut down on your drinking."

O'Brien beamed and leaned across to pat her hand. "Whatever you say, my dear, whatever you say." He started to take another drink, but thought better of it and put it down.

"And maybe we should say a few words about poor Rudd," suggested Becky, "now that Drew is back with us and getting better."

O'Brien stared at his plate.

"Oh, I'm sorry," said Becky. "I shouldn't have said anything. I know you miss him, Edward. I miss him too." She turned to Stacy. "You would have liked him. He was so funny."

That revived O'Brien. "Damn right. He *was* funny, always ready with a good joke, or a good story. The best friend a man could ever have. Let's drink to that." He drained his glass again and made sure he didn't look in Becky's direction.

"He saved my life," said Steele quietly.

"You haven't talked about it much," said O'Brien. "Can you tell us what happened? That is if the ladies don't mind. I've been itching to ask you about it, but these two said not to bother you."

"Two men came up on us at night," said Steele quietly. "Rudd was wounded and I was trying to work my way above them, but they spotted me. Rudd shot at them, distracted them long enough for me to get away. Then they shot him."

Nobody said anything until O'Brien spoke up. "I guess that's the short version. Maybe you could tell me more about it some time."

"There was nothing you could have done about it, could you?" said Becky.

"I've thought about that a lot. Maybe I should have done something different. Maybe I should have stayed with him."

"And they both got away?" said O'Brien.

"The man named Shorty got away. I shot the other one."

"You killed one of them?" asked Becky.

"I had no choice."

"Well, good," said O'Brien. "At least you got one of them. Mark my words, that Shorty won't get away with it. And neither will Longmore. That's why I was gone this afternoon. I was at the marshal's office demanding he do something about Longmore. Arrest him or something. I told the marshal he should make Longmore admit he was behind Rudd's killing and Willig's killing and maybe Becky's father's death too. I've been talking to some of the other people in town too. They're all up in arms about what's been going on. This killing has got to stop."

Steele was silent, but O'Brien was watching him. "Well, what do you think?" he asked. "It has to be Longmore, doesn't it? I mean, who else could it be?"

Steele wasn't sure he wanted to answer. There was so much he still didn't know. Finally, he said, "I don't know, but I will find out. I won't leave this town until I do."

That left everyone silent and nothing more was said about it while they finished eating.

After supper, Steele sat on the front porch with Stacy while Becky and O'Brien took the dog for a walk.

"She's very young," said Stacy as they watched them walk away. "I was young like that when you met me."

"You're still young."

"I suppose so, but I don't feel young anymore. Some of the things I saw in Europe . . . Many women are having a bad time of it over there." She stared into the darkness.

"You're going back."

She turned to look at him. "You always know what I'm going to say before I say it. Oh, Drew, I have to. I only came back because my mother was ill. And then I found out about you being hurt here. But my mother is doing better now and so are you. We're making such progress over there. The whole society is ready for change. I want to be part of that."

"I understand," he said softly.

"But this time I want you to go with me. Will you? Will you give up this obsession with danger and come with me?"

"I might have gone with you the last time you went, if you would have asked me."

"I wondered if you would. I should have asked you. I didn't realize how much a man could do for us over there. Some doors can only be opened by a man."

"So you want me to go only because I can help your cause."

She smiled coyly. "Why else would I want you to go?" But then she reached out to take his hand. "No, let's not do that kidding thing. Not about this. You know I want to be with you. We can do some good over there, but we can have fun too. I discovered so many wonderful things there. Oh Drew, how long has it been since you were in Europe? Things are changing there, changing fast. There's wonderful new art and new ways of looking at things. And I met some wonderful people over there."

"I would like to see the art."

She frowned.

"And meet your wonderful friends too, of course."

She squeezed his hand. "All right, mister loner, I guess your kidding me means you're really are getting better. Maybe we can leave this awful place soon. Mister Lu keeps on talking about getting back to San Francisco."

"We've already talked about that. I have to stay."

"Yes, yes, I know you want to help Becky find her father's killer, but that's what they have law enforcement for."

"And what about Rudd's killer? Rudd saved my life."

"I know, dear, but he's gone now so there's nothing you can do for him. He was the one who hired you to come here. Now that he's gone, your job is done."

"Whoever killed them is still here. There's something going on in this town, beneath the surface."

"And they will just keep on killing each other after we're gone. Listen, the new trains to the east coast are much faster now. My father can get us a private railway car. We could be on a ship for London in two weeks. And then you could see your parents again. You've always said you should go back and apologize to them for running away when you were so young."

Steele gently touched her cheek. "Just give me a little time to find out what's going on in this town. Then I'll let you lead me anywhere in the world you want to take me."

She frowned, but took his hand to hold it tightly against her cheek. "You promise? When all this is over, you'll come with me? You'll go to Europe with me, even if there's another case waiting for you when you get back to San Francisco?"

"I promise."

She kissed his hand. "Let's not wait for them to come back from their walk. Let's go to bed."

"I'm ready."

She helped him up the stairs and after she'd locked the bedroom door, she helped him undress. Then she let him undress her.

She lit a single candle and he explored her naked body in its flickering light. "You're still as beautiful as ever."

"More beautiful than Becky?"

"Well, almost."

"Oh, you." Laughing, she tried to push him away, but he still had ahold of her with his good arm and he pulled her down on the bed. Then, he just held her, letting himself be carried away with the familiar feel of her body against his.

Their love making started out somewhat clumsily, not only because of Steele's damaged arm, but also because it had been so long they'd forgotten some of each other's ways. When they couldn't figure out where all those arms and legs should go, it got them giggling. But in the end, they found each other, and it brought back the sweet feelings and deep passions. They made long slow love.

After Stacy fell asleep against his chest, Steele lay staring up at the ceiling, holding her, not wanting to go to sleep too soon, not wanting to lose the moment. Soon she would grow restless and then she'd find a reason to go back to San Francisco. He wanted to believe she'd wait for him there, but would she?

Chapter 30

*T*he next morning Steele was again out on the front porch, but this time he was alone, except for O'Brien's old dog. Becky and Stacy had gone shopping and O'Brien had gone off on his horse. Cook had invited Mister Lu into his kitchen to try making something Chinese for lunch. Steele was enjoying a rare few minutes alone when he saw Doctor Fletcher coming up the road.

"So you're out of bed now are you?" said the doctor, putting one foot up on the steps.

"Yes, and I'm thankful."

"You should be thankful. You're lucky to be alive. How's the arm?"

"Much better. Thanks to you and to Mister Lu."

"Me? I'd of cut it off. You know that."

"You did a good job of cleaning out the wound. That gave it a chance to heal. Why don't you come up and sit for a while?"

"Naw, got patients to see. Thought I'd just drop by and see how you were doing."

"My feet are still bad, but getting better."

"That little Chinese guy treating them with his herbs and all?"

"Yes, he is."

"And they're getting better? Like your arm did?"

"Yes, slowly. Would you like to look at my arm?" Steele pulled up his sleeve.

The doctor put down his bag and came up the steps for a closer look. "Damn, it's not looking too bad at all. Well, if those herbs and things can save an arm that was that far gone, those Chinese must know something. I wouldn't have believed it if I hadn't seen it myself."

"I too was surprised, based on what I saw during the war."

"Yeah, we sure did cut a lot off a lot of arms and legs back then. I guess Becky told you about Charlie."

"Yes, too bad."

"Yeah, but he's doin' better now. I just came from him. Maybe if that Chinese guy would have got here sooner . . . Ah well, you know what that's like, you always wish you could have done more." He reached out to touch the scarred tissue on Steele's arm. "What's this oily stuff he's puttin' on it?" He put his finger to his nose to smell it. "Not much smell to it. But if it works maybe I could get him to send me some from San Francisco."

"I'll send you some myself, when I get back there."

"That'd be great. We could sure use it around here, what with everybody always shooting each other." He picked up his bag. "Guess I'd better get going. They tell me a boy's come down with the mumps. Out by the river. Maybe I'll earn me a couple of chickens or something. You got plenty of my tonic left?"

"Yes. And by the way, I haven't received a bill from you yet."

"Naw, not for you. No charge. Call it professional courtesy."

Steele shook his head. "I'll expect a bill soon. At your full rate."

"Hell, it's been so long since I charged anybody full rate, I don't even know what full rate would be. Usually I just sell them a few bottles of my tonic and call it even."

"I'll expect a bill, and more tonic."

"Right, right. You win. Keep drinkin' that tonic. There's nothing in it that will hurt you. Don't be surprised if people think it's what cured your arm. I'm not gonna tell 'em any different."

As the doctor went down the steps, Steele called after him: "Don't catch the mumps."

The doctor didn't look back, but he waved and called back over his shoulder: "Already had 'em. Last winter. Thought I was gonna die."

That evening it was hot and muggy so everyone adjourned to the front porch as soon as supper was over. O'Brien was saying he was almost ready to start digging his new tunnel on the other side of the hill. "If you hear some blasting tomorrow, don't be alarmed. First step is to loosen up the rocks and dirt over there."

"Oh?" asked Becky, "did you get some investment money to start digging?"

"Well, no, but I figure I should at least have the hole started. In case I can get somebody to come here to look at my idea."

"What is your idea?" asked Stacy.

"Time was, I had the biggest and best mine in this county. But then I hit water. I plan to dig a new tunnel on the other side of the hill. Start a new shaft at a lower level. That way, when I hit water again, it'll just drain off."

"Sounds like a good plan," said Stacy. "Maybe my father would be interested."

O'Brien scooted forward in his chair. "Do you really think so? I mean, it wouldn't take all that much money to get started. You know, test out the feasibility and all."

"When I get back, I'll talk to him about it. He's always interested in new ventures."

O'Brien turned and grinned at Becky. "Did you hear that? Nathan Moran himself might be interested. I told you it was a great idea."

She patted his arm. "Now, Edward, all she said was she'd talk to him about it. Don't get your hopes up too high."

Suddenly, O'Brien's dog sat up with a low growl.

"Hello the house. I'm coming up." It was a man's voice. Steele didn't recognize it.

The dog got up and began to growl more loudly, the hair on the back of its neck bristling. O'Brien held him back. "Easy, Roy."

The man stopped at the foot of the stairs. He was a big man, broad across the chest, with graying hair. He shook his finger at O'Brien. "Keep that damn dog of yours under control, O'Brien."

"Well, if it isn't Fredrick Longmore," said O'Brien. "I figured you'd come strollin' back into town as soon as all the trouble was over."

Longmore nervously slapped a pair of leather gloves against his thigh. "I need to talk to you, O'Brien."

"So talk."

"I'd rather talk in private."

"If it's about Rudd, we have nothing to talk about."

"It is about Rudd. I was out of town. When I got back, I heard he'd been here, but that he'd got himself killed. How did it happen?"

"I suspect you know more about it than we do, Longmore."

"Don't get smart with me, O'Brien. As I said, I was out of town."

O'Brien pointed toward Steele. "Steele here can tell you all about it. Why don't you ask him? He got shot too, barely made it out of the desert alive."

Longmore turned to Steele. "Is that right? How did it happen? I'm an old acquaintance of Rudd's. He was my daughter's school teacher."

Steele could see the man was nervous, but it didn't seem like he was lying. "Rudd and I went out to Gold Valley," said Steele quietly. "Two men ambushed us. They killed Rudd and shot me. "

"He nearly died out there," said Stacy. "He's still recovering."

Longmore looked at Steele for a long moment before replying. "Sounds like you are a lucky man, very lucky indeed. Did he . . . that is, was there anything Rudd said that might indicate why you were attacked."

"We talked about what happened when he was here before, about you . . . and Willig."

"Still claim you don't know anything about it?" said O'Brien.

Longmore turned to him. "What are you inferring, O'Brien?"

O'Brien pointed his finger at Longmore's face. "Come on, Longmore, don't play the innocent act. Willig gets killed while you're out of town. Now Rudd get killed and guess what? You just happen to be out of town again."

Longmore shook his head in disgust. "This is absurd. I had nothing to do with it. Why would my being somewhere else prove that I did something back here? I came here to tell you you're wrong about me, but apparently you've got your mind set." He turned to go.

"I believe you," said Steele.

Longmore stopped and turned back.

"What?" said O'Brien. "I'm tellin' you he—"

"If you don't mind, I'd like to walk along with you," said Steele, getting up.

"But you shouldn't be walking," said Becky. "Your feet." She got up to help him.

Stacy caught her by the arm. "Let them go. They need to talk."

Steele made it down the stairs on his own. "I hope you don't mind walking a little slowly. My feet haven't fully recovered."

"I haven't got all night," said Longmore, but he did walk slow enough for Steele to keep up.

When they were out of earshot of O'Brien's house, Steele said, "This is far enough. Would you mind answering a few questions?"

"Why should I?"

"It will only take a minute. I believe I have some information that will be important to you. It's about Rudd."

Longmore shrugged.

"Let me explain, Mr. Longmore. Rudd hired me to come back here with him. He wanted to clear his name and pay you back the money."

"So he finally admitted he stole it."

"He didn't steal it, Dutch Willig did."

"So you say. If Rudd didn't take it, why would he have to pay me back?"

"He still had hopes of finding the land grant. He wanted to make sure you didn't have any legal claim on it."

Longmore let out a gruff laugh. "Land grant. There never was any such land grant. It was just another one of Willig's tricks. Judge Barnes was about to lock him up again for land fraud when he got himself killed."

"So why were you willing to pay him a thousand dollars for it?"

"I never . . . Well, it doesn't matter now, does it?"

"So it wasn't your money. Who gave you the money, Longmore? Who did believe the land grant was real?"

"Nobody. Rudd was just confused."

"So you had no reason to kill Willig. But whoever gave you the thousand dollars did. I think you should tell me who that was."

Longmore shook his head. "I don't know what you're talking about."

"I think you do. Someone is trying to buy, or lay claim to, as much land as they can in this territory. They wanted the land grant and they want to own other land also. They knew in advance this town was going to be the territorial capital, but I don't think that was the only reason. Tell, me, Longmore, why do you spend most of your time down south when your gold mine is here?"

"That's none of your business."

He started to go, but Steele caught his arm. "I think you know exactly who is acquiring land in this area. It's whoever gave you that thousand dollars to buy the land grant. I think you're still working with them."

Longmore shook off Steele's hand. "Nonsense. You're guessing."

"They had Willig murdered, didn't they?"

"I don't have to listen to this."

"But you should listen. Otherwise I may have to tell what I know to the Federal authorities down in Tucson."

"They won't listen to you."

"Maybe not, but they'll listen to Nathan Moran."

"The railroad man? What's he got to do with this?"

"Moran is now more than a railroad owner. He's a member of the California legislature and may run for the U.S. Senate. Did you notice that attractive young woman back there at O'Brien's house? She came here to be with me. She's his daughter."

Longmore stared at him. "You're trying to scare me, but why would I care about some California politician? I haven't done anything against the law."

"I know you haven't. You just stand by while others do it. But I think you could be found complicit in the murder of a man named Laird. He was killed in the hotel, in exactly the same way Willig was. Surely you heard about it."

"I never met the man. It doesn't have anything to do with me."

"Oh, but it does. Laird was killed for the land he owns, by the same people you've been working with."

Longmore was silent for a few moments. Then he said, "You can't prove anything. My hands are clean."

"I'm sure they are. All I'm asking you is to tell me who it is. Who bought your mine?"

"My mine? What makes you think I sold my mine?"

"Come now, Longmore. You're hardly ever in this town anymore. I know your mine is playing out, but I suspect they offered you a good price and were willing to back your new venture downstate. What is it you're doing down there in Phoenix? Does it involve the acquisition of land?"

"I have nothing more to say. I've got to go."

"One more thing. Why did they have to kill Rudd? Was it because he knew about the land grant?"

"As I said, I was out of town."

"Yes, you were. Somehow they knew Rudd was coming. Did they tell you stay away while he was in town?"

"I don't have to stand here and listen to this." He turned away and started down the road.

Steele called after him: "I suggest you think about it. I'll be staying at O'Brien's. I'm not leaving this town until I learn what is going on here. Come back when you're ready to talk to me. Otherwise, I will go to the authorities."

Longmore hurried away into the darkness.

Steele slowly made his way back up the road to O'Brien's house. Stacy and Becky were waiting for him and helped him get back up onto the porch and into a chair.

"Well, what did you find out?" asked O'Brien. "Denied everything, didn't he?"

"He did."

"I knew it. But he's behind it all, mark my words."

"I don't think so. Someone is controlling him."

"Controlling him? Controlling Longmore? That's a laugh. He's the one behind it. I'm sure of it and I don't care what anybody says." He jerked open the screen door and went into the house. Becky followed him saying, "Now, Edward, you shouldn't get so upset about things."

After they were gone, Stacy said, "Well, find out anything?"

"No, but I didn't expect to. I just told him what I suspected."

"Which is?"

"That he knows who killed Becky's father, and Rudd too. I threatened to go to the authorities. I even used your father's name to try to scare him a little."

"What will he do next?"

"He will go to whoever is behind him."

"And then they'll come after you. You're trying to make yourself a target."

"What else can I do? I have to try to bring them out into the open. I can't figure out why they haven't come after me already."

"They did come after you. They shot you."

Steele shook his head. "No, they were after Rudd. They didn't even know who I was."

Stacy stared at him, frowning. "But you want them to know who you are, don't you. You're doing it again. Looking for danger."

"It's the only way to flush them out. I've talked to everybody in town and found out nothing. I can't stand just sitting here waiting."

"You're not waiting, you're recovering."

"While I'm recovering, the killers could be covering their tracks. What I can't figure out is how they can remain so well hidden. Nobody in this town seems to even realize there's anything going on."

"That's not possible in such a small town. It's got to be outsiders."

"No, the response is too quick for that. The orders may be coming from outside, but there is somebody here, somebody with enough money to get things done."

"Longmore?"

"I don't think so. Longmore was out of town when we arrived. Somebody here knew Laird was coming. They put him in a special room in the hotel, a room where they knew they could get to him."

"Well, there's nothing you can do about it tonight. Why don't we go to bed?"

Steele knew he wouldn't be able to sleep, but he went upstairs with her. She was asleep quickly, leaving him wide awake to stare up into the darkness. He listened to Stacy's soft breathing, thinking about his talk with Longmore. If Longmore was working with outside land investors, how did he contact them? He surely couldn't risk sending telegrams. The telegraph operator would have spread the news all over town. So he had to have a contact person in town, somebody with money and authority to buy land. Did that person also have the authority to order the killings, or did that order come from out of town?

Chapter 31

*T*he next morning, Steele and Stacy were awakened by O'Brien pounding on their bedroom door. "Wake up, Steele. Marshal Johnson is downstairs. He wants to talk to you."

Steele got up quickly and was already dressing by the time Stacy was fully awake.

"What's wrong?" she said.

"I don't know. O'Brien says the town marshal is downstairs."

"Wait for me."

"I'd better go on down. Come as soon as you're dressed."

Using the banister, Steele was able to limp down to the living room. O'Brien and the marshal were standing in the middle of the room, talking.

As Steele hobbled into the room, the marshal turned. "So, you're getting around better now, are you? Just how far could you walk if you had to?"

Steele sat in one of the overstuffed chairs. "What's on your mind, marshal?"

"Did you see Fredrick Longmore last night?"

"What are you up to, Johnson?" said O'Brien. "I already told you Longmore came here last night, and I also told you he didn't stay long."

The marshal ignored him. "Answer the question, Steele."

"If you're here to see me, you must already know I talked with him last night. What happened?"

"So you admit you were talking with him."

"Why would I deny it? Has something happened to him? Has he been killed?"

"Killed?" said O'Brien. "What's going on here?"

The marshal didn't take his eyes of off Steele. "Found dead this morning. Somebody buried a hatchet in his head."

"Holy Christ!" said O'Brien. "Murdered?"

Just then Stacy came down the stairs. "Murdered? Who's been murdered?"

The marshal glanced toward her, but kept his focus on Steele. "First it was Stew, now Longmore. Seems like people end up dead after you talk to them."

Steele nodded. "I see your point. I didn't think they'd kill him. I thought they'd just send him out of town."

"You didn't think *they'd* kill him?" said the marshal. "Who the hell is *they*?"

"I wish I knew, Marshal. Whoever Longmore was working with."

The marshal drew his gun. "Maybe we'd better go down to my office to talk about this."

Stacy moved in front of Steele. "Don't be ridiculous. He was with me all night."

Marshal Johnson looked her up and down. "I suppose you must be that Moran girl that everybody's talking about. Well, I don't care who your father is or who you chose to sleep with, but people have been dying ever since this man came to my town. I'm taking him in."

Now it was O'Brien's turn to step in front of the marshal. "Put that gun away, Johnson. She's telling the truth. Steele talked with Longmore for a few minutes, but then he left and that's the last we saw of him. Steele was right here all night. He can barely walk."

The marshal jammed his gun back into the holster. "All right, so maybe he didn't kill Longmore, but he'd better answer my questions. Who's this *they* he's talking about?"

"Why don't we all just sit down and discuss this in a civilized manner?" said Stacy.

"I'll tell you everything I know, Marshal," said Steele, "but much of it is conjecture."

"Con-jek-sure?" said the marshal. "What the hell does that mean?"

"It means he's just guessing," said Stacy, sitting down next to Steele. "Speculating."

"Well, why didn't he just say that?" The marshal dragged up a chair and sat across from Steele.

O'Brien pulled up another chair.

"I'm very sorry he was killed," said Steele. "Last night I tried to get him to reveal what he knew about the murders that have been happening in this town. I suggested it had something to do with land and I told him I knew they'd bought out his mine."

"What?" said O'Brien. "He sold his mine?"

"Conjecture," said Stacy. "Let him finish."

"I believe Laird's murder had something to do with his land. Rudd's murder might also have something to do with land. Someone is trying to acquire as much land as they can here, and they're not above murder if that's what it takes to get it."

"But why would Longmore sell his mine?" asked O'Brien. "It's not as productive as it used to be, but it's still operational. The only one in town that is."

"As I said, if they can't buy the land they want, they're willing to commit murder to get it."

"So they threatened him."

"Maybe, or maybe they approached him to buy his mine and he negotiated a deal. I think he was acting as their front for some kind of land development down in the central part of the state."

"But why did they need him?" asked Stacy.

"Good question. Clearly, they want to remain in the background. I don't know why."

The marshal took off his big hat and scratched the back of his head. "So you think he went to this mysterious *them* last night after he talked to you. And they killed him."

"I should have anticipated it. I thought he would go tell them what I said and they would send him out of town again."

"He was about to. He was all packed up and ready to go. Left word for his driver to pick him up before dawn. When the driver showed up, he found Longmore lying face down in his living room."

"And you say he was killed with a hatchet?"

"That's right. Buried in the back of his head."

"No wounds on this hands or arms?"

"Nope."

"Then there must have been at least two of them. One to distract him while the other one came up from behind with the hatchet. And you say they left the hatchet in his head?"

"That's right. It's a real mess down there."

"The hatchet must have been left as a warning."

"A warning to who?"

"To anyone who might think about revealing their identity."

The marshal stood up and put on his hat. "I'd better get back down there. But listen here, Steele, if you find out anything more about all this, I want to be the first one to hear about it."

Steele stood up to shake his hand. "You will be."

After the marshal left, O'Brien stood at the door watching him go. "Longmore's killing's got him all riled up. About the only time I've seen him act like a real marshal."

"I notice he didn't come around after Rudd was killed," said Stacy. "Or to ask about the attack on Drew."

"Who didn't?"

They all turned. It was Becky, looking sleepy. "Who didn't ask about what happened to Drew? Did I miss something?"

O'Brien went to her. "Nothing to worry about. Some trouble in town. Ready for breakfast?" He took her arm to guide her into the dining room.

She shook off his hand. "You're all looking upset. What happened?"

"It's that man who was here last night," said Stacy. "Longmore. He was killed."

Becky put her hands to her mouth. "Not another one."

She burst into tears and O'Brien put his arms around her. "Now, now, don't get so upset. He deserved to get killed. I told you he was—"

She pulled away from him. "No, no, no! People don't deserve to die. What's the matter with this town? First my father, then Rudd, and now another person." She turned to Steele. "Why? Why is this happening?"

"I wish I knew, Becky."

She wiped away the tears and stared at the floor. "I don't want to be here anymore. Maybe I'd better go home."

O'Brien put his arm around her. "You're safe here with me. I'll protect you."

"It's not that, Edward. I like being here. You've been so kind to me. All of you have. But I hate this town. I don't want to be here anymore."

"All right," said O'Brien. "I'll get you a ticket on tomorrow's stage. In fact, if you want, I'll go with you. I could help you get things straightened out down at your property."

Just then there was a knock at the front door. "Halloo. Anybody home?"

"Now who the hell is that?" said O'Brien. He went to open the door.

A very skinny, weather-worn man with a long gray beard was waiting outside, his beat-up old hat in his hands. "Is this the O'Brien place? They tol' me ta go to the big house on the hill with the paint fallin' off it."

"I'm Edward O'Brien. What is it you want?"

The man used his hat to point out toward the road. "I got a fella out thar in my wagon. Said you'd pay me to bring 'im here."

Steele limped out onto the porch. A rickety old wagon was parked out in front of the house. It was drawn by an exhausted-looking old mule. Another bearded man sat up on the weathered board that served as a seat. He pointed a crooked finger toward them. "Which one a you birds is Steele?"

Steele used the handrail to get down the stairs. "I'm Steele. Who is it?"

A weak voice called out from under a dirty old tarp in the back of the wagon. "Is that you Steele? Christ almighty, get me out of this damned wagon."

Chapter 32

*T*hat voice. It couldn't be. Steele limped to the wagon and threw aside the tarp. Inside he saw a face he thought he would never see again. It was Rudd, his face pale, his eyes red and blinking in the bright sunshine.

"So quit gawkin' and . . . Rudd coughed and winced in pain. "Get me out of this damned wagon. He coughed again. "My back is about busted from bouncin' around in here." He reached up with a shaking hand.

Steele grabbed it. "Rudd. I thought you were dead. I saw you shot down."

"I'm a lot . . . . tougher than you thought."

Steele turned toward the house. "O'Brien, come help me, quick. It's Rudd."

O'Brien jumped down the stairs and came running. "Rudd? He's not dead?"

"Tell that old . . . fart it's me," said Rudd, between coughs. "Back from the dead."

"Don't try to talk," said Steele. "We'll get you out of there."

"I may not be so heavy anymore," whispered Rudd. "I been on a kind of . . . diet. Hole in my stomach . . . I think."

Then Becky was there next to the wagon, crying and laughing at the same time. She took Rudd's other hand. "Oh, is it really you, John? I'm so happy you're not dead."

"Not yet," whispered Rudd. He closed his eyes. "Not yet."

With all of them helping, they got him out of the wagon and inside to the sofa.

Rudd let out a big sigh. "Made it," he whispered. "Didn't want to die in that wagon."

"Don't talk about dyin', old buddy," said O'Brien. "We'll take care of you." He turned to Steele. "What should we do?"

"Let me look him over. You run get the doctor."

O'Brien sprinted for the door.

"Becky get me some scissors. I've got to cut this dirty old shirt off of him. Stacy, tell Cook to get some hot water going."

They hurried away.

Rudd reached up to take Steele's hand. "I been throwin' up . . . blood." He cleared his throat and swallowed several times. "Am I gonna die? Tell me the . . . truth."

"Wait until the doctor gets here. Just try to relax."

"I been lying out there in Jake's bed, hopin' . . . I could get back here before I . . . kicked the bucket." He pointed toward the door. The two old men were still standing there, hats in hand.. "They saved me, Steele."

Steele looked at them. Standing next to each other, they looked like twins, both with dusty brown hats and full beards. The only difference between them was that one was a little taller, and seemed somewhat older, with more gray in his beard.

"Found him out by the river," said the older of the two. "Night, it was. Heard some shootin'."

"Thank you for saving him," said Steele, looking at Rudd. "We're glad to have him back."

"Weren't really all that much," said the younger of the two. "Time we got there, the shootin' was all over. Saw some men up on a cliff with torches. Rudd here was lyin' down at the bottom of that cliff. Looked pretty much dead, but we took him home anyhow."

Stacy came back into the room. Cook's heating water. What should I do?"

"See if you can find Mister Lu."

"He'll be at the Dragon House. Spends all his time down there now chasing after a girl named Suzie. I'll go get him."

After she left, Rudd said, "Is that Stacy Moran? How did she get here?"

"She came here when she heard I was wounded."

"I heard you and her . . . Now isn't that something. She came all the way here."

Becky came back with the scissors and Steele used them to cut away Rudd's shirt.

Becky went around behind the sofa to take Rudd's hand. "Can you help him? He must be in terrible pain."

"Not so bad . . . with you here," he whispered.

"Oh, you," she said softly, "always kidding me even when you're hurt terribly."

Steele leaned his head against Rudd's chest to listen to his heart. It sounded fairly strong. He looked for wounds and found three, the original wound on the top of his shoulder and two more in his midsection. The shoulder wound had torn a long furrow in the skin. Apparently the bullet had glanced off of his scapula and exited on top of his shoulder. It was already starting to heal and didn't look infected. But there were also two bullet holes in his stomach. That worried Steele. They too were starting to heal, but what had happened inside? If he was throwing up blood it was a miracle that he hadn't died from the internal bleeding already. Without surgery, he still might. "Would you let me roll you up a bit so I can look at your back?"

Rudd nodded and clenched his teeth.

Steele lifted him up just enough to pull the shirt away and look at his back. There were two holes where the bullets had exited, both much more ragged than the entrance wounds in the front. Somehow both shots had missed hitting his spine.

He gently let Rudd lie back flat again. "Both bullets went clear through. It's hard to say what happened inside. I don't know why you didn't bleed to death."

"Haven't been able to eat . . . at all," whispered Rudd. "Even water . . . hard. Maybe I'll get . . . skinny, like you." He smiled up at Becky and she patted his hand. She was trying hard to hold back the tears.

One of the two old men by the door cleared his throat. "Uh, we gotta get going, mister," said the younger one.

Rudd lifted a shaky hand to point toward them. "Gave up their bed to me," he whispered. "Hid me when Shorty came looking."

Steele turned to them. "A short man came looking for Rudd?"

"That's right," said the older one. "Mean lookin' little guy, actin' big. But then he noticed my brother in the window pointin' our shotgun at him. He rode away."

"You never saw him again?"

"Nope. Didn't see nobody else either. Gets mighty quiet out there this time of year. Real hot."

"Steele," said Rudd, gesturing for him to come closer. "Did you dig up the money belt?"

Steele nodded. "When I found it was still there I thought it meant you were dead."

"I figured that. Thing is . . . them two boys are itching to get back out to their claim. I promised them . . . a hundred dollars. Give 'em both a hundred. They deserve it. Took a big chance . . . hiding me."

Steele removed two hundred dollars from the money belt. He stood up and led the two men out onto the porch. "I want to thank you for saving him. And thank you for bringing him back to us." He gave them the money and shook both of their hands.

"Damn, look at this," said the younger man. "Ol' Rudd really did have a hunderd dollars. Damn, would you look at that. Real Yankee money."

"Uh, wait a second," said the older man. "This is two hunderd. He said he'd give us hundern. That's all we oughta get."

"Well, if he wants to give us more . . . ." said his younger brother.

The older man shook his head and his brother begrudgingly handed his money back to Steele. "We agreed on a hundred," he said. "We don't want to cheat Rudd. He's a good old boy. And he told us some great stories while he was healin' up."

But Steele wouldn't take the money. "He wants you both to have a hundred. It's what he wants."

"Now ain't that somethin'," said the younger brother, all smiles and staring at the money. He went back to the screen door and shouted, "Hey, thanks Rudd. You come back and see us some time, ya hear?"

They heard Rudd's weak reply. "I will, someday. You can . . . count on it."

The men hurried down the stairs and ran to their wagon. "Let's go get somethin' to drink," said the younger man.

"We got to get supplies," said his brother sternly.

"Okay, we'll get a drink and then we'll go get supplies."

"No we won't. We'll get the supplies and then we'll head for home. Before it gets dark."

Steele could hear them continuing the argument even after they had turned the wagon around and started back down the hill.

Steele went back inside and sat by Rudd. He seemed to be asleep. Becky was still holding his hand and stroking his hair.

Rudd opened his eyes and looked at Steele. "Thought I was dead, did ya? Well, I thought you were dead too."

"I was wounded," said Steele.

"How'd you get away?"

"I found Willig's mine. It was halfway up the cliff, not at the bottom."

"You found it?" Rudd tried to sit up, but grimaced and gave up. "No kidding? It really was out there? Did you find the land grant?"

"No. His mine shaft broke into a natural cave. There was a room in there where he'd been sleeping."

Rudd closed his eyes. "So that's it. No land grant. I should have known."

Steele put a hand on Rudd's arm. "You should rest. We can talk later."

"Yeah. Feeling real tired." But then he opened his eyes again. "What about that Shorty guy? Did you get him?"

"No. When I came out of the cave he was gone. I think he may have been looking for you."

At that moment, O'Brien burst in through the front door followed closely by the doctor.

"So, he's not dead yet?" said the doctor, coming to the sofa.

"No," said Steele, standing up. "He's been shot three times, but he's surprisingly alert."

"Well, let's take a look at him." He sat on the edge of the sofa and ran his finger between the two holes in Rudd's stomach. "Looks like to me you oughta be dead, fella." He turned to Steele. "He's gut shot. You know what that means."

"Internal injuries. But both bullets went clear through. And his spine is undamaged."

The doctor shrugged and stood up. "Nothing I can do. He's got to get to a hospital. Surgery. To see what's going on inside."

"You can't help him?" said Becky.

"Nope. Needs a proper surgery, not my miserable little place. He's got to be opened up and even then they might not be able to save him." He turned back to Steele. "What did your boys do when a soldier was brought in gut shot?"

"Surgery."

"Your boys had time for that?'

"Not always."

"So you put 'em in a bed to die, didn't you? Same as we did."

Becky came around from behind the sofa to confront him. "How dare you say things like that in front of Rudd? Is that all you can do is tell people they're going to die?"

The doctor put up both hands and backed away. "I didn't say he was gonna die, missy. But he will unless you can get him to a hospital."

Becky turned back to Rudd. "Then we will. If that's what he needs, then that's what we'll do."

"What will we do?"

They all turned to see who had spoken. It was Stacy, with Mister Lu in tow.

Becky ran to her. "The doctor says we have to get Rudd to a hospital or he'll die. Can you help?"

Stacy looked at the doctor. "A hospital? How soon?"

The doctor shrugged. "Sooner the better. He's bleeding inside. Look at how pale he is."

"Then I'll hire a special coach. We'll take him back to San Francisco. Mister Lu has been after me day and night, asking me when we're going back. I'll go hire a coach and driver right now." She glanced at Steele, but didn't wait for his approval. She hurried out the door.

Becky went to sit by Rudd. "Did you hear that, John? We're going to take you back to San Francisco."

"But, Becky," said O'Brien. "We can't all go. There won't be room. Besides, I thought you wanted me to go back down to your property with you. You should find out what's going on down there."

She nodded and turned back to Rudd. "Maybe we can't all go with you, John. But Stacy and Mister Lu will get you there and they'll fix you all up like new. Then maybe we'll all come and see you."

Rudd smiled, his eyes still closed. "I'd like that."

Steele walked out to the porch with the doctor. "Does he have a chance?"

The doctor shrugged. "Who knows? I've seen 'em pull through, but only if a surgeon gets in there closes up the damage. I'm not sure he can make it to San Francisco, but he might. Make him drink lots of sugar water, even if he doesn't want it."

"All right. Thank you, doctor. For all you've done."

"So I guess you'll be gone by morning. It was nice knowin' you, Steele."

"I won't be leaving. As I said before, I won't leave until I find out who killed Becky's father."

"You'd let your gal go off without you?"

"She understands."

"Then she must be some gal. Well, I guess I'll see you later then."

Chapter 33

*T*hat night Becky insisted on sitting up with Rudd so Steele and Stacy could get a few hours sleep before the coach arrived to take them to San Francisco.

When they were up in their room, Stacy said, "Can't I talk you into coming with us, Drew?"

"You know I can't leave yet. I'll come as soon as I can."

"But if Rudd is going back to San Francisco, doesn't that mean your job here is done? He was the one who hired you. He said himself he didn't want to look for the land grant anymore."

"Whoever hired those killers is still here."

So how long will you stay here? What if you can't find them. What it they've already left town?"

"Give me a few days to try. If I can't find out anything by then, I'll let the marshal take over."

"A few days?"

"A week at most."

"All right, I'll expect you in exactly one week. You promise you won't get yourself shot again?"

"I'll be careful."

"And then we'll go to London? You promise?"

"I'm looking forward to it."

She hugged him tightly and soon she was asleep, leaving Steele to stare up into the darkness, hoping he could keep his promise to her. He had the feeling Longmore's death would change things. O'Brien had said the town was finally getting stirred up. It was time to do some stirring up of his own.

O'Brien woke them early the next morning, saying the coach and driver had arrived. They went down and ate a quick breakfast and then they all got together to carry Rudd out to the coach.

Cook came running out of the house with sandwiches and dried fruit he'd prepared special for the trip. He also put in a large jug of sugar water for Rudd.

Becky fussed with blankets and pillows on the floor of the coach to make sure Rudd was going to be comfortable.

Throughout it all, Rudd seemed only half conscious, but after Stacy and Mister Lu were aboard and Steele was just about to close the coach door, he opened his eyes and caught Steele's arm. "You . . . aren't coming with us?"

"I've got a few things to finish up here."

"Not for . . . my sake. I'm done with . . . this business."

"I'll be along soon. You'll probably be out of the hospital and eating steaks by the time I get back there next week."

Rudd managed a smile. "Steaks. You sure know how to make a guy . . . hungry. But in case I don't make it, I . . . want you to know—"

Steele squeezed his hand. "We'll talk more when I get there. We'll look back at all this and have some good long talks. I'm looking forward to it."

Rudd smiled again and closed his eyes. "Me too."

Steele closed the stagecoach door and Stacy leaned out the window to give him a goodbye kiss. "See you next week. Remember, you promised."

"I remember."

Becky and O'Brien leaned in though the windows to give Rudd last minute encouragement.

"So long, old buddy," said O'Brien. "You hang on, you hear me?"

"We'll come and see you as soon as we can," said Becky.

Then they were off, heading down the road at a surprising pace. A few dogs chased after them, but the coach soon left them in the dust.

"Damn," said O'Brien, "I sure hope he makes it."

"He'll make it," said Becky. "I'm sure of it."

Chapter 34

*T*he next day, Steele limped downtown to begin another round of questioning the townspeople. Using a cane O'Brien had found, he made his way to the hotel to talk to the employees about the night Laird had been killed. Most of them were more interested in asking him questions about why Longmore had been killed.

Steele didn't answer any of their questions. Instead, he moved on downtown where he found many of the townspeople waiting for him. They were all full of questions, just as the people at the hotel had been. Most were sure the killings had been the work of outsiders. At least, that's what they want to believe.

Steele talked to many of them, listening to their excited theories, but it soon became clear nobody had any real information. He gave up talking to people and went to the gun shop to buy a box of cartridges for his Lemat revolver. The owner of the shop had even more questions. Was it true he and Rudd had fought off a band of outlaws out at Gold Valley? Could those outlaws have been the ones who came into town to kill Longmore? Steele disappointed the man by simply saying he had no idea who might have killed Longmore.

Next, Steele headed for the Dragon House, thinking about how upset and nervous the townspeople were about Longmore's killing. They hadn't been much interested in Laird's murder; he was only an outsider. But they all knew Longmore and the brutal murder of the town's most powerful man left them all confused and personally afraid. If he could be killed without anyone knowing the reason why, what else might happen? Could they also be in danger?

Outside the Dragon house, he took out his revolver and loaded five of the cartridges. He put the gun back into its boot holster and opened the door. The old Chinese woman was at her station by the door and Teng was behind the bar, but there were no customers. Apparently the excitement about Longmore's killing had drawn everyone away from the establishment.

Teng was behind the bar cleaning glasses. Steele went to the bar and sat on a stool. "The town is up in arms about the killing of Longmore. I suppose you heard about it."

Teng hardly looked up. "We hear."

"Did you know Longmore? Did he ever come in here?"

"Not come here."

"I see. Is Cousin Wang here?"

"Not here."

"Can you tell me where he is?"

"Not here. You come back tomorrow maybe."

Steele turned to look at the deserted room. Then he turned back to Teng. "Not much business today."

"No."

Steele watched the man calmly and efficiently clean the glasses. It reminded him of the old Chinese servant that worked in the Moran household. Nathan Moran had told him the old servant had been one of the first he'd brought over from China to work on his railroad. The old man had lost part of his hand in a blasting accident and Moran had taken pity on the old fellow and brought him in as a servant. Whenever Steele was at the house dining with Stacy and her father, the old servant always kept himself busy in the corner, wiping and rewiping the glasses, just as Teng did. Steele had always thought the man was staying close so he could listen to the conversation.

"Tell me," said Steele. "Did you originally come to this country to work on the railroad?"

"Yes. Come on big ship."

"But then the white workers wouldn't work alongside you, would they?"

Teng didn't look up. "It long time ago."

"And then the other day, when I came here looking for Cousin Wang, you said he was up at the mine. The only mine in operation here is Longmore's mine. But that day you told me the mine owner would no longer employ Chinese workers, isn't that right?"

Teng didn't reply.

"So what was he doing up there, Teng? Visiting Longmore?"

Teng continued to polish the glasses.

"Tell me, Teng, when you worked on the railroad, as you say, a long time ago, did you know Uncle Chan?"

"No."

"But maybe that's how Cousin Wang knows Uncle Chan. Maybe they knew each other in China and were brought here together to work on the railroads."

"Ask Cousin Wang."

"I will. But you say you don't know when he'll be back?"

"Tomorrow. Maybe."

"All right, I'll come back tomorrow. Tell him I want to talk to him. Tell him it's very important. Tell him it's about what happened to Longmore, and what happened to Lucky Laird, the man who was killed in the hotel. Tell him it's also about Laird's land receipt. I have it right here in my pocket. You tell him that."

"I tell."

Steele left by the front door. As he slowly made his way back downtown, he continued to think about that old Chinese servant in Moran's household. He was always there, always listening, but hardly noticed by anyone in Stacy's family. Stacy had told him it was that Chinese servant who had suggested bringing in Uncle Chan to treat Mrs. Moran's various ailments.

Steele crossed the street to the town square park, but he did not go to join Billy on his bench. Instead, he found another bench where he could sit by himself to think. As he watched the people pass by, he realized that none of the people on the street were Chinese. One young Chinese man worked in the kitchen at the hotel, but other than that, Steele had rarely seen a Chinese person outside of the Dragon House. Did they intentionally stay out of everyone's way, or were they forced to stick to their own part of town?

It was Stacy's father, Nathan Moran who had brought many of the Chinese to this country. He needed them to work on his railroads and so he brought them in by the tens of thousands, accepting any able-bodied Chinese who was willing to get on a ship and come. But as soon as the Chinese workers appeared, the white workers sat down on the job, refusing to work alongside them. Moran still used them for dangerous tasks, like blasting, and on special projects like building the kind of trestles Rudd had described, but thousands had been fired and were left without employment of any kind. Many of them had ended up in Chinatown, but many others had spread out across the West. Few white people were willing to hire them, so they started their own businesses. They took in laundry, sold homemade liquor, or cooked meals. In the process, they had established a foothold on the periphery of nearly every town in the West. But the white people in those towns hardly noticed them.

Steele remembered Doctor Fletcher saying he got a loan from the Chinese. But had he gone to them, or had they come to him when they heard he needed money? Had they also approached Longmore when they learned his mine was falling on hard times? Maybe that was why Cousin Wang was spending time up at Longmore's mine. How much money did the Chinese have? Enough to buy Longmore out? Enough to back his venture down in Central Arizona?

Steele watched the people pass by and wondered if any of them were indebted to the Chinese. Doctor Fletcher had said the Chinese loaned him money against his house, but the loan agreement came from a San Francisco company named the CTL Consortium. What did CTL stand for? Steele had never heard of any such company in San Francisco. Uncle Chan, as one of Chinatown's leaders, would know. Maybe he should have asked Stacy to talk to Chan when she got back there.

But that thought gave Steele pause. Uncle Chan was in contact with Cousin Wang. Wang had known Steele was coming to town. Could Chan be involved with Wang in some kind of business arrangement? Maybe Chan was part of the CTL Consortium. Thinking about what the nature of such a consortium could be made Steele wonder again why they referred to each other as uncles and cousins. Maybe it was more than a business arrangement. Maybe the family designations referred to some kind of familial relationship that went all the way back to China. It made sense that the first group of Chinese that had been brought over to work on the railroads would have stayed in touch with each other. Maybe they were all part of some kind of self-protective organization that had been originally formed back in China. The family designations could serve to formalize their position in the organization.

It suddenly occurred to Steele that there might be someone like Cousin Wang in every western town, someone who looked out for the Chinese interests, almost like a local union boss. Did the local Chinese boss, the "cousin," report back to someone in San Francisco's Chinatown? Perhaps to someone like Uncle Chan.

Steele thought back to his last day in San Francisco. After he had told Chan he was going to Arizona, he had said, "If a man takes a new path, he can certainly become lost." He had suggested that the trip to Arizona may not have been on "the path for which he is destined." Now it seemed more like a warning than a philosophical statement.

Steele got up from the bench and slowly made his way back up the hill toward O'Brien's house wondering if it was possible that the Chinese were behind it all. Throughout the West, it was the property owners who controlled the towns. But it was illegal for Chinese to own property. Was the mysterious CTL Consortium their way around that? Where they trying to acquire property at any cost? Where they willing to kill to get it?

Chapter 35

*T*hat evening at supper, Becky commented on how quiet Steele was. When he told her he was thinking, she said he must be missing Stacy. "Maybe you should have gone with them," she suggested.

"Maybe," said Steele.

That night, the bed felt very empty without Stacy lying there next to him. Several times, he got up to check the window, looking for that cigarette glowing in the dark. But there was no one out there and the town was quiet.

Finally, just before dawn, he was about to fall asleep when he thought he heard a sound from downstairs. It almost sounded like the familiar creak of the front door. But he had warned O'Brien to make sure all the doors were locked. Had someone gone out?

He quickly got up and dressed. He opened the door to the hallway and listened. Nothing but the clock ticking downstairs. He went out into the hallway and looked down the stairs. The front door was standing open. He made his way painfully down the stairs and out onto the porch. There he almost stepped on something dark, lying on the porch. He stooped down and saw it was Roy, O'Brien's old dog. His eyes were open, staring at Steele, as if asking for help. His throat had been cut and it was still leaking blood across the porch. The old dog's legs were still twitching, but it was too late to help him.

Steele stood up and looked around. The street was deserted. How could someone have killed the old dog without him hearing it? He had been lying in bed listening to the night and hadn't heard a sound until he heard the front door creak.

He took out his pistol and went back into the house. Ignoring the pain in his feet, he hurried up the stairs and turned up the hall lamp. The door to Becky's room was standing open. He looked in, but she wasn't there. He went next door to O'Brien's room and pounded on the door. "O'Brien! Is Becky in there with you?"

He heard a muffled sound and then O'Brien opened the door. He was in his nightshirt. "Jesus, Steele. What are you doing with that gun? What's the matter?"

Steele turned and ran back down the stairs, yelling back over his shoulder. "Becky's gone. I think somebody's taken her. Get help."

Steele limped out into the street. The first light of dawn was filling the eastern sky. He was about to go down toward the center of town when he heard a sound further up the hill. Was it a woman's scream? He hurried up the hill to the end of the road. There was a bit of moon in the western sky, but it wasn't giving off much light. He followed the horse trail that led up into the trees. When he came to a dusty place in the trail, he kneeled down. There was just enough light to see a woman's bare footprint. It had to be Becky's.

He started up the trail, moving as fast as his injured feet would allow. He rounded the side of the hill just in time to see someone running across a meadow ahead: two people, a man and a woman. The woman's white nightgown stood out against the new spring grass. It was Becky. But who was the man? He was pulling Becky along behind him, but she seemed to be resisting.

Steele headed toward them, hoping the man hadn't seen him yet. Suddenly, Becky screamed and broke free, but the man quickly caught her and knocked her down. Then he pulled her up by the hair. He yelled something and pushed her forward at the point of a gun.

Steele stopped. That gun meant he had to be careful. So far, the man hadn't seen him.

If Becky continued to struggle, she might be able to slow the man down. He might be able to get up on the hill above them.

Just then Becky broke free again. The man was caught off guard and hesitated before chasing her. Steele knew it might be his only chance. He went down on one knee to take careful aim. But then Becky fell and the man was on her, holding a gun to her head.

Steele decided he had to do something quick. He ran toward them yelling, "Stop! Let her go."

The man turned and as Steele got closer he saw it was Carson. Carson raised his gun and Steele dove to the ground. Two shots tore into the dirt very close to Steele's head. He quickly rolled to the side, hoping the movement of the tall grass wouldn't give away his position.

But no more shots came. "Stay back," yelled Carson. "I'll kill her. I swear I will."

"No you won't," yelled Steele. "Because then I'd kill you."

Steele lifted his head enough to peer through the grass. Carson had his arm around Becky's neck and was backing away down the hill.

Steele stayed where he was, keeping Carson in his gunsight. But Becky was still too close to him. "Let her go, Carson," he yelled. "Just let her walk to me and I'll let you go."

"No you wouldn't. You'd shoot me sure as hell."

"No, I won't. Let her go and I'll take her back to town before I come after you."

"Like hell," yelled Carson and he fired another shot that hit just a few feet from Steele's position. Steele kept his head down and didn't move. He waited, listening.

By the time he looked up again, Carson was moving on down the hill. He had Becky by the wrist and was dragging her along. She was barely able to keep her footing. They were already out of the meadow and onto a washed-out road that led up into a narrow canyon. Why was Carson taking her up there? Did he have a horse hidden there?

As he ran, Steele kept his eyes on Carson, ready to hit the ground if he started shooting again. But Carson was busy trying to control Becky who was fighting him at every step. Carson was still heading for that canyon, but with Becky slowing him down, Steele wondered if he could get into the canyon ahead of them. There was a scattering of boulders that lined the bottom of the hill. If he could make it to those rocks, he could keep them between him and Carson while he worked his way up the backside of the hill.

Despite the pain in his feet, Steele ran toward the rocks as fast as he could, expecting a shot to come at any moment. But Carson must have been too busy trying to keep ahold of Becky.

Steele peeked over the top of a boulder just in time to see them disappear into the canyon. Steele knew he had to get up to the top of the hill before they did. He scrambled up the hill through the loose shale. When he reached the top, he carefully moved forward to look down into the narrow canyon on the other side. Two horses were tied behind a falling-down old shed with a rusted tin roof. It was an abandoned mine site. Old machinery and heavy wooden beams littered the hillside.

But where was Carson? Had he taken Becky inside the shed?

Steele cautiously moved down the hill toward the shed, being careful not to dislodge any rocks that might give away his position. But before he could get down very far, he heard a shot and at almost the same instant the bullet glanced off a rock right next to him.

Steele dived behind a large boulder just as another bullet hit close behind him. He waited, breathing hard.

"Did I get ya? I bet that one got ya, didn't it?" Carson laughed and the sound echoed off the other wall of the canyon.

Steele kept his head down. "You didn't hit me," he yelled. "What's the point of this, Carson? Just let her go and I'll give you the land receipt."

"I don't give a shit about that land business anymore. Don't mean nothin' to me now."

"Then what do you want?" shouted Steele.

"I already got what I want. But don't you think I won't hurt her if I have to." Steele peeked over the top of the boulder to see Carson leaning out of the doorway of the shed, his revolver pressed against the side of Becky's head.

"Why did you take her?" yelled Steele. "She hasn't done anything to you. Are they paying you for her?"

Again, Carson laughed. "Payin' me. That's a laugh. You don't know nuthin', Steele. This Yankee bitch is mine now."

Did Carson think he was within his rights to capture her if she was from the North? Was he still fighting the war? "She isn't a Yankee," he shouted. "She was born in Texas."

Carson looked at Becky and then back up at Steele. "You're a liar. You're tryin' to trick me. You Yankees killed my pals, every one of 'em. She's your gal so she's one of 'em too."

"You made a mistake killing her father," shouted Steele. "He was also good southern man."

"You're a damn liar. They said he was a land grabbin' Yankee so I was just doin' what needed to be done." He fired off another shot that buried itself in the ground just below Steele's position. Steele knew he must be just about out of bullets. Should he move closer?

"He's reloading," shouted Becky.

Steele heard Carson mutter something, but Steele didn't wait. He scrambled further down the hill and took up a new position behind a low, wide ridge of rock.

Another shot came, but it sounded too high up the hill. Carson must not have realized he'd moved.

"I'm gonna hurt her," yelled Carson. "I'm not kiddin'. Toss out your gun before I hurt her real bad."

Steele peeked between the rocks and saw that Carson had gagged Becky with a red handkerchief and he was tying her hands to the top of the shack's doorway. She kicked at him and tried to yell despite the gag in her mouth. He pulled the cord so tight she was almost lifted off of the ground.

"Southern girl, my ass," yelled Carson. "She's a Yankee if I ever saw one." He reached around from behind her and tore down the top of her nightgown. "What do ya think of your fancy girlfriend now, Steele."

Becky gasped and angrily tried to kick back at him, but her toes were barely touching the ground so it just caused her to spin around.

"Look here at what else I can do," yelled Carson, grabbing one of Becky's exposed breasts. "Why don't you come down here and try to stop me."

Steele kept his gun aimed at Carson, but Becky was still too close. "Listen, Carson, let's just leave her out of this. If you move away from her, I'll stand up."

"Oh sure, you want me to get away from her so you can pick me off."

"No, look here. I'm coming out." Steele stood up, pointing his pistol toward the sky.

"So you really are sweet on her, aren't ya? You think I can't hit you from here. I bet I can." He slowly began to move toward Steele's position.

Becky was frantically shaking her head.

Steele focused all of this attention on Carson's pistol, ready to dive for cover at even the slightest movement of his trigger finger.

But Carson didn't fire. He continued to move slowly forward, keeping his pistol trained on Steele. "All right, Steele, you want her? You can have her. The hell with all of you." He raised his pistol and fired.

Steele felt the bullet hit his hip. It turned him and threw him to the ground and that may have been why Carson's second shot missed. More shots came and the bullets tore into the ground very near his face, but Steele knew he had to get up and fire back or Carson would be on him.

He stood up fast and the movement seemed to startle Carson. Steele aimed and fired before the man could react. Carson went down hard. Steele could have fired again, but hesitated. Carson quickly crawled behind some rocks. Steele also ducked back down. He waited. No more shots came. How badly was Carson hit?

Steele cautiously peeked over the top of the boulder, but he couldn't see Carson. Becky was still dangling from the doorway, struggling to free herself.

The momentary pause gave Steele time to check his wound. It looked like the bullet had clipped the tip of his hip bone, tearing a shallow furrow in the flesh. Luckily, it wasn't bleeding too badly. He tore off a piece of is shirt and used it to put direct pressure on the wound. Then he turned his attention back to Carson. "How bad are you hit?" he yelled.

The response was quick. "I'm not hit. Who do you think you are, Sandy Sure-Shot?"

"I know I hit you, Carson. Listen, this is ridiculous. We're both wounded. Let me take you back to the doctor in town. He can help you, help both of us."

"Oh right, he'd patch me up so they could string me up. I'm not gonna hang, not in some damn backwater town like this. If you want me, you'll have to come down here and get me."

Steele waited, watching Becky struggle to untie her hands.

"Ya know, I can still see your girl from here," yelled Carson. "I could shoot her right between them pretty tits."

"You won't do that," said Steele. "I know you are a smart man, Carson, smart enough to have survived all these years since the war. You're smart enough to know that shooting a pretty southern girl won't get you anywhere. This is between you and me."

Becky finally got her hands loose. She looked up at Steele and he waved for her to go back.

She moved back into the darkness of the shack.

"Why were you after Becky?" yelled Steele. "Was it because she was nice to you on the stagecoach?"

No response came.

Steele decided to try again. If he could get Carson to talk, he might get a better idea of how badly he was wounded. "Why did you leave the stage in Camp Verde, Carson? And why did you shoot Charlie, the stage hand? He never did anything to you."

There was silence for a few moments, then Carson replied: "Too bad about that stage man. Didn't mean to hurt him."

"So you were shooting at somebody else, and you missed."

"The hell you say. If I'm shootin' at somebody', I hit 'em. That stage musta hit a bump or somethin'. And besides, I wasn't trying to hit anybody. I was just trying to put a scare into you city types. I'll bet you were all scared shitless in there, weren't ya?"

Steele saw Becky peek out of the shack. "Can you see him?" he yelled. "How bad is he hit?"

Becky pointed to her own side and then to her wrist.

"All right, I understand," yelled Steele "Get back inside."

She ducked back into the darkness.

"So I did hit you," said Steele. "Are bleeding badly?"

"Don't you worry about me, buddy boy. You'll best be worryin' about your own self when I get done with ya."

"Listen to me, Carson. The wound in your wrist may be a bigger problem than the other wound. If you're hit in the wrist, you'd better quit talking and throw out your revolver before you bleed to death."

"So now you're all-fired concerned about my health are ya? First ya want to shoot me and then you want to help me out."

"All I want to do is take you back to town. Neither one of us has to die over this. You can get a fair trial back in town."

"Fair trial my ass. They'd just string me up from the nearest tree. I seen it before. My pal Funny Jack got it that way. They strung him up while I watched from up on top of a hill. He was kickin' like a mule and his face turned all black. They'd of strung me up too if they would of found me."

"So you left him there."

"Wasn't nothin' I could do. He was already stopped kickin', and they'd of strung me up too if I'd gone back in there."

"I'll make sure you get a fair trial. Just throw out your gun."

Becky was again peering out of the shack.

Steele waved her back "Stay inside. Are you all right?"

"I'm all right," she called back. "I think he's hurt bad."

"I am not," yelled Carson. "Just you wait, missy. Soon as I'm done with your boyfriend, I'll come up there and I'll show you some fun. Just you wait."

"Talk to me, Carson," said Steele. "How bad is it?"

Carson was silent for several seconds before answering. "I had worse."

"Becky said you were hit in the wrist. Is the blood seeping, or is it spurting out?"

"I got a cloth around it. That'll fix it."

"Take the cloth away for a second. Just long enough to see how the blood is coming out."

There was another silence, then, "Coming out in little blobs. Like off and on."

"Listen to me, Carson. It means an artery has been opened up. An artery carries blood away from your heart. You can only stop it with a tourniquet. Wrap a cloth around your arm above the wrist and twist it tight. Use a stick or something."

"Got no sticks down here."

"Then use the barrel of your pistol. You have to stop the bleeding or you'll die."

"You're tryin' to trick me. You want me to tie up my own gun so you can rush me."

"I'm telling you this to save your life."

After another long silence, Carson said, "It's comin' out both sides."

"Do you mean the bullet went clear through?"

"Yeah, bigger hole on the backside."

"Then you'll lose blood even faster. You have to make a tourniquet to stop it or you'll die."

"Maybe you know what you're talkin' about, and maybe you don't. But I'm not goin' back to that Goddam town. Not while I'm still breathin'."

"I don't think you have any choice now, Carson. "You'll bleed to death if you stay where you are. Better just throw out your gun and I'll come down there and help you."

"I got a choice. I still got a Goddam choice. I can come out shootin' and we'll see who's best. Better to get it here than hang from the end of some damn Yankee rope for 'em all to see. They were all laughin' at Jack. Damn 'em to hell. He was all black-faced and snappin' around and they just laughed. Some kids were there, pokin' at him with sticks."

"That won't happen to you, Carson. You'll get your chance to tell your story."

"Hell you say. I got paid to take care of some Yankee trash and I done it. You think they'll let me go after that?"

"That will be up to a judge and jury. At least you'll have a chance."

"Shit, if that's a chance I don't want it. I'll take my chances . . . right here."

Steele thought Carson's voice was sounding weaker. "Is it still pumping out blood?"

It was several seconds before Carson answered. "Yeah. Won't . . .stop. Feelin' a mite . . . pesky . . . now. But I still got . . . gun. Don't be tryin' to . . . sneak down here or nuthin'."

"Carson, listen to me. There is no reason to die out here. I worked in a field hospital during the war. I can help you."

"One of them damn Yankee doctors. I shoulda knowed it. But you won't help me. Nobody ever helped . . . me. Not even my old man. He kicked shit outta me. Til I run off. Hell with 'em. Hell with . . . all . . . a . . . ya."

Carson was starting to slur his speech. It meant he must be losing blood fast. "Are you still awake, Carson?"

"Most of 'em . . . gone . . . now."

Carson mumbled something else, but Steele couldn't hear what it was. He used the opportunity to move down closer, being careful not to dislodge any of the rocks that were underfoot.

"Goddam . . . Yankees. Almost froze. Like rats ina . . . hole, we was. Hey . . .Steele. You got any chew?"

"No," said Steele. "Sorry."

"Damn. Wish I had . . . chew. Chinese kept me . . . hid . . . damn old . . . cabin. Made of . . . rocks. Cold. All alone. Ran out of . . . smokes. Always . . .alone."

"So it was the Chinese that hid you," said Steele, moving even closer. "Was it the Chinese who hired you to kill Laird?"

"Nobody cares. Nuthin' but . . . rice ta eat. Wet . . . damn . . . cold . . . cabn. Wouldn't lemme hafa . . . fire."

"Who hid you? Was it Cousin Wang?"

"You know Wang?" Carson's voice grew a little stronger, almost cheerful. "Why's he called . . . that? Whose . . . Cousin?"

"Was it Cousin Wang who hired you to kill Lucky Laird?"

"Lucky? He wassin lucky. Dumb name."

Carson's voice was getting weaker, and he was slurring his words even more.

"And Swill? The coal man out by the lumber mill? Did you kill him too? To keep him quiet?"

"Dumb shit. Cried like . . . baby. Did'm . . . favor."

"Carson, listen to me. Did you meet anyone else in town? Anyone besides the Chinese? Did you meet a man named Shorty?"

"Stupid Chinese. Cousin Wang. What kinda name . . . izat? Told me . . . go way. Leave ya . . . alone. But . . . I showed'm. Dumb Chinese."

"How did you show them, Carson? How did you show the Chinese?"

"Cousin Wang. Dumb Chinaman. Said . . . drink tea. Don't like . . . tea. Lackey tried . . . sneak up . . . hatchet. Saw't comin'. Can't sneak up . . . on me."

"Teng attacked you? With an ax?"

"Too smart . . . for 'em. Gut shot 'em. Watch 'em squirm . . . on floor . . . dead. Good 'n dead."

"You shot both of them? Was that this morning? Before you went to O'Brien's house to get Becky?"

There was no answer.

"Are you still awake, Carson?"

Still no answer.

Steele picked up a rock and threw it down toward Carson's position. No response. He got up and began to move down the hill, his pistol cocked and ready.

Becky came out of the shack and pointed. "He's lying down, but he's still got his gun in his hand."

Steele waved her back and continued down toward Carson's position. When he got there, he found Carson lying on his back, his eyes closed. His wrist was wrapped with a blood-soaked cloth, but he still had his revolver in his other hand. Steele put his own gun away and then he knelt down next to Carson and took the gun out of his hand. Carson's eyelids fluttered, then opened, but he didn't seem to be seeing clearly.

"Steele?" he muttered. "Izat . . . you?"

"It's me," said Steele. "Let me try to help you."

Carson closed his eyes again and turned away.

Becky came running, trying to hold up the torn front of her nightgown. Steele stood up and she fell into his arms. She was shaking. "I knew you'd come," she whispered. "I knew you'd come."

"You were very brave," he said softly. He kissed the top of her head.

She looked down at Carson. "Is he . . . dead?"

"He's lost a lot of blood, but we may be able to help him." He sat down next to Carson.

Carson slowly turned his head to look at Steele. His mouth moved, but no words came out.

"Just lie still. Let me look at your wrist."

Steele reached for his arm, but Carson tried to pull it away.

"Just let me look at it," said Steele. He removed the cloth from Carson's wrist. The blood was still seeping out, but very slowly. Steele tied the cloth around Carson's forearm to make a tourniquet. He removed the bullets from Carson's revolver and used the barrel of the gun to tighten the cloth until the blood flow stopped. How many tourniquets had be made in the Army field hospital? Too many to remember.

As the tourniquet tightened, Carson reached up and touched his hand. "No . . . don't."

Steele pushed the hand away. "I've got to get the bleeding stopped. It's your only chance."

"No," whispered Carson hoarsely. "Lemme die . . . here." He closed his eyes.

"He doesn't want you to save him," whispered Becky.

"It may be too late anyhow," said Steele. "He's lost so much blood."

"We can't just let him die, can we?"

At the sound of Becky's voice, Carson seemed to rally. He opened his eyes and looked at her. "Sorry, ma'am. Diden know . . . youer from . . . Texas."

Becky sat down in the dirt next to him and stroked his head. "It's all right. Drew will get the bleeding stopped. Then we'll get you back to town."

Carson slowly reached out to take her hand. "No ma'am. Don't . . . want to. Make'm . . .stop. Leave . . . me . . . here."

"We can't leave you," she said. "No matter what you've done."

Carson closed his eyes and sighed. Then he opened them again and stared at her. "Your . . . father. Didn't know . . . Texas."

Becky nodded, trying to fight back the tears.

"They . . . lied . . . to . . .me."

A tear slid down her cheek and fell onto Carson's face. She gently wiped it away with her thumb.

Carson still had ahold of her hand. "Make'm . . . stop. Lemme die . . . here. For yer . . . father." He closed his eyes again.

Becky turned to look at Steele. "He wants to die here," she whispered.

"He's afraid of hanging," said Steele. He saw his friend hung."

Through her tears, Becky whispered, "Maybe we should . . ."

Steele thought about it. Did he have the right to make this kind of decision? During the war, the doctors had often been forced to make those kinds of decisions. They helped the ones they thought they could save and they left Steele to sit with the ones who couldn't be helped. Many times he had heard men whisper their last words. Not one of them had ever wanted to die. Carson wanted to die. He would rather die there on the rocky ground than be taken back to die by hanging. There was no doubt that he would be found guilty. He would be sentenced to death by hanging for Laird's murder, if not for killing the two Chinese men.

Becky reached out and touched Steele's hand, the hand that was maintaining pressure on the tourniquet. She looked into his eyes and Steele knew what she wanted him to do. He nodded and removed the tourniquet from Carson's arm. Blood again began to slowly seep from Carson's wrist.

Carson's eyes fluttered, then opened slightly. "Thank you . . . ma'am. Sorry."

She patted his hand and leaned close to whisper, "We'll stay here with you."

Carson closed his eyes and held onto her hand.

Steele and Becky sat there silently, waiting for the inevitable. Carson never opened his eyes again. After a while, his hand dropped away and they knew he was dead.

Steele stood up and helped Becky to her feet. That was when she noticed the blood on his hip. "Oh, no, you've been shot."

He looked down at his hip. "I don't think it's serious. I was lucky."

"But we've got to get you to the doctor. Can you walk?"

"When I was up on the hill, I saw two horses tied up behind the shack. We can ride them back to town."

They started back up toward the shack, but Becky's feet were so torn and bleeding, he had to carry her. They were almost to the shack when they heard horses coming. Steele turned back. It was O'Brien, along with the marshal and two other men. They reined in their horses and Steele put Becky down. She blushed as she struggled to hold the torn front of her nightgown in place.

"Hey, what's going on here?" said O'Brien. He jumped down from his horse and went to Becky's side. "We've been looking everywhere for you. How come he was carryin' you?"

"My feet got hurt. Oh, Edward, it was Carson, the man I told you about from the stagecoach. I was asleep and he came into my room and took me. Drew came and saved me."

O'Brien turned to Steele. "Somebody killed two of the Chinese. The town's all riled up. Was it him?"

"Yes," said Steele. "He admitted it."

"Where is he? Did you get him?"

"He's over there behind those rocks," said Steele, pointing. "He's dead."

"Well, good. Is he the one who did in my poor old dog?"

"I'm afraid so," said Steele.

"I'm so sorry, Edward," said Becky. "He was a really nice dog."

O'Brien nodded sadly. "Yeah, I'm sorry too. Damn good dog. Is this Carson guy the one who killed Becky's father?"

"Yes," said Steele. "The Chinese paid him to do it."

"The Chinese?" O'Brien took off his hat and scratched his head. "I'll be damned if that makes any sense. But why did he take Becky?"

"I'm not sure," said Steele. "Maybe he just . . . fancied her."

"Looks like he done tore her nightgown too," observed the marshal. "I'm not surprised. Pretty gal, white gal, dressin' like that in these parts."

Becky turned to scowl at him. "He took me out of my bed."

The marshal shrugged and turned his horse to head down toward Carson's body. The other two men followed him.

Steele retrieved Carson's horses from behind the shack and he and Becky followed O'Brien back to town.

At O'Brien's house, there was a crowd milling around outside and they all surged forward when they saw the horses approaching. Everyone started asking questions all at once. O'Brien held up his hand. "It's all over. The marshal has things in hand. They're up at the old narrow canyon shaft."

Someone shouted, "Did they get the killer? The one who shot them two Chinese?"

"Yes, he's dead," answered O'Brien. "Steele here shot him. It was a guy named Carson. The marshal will bring him down."

That stirred the crowd into action. Most of them headed back down toward the center of town, talking excitedly, but many of the children took off at a full run toward the hills.

Steele touched Becky's arm and pointed after them. "The children. They're so curious about death. Carson said the children poked at his friend's body after they hung him."

"Maybe that's what he was afraid of," she said, watching them run up the road. "The children's eyes."

Chapter 36

Later that morning, the doctor arrived to look at Steele's hip wound. He stitched up the wound, pronounced it minor, and gave Steele more of his special tonic to drink. He didn't seem in any hurry to leave so O'Brien invited him to stay for lunch.

During the meal, both O'Brien and the doctor were full of questions about what had happened up at the old mine site. Becky told them how Carson had admitted that he had been hired by the Chinese to kill her father. They turned to Steele for an explanation of why.

"They were trying get his land," said Steele. "With him dead, they probably thought Becky would be forced to sell."

"Damn," said O'Brien. "I was sure Longmore was behind it all. But then he ends up dead too. Do you think Carson killed him?"

"Carson was a hired gunman," said Steele. "Longmore was killed with a hatchet, and Carson said the Chinese tried to kill him with a hatchet."

"So the Chinese killed Longmore?" said Becky.

"It would appear so."

"But why did they want Becky's land so much they were willing to kill for it?" asked O'Brien.

"The railroad is going to build a new line from Yuma to Phoenix in Central Arizona. Becky's land has the only water on the entire route."

"Hey, wait a minute," said Doctor Fletcher. "They were trying to buy up land here too. Maybe it means the railroad is coming here."

"A railroad?" said O'Brien. "That could turn this town into a real city overnight."

"It's hard to believe those two Chinese were behind it all," said the doctor thoughtfully. "Where did they get the money?"

"The Chinese have established a foothold in nearly every town in the West," said Steele. "Tens of thousands of them were been brought in from China to work on the railroads. They are a very close-knit group. The Chinese in this town may be part of a larger organization that was providing them with money and instructions."

"So somebody else was giving the orders," said O'Brien. "Have you figured out who it was?"

"I have a suspicion," said Steele quietly. "I couldn't understand why the killer hadn't gone after me. I tried to tell everyone in town that I had what the killer was looking for, Becky's land receipt. But now I think I understand why they didn't try to get it from me. There's a powerful Chinese man in San Francisco known as Uncle Chan. He has been trying to get close to Stacy's father. Because of my connection with Stacy, he must have told Wang and Teng to leave me alone."

"So this Chan guy could be behind it all?" said the doctor.

"I think so, but he too probably reports to someone higher. They go by familial code names like Uncle and Cousin, probably to indicate their rank in the organization. It may be related to the ancestral ruling families back in China."

O'Brien shook his head. "I've lived in this town for more than twenty years. When the Chinese came in, nobody really noticed. Then they started that whore house. Most of the miners who worked for me went there just about every night."

"Those women were probably instructed to listen to everything those miners talked about," said Steele. "That's how they knew everything that was going on in this town."

"My god," said O'Brien. "They were doing all that right under our noses. Well, now that we're on to 'em they won't be going around killing people any more. We'll run every last Chinese out of town."

"Most Chinese are honest working people," said Steele. "You can't punish them all for what a few Chinese men did"

O'Brien frowned. "Well, we'll see about that. At least you can bet we'll keep a closer eye on 'em from now on."

Chapter 37

*E*arly the next morning, Steele went into the forest to dig up Becky's land receipt. When he gave it to her at breakfast, O'Brien said the traveling judge was in town so he would accompany her down to the courthouse that very morning to transfer ownership to her name. "Let's do it as soon as we finish eating," he said, "and then I think it's time we went down to your property to see about those orange trees I've been hearing so much about."

"Oh, should we, Edward? I so want to know how things are down there. I've been thinking about it all the time."

"Why don't we go today?" said O'Brien. "Why not? There's a stage heading down that way this afternoon."

Becky jumped up. "I'll be ready in no time," she said. "Just give me a few minutes to pack my things." She started to leave the room, but stopped at the door and turned back. "And you'll come too, won't you, Drew? There's nothing left for you to do here now. I want to show you how we brought water down from the mountains to our orange trees."

"I'd like that," said Steele. "But I've still got a few things to finish up here. Draw me a map to your place and I'll stop by to visit you two on my way back to San Francisco."

Becky frowned. "Well, as long as you promise to come soon." Then she hurried off to pack.

"You can stay here as long as you want," said O'Brien. "Cook will take good care of you."

"Thank you," said Steele. "Let me ask you about something. Rudd told me the only law in this town at the time old Dutch Willig was killed was a judge named Barnes."

"Yeah. He was some tough old judge too. Ruled with an iron hand. But he hadn't been in the best of health for the past few years. Died in his sleep last winter."

"Was he married?"

"Yeah, he married a Mexican woman. Real pretty when she was young. That's what I heard anyhow. They had a couple of kids, but like most kids, they got out of this town as soon as they were old enough. The widow Barnes still lives here, up on old hill."

"Old hill?"

"Yeah. It's the old part of town, over on the east side. She lives in a little white house. Green trim, as I recall."

"Maybe I'll take a walk up there this morning," said Steele. "She may remember something about Willig's murder."

After O'Brien and Becky left for the courthouse, Steele sat on the front porch and took out the paper he had found in Willig's cave. Even in the bright sunlight, the words were faded and unclear except for two partial phrases, "Lands in perpetuity" and "By order of the king." Could it really be Willig's copy of the original land grant? Or was it just another one of his planned hoaxes?

Steele put the paper back in his pocket. He knew the Prescott chapter of his life was nearing an end, so why had he told O'Brien and Becky he couldn't leave just yet? Rudd wasn't interested in the land grant any longer, so why should he continue to look for it? All the evidence seemed to indicate it was just another one of Willig's land hoaxes, but some things still didn't add up. The Chinese must have hired someone to kill Dutch Willig, just as they hired Carson to kill Lucky Laird. But the break in at the records vault indicated they were still looking for it even after Willig's death. It meant they thought it was real. So, if it was real, what happened to it after Willig's death? It was possible Judge Barnes had been the last one to see it, when he arrested Willig for trying to register it. The judge was dead, but maybe his wife might remember something about the case.

He got up and headed for town. As he passed the row of bars downtown, he stopped to look into the window of Ham's Saloon. As he had expected, Gibby was sitting on his usual stool. At that time of morning, he was the only customer in the bar.

When Steele pushed open the door, both Gibby and the bartender looked up.

"Hey, if it ain't the man hisself," said Gibby, raising his beer mug. "Just the man we were talkin' about. Weren't we Ham?"

Steele joined Gibby at the bar and shook his hand.

"Seems like I owe you a drink," said Gibby cheerfully. "Sit a spell with me." He patted the leather covering of the barstool next to his own.

"I believe it's me that owes you one," said Steele. "For helping me with Rudd that night."

"Well, by God, I ain't never been one to turn down a free drink." He turned to the bartender. "Set us up a couple of whiskies here, Ham."

"I'll be glad to buy you one, Gibby, but I'm afraid I don't have time to drink with you today. I just came in to say goodbye. I'll be leaving town soon."

"Oh, too bad. Well, then make it one whiskey, Ham. I got to drink to this man. He's a genuine hero."

The bartender, poured the drink without comment.

"Here's to you," said Gibby downing the shot of whiskey in one gulp. He made a sour face. "Yessir, you knew how to deal with that dirty killer. That's the way. Take care of 'em with a bullet, then it's over and done with, once and for all. Tell us all about it. I heard it was a big shootout. Isn't that what you heard, Ham?"

Ham didn't reply.

"There isn't much to tell, Gibby. You've probably already heard what happened. I just came in here to thank you for helping me with Rudd and to ask you both again if you'd seen that Shorty fellow since that night."

Gibby shook his head. "Nope, we still haven't seen hide nor hair of 'em. Have we, Ham?"

The bartender shrugged.

"Don't mind Ham," said Gibby. "He don't say much. But if your man was in this town, old Ham, he'd know it. I'll bet that Shorty guy's pushed on."

"Yes, I expect so," said Steele. He paid the bartender for the drink, shook Gibby's hand again, and left the bar.

Outside the dark bar and back into the sunshine, Steele went on down the street wondering if Shorty had ever made it back from the desert. The young Indian had hinted that he might go try to take the string of horses away from Shorty. But O'Brien's two horses had made it back to town on their own so the Indians didn't get them. Did it mean Shorty was still alive out there somewhere? Maybe he'd heard about the killing of the Chinese and gone into hiding.

He stopped at the corner and saw that the nice weather had brought a lot of people to the town square. They were clustered in small groups, talking excitedly. Steele assumed they were talking about the murders. Billy was there too, alone on his bench, staring up into the trees, as usual.

Steele stopped at the general store and bought a dime's worth of the red penny candy and went to join Billy at his bench. He put his hand on Billy's shoulder to get his attention. "Hello, Billy, how have you been?"

Billy smiled very briefly at Steele before turning his attention back up into the trees.

"And how are the birds doing today, Billy? Are they still living out their busy lives up there?"

Billy pointed up toward the highest limbs. "Bad bird."

"Uh oh, is that bad blackbird causing trouble again?" He watched Billy for a moment and then added, "If you only knew what trouble their earthbound equivalents have been causing down here, Billy."

Billy didn't respond and Steele patted him once more on the shoulder. "I'm happy to have met you, Billy. I'll remember you." He handed the sack of candy to him and got up to go.

Billy was so excited about opening the sack to look in at the candy, he hardly seemed notice Steele leaving, but when Steele looked back, Billy was watching him. Steele waved, but Billy went back to playing with the candy.

Steele was still thinking about Billy's simple pleasures as he headed down the path toward the Dragon House. Even as he approached the building, Steele could see it was closed. The windows had all been broken out and hastily covered with old boards. He tried the front door, but it was locked.

He went around to the back of the building and found the tiny old Chinese woman attempting to chop firewood. The axe she was using was way too heavy for her. Steele watched while she positioned a large piece of wood on the chopping block. She struggled to lift the ax above her head and then let it fall of its own weight onto the piece of wood. The block of wood appeared to be completely unmarked. Were there no men left at the Dragon House? Steele stepped forward to help her, but she turned on him and attempted to lift the axe again.

"What you want?" she demanded. Hate burned in her dark eyes.

Steele, for the first time, wondered if Teng might have been her son. He knew she wouldn't be able to hit him with the axe—she could barely lift it over her head—but he kept his distance anyhow.

"I'm looking for Suzie," he said. "Su-Zee?"

"Gone. All gone."

He glanced at the back door, but decided not to check for himself. Either they had all left town, as the old woman said, or they were hiding. Either way, there was nothing left for them in Prescott. They would all be gone soon. The real question was whether the Chinese owners in San Francisco would try to reopen the Dragon House later and whether the people of the town would allow it.

"If you see, Susie, tell her goodbye for me. I will be leaving town soon."

The woman ignored him. She was again trying to chop the large piece of wood, but without any success.

Steele followed the path away from the Dragon House until he came to the old stone cabin. The door was standing open. Inside, in the dim light, he could see a mattress on the dirt floor, an empty bottle, and a few scraps of dirty cloth. This was where Carson had been hiding. He had an image of Carson sitting in there all day, only coming out at night, wandering the town, smoking his cigarettes in the darkness as he waited for his orders from the Chinese.

Steele walked back to town and headed for the east side. As he made his way up the east hill, he soon saw why O'Brien had called it "old hill." The houses were much older than the rest of the town. Some of them were made out of roughly-hewn logs, although many had been added onto using more modern wood-frame construction. There was one house that stood out from the others because it was so well kept. It was a small white house, with newly-painted green trim around the windows and doors. An elderly Mexican woman was down on her knees, tended a neat row of flowers in front of the house. Was this the judge's wife? She was a short woman, rather plump, smiling to herself as she worked. She obviously enjoyed what she was doing.

When Steele stopped to watch her, she looked up. "Do you like flowers?" she asked.

"Yes I do. Very much."

"The tulips are almost done for this year. It's a shame they don't last longer."

"They're very nice," said Steele. "You must take very good care of them."

"They do take some time, but all I have now is time." She stood up and dusted off her knees.

Steele nodded. "My name is Drew Steele."

"You're the one everybody is talking about. The one who got that murderer." She shook her head. "It's too bad things like that have to happen. It almost seems like the old days come back again. Terrible for this town. My husband could have used a brave young man like you. He tried so hard to keep order in this town, but there were so many strangers drifting into town back when the gold was first found."

"Your husband was Judge Barnes?"

"Oh, so you've heard of him?"

"Yes, my friend John Rudd mentioned him."

"Mr. Rudd, the schoolteacher?"

"Yes. He and I came to town together. He was shot and is in grave condition. They took him back to San Francisco. To the hospital."

"Oh, dear, I'm very sorry to hear that. I remember him. Friendly man. I don't think he ever appeared before the judge. I would remember that."

"Did your husband always talk to you about his cases?"

"Oh yes, he'd come home at night, sometimes very late, and tell me all about his day. He never could go to sleep until he did that. I would make him something nice to eat and he'd tell me about the men who came before him. He was often very sad about it."

"Did he every mention a man named Dutch Willig?"

"Oh, yes, of course. He came before my husband a number of times. The judge kind of liked him though. Called him a sly old fellow. Say, Mr. Steele, would you like to come in for a cup of tea? I was about to have one myself."

"Thank you," said Steele, "that would be very nice."

She led him into the house and he could see that it was as neatly maintained as the exterior. The furniture was old, but clean and in good shape, and there was a tall, ornate sideboard made out of dark, polished wood that must have been quite expensive in its day.

She led him into the bright kitchen and gestured for him to sit down. "I don't get many visitors anymore. People are so busy with their own lives. And now that my children have moved back east . . . "

"They don't visit you?"

"No, it's such a long way. I suppose they'll come when I die. If they can."

Steele was silent for a few minutes while she made the tea and poured it into two fragile-looking white teacups that might have come all the way from England.

Steele took a sip. "You were saying your husband mentioned Dutch Willig to you?"

"Yes, I got the idea he was somewhat of a scoundrel, always getting himself into trouble."

"Your husband must have investigated when he was killed in the hotel."

"Why yes, I suppose so. A terrible thing. Poor Dutch Willig. They never did find out who did that to him."

"No, and recently another man was killed in the hotel in much the same way."

"Well, now yes, I did hear something about that. My neighbor comes by talk to me sometimes when I'm out tending my flowers. She told me about it. I just hate to hear about that kind of thing starting up again. You just can't imagine what it was like in this town back then. Men were being shot, and stabbed, it seemed like every other day. My poor husband was busy all the time trying to bring some order to it all."

"I'm sure he was. But he never said anything that might indicate who was behind the killing of Dutch Willig?"

She shook her head and sipped her tea. "As I said, that one was never solved." She took another sip of tea. "My husband hated that. Unsolved crimes, I mean. He believed very strongly in justice."

Steele nodded, studying her features. She was probably in her late fifties, maybe older. She had a weathered face, probably from the years of tending her flowers out in the sun. "Would you mind if I drew your picture," he said, taking out his drawing pad.

"Oh my, do you know how to draw? I guess you can draw me if you want to. My daughter studied art, at some school back east. At least that's what she wrote to me. I never got to see any of her pictures."

Steele began to sketch the woman's face. It was the face of a somber woman, but she didn't seem to be unhappy. Maybe she had just seen too much of the troubled side of the world through her husband's cases. He quickly sketched in her chiseled face, her tightly pulled back black hair, streaked with silver. She was a tidy woman. Her appearance showed it, as did her neat little house. But there was something else, something behind her bright, watchful eyes. Did she have secrets?

"I'm not sure how to be," she said. "Should I remain very still?"

"No, just keep on talking. I'm only doing a quick sketch." Steele remembered Becky saying the same thing when she had posed for him in the park. He looked at his drawing. He had not captured that mystery behind her eyes. "Did your husband ever talk about the Chinese?"

"The Chinese? No, not that I can remember. They seemed to stay out of trouble. People at church complained that such places shouldn't be allowed. They never understood why the judge let them stay in business."

"Why did he?"

"Why? Well, the judge tried to . . . keep an even hand. That's what he called it. He said there were very few women in this town and . . . well, you understand."

"Yes, I understand. He was doing what he thought was best for the town."

"Yes," she said firmly. "That's it exactly. He always did what he thought was best for the town."

Steele turned the pad around so she could see his sketch. "I'm afraid I didn't do a very good job on it."

"Oh my," she said, putting her hand to her mouth. "Do I look like that? The years do go by, don't they?"

"No, no," said Steele, "my drawing makes you look older than you really are. I spent too much time working around the eyes."

"Oh now, you don't need to flatter me, young man. I may forget to look in the mirror very often these days, but I know what the years do to a person. My husband used to say . . . ." Her words trailed off and she stared out the window.

"Maybe you would remember," said Steele quietly, "if your husband ever said anything about an old land deed. It would have been related to the death of Dutch Willig."

"No, no," she said absently. "There were so many things like that. Arguments about land, about mining claims. Sometimes they'd even shoot each other over them."

Steele nodded. "Well, I'd better be on my way," he said, standing up. He tore the drawing out of the pad and left it on the table for her.

"Oh, you haven't even finished your tea."

"It's very good," said Steele, picking up the cup and finishing it. "But I'm sure you have other things to do. Your flowers," he said glancing toward the front of the house.

"Oh yes, my flowers. Aren't they nice?" She had a troubled look on her face. "I wish I could have been more help to you. After what you've done for this town. Maybe you could find something about what you are looking for in his papers."

"His papers?"

She looked up at the ceiling. "They're still up there. The judge never threw anything away."

"His papers are still up in the attic?"

"Well, it's hardly an attic. More like a little space between the roof and the ceiling. After he died, someone broke in and searched the house. And then last month it happened again. This time, when I got back, the place was in a mess. They looked everywhere, but they didn't know about his secret little place."

"Could I take a quick look up there?"

"Of course. If you really want to. I was going to clean it all out and burn everything anyhow. But I just never quite got around to it." She glanced toward the back of the house. "He had a little ladder. It's still out back."

She led Steele out the back door and pointed to a short ladder. She led him back inside and showed him where to lean it against the wall.

"The whole panel lifts out of the way," she said, pointing up at the ceiling. "He built it that way so no one could tell it was there."

While Steele positioned the ladder, she went to get a lantern.

When she came back with the lantern she said, "Take your time. I'll be out front. With my flowers."

Steele climbed up the ladder and pushed aside the ceiling panel. Dust showered down.

She handed him the lantern. "If you find anything you can have it. Just take it with you. Like I said, I was going to burn it all anyhow." She turned away and disappeared through the kitchen door.

Steele climbed up into the low space under the roof. He was able to sit cross-legged with his head almost brushing against the roof. He hung the lantern on a nail.

The entire space was nearly filled with stacks of papers. Dust and undisturbed spider webs showed that it had been many years since anyone had looked at them. He looked through a few of the stacks and found that they were mostly court records. But there were some other types of documents mixed in, handwritten copies of deeds and business agreements. The judge must have settled business matters himself and kept the documents as evidence. Why hadn't he put them in the records vault? Were they secret deals? Maybe he keep them himself to maintain peace between feuding parties. As he finished with each stack, he pushed it back to its original position.

Finally, he came to a stack that was mostly about land and mining claim disputes. He started to leaf through them and saw Willig's name on a mining claim. The next document was also a mining claim, and Willig's name was on that one too. He found several more, and then he saw the edge of a document about halfway down in the stack that was thicker than the others. He touched it and from the feel he knew immediately it was parchment. He carefully removed the papers that were on top of it and brought the lantern closer.

There it was, a yellowed old land grant on thick parchment, with hand-lettered Spanish words in a bold and ornate script. So it really did exist. The long-lost Spanish land grant that so many had talked about was real. Steele translated from the Spanish as he read: "Hereby granted to J. A. Rivera the lands herein described in perpetuity." The words were the same as on the piece of paper he'd found in Willig's cave. Willig must have been trying to make a handwritten copy before he registered the real land grant.

Steele read it over. The document included a detailed description of the lands covered. The rest of it honored the king of Spain and warned that his rule over the properties described in the document was both sacred and absolute.

Steele held the parchment document close to the lantern, looking it over carefully. It looked completely authentic. It even had some remains of the original red wax seal just below the king's signature. And at the bottom, in a shaky hand, someone had written out a poorly-worded note that in essence relinquished title to the land, giving it over to the bearer of the document. There were two signatures, Juan Rivera, followed by the Spanish word *"dueño,"* meaning "owner," and Juanita Rivera, signing as a *testigo*, a witness.

Steele stared at the land grant, still finding it hard to believe an old prospector in a remote part of Arizona, really had come into possession of one of the most sought-after documents in history. A court of law would have a hard time disputing the authenticity of the document he held in his hands. If the signatures of the Riveras were found to be authentic, the bearer might be able to lay legal claim to most of the Arizona territory. That must have been what Willig planned to do. Or maybe he wanted to register it in order to sell it to the highest bidder. But before he could carry out his plan, he was murdered by the Chinese. The judge must have brought the document home, along with the rest of Willig's fraudulent mining claims. Was the judge planning to investigate the land grant, or did he hide it to avoid the trouble the document was certain to cause in Arizona?

Whatever his plan, apparently he never told anyone else about it and after his death it remained hidden in this secret place.

Steele put all of the other papers back where he had found them and stuffed the land grant inside his shirt, realizing that he was now the legal bearer of the document. But he wasn't sure what he should do with it. Should he give it to Rudd? But Rudd really had no legal claim to it. Apparently, now that Willig was dead, no one did. The Riveras had legally relinquished their claim to the land long ago. It truly did belong to the bearer.

Steele lowered himself down out of the little attic and replaced the trap door. He put the ladder back out behind the house, then he went around to the front where he found Mrs. Barnes still weeding around her flowers.

She looked up as he approached. "Oh, you're all dusty. I'm sorry. I should have known it would be all dirty up there."

"It's no problem," said Steele, dusting off his pants.

"Did you find what you were looking for?"

"Yes, I did. I found a document that might have belonged to Dutch Willig. Would you like to see it?"

"Oh no," she said, turning back to her flowers. "They have nothing to do with me. Like I said, I was just going to burn all those old papers anyhow."

Steele stood watching her as she focused on finding and digging out every little weed that might threaten her flowers. He wondered if he could even explain to her the significance of what he had found in that dusty little crawl space. How could he explain that the old parchment was something that men had died for? "I'd best be on my way then," he said.

"It certainly was nice meeting you," she said, shading her eyes from the sun with her gloved hand. "If you ever need a cup of tea, you can come back by any time. And I hope you won't think too badly of the Judge. He did things his own way, but he was trying to do what was right. I know what they called him, but he didn't really hang very many men. And he suffered every time he had to do it."

Steele waited for her to say more, but she turned her attention back to her weeding, as if he'd already gone.

Steele turned and headed back down toward the center of town. As he walked, he could feel the rough edges of the parchment document under his shirt. He had the odd feeling that Dutch Willig had once walked those same streets feeling the roughness of that parchment against his skin.

Chapter 38

*B*y the time he got back to the house, O'Brien and Becky were gone. There was a note on the dining room table telling him to make himself at home. It included a map showing how to get to Becky's property when he was ready to come.

Steele spent the rest of the day sitting on the front porch, thinking. Several times, he took out the land grant to look at it. He almost wished he had left it hidden in the judge's secret hiding place. But she'd said the house had been broken into twice already. It meant somebody was still looking for it, maybe the Chinese. Sooner or later others would come to look for also. What would happen if they found it? Would the killing start again?

The next morning, he saddled a horse and started out toward Gold Valley. Cook had packed him some food and this time he brought along extra water, matches, and a lantern. He followed the same route he and Rudd had taken, but this time, no matter how often he looked back, he didn't see any dust.

Along the way, he looked for clues as to what might have happened to Shorty. Trying to reconstruct his walking route, he eventually found the place where he'd met the Indians. Not much farther along, he came upon Shorty's body. Or what was left of it. From the clothes and the short stature of the body, Steele was sure it was him, but the coyotes and vultures had been at him so there was little left. Something had torn open his shirt and eaten out his guts, and long lines of ants were gradually finishing off the rest. His revolver was missing and so were his boots.

Steele didn't have a shovel, but he used a stick to dig a shallow grave and cover over the body as best he could. Then he rode on down to the river and worked his way upstream until he came to Willig's campsite.

He untied the lantern from the saddle and climbed up the ridge. Then he made his way down from the top of the cliff to the mine shaft opening.

Inside, he found the body of the man he'd shot. It was stinking badly and the worms were already at it. When he moved the body aside, the maggots poured out of the eye sockets.

He lit the lantern and continued in. When he got to the cave, he hurried down to the underground river. He was surprised to discover the water level was so low he was able to wade across the dark water and duck under the rock ceiling to get into Willig's secret cavern. He realized this was how Willig had discovered it. The water level must rise and fall with rainstorms in the mountains.

He held the lantern up high. The room was as he had left it. He stared at the bed and remembered how cold he had been. The dirty old mattress looked even dirtier and more moldy than he remembered. He pulled the parchment land grant document out of his shirt and placed it on the wood planks that Willig had used as a table.

Then he opened Willig's dynamite box. He took out only one stick of dynamite, being very careful not to jar the old, decaying explosives. He held the lantern up high and looked toward the back wall of the cavern. He didn't see anything unusual. Nothing there but a damp rock wall. Had he imagined the sparkle of gold back there? During that terrible freezing night in the wet cave, he was sure he'd seen a vein of bright gold color by the light of the flickering candle. He imagined old Dutch Willig seeing that same illusive sparkle by candlelight. Maybe it was something about the cave. Maybe it only appeared if you looked under just the right conditions. He could imagine old Willig being driven mad by something so close, so beautiful and valuable, yet impossible to find if you went closer. Steele picked up the lantern and made his way back out of the cave. He didn't look back.

Back outside, he buried the stick of dynamite in the loose earth just above the mine's entrance. Then he climbed back up the cliff. From a position further down the ridge he could just make out the end of the red dynamite stick protruding from the earth. He took out his pistol and got down flat on the ground. He steadied his gun against a rock and took careful aim. He squeezed off a shot and the resulting explosion was quite a bit larger than he had expected. He put his face down and covered his head with his arms as rocks and dirt rained down around him.

When it was all over, he went back to inspect the result. There was no sign of the mine shaft anymore. Using his feet and a large stick, he smoothed out the dirt around the place where the shaft's opening had been. He climbed back up to the top of the cliff and looked down. No one would be able to tell that the area had ever been disturbed. The coming seasons of wind and sun and winter rain would soon cover the spot with weeds, and eventually cactus would also take seed there and grow.

He got back on the horse and started back to town.

The next day, back at O'Brien's house, Steele said goodbye to Cook and walked down to stage office. He bought a ticket and was told he was going to be the only passenger.

After the cargo was loaded, he got inside and the stage quickly began to move. As it picked up speed, he leaned out the window to watch the town recede into the distance. Somehow the place seemed very different from the town he had seen that first day when he arrived.

Soon the horses began to kick up so much dust he had to duck back inside. He settled in, looking forward to the trip. This time he would be able to spend more time watching the scenery as it passed. And he would have more time to draw. He would try to complete drawings of everyone he had met in Prescott, people who had helped him like O'Brien and Gibby, Billy and his mother. He would also try to draw, from memory, portraits of the ones who were now gone, Laird, Carson and his partner, Longmore, Shorty, and the Chinese. Someday, he would take the drawings out and it would help him to remember them all.

Epilogue

Six weeks later, Steele and Stacy were living in a small, but comfortable, flat in London, not too far from the American Embassy compound were his parents still lived. Of course his parents fawned over Stacy, asking questions about her family and constantly pressing her to learn when she and Steele were going to get married.

Stacy tactfully ducked their the questions and stayed busy with her women's movement, leaving Steele to wander around the city. He haunted London's many fine libraries, reading about medicine and art and philosophy. He paid the library staff to carefully copy articles about recent medical discoveries and he sent the copies to Doctor Fletcher in Prescott. Every afternoon, he made it a habit to drop by the post office where he usually found a few letters to Stacy from her parents back in San Francisco, but that was all.

But one day, just a week before Christmas, he received a letter from Rudd. In the letter, Rudd wrote that he was gaining a bit of fame for his dramatic newspaper stories about their adventures in Arizona. He also wrote that people still tried to talk to him about that long-lost Spanish land grant, but he always told them to forget it. It didn't exist, and even if it did, it would only cause more trouble. He added a postscript that said Becky and O'Brien were to be married in the spring and that Stacy's father had partially funded O'Brien's new mine shaft on the other side of the mountain. He said the project would be underway soon and that O'Brien had high hopes for its success.

Steele put the letter in his pocket and went for a long walk along the waterfront, all the way down past the busy docks. As he walked, he felt a terrible restlessness. He hurried his pace, trying to shake off the feeling, but memories of Arizona flooded his mind. Had the railroad approached Becky about buying her land? If so, why hadn't Rudd mentioned it in his letter? Were the Chinese still trying to acquire land in Arizona? When he had gone to Uncle Chan to retrieve his wartime diaries, the old Chinese man had listened quietly to his accusations, but he had calmly denied any knowledge of what had happened in Arizona. Steele was sure Chan was lying, but there was nothing he could do about it. He was also sure the deaths of Teng and Wang would only temporarily stall the plans of the Chinese. Others would be sent to Prescott to take their places.

Steele stopped on a hill overlooking London's busy harbor. He watched as one of the White Star Line's fast new steam-powered ships headed out, undoubtedly bound for America. If he were to board one of those ships tomorrow, he could be in New York in a few short weeks.

www.ingramcontent.com/pod-product-compliance
Lightning Source LLC
Chambersburg PA
CBHW062028170626
46813CB00001B/330